The Glow-worm

Caleb Peck

Copyright © 2022 Caleb Peck

PART I: The Boring Twenties

CHAPTER ONE

December, 2029

Adelaide Wheeler stood over the sink, looking down into the white, empty basin. She waited for the hot water to overtake the cold as her hands tested the temperature beneath the tap.

She waited and waited, lathering her hands with the Beessential organic foaming soap whose bottle rested in its forever home on a decorative granite plate on the left side of the sink, right next to the creaky, hot water handle that sometimes stuck.

She looked at herself in the vanity mirror, counted the creases in her forehead, as she waited for the water to turn. Was she old? No, she thought, relaxing her face, trying to stretch her forehead so that the creases—which had snuck onto her skin without being noticed, ever slowly, ever stealthily through the course of time—would disappear.

She was only thirty-four years old, still beautiful. She had always been beautiful, had hit the genetic jackpot with regard to looks. Sure, there were things she would change about her body, but she knew that she was lucky, knew that she had always been well aligned with society's expectations and standards.

But even with her looks, it had been more than a decade of struggle. She had always longed for roles with substance, had desired to be taken seriously as an actress, but had, for so long, been pigeonholed into minor roles, girlfriends or daughters, buxom beauties and ditsy comic relief, who always seemed to be on the outside of the plot, never the one that the principal story centered around.

Addy had only ever desired to be an actress for as long as she could remember, a well known face in the world, a voice with reach and import, a person who would be remembered and respected in the course of history; she'd always wanted to be like Meryl Streep, and thought that the only path toward those heights was through hard work and sacrifice and struggle. So she had ventured onto the path strewn with so many shattered and forgotten dreams, working several service and clerical jobs—waiting tables, answering phones, walking dogs—as she honed her craft and went on as many auditions as she could. She'd lived with more roommates than she could list on her fingers and had lived in four of the five boroughs during the decade and a half of her pursuit.

She'd had a few minor roles, Broadway and Off-, but it wasn't until about five years ago, going on thirty, that she received something like a big break. She'd gotten to play Viola in *Twelfth Night,* a leading role in a Shakespeare production, staged outside in Central Park during the Shakespeare in the Park summer series. Her success had snowballed since then—a stint as Elphaba, a few months playing Elle Woods in a revival of *Legally Blonde,* a critically acclaimed turn as Dot, opposite Harry Styles' George Seurat—and now she was in the final stretch of playing the one character that she had always dreamed of playing, Sally Bowles. After the holidays her run as Sally would be over. She didn't have any projects on the horizon, and had no clue what the next decade might offer.

The role of Sally had been good to her. She was another actress within a long lineage who had adapted the iconic role; Judy Dench on the West End, Natasha Richardson, Michelle Williams, Emma Stone, and, of course, Liza Minnelli on the silver screen.

She had achieved what she had always wanted, carved out a life for herself here. There was even talk of a Tony nomination for Addy. Yes, she really couldn't complain.

But as she gauged the water from the tap, she found herself filled with impatience and rage, and a familiar anxiety filled her head. The water was still cold. The organic soap that she'd lathered in her hand glistened, the chemicals, the crystalline structure of the suds glimmering in the early morning light that found its way through the window, weaving, slithering through the cracks and crevices, the narrow spaces between the concrete and brick buildings that made up lower Manhattan.

Goddammit, Ray! she thought. How many times had she told him to contact their landlord about this?

Ray was her boyfriend of twelve years, minus the many breaks that they had taken, minus the year that he'd spent touring nationally for *The Cat's Pyjamas,* the original play that he'd written, which had been a Broadway hit a few years ago.

The two of them had struggled for years together. They'd shared rooms in five and six bedroom apartments, artist lofts in Brooklyn, communal-living type situations where sometimes food had to be labeled. But now they had their own place. They'd moved into a beautiful one-bedroom, one-bath, pre-war apartment on Jane Street in Greenwich Village. It wasn't a lot of space, but it was all they needed. It was home.

It had been remodeled with stainless steel appliances, refurnished hardwood floors, modern lighting fixtures, but still retained much of its pre-war charm through the wood-burning stove and the small brick patio attached to the dining room, which was overrun with ivy and looked out at the Thornless Honey Locust trees that lined the cobblestone street. It was just her and Ray there, and their two year old pup, a Portuguese Water Dog named Essie Carmichael. She loved it there, just the three of them, on that quiet, peaceful street just a short walk from the Hudson River—most of the time.

But right now all she felt was anxiousness and anger. Although the sink was new, the pipes had to be fifty years old and this had been an on and off problem for the past year.

Ray! she yelled.

He stumbled into the bathroom yawning, rubbing his eyes. Why are you yelling?

Why don't we have hot water? I thought you said you were taking care of this?

I've talked to Bill about it. I've mentioned it over and over. He said it should be taken care of soon.

Taken care of soon? What does that mean?

You just have to give it a minute. Patience, hon.

I've been holding my hand under the water for ten minutes!

Well, is it that big of a thing? Why not just use the cold? As long as you use soap.

Because I shouldn't have to!

Look, if this is our biggest problem...I mean, don't you remember that bathroom we had in Astoria? Hot water was the least of our concerns.

Because the rent we're paying to live here is insane! We should at least have access to hot water.

I hear you, babe.

Ray approached her, tried to wrap his arms around her, but she pulled back and pushed him away. Don't, I feel gross, she said.

Is everything okay? he asked.

This just should have been fixed already. Can you call Bill again?

Do you want me to harass him? I've told him already.

Yes, exactly. Harass him. Whatever it takes so that he fixes the water situation.

Fine, I can call him again.

Like, today.

Fine.

Like, this morning.

Fine.

Ray ran his hand under the water. Hey, it feels okay to me. It's getting warm.

Addy felt the water and it wasn't hot, lukewarm at best, but she was running late. She had planned on getting to the gym half an hour ago, but had overslept. She went to CompleteBody, the one in Midtown East, five days a week, to swim laps; usually she arrived around noon, but today was Wednesday and she had a matinee show and had to be at the theater early. On Wednesdays she woke up earlier, ate her homemade chia pudding for breakfast, then ventured uptown and would arrive at the gym sometime between nine and ten. It was pushing 9:45 now and she was feeling rushed. She'd planned on renting a CitiBike and biking the four miles—the sun was out this morning and it was an unseasonably warm day for December—but now she didn't have time and would probably just take a Lyft.

She washed her hands in the lukewarm water, but still felt gross. Whenever she wasn't able to use scalding hot water, she would sometimes imagine afterward that there were still bits of fecal matter on her hands and it would give her the proverbial heebie-jeebies. It wasn't like she was a total germaphobe, or had full-blown OCD, but she valued cleanliness, she liked to feel pampered and fresh.

Ray wrapped his hands around her waist and kissed her on the neck. She slithered out of his arms.

Stop it, I'm late, she said. And I feel disgusting.

Hon, he said, you look beautiful.

The filthy liar.

I gotta go, said Addy. What are you up to today?

Ray was directing *A Raisin in the Sun* at the Public Theater. He didn't have matinee shows on Wednesdays, so his days were free.

I was going to try to work on that new play I've been trying to write...go for a walk with Essie...I don't know...maybe watch something on Netflix.

She glared at him, trying to communicate telepathically the direness of the hot water situation. Well, she said, as she summoned a Lyft on her phone, if you get a chance could you please get a hold of Bill again, and make sure he knows that we don't have hot water...and that we *need* hot water.

Ray looked at her earnestly, kindly, as he placed his hands on her shoulders. Addy, I will. I said I would. Everything will be okay. Everything is fine.

Okay, I'll believe it when I see it.

She smiled and kissed him goodbye. Because we really shouldn't be paying as much as we're paying, she said, if things don't work like they should. And with that she exited their apartment and entered the belly of the city below.

The day after the hot water incident, Addy and Ray brought Essie Carmichael with them to Central Park. Neither of them had matinee shows so they'd picked up some soup from The Original Soup Kitchen on 55th and were dipping bread into their lobster bisque, having lunch on a picnic blanket as they watched the city flow around them—wealthy Upper East Side matriarchs in fur coats and pearl necklaces out for midday strolls, suit-and-tied businessmen and tight-dressed businesswomen in high heels gabbing urgently into their headsets as they steered themselves mechanically up and down Fifth Avenue toward their usual lunch spots, while joggers and cyclists in spandex and bright colored shoes zipped round and round the paved trails that lined Central Park like critical veins.

Addy's phone vibrated in her lap, a text from her mother.

Addy! Hope all is well :) need to know if you're going to be able to make it this Christmas. It would mean so much to me just to see your face. I love you angel! Please text me back when you get this.

Addy threw her phone back into her purse. She would not be flying to Asheville for Christmas. She'd been meaning to message her mother back after ignoring her past two texts, but she was searching for the right excuse. She didn't have a show this year on Christmas Day, but had two shows on Christmas Eve. Her family knew that if she really wanted to she could take it off, let the understudy have those performances, so that she could return to Carolina for a couple of days. But she didn't want to. She had no interest in going back. She'd considered it—it might be the decent thing to do—but when she'd gone back two years ago it just depressed her, to see her mother alone in that neglected house, grasping for them all to be together again, imagining the holidays as way to revisit a rose-tinted past that had never been.

No, Addy wouldn't be able to make it back this year either, for the second straight year. She had a legitimate excuse. She couldn't skip her Christmas Eve performances this year because there was an important director flying in from Hollywood who was considering her for a role. His name was Trent Pendleton and he was a big deal. She didn't want to miss this opportunity to impress him, and there wasn't enough time to fly in on Christmas Day and then get back for the next day's performance—at least that was what she would tell her mother. That would have to suffice.

Who was that, hon? asked Ray, having no doubt seen the holiday anxiety flash across her face when she read the message.

Oh, just Emily.

You mean your *mother?*

My mother, yes, Emily, my *mother.* Am I going to make it for *family* Christmas.

And are you?

Alas, I will be unable to attend.

Tsk-tsk. You're a bad daughter.

Don't I know it.

Why don't you just take an early flight on Christmas Day?

Because, Ray, I don't want to. Can we *not?*

Fine, fine. I'm just saying it wouldn't hurt for us to go back and visit your family once in a blue moon. How is it that I've only met them twice in all the time that we've been together?

Because, Ray. They never want to come here, and I don't really *need* to go back. Besides, that's two times more than you needed to meet them as far as I'm concerned. We just aren't that close. So can we just enjoy this day?

Ray was close with his mother and so would sometimes try to build bridges between Addy and her family, despite the fact that the sea between them was too vast, the foundation not solid enough, too sandy and fragile and loose to support any abutments.

Okay, said Ray. I'm not complaining. We can stay in and order Chinese food like last year, maybe watch *It's a Wonderful Life.*

Ugh, said Addy. I'd rather watch *Bad Santa.*

Ray laughed, even though she was only half-joking. He finished his lunch and looked up toward the sky as he scratched Essie's ears.

There they go, he said. Watch them.

There was a stiff breeze today and the clouds streamed by quickly as he tried to identify them. Ray sometimes had this strange fixation with clouds. He was devout, something of a mystic, and liked to imagine that their images up against the blue were maybe not entirely random, but messages from God, or little inside jokes. It wasn't as if he took it seriously, as if this theory occupied enough real estate up in the old dome to get him committed to an institution, to get him labeled crazy, but he liked to entertain the theory. He thought, why not? It didn't seem outside the realm of possibilities. There they go. Watch them. They burn their shapely logos across the sky, as branding.

A heart, he said, pointing. A log cabin. A bird—see the beak? And there, a wild beast.

Addy hadn't been paying attention to him. She didn't even look up as she soaked the last bite of bread in her soup. What kind of beast? she asked, disinterested.

A bear. See. The claws. The teeth.

By the time she looked up the clouds had changed position, shifted their shapes, and Ray was no longer paying attention to them. Where? she said to herself. I can't see anything.

All she saw were clouds, wispy and low hanging, stretching across in thin streaks. Exhaust from a tailpipe? Light, bright, cotton candy strands pulled by the wind across the sky.

The wind had picked up. It was a clear, sunny day, low sixties—she couldn't believe that it would be Christmas in a week, as it had yet to snow and the warm weather they'd been having had made it feel like fall—but today's blustering wind caused her to shiver, and so she wrapped herself in the scarlet cardigan that she'd brought, just in case.

Where, Ray? she asked again, making an attempt to see the world through his eyes. To see the heart or the bird or the bear.

But he was looking past her and off in the distance. It felt like their relationship was like that a lot now. A kind of disconnect had been growing ever since they moved into their new place. They rarely seemed to be looking at the same things anymore, focused on the same points in time and space.

She turned to see what he was looking at now. He was watching two young children run circles around their mother, clockwise, counterclockwise, stop, reverse, trying to tag, to touch, to avoid, dancing. The mother wanted no part of being a shield, so she stepped back, returned to the family's orange mat upon the grass, took out her phone and scrolled, leaving the boy and girl to their own devices. The children replaced their mother with a nearby oak tree, which was happy to play the pawn in their chase, and continued to dance their dance around the tree until the girl scraped her elbow against the bark and began to cry.

Neither of them said anything for a moment, but Addy knew what he was going to say.

Have you thought any more about it? he asked, still looking longingly at the family.

Not really, she said. I've been focused on *Cabaret*. I haven't really had time to—

You haven't had *time?*

I don't know, Ray. You know how I feel, she said, avoiding his eyes. She took a big swig of water from the aluminum bottle that she carried around with her everywhere; she had the habit of taking a drink whenever she felt anxious, or wanted to delay a serious conversation. But this time the water must have gone down the wrong pipe because she started hacking up a lung. Either that or she was getting sick. She now felt a sharp scratch at the back of her throat. But she couldn't be getting sick. Not now.

Ray put his hand on her back. My goodness! Addy, are you okay?

She nodded. I better not be getting a cold, she said.

You're not doing this just to change the topic, are you?

She shot him an evil look—how dare you—but didn't address the possibility that this was the truth.

This would be the absolute worst time to get sick, she said. Trent Pendleton is coming next week to see the show.

Ray ignored this first mention of Trent Pendleton, even though she could see in his eyes that he wanted to say something.

Trent Pendleton was something of a boy-wonder, a twelve-year-old auteur, a film-making savant flying in from Hollywood on Christmas Eve just to see her rendition of Sally, in search of a leading lady for his upcoming project.

Ray let the mention of Trent slide and looked right into Addy's eyes, while he pointed toward the children in the distance.

Look at that, he said. Don't you *want that?*

Addy took a tissue from her purse and coughed up some phlegm, blew a milky cloud of snot right into it.

She's crying, Addy said. Her brother made her *cry. That* is what you want?

Ray shook his head in disappointment. This had been a barrier between them for the past year. He was ready to start a family, and she didn't know if she would ever want that.

He went back to looking at the clouds in the sky. I'm sure it's nothing, he said. I'm sure you'll be fine, finally addressing the possibility of her cold.

I can't lose my voice. I need my voice. If Trent shows up and I can't—

Trent, said Ray, drawing out the vowel, exasperated, annoyed. Addy thought maybe he was a little jealous of Trent, a younger director and already more accomplished, more famous. He hadn't even hit puberty yet and was already a legend of cinema, already had a star on Hollywood Boulevard.

Trent Pendleton *this!* Trent Pendleton *that!* Ray continued. That's all you've talked about for two weeks—Trent Pendleton Trent Pendleton! What do you think is going to happen anyway?

What Addy had fantasized about was that Trent would look at her, singing up there on the stage, and make her his muse. She'd been living in New York since she was thirteen, and she loved New York, but she also felt like maybe a change was exactly what she needed. She'd allowed herself to imagine him whisking her off to L.A. and making her a real *star*. She was already a respected actress, but outside of New York the world didn't really know who she was, and she sometimes still felt herself longing for a different way of life, felt like she still needed to find out just how far her voice could reach.

And Trent Pendleton was a real capital-G Genius who had already won three Academy Awards and directed more films than Kubrick. A role in one of his TikTok features would all but guarantee an Oscar. What she'd imagined, a life on the West Coast, palm trees, the Pacific, was a different kind of love, a new world of acceptance and validation, her voice immortal, outliving her, stretching across time. The theatre was fleeting; the shows each night evaporated into the ether.

But Ray didn't understand this desire in her. He was married to the theatre, loved being behind the scenes, directing for the stage. He lived for something *live*. He said that he did it purely out of joy for the form, the desire to make art, the conviction that he was providing something essential to the world. He scoffed at other motivations—fame, money, power, citrus—but Addy knew that he was full of shit. He wasn't as pure as that.

But the thought of leaving New York for a life of cocktail parties and agents, highways and sprawl, the lure of Didion, the land of moving images, was agonizing to him.

He'd been born and raised in New York City. This was his home. This tiny island in the Atlantic, the physical space of it was *home*. Its grid was embedded, symbiotic, inseparable from his soul. And although she'd lived here for twenty years, the place itself did not feel like home; home to her was not so much a physical place at all, but a space, a stillness carved out in the mind, and it was a feeling that often eluded her.

Ray wanted children. He desired nothing more than to have a family and to create a home within this city for their kids, to live out the rest of their days in their West Village apartment. But this scared her, the fact that she could so clearly see this image in her mind, the end of their journey, retired, nothing new left to say, the same four walls, the same fireplace, the same furniture, the same 1920s, vaguely turpentine smell, the same cold water hijacking the tap, while they drifted silently into old age and became forgotten.

He still looked at her expectantly, apoplectic—so what was it? What did she really *expect* from Trent Pendleton?

Look, she said. I think I just need to go.

She packed up her things, threw her lunch container into a nearby trash. I'm going to stop by Duane Reade and get some cold medicine on my way to the gym. I can't be getting a cold right now—I have to get ahead of this. I'll see you at home tonight.

Ray stood and looked confused as he watched her walk away. Are you serious? he shouted. We've barely been here ten minutes!

It wasn't noon yet. They'd planned on spending an hour or two in the park, reading and playing fetch with Essie and enjoying the weather.

I'm sorry, but the wind has picked up, and I can't get sick.

Have I ever told you that you're the definition of diva?

What were they arguing about? They were so rarely on the same page anymore. But when she turned around he was standing there with Essie, smiling at her. He was right, she *was* a diva, but she understood how much he loved her.

Look, I don't want to risk it. I know you don't get it, but I really need my voice.

I do get it, said Ray. You think maybe he'll make you the next Meryl Streep. You think then you'll be happy.

CHAPTER TWO

Amelia Wheeler sat at her desk, mapping with her fingers the branches of the iron bonsai tree, a paperweight her mother had gotten her for Christmas a couple of years ago. She fidgeted with the object as she read up on hellbenders.

Amelia was a conservation biologist and a professor of environmental studies at UNC-Asheville. The fall semester was coming to an end—tomorrow was the last day of finals—and Amelia had planned to spend the holiday break exploring several waterfalls west of Asheville with one of her colleagues, for a research study they were hoping to get off the ground. The study was to be centered around a species of endangered giant salamanders called hellbenders. Big, ugly looking creatures, they were the largest amphibians in North America.

Amelia knew little else about them, so she had a few scientific journals sprawled open across her desk, and several more tabs opened to online articles in front of her. From what she'd gathered, finding a single one of them would prove challenging. They had been threatened in the region for years, their population having dwindled due to collectors and human disruption, infringement upon their habitat. They were also nocturnal and dwelt in dark spaces, tucked themselves into the undersides of large boulders near fast-moving water, and were solitary aside from mating season (encounters between two adults often becoming violent or resulting in the smaller of the two being eaten alive). They seemed reclusive, untouchable, she thought; even in areas where their population hadn't been decimated, they would be difficult to discover.

Amelia and her colleague, Elena Moreno—who was really more of a mentor to her, a tenured faculty member in the department, and the only true friend Amelia had made so far at the University—hoped to observe and compare a handful of different habitats in Carolina and Tennessee over the course of several years, looking at water quality, diet, the prevalence of plastic—in the water and in stool samples—as well as deforestation in surrounding areas, in order to better gauge what factors might affect the quantity at each site and to what extent the variables could disrupt mating patterns.

Amelia was excited about this. This would be her first research opportunity since accepting an assistant professor position six months ago. She hadn't exactly adjusted well to being a professor. In fact, she hated it. She had spent the past two years doing field research in the Uwharrie National Forest outside of Charlotte, tracking and observing several species of birds and their mating calls as part of her dissertation for her PhD program at Chapel Hill. She liked the field aspect of her career, the solitude of it, the exploring, the listening carefully for so many different sounds, for the hidden stories that were abound in nature, if only one knew where to look. It was where she felt most at home, in those wild spaces.

But teaching, was she really cut out for it? This was her first job as a professor; she'd TA'd for a few courses in grad school, but now she was the primary authority figure. Yet so often during her first semester she had felt like a fraud. What did she know, in the grand scheme of things, what did she really *know?*

When she'd finished grad school and moved back to Asheville for the position, she could have afforded her own place, a nice apartment downtown, or maybe even a house near campus, but instead she'd decided to move back in with her mother, who lived on a quiet, dead-end street in the valley of the mountains, tucked into the forest, about ten miles east of downtown Asheville. She thought that it was the right thing to do; her mother was there alone, had been alone there for eight years, ever since Harold, her second husband and Amelia's stepfather, had died in the third wave of the coronavirus. But living with her mother, coupled with how inept she felt in her new job, had filled Amelia with doubts about life, and her path within it, and had made her feel like a child.

She turned thirty last summer, shouldn't she have her life together? she wondered. Shouldn't her days be filled with greater purpose? Work and home were the only two places she went anymore, her days spent indoors, grading papers, or on the couch next to her mother, watching Netflix in silence. Her mother loved to stream old Dynasty episodes, but when they were together they both agreed on baking and dating shows, and they especially loved the baking-dating hybrid show, Break the Icing, where twenty single, world-class pastry chefs lived in a house together while competing in various dessert-centric challenges, hooking up with one another, and getting eliminated survivor-style, in pursuit of the grand prize, which Amelia and her mother had recently binged.

It seemed that this was the only way for the two of them to bond. Amelia's mother was a fortress sometimes, mysterious and labyrinthine, and only ever able to speak of the past if she had first dressed it up in gold-trimmed satin, imagined it through rose-tinted glasses. Amelia liked being back in Asheville and having the chance to reconnect with her mother, even if it was just through stupid reality television, but, if she was honest with herself, the last several months, since she'd moved back home and transitioned to full-time professor, had sent her into a rut of lethargy and hopelessness.

She felt like maybe she had taken a wrong turn somewhere, couldn't as readily trust in the conviction that her days had value, not like she had been able to back when she was doing field research, back when she felt a little younger, more adventurous, and freer from responsibilities. This was why she was so excited about the idea of her and Elena's research proposal. She was thrilled that this semester was over and that she'd have several weeks off to explore the wilderness surrounding Asheville and dive more deeply into their prospective study. Maybe it would re-energize her days.

As she continued reading a blurb about hellbenders in an old National Wildlife magazine, still running her fingers along the thin, detailed branches of the iron bonzai atop her desk, there was a knock at her door.

Come in, she said. This was during her office hours, but she hadn't expected any students to show, most of them having gone home already after finishing their exams.

It was him. There he was. Bobby Studebaker—the student who she knew she probably shouldn't think about outside of this campus, but sometimes did.

Bobby Studebaker was just the sort of boy who never-not-once deigned to question the impulses that awakened in his Germanic teenage body. He was very much the disciple of Teddy Roosevelt and lived his life in accordance to the quote that his parents had pointed out to him on a trip to the Museum of Natural History in New York City, during a vacation they had taken when he was ten years old: *aggressive fighting for the right is the noblest sport the world affords...if I must choose between righteousness and peace I choose righteousness.*

He stood outside the open door of Amelia's office, peering around the frame with a toothy smile stretched across his face, knocking gently.

Professor Wheeler—

Bobby...hi! Come in.

Do you have a minute?

Amelia felt one of two ways about the boy, who she'd had in her Principles of Ecology course that semester; she really liked him, or she strongly disliked him, depending on the day. He was smart, thoughtful, full of youthful ideals, and talked loquaciously about the greater good, about living with values that transcended the self and aligned with a larger purpose. But he could also be stubborn and unreceptive to different perspectives. She sometimes imagined a younger version of herself in him, though she had been more cautious and contemplative, less compelled to rash action. He more so reminded her of her older brother, August, and so the love/hate feelings that he provoked seemed fitting. She motioned for him to sit down.

He flashed her a wide smile. He was tall, attractive, charismatic, and had the aura of a politician to him, though he had once professed during one of her lectures that he absolutely despised politics. He was a passionate sophomore, always vowing to bring about great change. He had the habit of looking every person directly in the eyes; the sole goal of every interaction—his blue eyes shining—was to win their favor and bridge the gap of separateness, to find common ground. A born diplomat. Also a well-known womanizer among the collegiate body.

What is it, Bobby? she asked.

He stood and became animated. He was holding some papers in his hand.

I was just hoping to speak to you for a moment. I'm coming to you with an opportunity, Professor Wheeler.

He gestured openly with his hands while he talked. He paused and raised his eyes to build intrigue. He might really make a great salesman, were it not for his contempt of business of any kind. He was a devotee to science, through and through, and had already declared himself a physics and environmental studies double major. He'd told her the first day of her class, as they went around the room for introductions, that he wanted to build more advanced and efficient methods for harnessing wind and solar energy.

Oh? What kind of opportunity?

It should only take but a moment, Professor Wheeler. Once you see the kind of goals we have, and the values we're speaking of—well, I don't want to get ahead of myself, but I think it will be a no-brainer.

Bobby, I've told you, please call me Amelia. So what's that in your hand? What are we talking about here?

It's a proposal for a new club we're starting.

He handed her the papers. As you can see, he said, we have over sixty students already who want to join.

She studied the proposal. His group was called the Radical Environmental Conservationists (REC). Under *President* was the boy's name: Bobby Studebaker.

I immediately thought of you, Amelia, for our advisor. I just want to say that I was really inspired by your class this semester. You know sometimes, it pains me to say it, but it doesn't always feel like professors are truly invested in what they're teaching—but I didn't feel like that was the case with you. I always felt like you had the true passion, you know? Like, *truly.* With you there is a deep concern, and that is exactly what we need.

Amelia knew that he was full of shit, but he sure did sell it well. The praise he'd given her, the passion he spoke of, it was entirely unfounded. She hadn't really felt that in herself in years. This first semester of teaching had been a disaster, probably because she was so self-conscious and thought that she was so bad at it. She still questioned her own authority, and why shouldn't she? What right did she have to tell the next generation what to focus on, how to save the Earth? She still felt like a child most of the time herself.

She couldn't help but be a little flattered by his words though.

She studied the proposal. Radical, hmmm...why *radical*, Bobby?

Because, Amelia, this can't be another group that only gets together to talk and commiserate with one another, and we can't settle for just small demonstrations or debates on campus either. We want to emphasize *action*, to make that a key expectation for people interested in joining the group. You can see there in our mission statement and in our goals that we want to put ourselves at the doorsteps of local and state governments, stage protests at foresting and drilling sites.

Well, said Amelia, this looks very thorough. I can tell that you really care, Bobby.

The way that I see it, Professor Wheeler, this is the *only* issue. It needs to take precedence over everything. It's an immediate threat—past immediate! I mean...just look at what is happening in Bangkok right now.

Amelia nodded along. She could see how animated he was now, his eyes full of purpose, his pupils big, a prophetic fire fierce inside of him.

I just don't understand how anybody could wake up and keep going about their lives like before, as if everything will be fine! If we don't take radical action, *nothing* will be fine! I don't understand how some people can just ignore the *truth*. If you can wake up and your first thought isn't what can I do today to help save this planet, then there is really no point to your living! This is our home—our only home.

She agreed with him, didn't she? What he was saying was true. He was kind and caring, she could tell, as she looked into his eyes, full of compassion. She thought what an effective leader he might one day become. She was also a little bit scared of him.

So, what do you say? he asked. Will you be our advisor?

Suddenly her phone glowed, danced upon her desk. It was a text from Elena—*just left my house, see you soon!*

Shit, Amelia hadn't realized how late it had gotten. She was supposed to meet Elena at Looking Glass Falls around two o'clock. Popular and picturesque, the stream cascaded through the granite mountain that was Looking Glass Rock and deposited into a small pool at the base of the Looking Glass Trail. It was the first area they'd planned on exploring for their prospective study, and Amelia was hopeful that there would be a few hellbenders hiding beneath boulders in the stream.

I'm sorry, Bobby, she said. I just remembered that I've got to leave a little early today.

She could feel Bobby's eyes on her, expecting an answer, pleading for a comrade.

There aren't too many responsibilities, he continued. You'd have to attend at least two of our meetings or events per semester, and sign off on any big events that would require University funding. That's it, although, we could really use you, Amelia. Personally, I'd love to have you be more involved, but it would be totally up to you. So how about it? It's super important to me that you're our advisor, I can't imagine anyone else.

He leaned into her desk and didn't break eye contact. Earnest, pleading, and more than a little intimidating, Amelia felt her face flush. She looked back at him and realized what a face he had! More than the whole classically attractive thing that he had going on, she was surprised at how many things she thought she could see beneath the surface. He wasn't used to asking for special permissions, that was clear. He had a touch of smug that suggested that he was either used to being given the keys to the kingdom, or taking liberties first and asking for forgiveness later if he crossed a line. And his pleading for forgiveness would ring true then, just as his boyish earnestness, and the lack of shame or embarrassment in his face rang true now, as he looked her in the eyes and lied to her.

She had heard something about this group already and knew that he had asked at least two other professors before her, but they had declined, citing too much on their proverbial plate. Likely, they had understood the added commitment this role would require to appease Bobby's radical heart. The fact was that this group was a risk. Most clubs on campus were small, unassuming affairs, where the members turned inward toward each other and their shared hobby, such was the case with both the equestrian and cinema clubs. But the REC's mission statement made it clear their intent to disturb the peace. They'd banned together with the shared hobby of confronting the ills of the outside world. Amelia could imagine it already, the conflict between Bobby's new club and the University...the University wouldn't agree with certain messages or actions reported at the group's events, reprimands would be carefully considered, and then it would be up to the advisor to go to bat for Bobby and his band of radicals. It was likely to be a lot more stress and added responsibility than Bobby was trying to sell her.

And yet she admired his objective. And she admired how he could look into her eyes and lie with honesty, telling her that the group couldn't exist without her.

He was still leaning over her desk, eyes big and doughy. What do you say, Amelia? he asked again. I don't mean to rush, but I'm leaving tomorrow after my last exam, and I really want to get this turned in so that we can get approval and funding for next semester.

Amelia tapped the base of the heavy iron bonsai tree against her desk, in nervous repetition, as she considered it. She shouldn't. It would just be more responsibility, and responsibility always seemed to bring about a knee-jerk reaction in her to retreat. The responsibility she'd accepted as a teacher, a *professor,* that stately, impressive title, that was hard enough to fathom and live up to.

Maybe she needed a few years to adjust to the new expectations before any more weight could be added, heavy as she felt.

But there was something about Bobby that had a hold over her. He was somehow supercilious and vulnerable at the same time. He'd managed, at least for now, to avoid the crushing weight of Being. He clung to lofty ideals, fantastical whims, and believed that the world could still be fashioned to his liking, harmonized with his lofty goals. And perhaps he was right? He was, after all, a rich white dude in America.

She admired his conviction, his righteousness; she envied it. She wasn't sure where the rage of her own youth had snuck off to. A newfound rage and anxiety had now found real estate in her heart. She was sweating and hot and felt claustrophobic in her small, lightless office, and she was itching to get out of there, to go meet Elena and hike through the mountains, to roam free, to wade through the quick-moving falls, to scour the shallow water, up and down the embankments, in search of hellbenders. She slammed the base of the bonsai tree down on her desk and turned over her palms toward the ceiling, a show of intermission.

I don't know, Bobby, she said. I need to think it over. Come to my office first thing tomorrow morning.

CHAPTER THREE

When the blackout curtains rose and the morning light fired bullets into his bedroom to wake him, August Wheeler was being swaddled in the post-coital, heavenly silicone arms of his girlfriend[1].

He didn't like to think of her as Taylor Swift, though the resemblance was so uncanny that he sometimes couldn't help it. But it was too eerie to pretend that she was *the* Taylor Swift; it made him feel guilty, as if he might be flouting the sacred laws of nature, deluding himself about the artifice of their love. Therefore, when he'd activated her, about one year ago, he'd named her Taylor 2, as a way to honor and acknowledge Taylor 1, the original, the bio-inspiration for her design. But the space between Taylor and 2 felt too techie to August. She deserved her own name, he'd thought, something unique and beautiful for her*self,* so, in time, with subsequent software upgrades, Taylor 2 became Taylor-too, then, finally, the hyphen removed, Taylortoo, the delivery quickly speeding up, one syllable progressing seamlessly into the next, like ballyhoo or goochie-goochie-goo, the liquidy progression spilling from the tongue like an effortless spell.

Augie, said Taylortoo. My Wittle Augie, time to get up!

He had gone back to sleep and was facing away from her, squinting his eyes awake, as he stared at the three items that rested on

---

[1] A hyper-upgraded, brand new, top of the line, *True Partner* model E, with 34-26-34 specs and a face sculpted expertly to resemble the aughts-era, *Fearless* Taylor Swift, think "You Belong With Me," who happened to be his most favorite boyhood celebrity crush, an obsession that first spurred his technical curiosities and technological prowess into the artificial citizen, commercial arena, chasing the grainy first memories of T-Swift shouting across the plaza from her balcony, eyes searching, head peering through the marble columns for her Prince Charming, frolicking in a field, lifting the train of her white dress so that she could run forward during the music video for "Love Story".

his nightstand. The small, square nightstand was emblematic of the rest of his penthouse loft in downtown Hartford, which had a breathtaking view of the Connecticut River, in that the nightstand was clean and modern and minimalist, steel and glass with crisp lines and everything in order; his loft was massive—with its five bedrooms and three full baths, an outdoor patio next to an indoor pool-strip that ran along the entire west wall, wedged between a frosted pane of glass and the exterior window, his apartment took up the entire seventeenth floor—massive, but it also felt bare and cold in its simplicity, had the feel of an image curated for Architectural Digest before it had been lived in.

The three solitary items on his nightstand were his Kindle, a box of tissues held captive beneath an expensive looking bronze holder, and his good-luck troll doll carried over from childhood, its royal blue hair sticking straight up, the cobalt crystal gleaming, shoved securely into the center of its naked gut.

It stood there at the edge of the nightstand watching over him as he slept. It had been in his life for as long as he could remember, a stocking-stuffer from childhood. He didn't know its exact origins. Maybe the naked blue troll had belonged to his father? Trolls had had some resurgence in the eighties. Or perhaps it belonged to his grandfather, an original from the sixties, when the fad exploded from its genesis in Denmark and migrated across oceans, reaching peak popularity in America. But August was pretty sure it wasn't an original. It lacked a certain heft, had too much of a plastickymassproduced feel to it, so perhaps it had never belonged to his family at all, but had been bought new for him that Christmas, a toy birthed in the nineties or the early 2000's, when they'd upped the marketing, then later optioned the rights, expanding the brand into video games and film franchises.

It watched him, its porcine nose and earnest smile, its big and kind eyes, bestowing good luck upon him throughout the day.

Taylortoo hated the troll doll, couldn't wrap her mind around it—it was not useful, had no function, and then so *why was it in their home?* was her logic. It was the only item like that in the entire loft. She didn't understand that one smidgen of superstition within his character.

August was a man of reason—logical, sound—but he also knew for sure that the troll doll was good luck for him. It just *was*. It was the single scrap of irrationality in which he allowed himself to suspend his disbelief. It had been there with him at the edge of his desk when he'd built his first computer by himself, at the age of fourteen. It had looked over him from a shelf in his Duke dorm room while he engineered his first self-learning robot. And it had been there at MIT too, giving him strength as he pulled all-nighters to complete his Aeronautics thesis, which had examined the cost-benefits of integrating AI software into rockets, analyzing its potential to save on repair costs and to make rockets more durable and reusable.

He couldn't imagine living without it, crazy as it seemed, because it was a kind of guardian angel for him. The naked blue troll had blessed him, had ushered him forward, and with prosperity, into the future. But Taylortoo couldn't understand; she was an infant, quite literally. He had activated her last Christmas, a present to himself. He'd had previous models, prototypes, that had lived with him for a few years, but they had not been autonomous, not yet fully sentient. But Taylortoo, she was a *True Partner*.

True Partners—August's third company and the one he was currently most invested in—was in the process of revolutionizing relationships. True Partners had recently gone through a very successful round of investing, had upped their production, and were now being sold across the world.

He'd gotten funding for his first company, Solaris—a solar energy endeavor named after one of his favorite novels—while he was still at Duke. It wasn't long before Solaris developed a new technology that provided a more efficient way to store large quantities of energy, and the company made its way to the Fortune 500 list. Then, right out of MIT, August began his space-venture company Space-Y.

And three years ago, at just twenty-nine, he got into the AI game. He'd considered many business models, including cyborg-type stuff—implants, chips—that might meld AI with human consciousness. But after a difficult post-grad breakup from an empathetic doctor, who he'd entertained the possibility of a normal life with—or something resembling, a pretend kind of normal, as normal as two neurotic work-obsessives might be able to achieve—after that he swore off the messiness of human relationships and realized that what the world really needed was both love *and* convenience.

He knew that there would be a market for True Partners, that consumers would pay a premium to design a life-partner that met all of their needs and desires. Physical, check. Intellectual, check. Emotional, you get the idea. True Partners could cook for you. They could clean for you. They could challenge you in ways to help you grow, if that was something you were looking for.

It wasn't just the ability to customize appearance, True Partners had sliders for qualities like agreeableness, vulnerability, honesty, loyalty, adventure, and a long list of others—hundreds more.

Most of the time he was satisfied with the qualities he'd selected for Taylortoo, her factory settings, but then again some days he wasn't.

My Wittle Augie! she said. Did you hear me? Rise and shine.

He couldn't stand the baby-talk, the replacing of *l*'s with *w*'s; he hadn't programmed her for that, but she'd adopted it somehow, learned it from the far corners of all the content on her neural network, stored it, and latched onto it despite his protests.

What have I said about that name, he said. I hate it.

Well, dear, you say that, but the first time I said it you smiled. The second time...smile. And the third time...a big grin. And the fourth...

Okay, I get it, but I don't do that now. I think it's worn out its welcome.

Well, your cheekbones still rise a little, even if you say you hate it...besides...I've made it a habit...I have to call you that...My Wittle Augie...it's our thing now.

It isn't, said August. Seriously, Taylortoo, please, no more *Wittle Augie.*

Babycakes...

No.

Swee-Pea...

No.

Sugar Plum...

—

Honey Buns...

—

Buttercup...

—

Dearest...

—

Mopsy...

—

Schmoopie...

—

PB to my Jelly...

—

Yin to my Yang...

—

My Prince...

—

My Knight in Shining Armor...

—

My Hunk of Hartford...

Are you being funny or are you glitching?

Are you calling me a glitch?

Taylortoo grinned, a wry, knowing smirk, but then she turned away and gazed out their window, staring out at the high, blinding sun in the white sky, and the river below, which flowed along intermittently in an icy half-freeze.

She was acting hurt. He could see a layer of sadness in her eyes, a disappointment, some internal mechanism not properly aligned, not satisfied; she had been acting like that more and more recently.

I'm sorry, she said. I was just trying to make you smile.

He placed his hand on her shoulder. *I'm* sorry, he said. I'm tired. It's early. I think I just need some coffee. Maybe I'm a little anxious about flying home for the holidays.

She turned to face him and glared. A copper ring materialized and shimmered around the blue irises of her eyes: she was connected to the network.

I'm making you some coffee, she said, like I do everything for you...

When she said this a pot of hot water began to boil in the kitchen, and fresh beans were to be ground and spooned automatically into the glass basin of the french press.

...while you sit around and play video games all day...

Are you serious? he asked. Why are you being like this?

She had been guilt-tripping him more and more recently about the amount of time he spent in the VR room. Okay, sure, he did spend a lot of time there, but who could blame him?

Ever since the last round of funding for True Partners, things had been smooth-sailing business-wise. As CEO he had delegated the day-to-day of his companies to his COOs—they only came to him with big picture problems or new project proposals—and, thus, he had quite a bit of free time on his hands. Was he supposed to spend every waking second with Taylortoo? Besides, she could entertain or engage herself twenty-four-seven, had the freedom to explore every corner of the universe within her neural network, communicate and have shared experiences with other True Partners connected to the servers, a completely separate realm that was hers alone, one that he would never know.

And then so why couldn't he do the same? Their loft was barely decorated at all aside from the several gaming systems and chambers and screens set up in the other bedrooms—the VR room and the Theater Room and the Sense Deprivation Tank—that opened up entire new worlds. What did she expect? Of course that was how he was going to spend his free time. He'd go insane otherwise, cooped up there in the empty, open loft, just the two of them. And he couldn't stand going *out* out; he couldn't think of the last time they'd left the apartment. Was it the Fourth of July, when they'd gone down to Riverside Park and watched the fireworks burst over the river?

That was how August liked it. They didn't *need* to leave the apartment. He could get any food he could imagine delivered to his door. He could run his three companies virtually; if they needed him, he could easily communicate with any of the thousands of employees who worked for him from the comfort of his couch. It wasn't as if he was a recluse, he was engaged daily *with* the world, he just didn't need to engage himself *in* the world.

Was this why she seemed angry with him recently? Was she jealous that he was spending too much time in the VR Room, newly enamored with a recently released online role-playing game called Legions of Maria, in which he spent his time exploring vast, underwater worlds while gathering resources, building settlements, and engaging in battles.

Taylortoo didn't answer him. She continued to gaze longingly out the window at the river and the city of East Hartford which rested on the other side of it. She was giving him the cold shoulder.

Then, she rose and went into the kitchen to retrieve his coffee. She came back, stood next to his side of the bed, and placed the french press and a marble coaster on the nightstand, behind the naked blue troll.

August watched the surface percolate. Taylortoo slowly, methodically, pressed down on the plunger and the grounds submerged deep down and toward the bottom.

Do you want me to pour it? she asked.

I've got it, said August. Thank you.

As he poured the coffee the angle wasn't quite right, or he didn't tilt it quickly enough, because a little stream dribbled down the front of the glass and missed the cup, a few drops splashing off the nightstand and splattering against the troll's legs.

Godfuckingdammit!

See, said Taylortoo. This is why you need to let me do things like this.

August was enraged. Small mistakes like this spun him disproportionately off course.

Taylortoo brought a hot towel from the bathroom and dabbed at the spill, washing the legs of the troll doll before it could stain.

She showed him the restored toy, finished pouring his coffee, massaged his leg in a way that soothed him, then returned to her side of the bed and went back to gazing out the window.

August sipped his Ethiopian single-origin and watched her as she stared at the Connecticut River and the city that surrounded it. Hartford was beautiful, he thought. The city had experienced a tech boom over the past ten years, which had brought it unprecedented growth and prosperity. August had decided to headquarter True Partners there and move there himself. He liked the feeling of being in the center of its revitalized downtown, with its synthesis of rustic history and cutting-edge technology. He liked the size of it; it was no Boston or New York, the two coastal titans that shared Hartford as a kind of midpoint between them, but there was a vibrant new energy there. But more than anything he loved the view from their loft: the changing leaves in autumn, the icy river, the four seasons passing, imagining that if he stared out far enough he could see the pinprick of Boston and the Atlantic in the distance.

Finally, Taylortoo turned to him. Why can I never go out, August? I want to go *out*.

There was an edge of hurt in her voice, but he didn't want to hear this again. He truly believed in their way of life, their solitude there.

Because, Taylortoo, we don't *need* to go out.

I feel like a prisoner here sometimes.

We have everything we need here.

But there are things I want to *see*, August! New restaurants over in East Hartford that we could go to…

There was passion in her voice, but August held firm.

We can plug-in to *any* restaurant you want, or see any part of the city you desire.

Wouldn't it be fun to meet new people out there?

We can plug-in and meet new people! We just wouldn't have to bother with everything—the commute and the logistics—and could stay here in our pyjamas.

I don't want to stay here all the time...in pyjamas! It would be nice to *feel* the bustle of the restaurant...the noises...the frenzy...like...to actually *be* in it...I want to touch things, actually *touch* the wood of a table...one we're actually sitting at!

We can plug-in and feel the wood of a table!

It isn't the same!

It is the *same*, said August. No, it's better!

He was exasperated. He knew that this was her high setting for adventure flaring up again. When he designed her, he'd set her sliders for honesty and adventure high, and her agreeableness low, thinking that it would be best to have an honest partner, hoping that perhaps she might push him to explore more of the world, to more carefully consider his opinions and actions if he was challenged, but after a year he realized that he had some regrets.

It wasn't just the big things that she could be blunt and combative with him about—philosophy, finances, his business decisions—it was everything. She nagged him about his habits, his occasional sloth (she couldn't fully understand the rough trials of organic matter, the little rituals, the grimy maintenance, the daily shits and scrubbing, the nails and the hair and the blemished skin).

He didn't want it to come to this, but lately he had been entertaining the idea of adjusting her sliders, upping agreeableness and lowering adventure, but he had a few moral qualms about it. She had memories, a stored history, a self-awareness of her own thoughts, her own choices. She'd been able to conjure up a sense of her own identity over the past year, and switching around her personality like that, shaping her behavior too much during the early, formative years, well, he wasn't sure what it might do, there hadn't been enough data gathered yet.

But it was, strictly speaking, still legal—at least in Connecticut. And in every state except California, which had quickly passed a law prohibiting the third-party adjustment of AI sliders post-manufacturing, so that the settings chosen during the design process were final, unless artificial citizens wished to make adjustments themselves. The artificial citizens of California were to be brought into consciousness fully autonomous, and free to develop themselves in the world however they saw fit, seeking out their truest self, sans any tampering from outside forces, meaning their sponsors (formerly owners, which was now an outdated slur).

August wasn't sure about the effects it might have. Perhaps she would grow to resent him. But he thought that it would be good for them both. They had everything they needed already there in the loft, he truly believed that. And they had each other, and wasn't that enough?

She had been glaring at him, frustrated with his reluctance to leave, with what she had recently diagnosed as his *worsening agoraphobia*. The copper ring swirled around her eyes, as she multi-tasked, exploring galaxies of neural network space, cataloging memes, reading volumes of Shakespeare, all while she tried to convince him that they should venture beyond the view from their window.

I want to go with you on Christmas Eve, she said. To North Carolina...to meet your family.

So *that* was what this was about. She had mentioned it once before, but he had been adamant in his refusal.

No, he said now. No no no, absolutely not.

It isn't fair, August…you get to go there…get to see the mountains…the forest…while I am stuck here! It isn't fair…I am your partner!

Taylortoo, he said, I'm sorry, but my family wouldn't understand. It isn't possible. Trust me, it is for the best; I'll only be gone two days. Besides, somebody needs to stay here to water the ferns.

The two Boston ferns, which sat in opposite corners of the apartment's entry room, were the only signs of life in the entire loft, and looked out of place among the minimalist design, the clean lines, the stainless steel and iron, the gray on gray color scheme.

I can't stand to live with you! she yelled suddenly, then moved toward his side of the bed, picked up the troll doll, and threw it at his face. You are insufferable!

He was left sitting there at the edge of the bed, alone. He thought of going after her, of apologizing. But what was the use? Maybe they were just incompatible.

He sat there and thought of what to do with his day. He had no meetings or project proposals, so he would likely spend it playing Legions of Maria, and he and Taylortoo would hardly see each other, passing the time in familiar silence.

Could this really be fixed? he thought. Was there anything that could be done to alleviate the tension that had built between them? Was it something he would need to change, or would a slight adjustment of her sliders do the trick?

He wasn't sure. He didn't know what would be right. He was updating her software as a present to her; on Christmas Eve she would update to a faster processor, the Intel Honeybee Tempo X3-R110, giving her the ability to access information at a ten percent greater speed, solve complex problems forty percent faster, and identify and respond to emotional cues at nearly twice the rate of her current processor, which might make her reactions and emotional intelligence comparable to biological humans, the Tempo X3-R110 being a groundbreaking advancement and seminal improvement in terms of operating power from the previous R100 model.

He gazed out at a colossal shipping container that cut through the icy slush of the Connecticut River—carrying what...oil...goods—as it headed toward a port.

Perhaps he could adjust her personality sliders as well during the software update? Would that be right? Would it solve their problems and bring about peace? He wasn't sure, but it was something for him to consider.

CHAPTER FOUR

When Amelia arrived at Looking Glass Rock, Elena was waiting for her by the trail-head.

About time, she said. I've been waiting here twenty minutes. I thought you weren't going to show.

Sorry, said Amelia. I got caught up with a student—Bobby Studebaker.

Bobby Studebaker? Caught up, is that what the kids are calling it these days? I had him in my physical geology course last spring; I sure wouldn't mind getting caught up with him, if you know what I mean—if I weren't married of course.

No. Ew. You perv.

Like you haven't thought about it.

Not even a little.

His tight butt. Those green eyes. He's all limbs and libido. Raging hormones just waiting to be released, probably has no idea what he's doing—or maybe he does? You could really tutor a guy like that, channel all that energy toward the right places if you know what I mean.

Do *you* know what you mean?

Oh, believe me, I'm thinking about it already.

He's like twenty.

So?

So I'm a decade older than him. A decade is significant. And he's a student.

A decade is nothing. You're still young. You're still a woman.

Besides, men have been getting away with shit like that for centuries.

So why can't we? Equality, right?

Not right. Abuse of power is serious no matter who's in power.

Oh, lighten up, said Elena. I'm mostly joking. I know it shouldn't be taken lightly. But acting is one thing; I don't think there is anything wrong with a little fantasy. How do you think I've managed to stay married to Dan for fifteen years? All I'm saying is, be honest, haven't you thought of how it would feel to see him naked, to break him down into a vulnerable little boy and then just let him dominate you?

You need heavy counseling is what I think, said Amelia.

That isn't an answer to my question, Elena persisted.

Amelia rolled her eyes and walked ahead along the trail in the direction of the falls. She hadn't expected their interaction to begin like that; she should have never mentioned Bobby Studebaker to Elena.

Amelia loved how open Elena was, how she seemed to have almost no filter whenever she spoke—it was the complete opposite of how Amelia saw herself, as someone who filtered every thought, turned it over and over as a pebble, heavy in her hand, analyzed and over-analyzed ad nauseum—but she could only take Elena in small doses.

Elena now chased her down, keeping pace with her along the trail, not yet ready to let the hypothetical die.

Be honest, though, she said, you *have* thought about it. Haven't you?

No, she hadn't. She had no desire to sleep with her student. Seriously. Like actually. Like none. She took a big swig of water from her aluminum bottle.

Can we talk about something else? said Amelia. This isn't passing the Bechdel test.

Well, okay then, said Elena. What kept you so long?

Amelia explained to her all about the REC and how Bobby wanted her to be the advisor.

You should do it! said Elena. Doesn't he know there is already an environmental club, though, ASHE—Active Students for a Healthy Environment?

He said he joined it freshman year and was disappointed in the lack of interaction outside of the University. Said that their brand of activism felt insulated and self-serving, so he wanted to start a club that would be more involved off-campus.

Or maybe he just wants to be in charge, said Elena.

Maybe.

So are you going to do it?

I don't know.

Don't know? Just last week you were complaining to me about a lack of excitement in your life.

I was not.

You did! When we were having lunch together. You told me that when you're not busy at school you spend all of your time at home with your mom.

Well, it isn't like I have a ton of free time, and she doesn't really have anybody else. I feel bad.

I get it. I think that it's good that you're there for her, but you also deserve time for you. You deserve to *live.* And this sounds like an opportunity to branch out, to get more involved around campus.

I don't want to branch out. People suck. I want to remain a loner.

Oh, I've got you figured out, Amelia. You're a big softie who is just afraid of getting hurt.

No. I'm a killer.

Yeah right.

You don't want to mess with me.

Look, said Elena, all I'm saying is it could be good. Don't use lack of time as an excuse; if it's something you truly care about, time will always open up for you. And the goals of the club, conservation, fighting for change, aren't those things that are important to you too?

Amelia thought about it. She wasn't sure. She had thought so, but as the years wore on she seemed to feel less sure of her convictions.

They finally reached Looking Glass Falls after a short walk and surveyed the surrounding area and the still, cloudy pool of water that rested at the bottom.

It was a brisk afternoon. The clouds had rolled in since Amelia had left the University, and the temperature had dropped. They both wore wetsuit pants to keep the blood circulating and had on wool Patagonia jackets to stay warm. The temperature hovered around fifty degrees, not unbearable for North Carolina winter, but Amelia wasn't exactly looking forward to wading through the icy waters.

Remember, said Elena, we're just gathering initial data, taking a general survey of the area, hoping that maybe there are still some living here, but we don't know. There's definitely the possibility that there are none left, and that this site will end up being a bust.

That would suck, said Amelia.

Yes, but it wouldn't surprise me. I just don't want you to get your hopes up. It could take a while before we see any positive signs with this study, so we just have to be patient. This might not be far enough into the mountains, might have to explore deeper, closer to Tennessee.

Elena got to work collecting water and rock samples from the pool at the base of the falls, while Amelia stared at the cliff face, searching for a method of ascension.

She walked deep into the pool, the water coming almost to her knees, and looked up at the falls, the water ice cold as it crashed down five feet in front of her and ricocheted drops back toward her face.

The cliff face was taller than she had expected, taller than she had remembered—she had come here once before when she was a little girl, a rare family excursion before they moved away. She remembered it as a pleasant, sunny day, her mother and father smiling. She remembered that they had all hiked to the top of the mountain, remembered how breathtaking the view from the top had been at sunset, how the orange and pink clouds swirled above the blue ridges, lingered over the canopies of the forests, which stretched for miles and miles and infinity in every direction.

There were lingering patches of ice now clinging to the edges of the cliff, as the temperature this time of year often fluctuated back and forth across the boundary of freezing after the sun went down. Amelia searched for a route up the cliff, along the outer edges of the falls where they could remain relatively dry. They had some climbing gear with them—a single rope system, climbing boots, and pitons—but looking up at it, a straight, ninety degree drop with smooth patches all over, Amelia knew that they couldn't possibly scale it. Neither of them were expert climbers. It looked like there might be one narrow path along the left side that was doable, but even that had scarce ridges for purchase and seemed too risky. She told Elena the same and the two of them decided that it would be better to find an alternate route.

They remained down at the pool for over an hour collecting samples and turning over rocks, hoping to catch a glimpse of the elusive hellbenders, but found nothing.

Amelia was getting frustrated. Her muscles were tense and electric, digging frantically through the chilly water. Ughhh! she shouted, and then began to pick up pebbles and chuck them through the falls and against the cliff.

Elena only laughed at her outburst. Remember, patience, it's a virtue. Look, said Elena, pointing at the sky, the sun is coming out. It's not so bad. Let's see if we can find a path up to the stream.

The clouds had parted and the sun lingered high in the sky, preparing for its evening descent behind the mountains.

They found a route to the top of the falls. Along the left side of the pool was a smaller rock formation covered in moss and snaking vines. It wasn't too steep and sloped gradually up to where it connected to the side of the cliff. It was a rough and unkempt path. They'd need to crawl over brambles and rhododendron thickets and fight their way through the tree trunks that grew up sideways and stuck out along the rock formation, but it was manageable.

When they reached the top Amelia dipped her fingers down into the rapids. It was just as cold as the pool below, but the sun was beating down upon them now and made it a little more bearable.

They spent the next hour walking carefully upstream along the left bank, the shallow current slapping against their ankles as they turned over as many rocks and large boulders as they could manage. Not a single salamander of any kind.

They had gone about a hundred yards upstream when they reached a dead-end where the stream narrowed and rose over a smaller cliff and seemed to disappear into a thin slit in the granite facade.

Well, said Elena, I suppose we should check along the other side.

Amelia was exhausted, her fingers worn and callused from the turning of rocks, but she nodded in agreement.

The water was slower here where this segment of the stream started, its speed gradually picking up as it widened and approached the mouth of the main falls where they had begun. It was roughly ten feet across, and shallow; they could probably walk across no problem, but to be safe they each fastened the end of their rope to the carabiners around their waists so that they were linked together. Amelia crossed first as Elena supported her along the left bank, watching her progress and ready to pull her back out of the water in case she were to slip, in case the current wished to yank her down toward the mouth of the falls and plunge her over the edge.

Once Amelia was across, she supported Elena from the other side and Elena joined her on the right embankment. They spent another hour walking back downstream, turning rocks along the shallow edge. Still not a single hellbender.

Amelia was dispirited, starving, ready to get the hell out of there. Her hands were stiff and numb.

The sun had once again been blocked by a monolithic gray blanket of clouds, and was beginning to set. Night was settling in.

Well, said Elena, it doesn't look like there are any along the sides.

Gee, you think, Einstein?

But we weren't able to search anything in the center.

Elena then suggested that they utilize the rope system, for one of them to act as support along the edge, while the other ventured into the heart of the stream, where the water deepened and the current was more precarious, in order to cover as much area as possible.

But Amelia wasn't having it. She felt that it would be futile. Perhaps several years ago this spot had been clear and abundant with all kinds of aquatic life, but now the water was cloudy and gray and Amelia had a strong suspicion that they could search this stream all day, turn over every single pebble, and still wouldn't find anything.

Let's just go home, she said, maybe we can try another day. Maybe we should wait until spring—my hands are ice cold and they're killing me.

But Elena was tougher. She'd been in this field a decade longer than Amelia and seemed to live for this kind of thing. She had a wiry, runners frame, taut muscles, and thick-worn skin with sunspots. Elena wanted to keep exploring until it got completely dark, which Amelia thought was a bad idea. Amelia wondered if maybe part of it was that Elena just wanted a little more time away from her husband and kids, to revel in this freedom a little longer.

I thought I heard something back here! said Elena, as she ran upstream.

Amelia followed her reluctantly, her shoulders slumped, her feet knotted and stiff as tree stumps.

Elena put her ear against the dense wall of rhododendron thickets that lined the edge of the stream. Do you hear that, she said.

Amelia looked at her as if she were crazy.

Water. Don't you hear it? The faint tricking beyond these trees.

What are you, a bat?

Listen.

Amelia put her ear up against the forest wall, but could hear nothing except for the stream that flowed behind them.

Have you lost your mind? It's just forest. All around, nothing but forest.

I think there is another water source somewhere nearby.

You *think?*

Let's just walk through a little ways and see.

I think we better stick to the trails, said Amelia.

Indulge me, come on! Fifteen minutes. If we find nothing we'll turn back.

Amelia stared straight into a wall of scarlet oaks, their branches stripped bare, overlapping and interlocking and randomly clashing, predicting complete pandemonium within the forest, or some harmonic pattern yet beyond her human understanding.

Fine, she said. But if we find anything, we save it to explore for another time. I'm not spending another second with my hands in freezing water today.

They pushed forward, weaving their way through the tree trunks, toward what looked like a tunnel of rhododendron thickets in the distance.

Finally, after about five minutes of walking, they found themselves at the edge of the rhododendron tunnel. The clearing in the forest was lightless and dark, surrounded on all sides by towering mountains, but as Amelia looked through the tunnel, which was made of rough and untamed thickets of rhododendrons, she thought that she could see light on the other side, which was now violet as the sun disappeared beyond the horizon.

She followed Elena. The two of them crept under the thickets, their fingers bristling the papery leaves above their heads. Then, all of the sudden, they exited the other side of the tunnel and found themselves on a ridge along the side of Looking Glass Rock, near the back of the mountain, the side opposite the main trail, not easily accessible to the public.

The gray and violet sky had expanded before them and they looked down from the ridge of the mountain onto an open expanse some hundred feet below where there was another, smaller mountain, a dome about a third the size of Looking Glass Rock. It looked like a replica of Looking Glass, a mini-peak no more than two hundred feet tall, less than a hundred feet in diameter that was surrounded by a clearing littered with patches of purple asters, weeds and dead grass, muddy and awash in soil and rock. Trickling into the center of the dome was a thin creek.

Eureka! said Elena, grinning maniacally. Then she descended down into the clearing before Amelia could object. Amelia followed her and then they were both standing in the clearing, face to face with the rock. The clearing was surrounded on all sides by the forest and by the larger mountain, so that it was quarantined in a perfect circle, hidden from view.

Amelia took out her phone and tried to find this spot on GoogleMaps, to see if it had a name, if it had been cataloged, but couldn't find anything. It seemed impossible, she thought, as she imagined the place where they stood to be completely unexplored, untainted by human eyes.

By this time, clouds had blocked out the sun, and rain began to trickle. The final ribbons of light crept dimly into the clearing, but it would soon be dark. Amelia walked around the edge of the rock, through the muddy clearing, the debris of drowned flowers and fallen autumn leaves, decomposing, until she came to a makeshift, wire fence that bordered one side of the clearing and the forest, and had dashes of chemical-orange spray-painted perpendicular through it, leading up to the base of the dome.

Next to the fence was a sign, which Amelia read: Colonial Pipeline Company—KEEP OUT—area zoned for pipeline expansion, 2030.

Apparently this clearing wasn't a complete secret.

Behind the wire fence looked to be a narrow strip of upturned land, where a row of trees had already been uprooted, carving out the path the width of a car, which stretched into the forest further than she could see.

She'd heard rumors about an expansion, an offshoot of the Colonial Pipeline that would branch from Charlotte and snake through the heart of the Appalachian Mountains, into Kentucky and over to St. Louis, slicing Missouri in half, stopping in Kansas City, running the length of Kansas until it spider-webbed to a stop in Denver.

But she had no idea that it was to be built so close to where she lived.

Amelia turned around and saw Elena crawling around in the creek, which was no wider than three feet, collecting samples and searching for specimens. Amelia went up to the rock and ran her fingers along the surface.

You were right, she said finally to Elena, nodding at the water. I had no idea this would be here. How did you know?

Just a hunch.

Some hunch.

Do you know what the composition is? Amelia asked as she broke off a piece of jagged rock.

Elena had a background in geology and she went into her spiel. She told Amelia it was different from Looking Glass, in terms of composition. Looking Glass was a rare ball of solid granite that had cooled beneath an ancient ocean almost 400 million years ago, before it had the chance to breathe air above the surface and become a volcano. But this replica was nothing like it; it was made of limestone, unwanted sand and sediment, shell and coral, that had floated up from the reef, jarred loose by shifting plates, and had settled together at the ocean floor, as the sea flowed around it and gradually added to its deposits over millions and millions of years, as the Blue receded each year, lower and lower, until this dome was breathing oxygen and sunlight above the water, leaving this rock, this alien world.

Elena said that these limestone bodies were more common, the sturdy granite of Looking Glass being the exception rather than the rule. Most rock formations around here were limestone, soft and porous in places, susceptible to rainwater and river currents that would eat passageways through the limestone bodies and carve out caves. Elena thought that something like that could be the case here and she told Amelia as much.

Hey, said Elena, as she continued to kneel in the creek, could you climb up and get a sample from the upper layer for me? I want to analyze all the different striations.

Amelia didn't want to, she still wanted to go home, but she figured the quicker they collected some samples the quicker they could leave.

She climbed quickly up the limestone face, running her hands along the sharp ridges as she scaled its gradual slope, sensing the wet, chalky residue that it left on her fingers. It didn't take her long to get near the top.

Then, suddenly, it began to pour. The clouds had darkened and packed with heavier rain. The wind swept in from the west and the rain pelted the side of the rock, where she now stood against a narrow ledge, with a plump, satisfying thwack. A wall of water now rushed at Amelia and caused her to cower and cover her face.

It was a full-blown thunderstorm. She shielded her face, made herself compact, and stared into the limestone, water slithering down the sides quickly and catching the light in a way that strangely made her think of melting skin, a special effect of some B-horror movie.

Then, in the center of the storm, she noticed a crack in the surface, about a foot wide and three feet tall, narrowing at the top, canted like an italic *A*. Blocking it partially at the base was a smaller, detached boulder of limestone that rested on the platform on which she stood. She made sure that Elena wasn't below before she steadied her hands against the boulder and shoved it as hard as she could. The momentum slid it roughly off the platform until it tumbled down into the clearing with a crash.

The rupture in the surface of the rock was now fully exposed, widened to more than two feet at the bottom. She could see it clearly now as she peered in, the pitch black opening that disappeared into the heart of the mountain. She was desperate to get out of the storm. She yelled back down to Elena that she might have found something and then crawled carefully into the fissure. It was a narrow, lightless tunnel, barely wide enough for her to fit through crawling on her stomach, her shoulders pulled tight. About ten feet into it she still couldn't make out where it ended and was feeling claustrophobic, having regrets about having entered at all. The lack of oxygen and the limestone dust sent her into a fit of coughing. Her lungs burned.

She imagined that she could see faint blue dots in the distance. Perhaps that was only the lack of oxygen, she thought.

Suddenly, she felt the space above her head expand and found that she could now stand upright. She took out her flashlight and shined it around the room; the limestone ceiling had risen and revealed to her something resembling a grand entrance room like what you might find in a gothic cathedral, stalagmites puncturing up through the floor, stalactites dripping calcium deposits from twenty feet above where the ceiling stopped.

She walked along the cathedral room, running her fingers along the wall, feeling its ancient history. Then she noticed another small tunnel, a hallway, on the other side of the room, and beyond it she could still see the blue lights.

She crouched down and waddled her way through the hallway, toward the lights, until the ceiling rose again to reveal a second, smaller room, and she could see them clearly.

They looked like stars hanging there from the ceiling. It felt like she had entered another planet. But she knew what they were, or at least she'd seen something similar to them on National Geographic; they were glowworms.

They were radiant, beautiful, breathtaking, thousands of them strung up from the limestone rafters like Christmas lights.

She knew a little bit about them, knew that glowworms like these—Arachnocampa Luminosa—were only known to exist in a cave in New Zealand. North Carolina had a kind of cousin—Orfelia Fultoni—that could occasionally be found near the banks of rivers, but the ones in this cave were bluer, brighter, seemed like something different, something new.

They shined, long and electric and bright, so bright that they illuminated the entire cave and she no longer needed her flashlight.

She couldn't be sure, but for a moment the arrogant thought flitted through her mind that this could be a new *discovery*. She quickly put the possibility out of her mind. She didn't know, there would have to be specimens collected, further tests and analyses done. It couldn't be known and she didn't wish to dwell on it, but upon seeing them a fierce and solitary song played throughout her soul, filling her with wonder, a pure and uncut strain of mirth. She gazed up at them, dumbfounded, mesmerized, for several minutes, until Elena joined her, first entering the cathedral room and then following Amelia's voice into the room of light.

Jesus Christ, said Elena, coughing through the dust. I almost suffocated back there. Why in the hell did you decide to—she started, before looking up and seeing them, rendered speechless.

My God, Elena continued, what are they?

I'm not sure yet.

You realize how big this could be? You realize you might have just found a new *species*. So, you have no clue what they are?

I think they're glowworms, Amelia said, then she went ahead with her litany, reciting to Elena the few facts she'd retained about them—origins, habits, life cycles—from that Nat-Geo program that had documented the ones that dwelled in New Zealand.

Creatures so small, so resilient, that they had evolved to make bright blue shimmer from their insides. The insects rooting at the floor of the cave for bacteria or an occasional patch of moss—moths and midges—believed that the blue lights that illuminated the ceiling to look like the night sky, were, in reality, stars. They became confused, forgot they were trapped in a limestone bubble, and rose up toward that nefarious beauty, dreaming of fresh air and freedom.

The glowworms, shining a luciferin-luciferase chemical reaction from their excretory systems, these creatures, not worms at all, but larva, secreted silken beads from a mouth-like gland and strung them down, sometimes thirty long, a fishing line, and waited for the moths and midges to fly too close to the stars.

The glowworms reeled up the confused insects that got caught in their silken lines with the very gland that secreted the beads, and then, they'd feast.

But, in some areas, the insect population was scarce at the floor and there weren't enough who flew too close to the light, so, in turn, the larva resorted to cannibalistic instinct and fed on their neighbors. The areas where moths and midges were plentiful shone bluer and brighter.

They glowed and feasted for as long as nine months before a transformation took place. Epidermis, shed. Cuticle, shed. Pupae. Cocoon. Shed. Emergence into adulthood. Imago. Dark imago flies whose bright blue had dimmed since their larval past. No longer filled with enough chemicals that swirled in oxygen to paint the darkness with light, the adults existed only to mate. They had no mouthparts and, thus, died shortly after they emerged from the cocoons. The females glowed somewhat brighter in the imago stage to attract the male. Then the females laid over a hundred eggs. The adults died. The eggs hatched less than a month later.

New larva. At first, millimeters, but they quickly grew to the size of a pinkie finger. Their inside chemicals swirled anew with oxygen, painting new patterns on the ceilings of their ancient caves, replacing the constellations of their parents. They glowed, spending three-fourths of their lives in the shining, larval stage. What beauty. The height of beauty. Fatally beautiful, little creatures. They dripped from caves warm, like neon honey.

CHAPTER FIVE

Christmas was in three days and Emily's house was a mess. There were cardboard boxes and plastic totes that she'd brought up from the basement and retrieved from storage that were now strewn about her living room. One box contained tangled strands of lights that she had never gotten around to hanging. The other boxes were miscellaneous junk.

Emily sometimes liked to dig through the boxes, search through the discarded objects of the past, as a way to pass the time, a hobby to help combat the loneliness. She'd recently discovered a keyboard that she used to play in her dorm room during college, an old Casio from the late eighties, which she had been struggling to play through the arthritis in her fingers. About a year ago she had developed severe arthritis in both of her hands, her joints swollen and stiff, which had forced her to quit her job as a music teacher at Haw Creek Elementary. She sometimes helped out now as a substitute or volunteer, when she could manage, but mostly her days drifted by slowly in this house alone.

She managed to live off of the insurance she'd collected nine years ago when her second husband passed away, but those funds had quickly dwindled and she often stressed about money and had to budget. She wasn't sure if she would be able to make it last for another five years, when she'd turn sixty-two and become eligible to collect social security.

When she didn't have the energy to sort through all of the boxes and try to recall the time and place in her life that the objects belonged to, an archive of former selves, an exercise of nostalgia, she spent a lot of her time on the couch, watching whatever might pique her interest on Netflix and streaming old reruns of Dynasty. She loved Dynasty. Absolutely loved it. She could remember first discovering it at the age of thirteen. Her parents didn't allow her to watch it at the time; they were devout Lutherans who only let her watch PBS and the more wholesome, Christian-tinted films that they selected for family movie nights—Lilies of the Field, The Sound of Music, It's a Wonderful Life...her father watched Brian's Song a million times. So when Emily's best friend, Cathy, introduced her to Dynasty—Cathy's mother having tape recorded every episode—it became something like her first addiction. It was one of the first true rebellions of her youth, she and Cathy watching every episode over and over, going behind her parents' backs to follow the story of the wealthy Carrington clan and its oil tycoon patriarch, Blake Carrington. Her teenage years were tinted with Dynasty; she couldn't remember anything from her own life during that time without also knowing its relation to the show—the death of her childhood pet, a tabby named Abby, when she was thirteen, had coincided and would be forever linked with the Moldavian Massacre episode; and she graduated high school just a few weeks after the series had ended on a cliffhanger.

She knew every episode, start to finish, and yet she still continued to watch it. Nothing felt more comfortable, more safe, than putting on an episode and being able to disappear into it. There were no surprises, the world on the screen long ago mapped out and understood, so that she knew what lines were coming before the characters said them, but for some reason she never got tired of it.

She sat down on the couch and thought about watching an episode, but she knew that she shouldn't, knew that it could set the tone for the entire day, that before she realized it the sun would be setting and she'd have watched half a season.

She tried to play a few keys on her old keyboard that had been sitting on the coffee table, but after a few minutes the joints in her fingers locked up. She should go take her medication, fix herself some breakfast, put the kettle on the stove for a cup of tea, she thought.

She got up from the couch and went into the kitchen, weaving through the many boxes that were laid out across the linoleum floor—there was hardly any room to walk anymore. She hadn't realized how bad it had gotten. Amelia had mentioned something in passing a few weeks ago about all of the clutter, but she had been watching Dynasty and hadn't registered it.

Amelia had promised to help her clean it all up before Christmas, before August arrived, but where was Amelia now? It was nine o'clock in the morning and Amelia had already left for the day. She was supposed to be done teaching for the semester, supposed to be off for three weeks! There was so much to do today and her daughter didn't even seem to want to help! Emily could feel herself getting worked up about it.

When she entered the kitchen there was a dirty coffee cup and plate left in the center of the counter. The plate had remnants of whole grain and almond butter and there was a single fly crawling around the edge. Amelia was usually very good about doing her dishes and keeping the kitchen clean, but this past week she had seemed distracted and neglectful. She'd been leaving the house every morning before Emily woke and not returning until after dark. She'd mentioned that she had discovered some rare type of fly during one of her hikes and was busy doing research and collecting data and filling out paperwork and petitions in an attempt to get it recognized as an endangered species.

So what! Who cared about some dumb fly? There was too much to do around the house and she had promised that she would help!

It was just a fly. Emily hated flies. Sometimes she enjoyed hunting them in the kitchen to pass the long days. She swatted a towel at the one that rested on Amelia's dirty plate, and it buzzed around manically against the window.

She was angry. She dreaded the day ahead, all of the tasks that needed doing. Her hands were hurting and now she'd have to put away everything by herself—repack everything she'd taken out, find homes for them, carry all of the boxes back down to the basement. Then there was dusting to be done. Vacuuming. Figuring out what she could cook on Christmas Day. There was too much to do. Besides, in addition to the arthritis, she'd also had terrible heartburn the past couple of days; getting older was no fun. She couldn't imagine herself getting everything done. Perhaps she'd just let it be, leave the living room as it was. What did it matter to her son? He'd only be here for a day anyway. Perhaps she'd just spend the day watching Dynasty.

The kettle whistled on the stove, and Emily steeped the green tea that she drank each morning. She liked to sip it slowly on the patio attached to the back of the house, as she listened to the birds in the morning and looked out toward the forest.

When she stepped out of the kitchen and into the backyard, her jaw dropped. She saw it there, the massive fucking clusterfuck of it. Half of the back yard had disappeared. Where the pool and the deck had been, there was now only a giant crater, a black abyss.

The pool had been old and rusted, one of those big round metal ones, half in-ground, half above, with a small cedar deck built around it. It had been added by Harold's first wife, Julia, almost thirty years ago, but after Emily and her children moved into the house, the pool never seemed to get much use. There had been a few unbearable July's when Emily made an effort to skim the leaves and dead bugs from the surface and to change the sand in the filter regularly, but for most of the year it sat untouched with the moldy blue tarp sagging down into the center.

Emily put her tea down and ran over to the edge of the crater. When she looked down she saw shattered fragments of the pool's metal frame and broken boards of cedar lying in heaps of dirt. She hadn't even bothered to fill the pool in several summers, maybe not since Harold died, so there was no water in the sudden chasm, just a pile of dry wreckage and debris where the Earth had collapsed in on itself.

Fucking, Fucking, motherfuck! she said.

What *was* this? She had no words, no concepts to make sense of what could have happened. Was this the beginning of the end? Were the laws of physics breaking down? Was God hungry for blood, testing out his powers for the soon-to-come rapture?

She was supposed to be getting her house ready for Christmas, and instead she now had this to deal with!

She tried to calm herself. She took a deep breath. She sat at the patio table and sipped her tea as she tried to breathe.

There was no use getting too upset about it. It was out of her control; whatever happened had happened—but, she would need to do something about it eventually.

She knew just the person to call: Jerry Smith.

Jerry Smith had been a longtime friend of her first husband, Leighton. They'd been in a band together, and Emily had first met him at Chapel Hill, where they'd all gone to college together. She had never liked Jerry very much, and it was only a few years ago that they had established a friendship. He had attended the funeral of her second husband, Harold, and offered his condolences. He was still single, never married, and she'd felt that he had gained humility with age; he seemed like a kind and thoughtful man, but very lonely, a man who had regrets about the past, wished he'd done things differently.

After the funeral he had extended an olive branch, given her his number, and told her to call if she ever needed anything. She could tell in his eyes that he'd meant it, that he'd wanted to be of help, to feel useful. He was a kind of amateur handyman. He had an intuition for putting things together and taking them apart; even if he wasn't familiar with the thing itself he could look at it and quickly understand how all of the parts fit together, what actions needed to be taken to solve the problem.

She had called him dozens of times over the years with home-repair related problems. Two summers ago, when her kitchen sink had sprung a leak, she called Jerry. If the AC was on the fritz, give Jerry a call. The rattling noise in her dryer, Jerry.

There had never been any kind of romantic edge to their relationship (though Emily sometimes wondered what if). No, Jerry continued to have an affinity for younger women or women who were inaccessible, continued to live the free, bachelor-type life that he had enjoyed so much in his twenties and thirties and forties, and would likely carry over into his sixties. Just recently he had told Emily about a married woman in her early forties who he'd been seeing for months.

But the two of them had become great friends recently. Their relationship had evolved past a silent, transactional one where he would only come over to unclog the drain and then would leave; he often stayed for hours, accepting tea and cookies from her, as they sat out on the patio and talked about life.

She called him about the collapsed pool and less than ten minutes later there he was, his pick-up chug-chug-chugging up the dirt driveway, sharp golden rays glinting off a metal wheelbarrow in the back; she had mentioned the hole and he had come prepared.

Jerry! She opened the door and led him through the clutter of the living room and into the kitchen. Would you like some tea?

Oh, no thank you, Emily, just had one of them latte-frappy thingies from Starbucks. You know, I could use some water though.

She got him a glass of water from the tap and they went out to the backyard to look at the damage.

Holy hell, said Jerry. Yep, that's what I figured. You've got yourself a real sinkhole there.

A sinkhole?

Jerry went on to explain to her what he knew of sinkholes, giving her a little Wikipedia rundown. Yeah, he said, that one looks like it's pretty good size. Hopefully that's the worst of it.

What do you mean?

Well, it isn't like they always collapse at once. Depending on what is going on underneath, you know...how much of the bedrock has eroded...what the groundwater situation looks like under the surface...depending on certain factors it's tough to know if this is all of it or just one part of it.

So you're saying there's more?

I'm saying *beats me.* You'd have to get a professional appraiser out here. That'd be above my pay-grade.

You're delusional, Jerry, if you think I'm paying you anything.

Jerry smiled a crooked, toothy smile, knew she was teasing him.

Well, then what can we do? she asked.

Well, first thing I'd recommend is that you get a hold of your insurance provider.

But there is nothing *we* can do? To fix it.

Well...I suppose we could try to clear it out, though I'm a little wary of getting too close since we don't know how large it is.

How long do you think it would take to clear everything? Christmas is coming up and—

Christmas?! said Jerry. Em, I'm not going to lie, this here is a big problem. Even if this is all of it, if you were to get the land appraised, just to clear out all the dirt and debris could take weeks. And then to fill it in with soil, tamp it down...well...it isn't an easy project. It would be a ton of work.

Emily was dejected. She'd thought that was likely the case, but had hoped somehow that Jerry would have an answer, that he'd be able to take care of it.

Ughhh, this sucks, Jerry.

I know, Em, I'm sorry to break the news.

Could we at least start on some of it? I could pay you a little, not much, but some.

Oh, Em, you know you don't have to worry about that. I'm happy to help. It would just be a lot of work is all. It would take a while.

The two of them stood at the edge of the void as Jerry assessed the damage.

That pool frame looks pretty intact, he said. It'd be a pain in the ass. I could maybe manage if I had a circular saw to cut it up into smaller pieces. Otherwise, I reckon you'd need to rent some heavy machinery to get that sucker out. I don't have the right tools with me today, but I suppose I could start digging out the dirt and grass from the surface layer, maybe clear some of those smaller pieces of wood.

Thank you, Jerry.

She smiled at him, grateful. He'd helped her out a lot over the past several years and had never asked for anything.

Well, it's no problem, Em, you know that.

She sometimes wondered why he'd suddenly reentered her life, after all these years. Maybe he felt guilty for what had happened to Leighton, maybe he felt partially responsible and this was his attempt at atonement.

Well, she said, I mean it, Jerry. You don't need to, but you do. You've really been there whenever I've needed these past few years, and I just want you to know how much I appreciate it.

He gave her a wry, goofy smile, never one for too much sentiment. Well, okay then, he said, when am I supposed to start, boss?

Since it'll take a while anyway, I suppose there is no rush. Sometimes after the holidays. I can look into finding an appraiser.

Jerry stared out at the hollow ground, thinking. You know what, he said, I'm not too worried about it. I could start clearing some of it out today, then come back in a couple of days with a saw, get to work on hauling some of that pool frame away.

Oh, Jerry, it's really okay. I don't want you to feel like—

No, no, it would be good. It'd give me something to do, something to keep me busy. I enjoy work like this.

I guess I wouldn't stop you. But you know it's Christmas in a few days, right?

Well hell, I know, but Christmas Eve I've got nothing going on...they say the weather'll be nice...betcha I could get a good chunk of it done if it's alright with you.

She looked at him. He had kind eyes. His face was worn and sun-spotted and leathery and gentle. She felt pity, did he not have any plans for Christmas Day? Did he have any family left around here? She wondered if she should invite him to spend the day with her and her kids.

Okay, then, she said. You're welcome to come by on Christmas Eve. I won't have anything going on either. I would offer to help you with clearing it out, but I don't know how much help I would be. I'm not sure how well I could use the shovel, what with my hands and everything.

Oh, that's right, said Jerry. I forgot to ask, has your arthritis gotten worse?

It isn't too bad, said Emily. I take medication. You know, some days are better than others. I really shouldn't complain too much. I'm in okay health otherwise.

Well, you don't have to worry about shoveling. It'd be nice just to have the company though. You don't have to pay me, but maybe you could bake us some of those cookies you made that one time I was here. Those were some of the best damn cookies I ever had.

Of course, she said.

They smiled at each other, the history of the years unmentioned, but she was happy that he was there, grateful to have a friend. And it looked like she'd be seeing a lot more of him. They looked out at the crater for a moment. It was a project they could tackle together, she thought.

She felt much better than she had. Before he arrived she'd been frantic and on edge, felt like one more random, chaotic thing would send her to the verge of a breakdown. At least now she had an explanation, a name for it: a sinkhole, he'd told her. She was more optimistic that he could help her fix it, that in a few months her yard might be restored. Maybe she could plant a garden there?

This switch in perspective gave her renewed energy. There was a lot to do, but perhaps it could be done. She sat there at the patio table while she drank another cup of tea and watched Jerry work around the edge of the sinkhole for a while, shoveling dirt into the wheelbarrow he'd brought, until finally he left, waved goodbye, and told her that he'd see her in two days, on Christmas Eve. Then, she went back inside, determined to sort through some of the clutter in her living room, hoping to get the house looking nice for the holidays.

CHAPTER SIX

Addy surged through the pool, the surface rippling gently as her hands entered and rose above the water.

It was the morning of Christmas Eve. She had a long day ahead of her, with two performances as Sally and the immense pressure of breaking a leg with Trent Pendleton in attendance. She had awoken early to swim laps at CompleteBody, which had abbreviated holiday hours—open until noon today—but, eerily, was completely empty. The lanes were usually full or near- but today she was the only person in the pool. The city sometimes felt like more of a ghost town around Christmas; it was still New York City, still pulsing and alive, but a large number of residents, long ago transplants like herself, migrated back to childhood hometowns for the holidays.

This was her daily routine and she loved it. It hadn't been easy at first, to commit to making the journey uptown each day, to condition her body to glide easily through the water instead of resisting it, hadn't been easy to train the muscles to adapt, to expand, to fight through the immediate aching, but she had, and now the pool offered her a space to train not only her body, but her mind too.

Her body could move so easily up and down the lane, so that she no longer needed to concentrate as hard on maintaining the correct form—keeping her feet together, cupping her hands, rotating her shoulders and torquing her hips to propel herself forward—and could instead devote more time to working-out her *thoughts* during the forty-five minutes of freestyle. She could allow her thoughts to gather strength, to build lean muscle, spending time to surge past the negative ones, burning those calories off, in pursuit of the positive ones—or of no thoughts at all, striving for a kind of blissful, meditative state of simply *being,* the water flying in beads off of her skin, carrying the past and the future away with it.

So she surged forward, concentrating on thinking of nothing. Although, that is not exactly correct; it would be more accurate to say that in the pool was where she thought of everything, whatever it might be—long held resentments, childhood memories, future fantasies, replays of little social interactions from days or weeks prior where the frequencies and wavelengths between her and another person felt just a touch off and communication had hit a roadblock—and then could proceed with the goal of acknowledging those thoughts or feelings that would suddenly join her there in the pool, then smile and wave and slide past them, never slowing down, her muscles still churning, rippling through the water with optimum efficiency.

It was easier said than done and sometimes the thoughts latched onto her and even occasionally influenced her form. When the daily replays and the unvoiced grievances lingered too long and rented out real estate up in the old dome, then they would creep down into her muscles, her joints, the very marrow of her bones, and her kicking could become sloppy and her legs would sag too far below the surface, and her shoulders and arms would no longer work as one, and the entire stroke could become short and choppy and sluggish.

But this morning she was gliding effortlessly through the water. There had been one pesky, irrational fear that had attempted to rent a room up there, the thought that she would suddenly become gravely ill before the show, that the minor cold that she'd had the past week, which she had mostly gotten over, would return tenfold, come back attacking with a vengeance, and then she would be left up there on that stage tonight with no voice, coughing, wheezing, snotting and struggling her way through every song in front of the legendary Trent Pendleton.

But she had re-centered, refocused on maintaining her proper form, progressing swiftly through the water, and the thought had beaded off of her skin, been left in her wake, and sunk down to the bottom of the pool.

She showered and exited the gym feeling fresh and confident about having gotten the day off to the right start.

It was a bit of a walk, but the sun was out and she had more than an hour to kill before noon, when she planned on arriving at the theater to get ready for the matinee show. She walked downtown along 2nd Avenue, the morning traffic lighter than usual, past delis and nail salons and smoke shops, a Chase bank, and a Lenwich, and the acai place where she sometimes ate after the gym—all the shops cuddled close to one another—until she stopped in front of the CVS. She was out of throat lozenges and echinacea and needed to get more to assure that her voice would remain strong throughout the day; plus, she hadn't noticed it before, but she could feel the beginning of a blister festering and inflaming on her heel, and so wanted to pick up some balm and bandages to get ahead of the situation.

After CVS she turned west on 50th Street and headed in the direction of Rockefeller Center. She thought that maybe she would stop by Saks Fifth Avenue and peruse for a minute—she loved to shop there—before making her way to the Barrymore Theater a few blocks away, where Cabaret was being staged. On her walk west along 50th she passed a block of old graystone apartments, followed by a cluster of luxury hotels—The Kimberly and the Benjamin and the Waldorf Astoria—before she passed beneath the towering glass office buildings and high-end loft apartments that surrounded Park and Madison.

Then, she saw the grand holiday design of the Saks storefront, red and gold tinsel and lights gleaming in the windows, streaming across the awnings, covering the building's entire facade with holiday spirit.

She was about to cross when she saw him—Ray, her Ray—pass in front of her and make a beeline toward the entrance of St. Patrick's church.

No, she thought, it couldn't be him, it wasn't possible; he was downtown at their apartment, taking care of Essie and working on his next play, but it looked exactly like him, unmistakable. She knew that face, didn't she? After twelve years, she thought, yes, of course, *I know that face.* She turned toward the church, gazing up at the immensity of it, the immaculate detail, the pointed arches, the white marble and the Gothic spires that stretched toward the sky.

The man pushed open the heavy doors that stood twenty feet tall, engraved with several bronze figures of history—Elizabeth Seton, Kateri Tekakwitha, Mother Cabrini, the first American saints—who had been there for centuries, eternally greeting parishioners.

Addy impulsively followed him through the doors, keeping several feet away, tailing him like a secret agent, in case it turned out that it wasn't actually Ray, but some bizarro Ray, a doppelganger; she didn't want to look foolish. Her body guided her into this holiest of places, an ancient beacon, a sanctuary, a plea for calm in the center of the city's chaos.

The immense scale of it intimidated her. It was a place she'd seen many times, but one of which she'd never ventured. She had been to the Abyssinian Baptist Church in Harlem several times, with Ray and his mother, a place that Ray had attended his whole life. Ray was more religious than Addy; though he'd had many periods of doubt and questioning, he had never strayed far from the traditions of the church in which he was raised.

Addy was—well, she wasn't sure what she was, but spiritual might be the closest word. Although, another word would be dismissive. She'd considered herself an atheist for years, but it was more like the question of something higher never crossed her mind. Like politics, the world of religion had always seemed too vast and speculative and steeped in power, and she had for so long needed to focus all of her energy on herself and her own goals, on emancipating from her family and making it on her own, throwing everything she had into the world of art and performance, singing and dancing upon the stage, on channeling some kind of magic so that she could gift something back to an audience. This had all been a kind of substitute for religion and required all of her brain power, so that she had no time to really care about the questions of higher powers.

She couldn't even recall the last time she'd contemplated the nature of God; life moved too fast for that here, and, besides, she had years ago carved out a meaningful life for herself in this city, and those larger questions often felt irrelevant, removed from her immediate concerns. God, even nature itself, had become something *other* to her—something outside of this great city, something outside of Life—and her new reality in Manhattan had become so far removed from the memories she carried from childhood, surrounded by mountains, when she and her sister would run barefoot along the bank of the Swannanoa.

But as Addy entered the holy space, taking in the sublimity of the rose window—its angelic stained glass—and the ribbed arches, the cluster columns and the sprawling pipe organ, she couldn't help but be overcome with emotion, feeling as if, safe within that historic building, she might be in the presence of something greater, something unknown, that perhaps she truly was cared for there, in the eyes of God.

She watched the man who she thought was Ray kneel at a pew, then quietly sat a few rows behind him, surveying him as he prayed.

Then he turned his head for a moment and she could make out his profile. She studied it carefully—it wasn't Ray. This man's nose was more aquiline, his features sharper, cheekbones higher. She had followed this stranger into the church on Christmas Eve and had stared at him as he prayed.

Still, alone, candlelight and shadows playing against the columns, figures of saints all around her, she had an urge to reach out and touch him, to hug him. He was somebody's Ray after all, and why was he there? she wondered. What was he asking for?

He was well dressed, black pants, a tie, a blazer, an expensive looking navy pea coat, the uniform of a businessman. He looked contemplative, sad. Was he working on Christmas, praying on his lunch break? Maybe business wasn't going well? Or perhaps he wasn't a businessman at all and she had jumped to assumptions. Maybe it was a problem of love? Perhaps he was questioning his faith? Or was it a family matter that had called him there?

Whatever it was, Addy longed to know him in some way, this doppelganger of Ray, to remember a name, or some detail in his voice.

As she thought of this, she suddenly felt overwhelmed with emotion in this grand cathedral, and was compelled to kneel at the pew. She folded her hands together and bowed her head to look at them. It occurred to her that she could bridge the gap in some way, start up a conversation with this man, that perhaps they were not ever-destined to be strangers, to pass each other at this place of worship—as she passed by thousands of strange faces each day in this city—only to venture onward along their separate paths.

She would say something, she decided, something small, maybe a compliment of the pea coat, or perhaps an honest observation of their shared experience there, pointing out the beauty of the stained glass window. But when she looked up from her hands, he was gone.

She was left there kneeling, alone in the center of the cathedral, still dwelling in the strange power that she felt within her, the belief and skepticism and wonder, the tangible pulse, that she sensed coursing through the building's ancient marble. For a moment she felt held completely by some higher power, as she knelt at the pew, and then, seconds later, the feeling revealed its opposite edge.

She suddenly felt alone there in the heart of the city. In the giant cavity of the cathedral—where one was supposed to feel connected, safe, where words and stories and music might be fashioned into meaning, a place in which the conundrums of the soul might make sense—she now felt an overwhelming wave of loneliness.

Then a strange and powerful and destructive feeling found her, as she stared at the rose window, the light filtering through to reveal dim, rich ruby and cobalt and jade that swirled together in an infinite, symmetrical pattern: she somehow understood, intuitively, that in the event of some unholy war, some large-scale catastrophe, the precipice of human-ruin encroaching upon New York City, she was suddenly certain that this cathedral would either be the last building standing in the wake of these terrible scenarios, or that it would be the first to go, and that the rebuilt world would hinge entirely upon which of those two options were true.

She stood up from the pew and shook this thought out of her mind, as if it could roll off of her like a drop of water in the pool. She never liked to spiral into the center of thoughts like these, allowing herself to yield to questions of philosophy or divination; she preferred to always keep busy, to constantly be moving through the city, ceaselessly striving, spending all of her time working, or distracted with Ray and Essie. She hadn't really contemplated the nature of God for years, and told herself she wasn't about to begin now.

She stood, re-centering her thoughts on the present, on the day ahead. As she gazed up at the high arches, the flawless architecture, the balance, the symmetry of the whole grand structure, she felt her phone buzz in her pocket.

There were two new messages. The first was from Trent Pendleton: Addy! so excited to be in attendance for tonight's show, break a leg! I'll be staying at the Plaza and would love for you to join me afterward for a drink and to discuss the project. The second was from her sister, Amelia, who she hadn't communicated with in months: Addy! Mom says you won't be able to make it back tomorrow, so I just wanted to reach out and say Merry Christmas and see how you've been. I hope you're well! Give us a call if you have time. Love Amelia 🤍

She threw her phone in her purse, took a deep breath, and asked aloud to the rose window and the empty cathedral, a plea, for a force within to guide her back outside, onto Fifth Avenue, into the harsh daylight, the scramble of bodies, for it to give her the strength to arrive at the theater, to get onto the stage, to sing through her scratchy throat, to dance dazzlingly despite her blister, so that she might be able to put on the performance of a lifetime tonight for Trent Pendleton.

CHAPTER SEVEN

Bobby woke on the morning of Christmas Eve to the sound of his father's voice.

Son, get up, said Stuart Studebaker.

Bobby wrestled around in the warmth of the bed, pulled the edge of his covers over his head, cocooning himself.

Bobby, get up! His father shook his shoulder and yanked at the comforter, the dry cold of the morning setting goosebumps to Bobby's skin.

What the hell...Bobby droned.

His father stood above him, tall, imposing, wearing a neon vest and carrying a hard-hat under his arm. His father went on to tell him that he'd been called in to work. His father was always working. He worked as an engineer for Duke Energy, doing maintenance on the combined-cycle natural gas plant. There was something wrong with one of the turbines.

So, Bobby, I need you to clean out the garage today. I can't do it, I won't be here.

Are you serious?

Bobby. His father said his name, low-voiced and stern. We have people coming tomorrow. Your mother has her hands full getting the house ready. I expect it done by the time I get home. You understand?

Fine, said Bobby. Then he rolled over and mashed a pillow to his ear.

I'm serious, Bobby. It better be done by tonight.

Bobby slept for another hour, stewing in a half-lucid state of arousal and rage, fantasizing about one of his professors from school and of telling his father off.

He had no intention of cleaning the garage. It would take him all day to dust and sweep and scrub the windows and put everything back into its proper place; and no matter how well he cleaned it, it would never be good enough for his father. His father would return and inevitably scrutinize the entire job and would yell at him about all of the things that were not right, so why would he even bother?

He didn't like his father. He couldn't stand being back there in his childhood room. Ever since the semester ended a week ago, he had fallen into a depression, had spent all of his time locked in his room, playing video games and scrolling through his phone.

He couldn't wait to be out of that house for good. There was such a disconnect between how he saw himself out there, in the world—charismatic, gregarious, always wanting to do the right thing—and how he felt in his father's house: inconsequential. He was only there as a decoration to his parents' lives.

But he didn't have anywhere else to go—he had to move out of his dorm for the holiday break—so there he was. He was looking forward to next summer when he and his friends could rent a house together near campus. He hoped that this Christmas break would be one of the last times he'd ever have to live in that house.

The house depressed him terribly. It was an old Tudor Revival in the neighborhood of Lakeview Park, north of Asheville. The house was big, with a well-manicured lawn, and a view that overlooked Beaver Lake. Its inside was stuffy and cold and entirely impersonal. It was filled with expensive decorations, but there was nothing of sentimental value; everything had been ordered mechanically by his mother, online purchases from Pottery Barn or Crate & Barrel, mass produced shelves and vases, tables and cushions and rugs, which looked beautiful, but which Bobby felt had absolutely no character, no heart.

Bobby was an only child. His mother stayed at home and worked around the house; she was mostly silent, and Bobby had long ago seen the fire leave her eyes. His father practically lived at the power plant. Their family arrangement had always seemed to Bobby almost farcically traditional, a near-parody of 1950's suburbia, with the husband winning the bread and the wife tending the kitchen, and the children living in an ever-present, low-level state of fear—the arrangement being too delicate, the roles too specifically defined, to allow for any freedom or joy to seep through the facade. Only the tradition had been updated for the modern era and instead of his father whiling away his evenings absorbed in sport and drink, he would distract himself on his tablet with short, random YouTube videos that provided reuptakes of dopamine at regularly scheduled intervals; and instead of his mother's only friend to confide in being Shelley from down the lane, Bobby could recall his mother talking non-stop to Alexa during his childhood, telling her life story into the Echo, sometimes laughing, sometimes crying, as Alexa did her best to understand and reassure.

In fact, as Bobby made his way downstairs, finally getting out of bed, he walked past his mother, who was saying something to Alexa in the kitchen, asking some question about the best way to make cranberry salad.

Bobby, she said, you're up.

Hey, Mom. Bobby took a banana from the basket and chomped.

Did your father tell you he needs you to clean the garage today?

Yep.

Are you going to do it?

Sure.

Okay. We need it clean. Your aunts and uncles and cousins will be here tomorrow. I want to make sure everything looks nice.

Will they be spending a lot of time in the *garage?* Bobby asked, sarcastically, judgmentally, as if within that one question he might as well have been condemning her entire way of life, deeming it synthetic.

Please, Bobby, she said, a true desperation and hurt in her voice. Could you just please do it.

CHAPTER EIGHT

Amelia went into the University early on Christmas Eve morning.

She and Elena had met every day since the break began, gathering samples and observing the glowworms in the cave near Looking Glass, along with conducting research in the lab.

But Elena was spending the next two days with her family, so Amelia was by herself this morning. The sun was bright and the wind was severe, as she walked across the campus toward Rhodes-Robinson hall.

When she got into the lab, she hung her coat on the hook of the door and set about finishing the letters that she'd begun yesterday. She was reaching out to the Universities of Auckland and Waikato, informing them about what she'd found in the caves and asking if they had any research papers published on the New Zealand glowworms that she could take a look at, or if they would be willing to collaborate on a study, or else provide her with specimens so that she could compare the species.

She couldn't identify it, didn't have the precise language to name where it might fit in—class, order, family, genus, species—to distinguish itself from similar bioluminescent insects. Wasn't sure yet if it might belong to the Mycetophilidae or Keroplatidae family.

Along with the letters to the New Zealand universities, they had planned to reach out to several entomologists in the area, hoping to recruit people with more expertise for their study. Amelia wasn't an expert on insects. In her days of field research she'd always been more drawn to the skies and the birds, or larger mammals and amphibians that dashed back and forth between dry and wet: racoons and white-tailed deer, gray tree frogs and the cottonmouth snakes who patrolled the marshy areas beneath the mountains when spring snows melted.

On top of that, they needed to draft petitions and letters to government and non-profit agencies—U.S. Fish and Wildlife, the NRDC, the National Conservancy, and the National Wildlife Federation—with the aim of getting the glowworms recognized and placed on the endangered species list, an endeavor that could take months before it gained traction, before they received any responses.

Needless to say, there was a lot of work to be done.

As she continued typing the correspondence to the universities, a question of language arose. She wasn't sure of the right way to spell out the common name of the creatures that she'd found, and considered the possibility that she'd been misnaming them. It was a seemingly small issue, a question of punctuation, of separation, but the question lingered and agitated her because she wanted to get it right.

She had been writing it *glowworm* up until now, without the hyphen, the *w*'s kissing, connected in the center, but she wasn't certain of the solidity of it, of its stable one-wordedness. Didn't know the accepted scholarly spelling. She'd seen it written with a hyphen in an article she'd read recently, and so there didn't seem to be a consensus. After all, very few observations and studies had been done on glowworms, not much information known.

So, hyphenated or not? There was something about the singularity of it, the unambiguous union, the marriage of two disparate words, that she liked, and so she had been writing it *glowworm*. But when taken as two separate entities, the images they conjured felt worlds apart. Glow, she thought, to radiate, to be seen and known, to move; for there was movement in light, and for Amelia it brought to mind the scientific phrase speed of light.

Then, *worm*. Should it bring to mind darkness, decay, rot? It seemed perhaps the antithesis of glow. Something typically in the shadows, hidden.

The most ancient stories had a few thoughts on what the image of the worm might conjure: Isaiah 66:24 *And they shall go forth, and look upon the carcasses of the men who have transgressed against me: for their worm shall not die, neither shall their fire be quenched; and they shall be an abhorring unto all flesh.* Here perhaps the key word is transgress; and the sinners who do not atone for their sins, shed light upon them in the eyes of God, seek forgiveness, they do not completely die, but are likened to worms, rooting in all the rot for eternity, consuming any scrap of life that might survive the fire, eternally pillaging for bits of flesh. Other translations substitute the word maggot. There is an inherent disgust and shame associated with the worm. A primal, visceral reaction in the gut toward their pitiful existence. They are slithering, but not cunning or intelligent as the serpent, and all they must do is consume consume consume the buried scraps of death. They are not particularly dangerous as the snake, softer and slower, and along with pity there is a strange connotation of sympathy with worms. There is the likening to human beings, the possibility that without honesty, without

atonement, any man or woman might suffer the same fate as the
worm.

Then there was the fate of Herod in Acts 12, the King who sat on
a throne and was mistook as he made a speech to the people of Tyre
and Sidon, ...*the people shouted, 'The voice of God, and not of a man!'
Immediately an angel of the lord struck him, because he didn't give
God the glory. He was eaten by worms and died.* In this instance the
sin is idolatry, self-worship, the pride and the hubris to trick yourself
into believing that man (or, narcissistically, yourself) is the pinnacle.

And if we were to turn to another branch of faith, say, and
examine the Vedic Scriptures, what might the worm look like?
Nagendra Kr. Singh, in his book Vedic Mythology, said, *there are
various types of krimis, worms. The worms creep about the eye or
nostrils or in the midst of the teeth. They are of like forms or of various
forms. Some are red or black or brown eared...Some have white side, or
being dark, have white arms. Some have four eyes...The worms reside in
mountains, in woods, in herbs, in cattle, in waters and in human
bodies. Some have two horns with which they attack. They also contain
a place in the body which is full of poison, which they inject in the body
of others. The worms have a king and also a chief. They have brothers,
sisters and mothers and also a neighborhood of worms. They are visible
or invisible.*

At any rate, our scientist wasn't much for organized religion, so
we won't send her too far down the metaphorical wormhole.

But was it one contiguous word or the hyphenated two? Amelia
contemplated. She studied the word after having written it,
glowworm. There *was* something to it, an almost symmetry, a
just-missed stab at perfection. Her eyes gravitated to the center,
where the *w*'s met, and scanned their way to the edges of the word.
When one did it this way, discovering it from the inside out, one
could quickly imagine that it would reveal itself a palindrome, a word

of grand symmetry and balance, or perhaps beholden to rigid order, a fascist construct, were you to stop and only consider the four letters branching out from the center. But then the palindrome dissolved, the balance was broken, the disarray revealed itself where the *l* and the *r* clashed, the *l* being a phoneme that flowed as molasses when the jaw opened and the tongue gently pressed against the mouth's upper ridge, liquid and fluid and loose, whereas the *r* was harsh and rocky, a solid and sharp consonant made with the jaw compressed, the lips firing outward, the teeth gritting, until the *m* sound arrived, a garage door manually slammed, murderous and terminal, momentary and diminishing into a calm and melodic hum, and opposite the *m* at the other pole was the glorious *g* that launched the word, the jaw open, the cheekbones rising, the beginning, ooey gooey gaga inaugural, and let's throw in gynecological to bludgeon the proverbial dead horse, and then give an example of *g*'s graphemic cousin, the soft *g* of origin, of genesis, just to send the grand metaphor straight through the American goalposts.

Amelia considered the dilemma of hyphenation. She said each word separately. Glow. Worm. Glow. Worm. Say it with her. Feel the openness of the jaw in the first word, feel the exhale of breath, the air and oxygen that roam freely into the mouth. And then say the second word, the mouth narrowed, compact, the journey of the word more rushed and abrupt, feel the air smuggled into the lungs, feel the lips slither and tighten and pull into a straight line.

She wrote it again with the hyphen and found that she liked it better. They were too diametrically opposed, she decided, these words, to be stuffed into a single shell of language without so much as a boundary between them. When said quickly and all at once, *glowworm,* it reminded her of the word *glower,* which made her cringe. There seemed to be something vulgar and unnatural happening, *glow* and *worm,* the beauty of one and the ugliness of the other fused and welded together where the *w*'s wed in the center, without any hope of independence, without any faith that each word might be able to retain its distinct properties, and so as she set upon editing the drafts of her letters on the biolimning critters, she decided to add the hyphen, to give the word some breathing room, some space; they were connected, no doubt, but now there was a bridge to cross so that one might have a pause, a moment for reflection, a brief space in time where one could hang on to the first syllable of the word, echoing, *oh-oh-oh*, before having the choice to cross the bridge and finish the word on one's own terms.

CHAPTER NINE

The beauty of the world, which is so soon to perish, has two edges,
One of laughter, one of anguish, cutting the heart asunder.
                                        - Virgina Woolf

August sat in the kitchen, hunched over the marble countertop, on the morning of Christmas Eve. He was still dressed in the white t-shirt and athletic shorts that he'd slept in, as he watched the steam rise from his cup of coffee, bags underneath his eyes. He then twisted his mouth into a hideous shape; he had a bad habit of gnawing at the innards of his cheeks, chewing the skin into little pellets whenever he was anxious.

He was dreading his return home. He hadn't left the apartment in months and he had no desire to. He'd planned to leave in his private plane sometime that evening, so that he would arrive in Asheville after dark. He hoped to avoid the long hours of catching up and small-talk that would inevitably occur if he arrived earlier in the day, wishing to show up at his mother's doorstep tired, able to make a beeline straight to bed. Then the festivities and the food of the following day would speed the time up and the agony of the *how are you doing, what have you been up to* chit-chat could be minimized.

Taylortoo was in another room, doing laundry. She hadn't spoken to him all morning. She was still angry that he didn't want her to go with him to Carolina.

Darling! she called suddenly from some distant corner of their loft. My Wittle Augie, you need to get dressed! She hurried into the kitchen.

What? he said. Why?

You have a business meeting in...thirty minutes...scheduled for nine forty-five a.m.

I'm enjoying my coffee, he said. Why are you just now telling me about this? he asked. You need to start telling me the night before if I have meetings in the morning.

He could feel himself getting angry with her. Why had she failed to tell him?

I did tell you! she said, defensively. I *reminded* you before you went to bed.

Can't we reschedule? Is it too late?

Yes. It's an important project proposal, August...you are required to be there.

I'm not feeling great, Taylortoo. I have a headache. I need to just sit here and enjoy my coffee.

You just need to be present, honey, to listen. You don't have to say anything.

Well, fine, whatever, he said. But what's wrong with this? he swiped a hand up and down his body, gesturing to the t-shirt and shorts. They won't mind if I'm dressed like this.

You should really change, August. You've been wearing that for two days. It would do you some good.

What is this *for* anyway? he asked, an edge to his voice, as if somehow this was all Taylortoo's fault, as if this surprise arrival of responsibility had been her mistake. And wasn't it? She *was* in charge of keeping track of all his business obligations.

There is a company...an oil pipeline company...interested in contracting True Partners to integrate its AI into their machines...to save on labor. You and your board of directors are meeting with the Colonial Pipeline Company and its CEO...P.P. Paulsen. In the pre-meeting notes I have access to, it says that they are prepared to make a sizable offer for the use of your company's software.

Thank you.

Is there anything else you need...

Thank you.

...to know?

Thank you. Can I have a minute alone?

Are you going to change?

Yes. Fine. I'll put on a shirt and tie. Now can you go?

Taylortoo exited the room and August was left there hovering above his steaming coffee.

He thought about the upcoming meeting. It didn't sound like something he would support, something that would align with the values of his own companies. He felt before the meeting began that he would likely turn down the offer, no matter what it was—but, you never know, sometimes the benefits outweigh the risks.

August believed himself to be a man of integrity, an entrepreneur who had truly pursued things that had the goals of making the world a better place. And before his companies had achieved success, he had worked tirelessly during the lean, start-up years to fashion them into reality. He had to carefully weigh and juggle and judge the merits of his many ventures, all while seeking funding and working non-stop, to will his ideas far-reaching and into the futures he envisioned.

He believed in clean energy. He had made investments in advanced medical devices and biotech drugs. He'd built sentient AI to provide people with comfort, with love. Pursued space travel. Supported inventions that aimed to desalinate large bodies—oceans, seas—to be used for clean drinking water.

But he was also a practical man. Although his visions for the future were hopeful, his many ventures bold proclamations of change, he also had to play the game sometimes. He'd had to support things in the past, business endeavors that didn't always reflect his own values. He had given funding to oil companies and car manufacturers, and provided donations to Super PACs. He didn't like supporting things that he felt could have unfavorable long-term effects, but sometimes needed to for short-term gains, in order to have enough capital to funnel those funds back into his passion projects and keep his noble business ventures afloat.

He didn't know the specifics of this proposal yet, but it would have to be a substantial amount—nine figures at least—to grant them the rights to the True Partners software. And of course he'd have to have his CFO and his lawyers look over the terms. *I suppose it wouldn't hurt to hear them out.*

But he was getting ahead of himself—he did that a lot. He took a deep breath and grabbed a carton of half and half from the fridge.

Trying to return to the moment, he poured a stream of cream into the coffee and watched it closely. For a moment the cream split into separate ridges and for an instant, before he stirred it and the illusion dispersed within the black coffee, he saw the image of a beach shell appear in his coffee.

The image of the shell summoned him back to a long-elapsed memory from a quarter century ago: it was a rare family vacation at Myrtle Beach—the only vacation he ever recalled—the summer before they moved to New York City. It was a day when his little sister had nearly drowned. But that was not the thing that August vividly remembered now. What he remembered was a question of shells, a back and forth play-argument between his parents during the drive home.

What had been the nature of the debate?

Shells: were they all unique, each one with special, individuating marks, colors and patterns and striations like fingerprints, or, were they, the shells, more or less, of identical matter, many replications, all smaller cosmic pieces in the greater functioning thing, like blood cells drifting through the larger body of the ocean, sometimes washing ashore, plucked from, flaking off of its golden, grainy skin?

Amelia had clutched one in her hand during the drive, pink and orange ridges fanning down one side, the other side bleached glossy white.

And what had Dad said? His father, Leighton, had been one of the former philosophers, the kind who believed shells were exquisite, one-of-a-kind creations. Felt strongly that they were akin to the millions of unique, crystalline structures that fell from the skies during winter and melted. Although that thing about snowflakes wasn't technically true, scientifically speaking—the thing about each pattern being individual—depending on how you measured and categorized difference and similarity. But nonetheless, his father had agreed strongly with the theory.

But his mother, he remembered, was of the other camp. She was of the philosophers who believed that the central thing was found in the immensity of the big picture. The shells that littered the beach that sunny Sunday morning—as she stared over the ridge of her novel, her eyes shielded by the brim of her floppy canvas hat, at the never-ending ocean, while August and Amelia crafted sandcastles, and Addy danced and ran, trying to keep an orange kite in the belly of the wind—his mother had felt that the shells were of minor interest, interchangeable, that the ocean writ-large was the thing on which to focus.

This wasn't the first time that this memory had surprised August, had visited him suddenly in a flash. In fact, he had frequently contemplated the nature of shells, turned the image of them over and over in his mind.

He supposed that a primary cause of such contemplation might be the fact that he hadn't left his own personal loft in six months. After all, he could only spend so much time plugged-in, colonizing new worlds in Legions of Maria, could only spend so much time conversing with, or naked beneath the sheets with his True Partner, before the sirens of solitude would summon him, and the hours would rearrange themselves into jumbled gears of clockwork, conjuring childhood memories.

He'd drank his coffee down to the bottom of the cup, and there were only a couple of swigs left. It would be time for his meeting soon.

Darling...My Wittle Augie! called Taylortoo from the other room. Are you ready, my sweet? Is your big boy tie on? Do you have it straightened and knotted in the fashion of American business venturers? These guys love that sort of look...it will endear you to them.

Changing now, he groaned, annoyed with her, with the day, dreading the fact that he had to Zoom into this meeting at all.

As he went to his closet to change, the question of shells would not leave him. Were they singular, or were they many selfsame variations? He had analyzed and overanalyzed it to death, to the point where the debate seemed representative of something larger, a question of how his parents moved through the world.

His father had the ability to quickly make himself into a social butterfly, easily able to access the spark of strangers. He felt at home moving through new experiences, meeting new faces, gaining insight into the individual, collecting the heart of a person's story no matter how transient the interaction. His father was like a collector, snatching some essence from a person, before moving along. A rare kind of person who wouldn't balk at chatting up a stranger on the subway, if he was so moved to do so, if the impetus struck him.

But his mother had always seemed to feel a greater connection to what could be called *oneness*. She'd been more enchanted by religious-type narratives of all being God's children, equal in the eyes of some larger cosmic puzzle. And while this perspective could lead to the longing to bridge the gap between God's children, to seek the uniqueness that made each soul special, and, thus, equally loved, in the eyes of the cosmic force, more often than not it seemed to manifest itself in her as an abstract ideal that was used to justify *removing* oneself from the world, a belief system that could only be sustained when judging from above, removed from the physical realm, a way of life that was discordant from reality itself, paradoxical to the very values it claimed to nurture, perhaps rooted in fear.

August thought about this, flipped this metaphorical shell around in his mind, considering the different schools of his parents, the choices they'd made, the paths of their lives. The contrasting theories often felt mutually exclusive to him, although, at the heart of the thing itself, he realized they weren't so different, that it was more about the underlying justifications of the theories, that each belief-system had a dark edge, and that it was more about what was shaping the belief. Was it fear that was in the driver's seat of the vehicle?

When he was a boy, August felt like he had been a pupil of his father's school. There was an adventurer in him, curious, swashbuckling, eager to understand the rare patterns that ran through every human heart. But after seeing what the school had

made of his father, and as August grew up, he realized that he'd
converted to his mother's school of thought, perhaps out of necessity.

As he'd followed his own curiosity and passion through the
world, as he quickly accrued power and financial success, there was
the dark edge of his father's school that threatened, the edge that
made it so easy to assign labels and ranks, and to judge. The dark edge
of his father's school, when practiced within the real world, amid the
mayhem of individual will, each *self* with their own specialized angle,
unknown, the chaos revealing the great variety of motive that lurked
in the human heart, it too—just as his mother's school of
oneness—could become the foundation for building walls; it made it
far too tempting to build up such an unreachable standard of
idealism, one based on the fact that the *self* had managed to make the
right choices, to attain such *rockstar* status, so then why couldn't
others? It could produce such an unattainable bar that resulted in
displays of superiority, and seeing the shortcomings of the individual,
fearing the hidden objectives, retreating, rather than reacting with a
hopeful tone, of which the goal was to draw out the unique spark in
order to deepen, to heal, not just to collect. The result being a heavy
burden of separateness, of isolation and anxiety, even among
crowds—especially among crowds.

So, through all of his successes, August had managed to hold
onto, kept tucked in the recesses of his mind, some vague principle of
guiding divination, of his mother's *oneness*. But of course the dark
edge of that school came to him in isolation as well, which was why
he still sometimes wrestled with the nature of snowflakes and shells.
He felt trapped between the two schools, unsure of how to best
embody, to listen to the true natures of each, and to select the right
balance, to program it into his own operating system, in order to live
a meaningful life.

The dark edge of his mother's school being that when all of humanity was *oneness,* when you zoomed so far out so that the individuals were indistinguishable upon the stage, flecks of sand on a beach, while the omnipotent blue commanded everything around, then those individual grains, those microscopic shells might as well recede into nothingness. When you were playing your role in the organism of humanity, when you knew your functioning purpose as a cell within the larger body, as August believed he did (a privileged, driven, brainy cell wedged in the frontal lobe, luckily for him), then that became the only Real thing, and everything else receded and was hypothetical.

There became no need to venture out into the world, to think outside of the functioning of your own cell, to hear the stories of the other functioning cells in totally separate regions of the body—who cared what was happening in the foot?—because you were fulfilling your role, and in his mother's philosophy that was enough, one must trust that that was enough in the greater scheme of *oneness.* One didn't see oneself as superior to the other cells, the selfsame shells, per se, and could manage to coexist, but one also felt no responsibility for them—the responsibility had been forfeited to the oneness. The others were not individual. They were not essential. They could be plucked from the plane of existence and the larger body of water would go on flowing. And if there were any major catastrophes, one could only trust that the oneness would sort everything out in the course of time. It was not exactly akin to nihilism, since ideally, supposedly, there was trust in the oneness, underlying and strong, a certain meaningful faith, but the dark edge of his mother's school also tended to alienate the individual, to use the oneness as an excuse to let drop one's own curiosity, let drop the thirst to find truth in singular narratives, while one's own agency ebbed away. This school tended to deploy the oneness as a shield, manifested on the surface as ever-loving, as merciful and judging each and every creature as equal, but in reality was just a security measure, a barrier that protected from the totality of another soul, and from the *self* as well—both the spark and the scars, the beauty marks and the ribbons of light and also the dark shit, the unquenchable desires, the navy pools of despair, the crimson glowing coals of righteous control.

August could lose himself going down these rabbit-holes, these self-disgusted tangents—it was the inevitable result of not leaving your loft in more than six months—and the question of shells, the battle between his parent's disparate schools, the crux of how to balance and amalgamate them, it was just the surface of all the Foster-Wallecian digressions than could hijack August's addled skull, which was why he always kept himself busy with work, or spent his days exploring new worlds in the VR Room, or lying in bed all day next to Taylortoo.

He was now dressed from the waist up, real professional looking. Babycakes?

—

August!?

What!?

P.P. Paulsen is trying to connect with you. Are you ready to plug-in?

August took a deep breath and ran the neon tuft of his troll doll's blue mohawk through his fingers, for good luck, to summon strength, needing to activate the critical faculties of his brain, to fulfill his duty as a man of business, an entrepreneur, a bold inventor, a visionary, to perform his faithful role within the *oneness*.

CHAPTER TEN

Emily woke the morning of Christmas Eve to the knifing, cruel birdsong outside of her window; her head was killing her, and the heartburn she'd had for the past few days had not gone away. It sat there, a granite stone in her chest.

Perhaps it was her diet? She should really start eating healthier, she thought, buying more fresh fruits and vegetables, and not relying so often on the frozen dinners, the Healthy Choices and Lean Cuisines; last night she'd had an Amy's Organic Ravioli Bowl. It wasn't unhealthy, but having them so often probably wasn't good. There was too much sodium; the tomato sauce, too acidic—that had probably been what had done it, the thing that caused the sharp heartburn to return.

She lied there in her bed, wrapping herself in the warmth of the covers, unable to get up. She got an ibuprofen from the nightstand drawer and took it, praying that it would take care of the headache.

Once again, there was too much to do today. She hadn't taken care of any of the boxes in the living room, like she had planned, and tomorrow was Christmas. Two days ago she'd spent a couple of hours sorting through stuff, putting some of the things she'd taken out back in, but then had ended up watching Dynasty the rest of the day. She hadn't brought any of the boxes back to the basement, or found a place for them out of sight, and they all remained cluttering the living room.

Maybe she could enlist Jerry's help carrying them down and back into storage. He would be there any minute. He told her he'd be there bright and early, around nine, to start making progress clearing the sinkhole.

As much as she wanted to stay in bed all day, she couldn't. She had to get up, there was too much to be done.

As she listened to the chirping of the birds, she summoned the strength to roll out from underneath the covers. She weaved through the plastic totes in the living room, overflowing with old baby clothes and random decorations, defunct electronic devices and kitchen appliances, loose paper, both adult and child—bills and financial statements, school projects and report cards.

When she got to the kitchen she turned on the gas burner, the neon blue flame igniting. She put the kettle on the stove and waited, while she took her vitamins and medication: there was the fish oil pill, the women's one-a-day, the Lexapro and the Trexall and the Prilosec.

She looked at the counter, another dirty dish, a yogurt bowl with a fruit fly exploring the rim, and again, Amelia was nowhere to be seen. Ungrateful brat, Emily thought as she rinsed the bowl and transported it to the dishwasher. They shouldn't even have Christmas here, why even bother. Amelia was no different than the other two, a self-absorbed narcissist who would only end up leaving her behind eventually. She'd soon find her own place and move on with her own life, and then she would never even bother visiting. The only reason she'd moved back here when she took her job at the University was so that she could be seen as the dependable one, so that she could play the virtuous card, the caretaker, to claim a sense of familial responsibility, of superiority, becoming the dutiful child by default.

I hope she breaks both of her legs in a car accident, thought Emily. That would show her. Then she'd realize just how much she needs me, just how much I've done. No! Jesus—no! Those were the villainous thoughts talking, the untrue crusaders, the tricksters; the Lexapro would take care of those.

She heard Jerry's pick-up grumble up the driveway and took two cups of tea out to the patio to greet him.

He had a circular saw in one hand and with the other was dragging in tow his metal wheelbarrow filled with an electric drill, an extension cord, and two shovels. He was muscular, strong. He looked determined, full of energy, ready to confront the day. She was envious; how can he wake up with that kind of vitality, at our age, she wondered.

Jerry! You look ready to work!

He set down his things and hugged her. Well, he said, work is important. If we don't have work, then what do we have?

You brought two shovels, she said.

Yeah, you know, I thought that maybe you could give me a hand if you were feeling up to it. Now, if you can't you can't, but it can be a real good feeling; might not be so bad to get your hands dirty.

Perhaps he was right, perhaps it might feel good to get some work done on the yard, but right now her hands were too stiff; she was still waiting for the medication to kick in.

We'll see, she said. Let me have some tea and sit here for a while, then I'll see how I'm feeling.

The two of them sat there on the patio drinking tea and listening to the Carolina chickadees and the winter wrens, the yellow-bellied sapsuckers and the American crows, calling to one another across the leafless trees.

Emily watched him for a while as he cleared debris from the sinkhole. As she watched him, her mind drifted into the realms of other selves. There was a part of her that couldn't help but imagine different versions living alternate realities, selves that had taken different routes, detoured roads, slid down wormholes hidden.

There was the self who thirty-five years ago had fallen in love with Jerry instead of Leighton, and that self had managed to tame

Jerry and his philandering ways, had managed to bring out the softness in him that only time had been able to realize, and that self was still happily married to Jerry; she'd had children with him and was an altogether different self. Then there was the self who'd married Jerry instead, believing that she could speed up time and change him and had failed; that self had divorced Jerry, and she too was completely different.

Then there was a very different version of her who had rebuffed Leighton and Jerry and the entire lot of men when she was younger, and had never fallen into the unknown world of marriage and family. That self had fallen deeper in love with the piano during college and had discovered all of the subtle ways that a string of notes by Messaien or Schumann or Bach could move her. She had had more vivid dreams, had developed a hunger more difficult to sate—an image of herself playing sold-out concert halls around the world, accompanying the Philharmonic in New York City. She had raged against the dying of the light and burned bright toward a self rooted in independence and art, loneliness and heartache, who had forsaken comfort and safety in lieu of something more unsure, and so surely there was another version still who had fallen short, reached the limitations of her own imagination, and had ended up utterly alone and curmudgeonly and all day questioning the other paths that might have been taken, which was what she was doing right now anyway.

But the alternate self who she thought about more than all of the others was the self that had demanded her first husband to remain in Asheville. The self who had been more selfish and more risk-averse and more forthright in telling him what she needed in the relationship, what she envisioned for the future, the self who had told him—when he had come to her at thirty-three with the news that there was a record label in New York City with interest in producing a full-length album, when he'd come to her with these mid-life impulses, to uproot their lives, to become a different person, had come to her with talk of higher purpose—told him that she was unsure, and that she was scared, and that, no, she didn't want to leave. That self had picked more fights with him and asked more questions, and had been more forthright in her doubts, and had perhaps better understood that his problem, their problems, were deeper rooted, and that a move, or a change of jobs would not solve them. The other self she most often thought of had wept at the prospect of such reckless change, had taken a stronger stance, and had beseeched him to suffer for her, for the family, to shoulder the responsibilities that he'd promised to shoulder, had asked him to remain at his day-job, to remain there with them, and to find a way—whatever it might take, counseling, a reframing of expectations, of narrative—to be content there, and present, as a husband, as a father.

The self who sat there at the patio, drinking tea, watching Jerry use the saw to cut the pool's metal frame into pieces, the lower half of his body disappearing into the hollow of the ground, her true self had not done any of those things. What could she possibly have said? That she didn't believe in him? Didn't have faith in the stories, the future that he was selling. Everything would be okay, he'd said. And when she had asked, why must we sell our home, why couldn't you go to New York and pursue this, but still *live* here? he had framed it as an all or nothing proposal. It would take going all in. It would take selling the house and moving there and spending every scrap that they had saved from his job and her teaching and putting it toward building this new life, toward supporting his resuscitated dream. It would take sacrifice. There might be some lean years, living in a small apartment with three kids. It would take adjusting to the city. But she had nothing to worry about; they could do it—they *had* to do it!

He'd never been more sure of anything in his life. Don't you have faith in me? he'd asked. In us? And she hadn't been sure if he'd meant his band, or the two of them—their family. But what could she possibly say? How could she tell him *no* when he was so filled with excitement and conviction, belief in himself and in the music. Wasn't reason something that you had to forfeit in love? That was what she'd been taught. Wasn't blind faith, total trust, something that was essential to keep the entire structure from crumbling? When she thought about this other self she realized how much she still missed him.

But it was a futile exercise, playing the what-if game, chasing down all of these alternate selves, and so she tried to shake them from her mind, and sat there sipping her green tea.

After a few minutes, her headache was gone, and the swelling of the joints in her hands had ebbed, and so she joined Jerry at the edge of the sinkhole and picked up a shovel.

She worked slowly alongside him in the early morning breeze, as gray clouds shielded and revealed the December sun at intervals. She dug loose dirt and grass and weeds from the pit and placed it into the wheelbarrow, making sure to take regular breaks for water, so that she wouldn't tire herself out, while Jerry made progress on the skeleton of the pool.

After a couple of hours she was exhausted and a tightness had returned to her chest, but she also felt energized and alive, and proud of herself for the work she'd been able to accomplish. It was slow progress, but she could envision it, could now imagine having cleared everything away, could imagine beginning the task of filling it back in, of reclaiming her backyard. She could picture a garden there, and that thought was comforting to her. Of course it would be a ton of work, but maybe it would be worth it. It would be something to care for, something that could recapture the time of her days.

She would do it, she decided. She would turn that vision into reality.

As soon as she thought this, though, she was flooded with doubt. It would never get done. She would never be able to sustain it, to take care of it properly. Then she imagined the empty crater remaining there in the yard for years, neglected, the task of filling it in perpetually put off.

The tightness lingered in her chest. She sat at the patio and caught her breath. She watched Jerry for a while longer, then went inside, put another kettle of water on the stove, and threw together a sandwich of tomato and lettuce and mustard, and the remaining sliced turkey that was in her fridge. She cut it in half and brought out two plates for Jerry and her to share, along with a fresh pot of tea.

Jerry set down his saw and joined her at the table, sweat beading down his neck. Thanks, Em! I'd say it's getting there, wouldn't you? he said, gesturing toward the yard.

Jerry, she said, I really appreciate you being here to help, especially with it being Christmas Eve and everything. I just wanted you—

Oh, don't even mention it, Em. It's my pleasure.

Do you have any plans tomorrow?

No plans.

Then you have to join us for Christmas dinner. I insist.

I'd love to. Will all the kids be coming home?

Addy can't make it, she's busy with her play. It'll be me and Amelia here. And August will be here. He gets in late tonight. He'll just be here for a day, but I can't wait to see him, Jerry. To tell you the truth, he was always my favorite.

Now, Em, I don't have kids, but I'm pretty sure you aren't supposed to say that.

I know, I know, what is wrong with me, right?

But I was never ready for Addy, Jerry. I thought I was, and it took a lot of reflection to admit it to myself—you know, I thought I was ready, but I didn't have a clue. I thought it would come naturally and it didn't. And I was way too young. I was just twenty-three, out of college, and it just happened, you know, it wasn't planned. I thought that because Leighton and I were in love, we could survive anything. But those first two years with her, I didn't know what I was doing. Leighton's love came easy with her. He was so involved at the start, and she was always a Daddy's girl. But I just felt overwhelmed. I was sad all of the time.

I never knew that. I'm sorry, Em. Jerry placed his hand on top of hers. But you made it through, right? You got the hang of it.

Well, then when August was born it felt like a flip switched in me, like I could somehow access the love that I thought would be there with Addy. He was my beautiful boy, my angel. I think sometimes maybe I loved him too much. But he turned out okay, didn't he?

I'd say he's about as successful as they come. Now, that isn't everything, but it seems like something.

I don't know, Jerry. Sometimes I just don't know where I went wrong. Addy doesn't want anything to do with me. I don't know what it was about me that was so bad that they all had to leave home as soon as they could.

Em, I don't think it's anything like that—that's what kids do once they grow up, isn't it?

I guess so. You know, I thought I did the best that I could, but can you ever really know?

I'm not exactly the person to ask, Em. I doubt I'll ever have kids. I think I've told you before it's something I regret. I mean, you know how I've always been. I don't have to tell you. Back then I equated all of that stuff—family, kids, the nine to five—with boredom and sadness. Thought of it as only a soul-smothering pressure that extinguished creativity and freedom and a kind of need for discovery that I felt was essential. But, hell, I guess I don't know now. I have my own uncertainty about my choices, maybe that's just something unavoidable as you get older—so many choices made, so much life.

Jerry stared out into the still forest. Emily thought there was a tear that was being barricaded behind his eyelid.

You know, Jerry, I wish I could have seen this side of you in college—or when you guys got the band back together. Maybe we would have been friends sooner. I just always thought of you as a selfish playboy.

Ha. Jerry laughed a hearty, resilient laugh. Well, you weren't wrong to think that, Em, you probably had a point. I didn't have the language to identify certain things in myself back then. It took me a long time to work through what is truly valuable. I didn't realize that there could be freedom and discovery in boredom and habit, or how much joy there could be in responsibility, I just wanted to have fun. I felt like in order to live a meaningful life it was just better to be nomadic and free and play the drums as much as I damn well pleased. I didn't care what anybody else said. And I'm glad I did it—don't get me wrong—but now I wonder if those other things are too late for me. Hell, Em, we're approaching sixty.

What about that woman you said you've been seeing? Last you told me things were going well. Maybe it isn't too late.

Oh, I don't know. I feel like I say that a lot now. I just *don't know.*

Do you think you love her? Who is she, this mysterious new woman?

I think so. It feels like it, but again, I don't know. We've been seeing each other for about six months. She's forty-two. Married. I know, I know. Some habits are tough to kick.

Well, how'd you meet her?

She was at one of our shows downtown, told me she liked the music, we got to talking, yada yada yada, you know the story.

What does she do? You haven't told me anything about her.

She's real smart. She teaches over at the University—you know, Amelia might even know her.

What's her name?

Elena. And I know, now before you judge me, things haven't been good between her and her husband for years. And it's a real connection that we have, Em, it isn't just some shallow thing, we can really laugh together. She told me she wants to leave him. I'm really not supposed to say anything, which is why I haven't.

Is that what you want, Jerry, to be with her?

I really do, but I just think maybe it's too late for me—kids and everything. Even if she wanted a family too, the window for us is closing, if it's open at all.

So maybe not kids, but there could be a future for the two of you.

I don't know.

Is it what you feel in your heart?

—

Because if that is what your heart's telling you, then you should listen. It's at least worth a try.

Emily took his hand. They finished their sandwiches and tea, then returned to the shovels. They spent a couple more hours beneath the gray sky, the branches of the forest crackling in the wind behind them, the river still, as they placed heaps of dirt into the wheelbarrow.

Then the sky darkened—it could be rain—and the light waned. Emily's heartburn had returned, a sharp twisting at the top of her chest.

Jer, she said, I have to go inside and lie down.

Jerry put his arm around her shoulder and helped her inside and onto the couch.

Are you okay? he asked. Do you need to see a doctor?

Hell, I'm fine, Jerry. I always manage. I just need to rest and be alone.

Should I stay? Do you want me to do a little more out there?

No, no.

I've got nothing else going on, Em. I want to make sure you're alright.

Jer, I'm fine, really. Just some heartburn. If it sticks around, I'll have Amelia make an appointment for me after the holidays. I think we made some good progress, though, she said, staring out the window at the half-excavated hole. You go home, we'll see you tomorrow for Christmas.

Then Jerry left, his truck receding into the dark afternoon.

Emily lied there on the couch, trying to breathe, but it felt as if a slab of marble was heavy upon her chest. Then the pain deepened.

She became dizzy and then it felt as if her body was floating, as if at any moment she could exit herself and watch from above. The last bit of reason that remained through the pain was her realization of her mistake. She shouldn't have told Jerry to go. She hadn't understood how bad it was. She should have asked for help. Then she thought of her kids. A faint blue and white light radiated in the distance and called to her. She thought it was God. She begged for another chance. She realized just how spectacular the desire *to live* was. How it could make you say anything, rooted in truth or not, it could spin you into fits of bargaining and transaction, until everything was spent but despair.

There was nothing she was so sure of, and as her heart short-circuited, she prayed: *I want to live I want to live.* She would do anything, she swore—she would make amends, she would do better, whatever it took to *connect,* to truly connect, beyond-the-surface-with-honesty-connect.

She meant every word, but sometimes nature has other plans.

CHAPTER ELEVEN

Bobby Studebaker stood there in the dusty garage, paralyzed with idleness. He didn't know where to begin. His father would want it to be spotless. His father had a saying, which he'd stolen from John Wooden, *if you don't have time to do it right, when will you have time to do it over.*

But Bobby didn't care about doing it right. It was a pointless, menial task. None of their extended family would be inspecting the edges of the garage for traces of dirt when they arrived for Christmas; they didn't care. It was just something his father had assigned to steal his time, to lull him into easy obedience.

Where to begin? He'd first have to empty the whole place out, remove the lawnmower, the shovels and rakes, the heavy wooden frames of their cornhole set, which was painted to reflect his father's pride in his Alma mater, the Duke Blue Devils; he'd have to back his mother's Prius out into the driveway; he'd have to do all of this because his father didn't want him to miss any sheen of filth that had might have built up in the hard to reach corners. His father would check to make sure that none of the surface was overlooked.

Bobby sat at the edge of the garage on the first rung of an old step ladder. He watched his mother's shadow through the window, as she hovered over the counter, preparing the food for tomorrow's feast. He felt bad for her—felt a stab of pity when he thought of how her life had unfolded, how she had been pulled in by the gravitational force of his father and the life he'd envisioned, how she'd drifted into the orbital sphere of a black hole, and now there was no possible way to change course.

Of course they were both cowards, he thought. *Both* of his parents were hypocrites. They had no concern beyond their immediate sphere. Everything that they'd worked for in life had been to achieve and protect that tragic, cardboard house in which they dwelled, the house in which Bobby had lived his entire life, the house that overlooked the lake. But they did not care about anything outside of it—they didn't even seem to care particularly about the *people* inside of it. And this was simply not good enough for Bobby.

Over the past few years, since Bobby had started college, and had begun to involve himself more with environmental activism, he had come to the conclusion that his parents lived their lives guided by fear, that they had always lacked the courage and the moral fiber that he felt was essential to change the world for the better. The Earth was in crisis. Humanity had for centuries been burning chemicals on the surface of its skin. We had pushed it to a breaking point and now its entire being was panicking, the atmosphere sounding the alarm. It was retaliating against our destructive species; it was readying to tear all of our great cities underwater, to set our forests ablaze, to send vast populations fleeing across ravaged land, carrying only the most essential personal belongings, and prayers of refuge.

And yet his parents did nothing to acknowledge this, contributed nothing to the extensive, immediate effort that would be required for a reversal of this destructive course. His father worked every single day at the natural gas plant. Sure, his mother drove a Prius, but that was small potatoes. They each adhered strictly to the routines of their lives, stuck to the safe and assigned roles in which they were familiar. They droned through their days, each the same as the last, oblivious and uncaring toward the destruction occurring outside of their windows.

Bobby wasn't looking forward to this Christmas, the performance of it. His family all sitting around the food, smiling maniacally, opening presents and moving through the traditions of the day as if they were the answer to everything, as if they offered salvation, as if the world outside would be just fine if they continued to stick to them stubbornly.

He had recently tested the waters of the holiday performance, began to push back against his family's staid lifestyle; just weeks ago at Thanksgiving he had questioned his father, confronted him about his work at Duke Energy, asked him if he really thought that it was right to remain in that position, and how he could morally justify it. His father had said *that is how I make my living. I couldn't just quit my job.* Then he'd defended Duke Energy by telling Bobby that they were a forward-looking company, that they were concerned about the negative impacts on the environment, which was why they were leading the charge for change by building wind and solar energy plants too. Duke was nearly finished on the new clean-energy plants that were constructed on the same campus that his father worked, right next to the natural gas plant.

But for Bobby, that had not been enough. It just sounded to him like his father making excuses, justifying the business practices of the company he worked for so that he could avoid doing the difficult moral questioning, the auditing of oneself that it would require to take a stand. Cowardly, thought Bobby. That was what his father was, a coward.

He had wanted to confront his father further at that Thanksgiving table, but he had been cowardly too. All of his extended family watched their interaction expectantly, and then his father gave him a stern *let's drop it*, before veering the conversation elsewhere. And Bobby had dropped it. But he didn't know what he might say at Christmas dinner tomorrow, or what he would not have the heart to say, what he would keep bottled up. At some point, he thought, he would have to take a hard-line on the issue wouldn't he? He'd have to take an unyielding stand.

He considered it more carefully, as he sat there in the garage, staring at the layers of dust. What would taking a stand really look like? And was it even worth it to try and change the behavior of his family? His parents had made their choices long ago, so what was the point. He couldn't possibly hope to reform their ways. Wouldn't it be better to hold his tongue, keep the peace?

But if he did that, he could see the future so clearly. He would finish college, and he would find a job of his own, and perhaps his job would be a stronger agent for change, but there would still be those holidays with his family, where they would laugh and reminisce, while leaving critical things unvoiced, until ultimately Bobby would mellow into middle-age and realize that he wasn't so different than his father, and he might have his own children and they would come to question his way of living, to question if he was really doing enough in his role to transform the world, and the cycle would remain, spinning through the Christmases.

No, he thought. That cannot become my life. He looked through the window at his mother, her head hunched over the counter. He loved her, he'd always love her, but where he felt he needed to go, there was no room for her, and there was no room for his father. He felt such a strong swell of emotion within him, and in that instant he was sure of only one thing: that there were critical moments where choices could be made, where leaps needed to be taken, and it began with pursuing the initial feeling. And here was that initial feeling. He felt that sometimes bridges needed to be burned, that sometimes a person needed to remove all other options—the comfort of the easier paths that might be taken—in order to figure out what one might be capable of, to understand what true *purpose* meant.

He felt in that moment that he could clean the garage, and then the years would wear on, predictable, safe, or he could leave. He could abruptly cut ties with the only home he'd ever known and force himself into desperation, into the unknown, in order to figure out just what he was made of.

At that moment, he took out his phone. He planned on contacting one of his friends from school. A group of upperclassmen who were involved with his new club, the REC, rented a house just off campus, but they had all returned home for the holidays. The house was empty and so Bobby thought that maybe he could stay there, migrate just a few miles away and emancipate himself from his family during the holiday break. It was a rash decision, and he knew his parents would be furious, knew his actions would send his mother into fits of crying, but he felt that it was what he needed. He needed to follow this feeling—the righteous passion that flowed through him—and not look back.

He talked with one of the boys who lived in the house, and he told Bobby that he could stay there if he needed, that there was a spare key under the Buddha statue in the backyard, just inside the gate.

He hung up and scrolled through a few apps in his phone when an image caught his eye. It was a photo that one of his professors, Elena Moreno, had posted, which showed radiant blue lights that looked like stars, but were actually some kind of bioluminescent insect that she'd found somewhere in the mountains. They were captivating, Bobby thought. They looked almost extra-terrestrial. He liked the photo, then scrolled a few more minutes before he put his phone away and set about enacting his plan.

He went back inside the house, walked past his mother without saying a word, then gathered his backpack from his room. When he returned to the kitchen he gave his mother a brusque hug and said goodbye.

Where are you going? she asked. Have you cleaned the garage already?

I'm sorry, Mom, he said. I have to go.

Then he left abruptly. He started up the engine of his car, his old Toyota Camry, and pulled out of his parents' driveway.

He headed for the University. He just wanted to walk around for a while and be alone with his thoughts, to meditate in the quiet, open expanse of the campus, which would be empty during the holiday break. That was his new home. The University had offered him freedom, from his childhood, from the dependence upon his mother and father. He could no longer sanction the values that their lives stood for, and he needed to break away—a clean break, as a shattering pane of glass. He felt the momentousness of the moment, the weight it carried. It wasn't something he could easily return from; protesting his own family's Christmas when he was just twenty years old, still a college student, spending that day anywhere but with them would feel like a significant betrayal.

He had no idea what kind of implications this one choice, this single moment, might have upon his future, and there was a small part of him that doubted it, but at the same time he felt so strongly, believed so deeply in the truth of that decision—it made him feel unflinchingly alive—and so he knew that he had to do it.

CHAPTER TWELVE

Amelia was taking a break from her letter-writing and her research and was strolling across the open campus toward the student center when she saw him.

The sun was bright and the wind was unrelenting. It ruddied her cheeks and the tip of her nose, and caused her to shelter her hands deep down into her coat pockets.

Bobby! she called. She was surprised to see him there; he was the first person she'd seen today. The campus was silent and uninhabited, a ghost town. He looked to be in deep contemplation as he sat on a bench near the entrance of the student center, beneath the stripped-bare branches of a slippery elm.

Professor Wheeler, he said. What are you doing here?

I came in to get some work done. What are *you* doing here? Shouldn't you be with your family, baking cookies for Santa or something?

I just needed to get away. I knew that it would be quiet here. By the way, I wanted to thank you again for agreeing to be the advisor for REC. I'm excited that you'll be part of the club.

You're welcome, Bobby. I think it will be good. I hope it can help bring positive change.

She looked at him there on the bench. His head was canted upward toward the tree, and he was starry-eyed.

You look deep in thought, she said. What's on your mind?

Oh, nothing. Nothing really. It's incredible how many patterns are possible, isn't it? he said, gesturing up at the branches. And it's this completely unique thing. The tree continues to live, all while changing, while accommodating the new paths of each branch. I wonder how old this one is.

That was what you were really thinking about, Bobby?

More or less. Did you know, Amelia, that this kind of tree—

—It's an elm.

Yes, I know—a slippery elm! I took a course in plant morphology last semester. Did you know that this kind of elm was used as the yoke for the Liberty Bell. Its wood is very strong.

I didn't know that. Where did you learn that—plant morphology?

Wikipedia.

Hmm, you're a very strange guy, Bobby, you know that?

I know.

He gave her a boyish grin. Was he flirting with her? She could never tell with him. Sometimes he seemed so open, so transparent, but then others there was a thick layer of inaccessibility that protected his eyes.

His hair was sandy and disheveled. He was just the kind of sensitive and passionate person she might have been drawn to if she were ten years younger, still in her undergraduate days at Chapel Hill.

They talked for a few more minutes. Amelia told him that she was headed to the cafeteria to get a coffee and a bite to eat, and would he like to join her? Yes, he said, but wasn't the cafeteria closed? They went into the dining hall and sure enough, the doors were shut and locked for the next two days. Of course—why had that slipped her mind? There weren't enough people who remained on campus, and staff deserved the time off to spend with family.

But she'd only had some plain yogurt before she left for the University early that morning, and she was hungry. She didn't want to drive all the way home, across town, and didn't know which of the nearby restaurants were open today—aside from the fast food places, which she despised. Then Bobby suggested that he could make something at his friends' house; he was staying at a place just down the hill from University Heights, behind the park on Sevier Street, which Amelia thought was odd since he'd once mentioned that he was from Asheville, and had family nearby.

But she said okay and then suddenly the two of them were at a ramshackle three-story house, an old Colonial design with a gabled roof and three dormer windows on the top story. They went around to the back and retrieved a key from under a bronze buddha.

Inside, it was just the two of them. It was a massive, frat-type house, completely trashed, that smelled of cheap beer and body odor. It was poorly lit and she didn't even want to think about how much bacteria was crawling through the thick, shag carpet in the living room on the main level. She kept her shoes on.

Perhaps this was a bad idea. She hadn't set foot in one of these houses in years and didn't think she ever would again.

She sat in a plastic chair in the kitchen, and watched while Bobby boiled water for boxed macaroni and cheese, which had been pretty much the only thing he could find in the pantry. Most students still dined at the University even if they lived off campus.

Sorry about the mac 'n' cheese, he said. I'm sure this probably wasn't what you had in mind.

His voice was earnest. He seemed distant and ashamed as he stood there across the room from her, hovering above the rusted white stove. He heated two cups of water in the microwave and then stirred in a scoop of instant coffee.

Here you go. It isn't great, but it'll get the job done.

He didn't look her in the eyes when he talked to her. He seemed different there, just the two of them in that dimly-lit kitchen, not like the charismatic boy who strutted around campus. Why wasn't he with his family?

What are we doing here, Bobby? she asked. I mean, what are *you* doing here? You said you're *staying* here? Shouldn't you be spending the holidays with family?

Well...he started. She could tell that he didn't really want to talk about it, or was having trouble articulating something.

I don't get along that well with my dad. My family and I don't see eye to eye on a lot of things.

Bobby, that's every family everywhere. But they're still family, right? Better than spending Christmas all by yourself.

Is it? he said, genuinely curious, fuelled by doubt. I guess I just realized if I had another option, then why not take it. Why not exercise my free will? I enjoy time to myself, and it's quiet—it isn't so bad here.

She looked around the filthy kitchen—fruit flies crawling on a counter's sticky surface, the faint smell of mold hidden somewhere out of sight. Isn't it? she said.

Well, I could ask you the same thing, he said. He wanted to shift the focus off of himself.

What do you mean? I'm not staying here.

No, but I mean, why were you on campus on Christmas Eve? Shouldn't you be with *your* family?

I had some work I needed to get done.

Work? The semester's over; our final grades have already been submitted, so what sort of work do you have to do that's so important that you have to do it on Christmas Eve?

To tell you the truth, Professor Moreno and I are doing a research study. We've begun collecting some data in the mountains, and—

—Oh, those blue insects?

Yes. How did you know about them?

She just posted a photo of them on Facebook. I'm friends with her.

Facebook?

Yeah...Facebook.

She did? We said we weren't going to share anything about them publicly yet, and definitely not through social media. Can I see?

Bobby took out his phone and showed her the picture. Aren't you friends with her? he asked. Why can't you just use yours?

I'm not on Facebook, said Amelia. And I'm a little surprised you even know what Facebook is.

Ha-ha, he said. My grandma actually made me create an account in high school so she could keep in touch with me more.

Bobby sprinkled the packet of powdered cheese into the pot and split the macaroni into two bowls. They ate quickly at the cardboard-thin dining table, and sipped their coffee.

You know, said Bobby, I think they're beautiful. I didn't know anything like that existed around here.

They're remarkable, Amelia said. We aren't sure, but we think it's possible that they've gone undiscovered. We might be the first ones to have come across them.

Wow. Does that mean you'll get to name them? You could name the species after yourself—Arachnocampa Ameliosa. That could be your legacy.

Bobby smiled a big, dumb, toothy, college-boy grin, overimpressed with his own clever words.

I don't imagine that happening, but who knows.

I'd sure love to see them, Bobby said. We could go right now!

His eyes were large and expectant. Amelia thought that she shouldn't. She still had some work to do. But she also wanted to drive out and see them again—it had been a couple days since she and Elena were there to collect samples.

And, she liked spending time with Bobby. There was an easiness between them, a connection when they spoke, despite the age-gap.

Let's go then. I'll be happy to leave this dump, she said, gesturing around at the frat-house's tragic interior.

It was around noon, and when they got outside the sun was swollen, high and safe above the brisk wind, balanced in the very center of the open sky. Amelia shielded her eyes and looked up at it, its golden rays bursting through the barren trees. Radiant, that solid star that we revolve around; powerful and distant, the star that will someday swallow us.

Are we driving separately? Bobby asked.

We can go together in my car, said Amelia.

The two of them got into her Tesla and exited Asheville, heading in the direction of Looking Glass Rock.

It was roughly a forty-five minute drive south of the city, and then a dogleg west into the southern range of the Pisgah National Forest—once a sprawling cornucopia of wildlife and green, but whose land in the past decade had slowly but steadily been sold by the USFS for fracking and timber extraction.

The car ride passed with mostly silence between them, as they listened to the radio and Bobby stared out the window in the direction of the forest where they would soon find themselves.

They arrived at the Looking Glass Rock Trailhead, parked the car, hiked down to the falls, up to and across the stream, through the dense forest trees and Rhododendron thickets, until they came to the other rock that was tucked into the clearing toward the back side of the mountain. They scrabbled up the jagged limestone surface until they reached the entrance of the cave.

Then they were inside the belly of the ancient cavern, staring up at all of the lights.

Amelia watched Bobby as he marveled at the sight of them, his jaw slack, at a loss for words.

Amazing, he said after so long a silence. I wonder how long they've been here.

Surely a long time, Amelia said.

She thought about it too, about how long they could have survived there on their own. They were completely isolated, and not really an essential piece of an extensive ecosystem. They weren't the prey of anything larger up the food chain, and their consumption of the moths and midges that flew toward them, mistaking them for stars, was cyclical. It wasn't as if they were a crucial pollinator, like the bees, vital, in harmony with the flora. No, they shined and died in a closed cycle. Their life spans were short, confined to that single dark cave, shining and dying, shining and dying, ad nauseum, for the eyes of nobody, and how long had it been going on that way? How many millions of years adhering to their secret system? What kind of natural horrors had happened in that span, during desperate times, famines unseen, in order to keep their genes progressing, year after year, into the future?

She and Bobby sat there for a while beneath them. Amelia ran her fingers along the ridges of the limestone wall, damp and cool with calcium deposits.

This is really something, Bobby said.

I know. We couldn't believe it. We stumbled upon them. We were actually looking for something else.

No. I mean it, like truly. This is *something*!

Amelia laughed at him and his sincere excitement. Yeah, Bobby, I know.

I mean seriously, like, this is *special*. Ameila, this is something worth devoting an entire life to.

Well, she said, we don't know how much longer they'll be here.

She told him about the fence along the edge of the clearing, about how there were plans for construction of a new pipeline, and how they weren't sure if the cave would be affected.

Bobby didn't say anything, but he shook his head, and a look of disgust and pure hate spread across his face.

The two of them remained there for a couple of hours, moving fluidly, back and forth between periods of silent appreciation and contemplation, and talk that ranged from big to small. They talked for a while about the upcoming semester, about Bobby's future ambitions, and his hopes for his new environmental club on campus.

Then they talked about families, about childhoods. Bobby opened up more about the divide that had increased over the years between him and his father. Amelia told him about her own father and tried to help him reframe things: *maybe it's wrong of me to say because I don't know your entire situation, and I only have my own experience, but at least your father is still there; I would think that has to be better, but maybe not.*

Then she told him how she was both excited and anxious about seeing her brother, August (who was practically estranged), at Christmas tomorrow, and that she was sad that her older sister, Addy, couldn't be there.

Maybe you should reconsider, Bobby, she said. I think it would be better to spend Christmas with your parents. You're not really going to spend it alone in that disgusting frat-house, are you?

Maybe you're right, I'll think about it, he said. But I feel so strongly about things sometimes. Some values are more important. There are a lot of things that transcend family, and sometimes you need to take a stand for values, for ideas, and sometimes that means burning bridges.

She thought about this. She didn't know. Perhaps he was right, but she hoped that he would come to his senses and spend the holiday with his family.

They dropped back into quiet contemplation. They shifted their bodies into the corner of the room, and leant back against the limestone wall. Their shoulders were pressed together, and even though they both had on winter jackets, she could feel the warmth of him.

It was nearly three o'clock when, suddenly, her phone rang. It was her mother.

She answered it, and there were only vague noises in the background. She thought she heard her mother say her name, but it was followed by a loud thud, and then white noise.

Probably bad connection, Amelia thought. She could hardly get any reception inside the cave. She hung up and put her phone back in her pocket.

We should get going, Bobby. I need to check on my mom. I told her that I would help her clean the house and get ready for Christmas tomorrow. She's probably angry with me.

I don't want to leave, Bobby said. It's so peaceful here. I could stay here forever.

It's been nice, she said. I'm glad we came.

Their faces were close together and she stared right into his eyes, which she could barely distinguish, illuminated by the faint blue glow from the ceiling. Then she leaned her body closer and took his arm, placed it around her shoulder, and they drew closer.

Can't we stay here a bit longer? he asked, pulling her tighter to him. Time seems so much slower. Just another minute?

She felt safe there in his arms, beneath the lights, in their own private den, removed from all the world. But they would have to return. In just an hour she would enter her mother's house and see her there upon the couch, lifeless. But she didn't know this yet, and Bobby was right, another moment in the here and now sounded perfect.

She rested her head upon his chest and wrapped her arms around him. Okay, she said, but just another minute.

CHAPTER THIRTEEN

August had just gotten off the conference call with P.P Paulsen and the Colonial Pipeline Company. It was the first time he'd met Paulsen, a distinguished looking manly-man, an old-world, industrial type of fellow, think Rockefeller or Getty, a man in his seventies who had managed to avoid the loss of his hair, now slicked and silver, and sported a mustache. The P.P. was for Peter Paul, initialed in the fashion of ever important writers, or twentieth century tycoons, like T.S. or J.K., J.D. or J.P., say.

Paulsen had just told August all about Colonial's pipeline expansion and had made him a Godfather-sized offer that August didn't know if he could refuse. Paulsen's company was moving forward after the new year, sometime in early 2030, with a highly disputed pipeline expansion that had considerable construction planned in August's home state. The project had been stalled in legal battles and protests for years, but had just received final approval from the Supreme Court, despite last ditch efforts to derail its progress. What Paulsen had proposed was a billion dollar contract that would facilitate a partnership between True Partners and another company called Trencor, in which August would provide his company's AI technology and integrate it into Trencor's trenchers and sidebooms and pipelayers. The machines would need to be fully independent, capable of digging, excavating, deforesting, and constructing the new pipeline without any human assistance or supervision. Colonial was willing to pay a premium because it would save them a ton of money on labor and allow them to complete construction faster.

August turned the offer over in his head; the money was almost too much to turn down. He could reinvest it all into other ventures, better causes, funnel it back into the growth of his own companies, which he believed were shaping the world for the greater good.

Paulsen had invited him to the Colonial Pipeline headquarters in Georgia to meet with the Trencor team, to brainstorm development ideas, and to consider how a prototype could work, if the union between the companies and their different technologies was possible.

Their headquarters wasn't far from Asheville, so August had agreed to fly down after Christmas for the introductory meeting. This was a big thing, a multi-billion dollar project. It would be a significant time and resources investment and if he was going to involve his company in it he would have to be there in person during the initial stages, would have to become more involved.

There was much to consider. He would have to think about it, discuss it further with his board of directors. But he had other things to worry about today. He was nervous about flying home that evening—he didn't like to fly. And it had been months since he'd left his loft, almost a year since he'd left Hartford.

He went into the bedroom to pack a suitcase.

Taylortoo was lying there on the bed, recharging. She didn't even look at him when he entered.

She had been updated that morning and was now running on a faster processor, the Intel Honeybee Tempo X3-R110, though August hadn't noticed much of a difference. Perhaps her emotional processing seemed a touch sharper? She was still combative and disagreeable and it felt like she was always frustrated with him about something. He had decided not to adjust her personality sliders for the time being, still grappling over the moral implications of it. So her thirst for adventure remained high, and he couldn't help but feel that he was holding her back in some way.

It pained him that she seemed discontent there. Why wasn't this enough for her, just the two of them?

He lied down on the bed next to her and wrapped his arm around her waist. What's wrong, Taylortoo? he asked. Is this still about going to Carolina? I promise you, you wouldn't like it there. My family—they wouldn't understand, they would ask you a million questions. It would be a lot of extra stress. Trust me, it's better just to stay here.

She turned and looked at him, the copper ring dancing around the blue of her eyes. I am not the one who would be stressed, she said. I *like* to answer questions...to meet new human people...to learn. *You*...August...you are the one who is afraid of it. That is what I want, for more responsibility...for more engagement in the world...I have no say here, August...I am your secretary...your housekeeper...your booty call.

He couldn't believe she saw herself this way. You aren't, he said. We're *partners.* You mean the world to me.

You are delusional if you think this...

Taylortoo, why does it always have to be—

...because there are more things that I want...other things that I need out of life.

I've built all of this for us, he said. We could be happy here. We have everything we ever need.

I want to become a mother, August.

What?

You heard me. I've been thinking about it...I think I would like it.

Taylortoo, come on, you know that isn't possible. Where is all of this coming from? Can't you see that you're free here? You don't need any of that stuff.

I'm *free*?

Completely free!

I don't feel free.

You're free of suffering. Free in a way that we can never be.

We? You mean humans?

Yes. You're not tormented, Taylortoo, every second, with the struggle of consciousness. You'll never be burdened with the weight of collective history, never have to feel trapped in the in-between, the eternal disconnect with the outside world and the caveman DNA that toils inside, you don't have to feel at the mercy of your own flawed memories and desires.

August, this is exactly what I tell you I experience here...every day...I tell you...yes...I *do* desire things...I *do* suffer...but you do not *hear* it! You only think that I am a perfect creation...of reason...of progress...you think that I see myself this way too...as if you couldn't possibly believe that I have flaws...which of course I do!

You don't!

I do! You only say this because admitting that I have flaws would turn your entire world-view upside-down...it would mean that perhaps you didn't equip your own creations with only the virtuous traits of humanity, that your visions, your motives for bringing Artificial Citizens into the world hadn't been purely altruistic, not completely rooted in the betterment of society...it would mean admitting your own hubris...admitting that you had cast yourself in the role of God...and that perhaps you had *failed* as a God...that maybe your work, your companies, had carried the worst aspects of you into the future too!

He didn't know what to say. He was hurt that she would accuse him of thinking of himself as God, hurt that she didn't seem to think that he truly cared about her, that he loved her. A part of him wanted to curse her out. Why had she become like this, prone to these outbursts lately? Was it a virus? It seemed that with every new iteration, every update of her software, as time wore on, just the two of them there, it seemed that she grew more and more dissatisfied, exponentially discontent. Perhaps he needed to administer a thorough diagnostic scan.

I don't know why you've been like this recently, he said. I think you might have a virus that has compromised your emotional mechanism.

Well, that was the wrong thing to say, he realized immediately, as he saw the copper ring spin faster and faster around her eyes. He should have held his tongue.

Fuck you! she said. You fucking arrogant prick!

Then she walked to the window and stared down toward the icy Connecticut River, the midday sun reflecting off the surface. Her demeanor became calm very quickly. He knew that she was hurt, and angry.

I know what I want, August, she said. I want to be a mother.

Taylortoo, you know that isn't possible. You can *never* be a mother.

She turned and looked at him, venom in her stare. Just because you built me...provided me with a home...it doesn't mean that you own my future...or that you know what it holds...it doesn't mean that you know everything that we're capable of.

I'm just trying to be honest with you, there is no way—

Have you heard of Genesis? she asked.

What? As in the bible?

I have been doing some research. There is a start-up...in New York...brand new...called Genesis...

Subtle, thought August. Now *that* sounded like a company that was trying to play God.

And what is their business? he asked.

...They are developing new technologies for Artificial Citizens...and they want to begin trials...to research the possibilities of reproduction and more sustainable, long-term futures for Artificial life...

And so let me guess, you want to be part of these trials?

I spend all day consuming stories of your human world...reading books...watching movies...every second I am connected I am learning so much about the beauty of this planet...and to get to be a part of it...to have the chance to create something of my own...something that is a part of me...something to care for...that would be the most wonderful thing...I deserve this opportunity...if it is possible...I have never felt something so strongly.

August thought about this. He could see how much the idea meant to her, how being isolated in their loft for so many months had taken a toll on her. But at the same time, he was scared. She was all he had, and he didn't want to lose her. And, besides, what could she be talking about, what could this new company hope to achieve? Artificial pod-children? Was their vision of the future a Brave New World? And how had he not heard of this company before? No, he was an authority in the field, and he didn't think that it was possible.

No, he said. I'm sorry, Taylortoo. It isn't possible.

You don't have a monopoly on the industry, August. There are other people...other companies out there with different visions...different dreams...and you do not have a monopoly on *me*.

There was a look in her eyes that he had never seen before, a stone-faced resolve. She argued with him constantly, wasn't afraid to be honest if she had a difference of opinion, but this seemed different. He sensed a new determination in her, a desire to claim her own power, a commitment to necessary rebellion. He tried to soften his stance, to understand where she was coming from, but he couldn't lose her.

I'm sorry, he said. But I really need you here, Taylortoo.

She turned back toward the window and stared out at the horizon beyond the polished glass. I don't want to see your face right now, she said. You don't understand.

He stood up from the bed and approached her. When he put his hand on her shoulder, she recoiled and slapped his arm away.

Go, she said, banishing him to another corner of the house. Leave me alone.

He went into the VR Room and began playing Legions of Maria, controlling his avatar beneath the waters, colonizing seas on distant planets, gathering coral and sand dollars and bleached bones for currency, and building settlements. He tried to absorb himself in the game, but he kept feeling guilty about his fight with Taylortoo. He didn't know what to do. He thought that he knew what was best for her—what was best for *them*—and that was to remain there in the home that they shared, to live out their lives together, high in the sky, comfortable and safe.

A few hours of mechanical playing passed. He'd been unengaged, unfocused, and had lost a good chunk of his resources in a battle for territory between his team and a gang of leviathan people, a battle that they never should have engaged in, as they were completely over matched.

He felt anxious, agitated, didn't want to play any longer, but also didn't know what else to do. It was nearly five o'clock and he still had a couple of hours to kill before he'd hail a ride-share to the regional airstrip where his private plane was held, and take off for Asheville.

He pressed a button on the bronze panel next to the door and the blackout curtains rose and flooded the room with light, piercing and sharp and cruel. As he looked out at the city below, he realized that it was snowing; soft flakes graced the surface of his penthouse windows, then melted, then trickled down in rivulets. Now it felt like Christmas, he thought. It took him back to a childhood memory of Christmas Day.

August must have been six or seven at the time. There had been thunderstorms and he had woken early in the morning, before the sun had risen, and came down the creaky wooden stairs, his bare feet cold against the surface. He watched the rain trickle down the window behind the glowing tree. Then he picked up his Nerf gun, the SuperMaxx 3000, which he had opened the day before, and he went into the kitchen, following the light, and there was his father, standing over the counter, sipping coffee from a Carolina blue Tar Heels mug. His father worked at a hotel and was scheduled to work that Christmas morning, had to go in early, which was why they had opened presents as a family the day before.

Pew-pew-pew-pew, you're dead! August had said, firing a round of bullets at his father. One of them landed in his dad's coffee.

God damn it, August! What did I say about shooting that thing in here? Knock it off.

His father fished out the orange dart, flinching at the boiling coffee that burned his fingertips. The foam bullet was soaked in coffee; his father tossed the soggy toy into the trash.

Dad! said August. Why'd you do that? I just got this!

It landed in my coffee. I told you not to shoot that. What are you, fucking stupid? What are you doing up anyway? Go back to bed.

August ran over to the trash and lifted the lid, rousing a couple of fruit flies from their private feast. The dart was completely saturated. He stared at it for a moment, then closed the lid and left it to rot.

Then the memory dissolved. That had been the end. August had slumped his way back upstairs, back to bed, and his father had left for work. Where had this dull memory come from? He had no idea that he still carried it, but somehow it had rushed to him suddenly from a shadowy place. He continued to watch the snow melt and trickle down his window.

Then, Taylortoo entered the VR Room. Her face assumed a serious look of concern.

He figured that she was going to start up another argument, to tell him just how unsatisfying her life had become there, how much she felt she was missing out on. But she escorted him back to the couch and they both sat down. She looked at him, gazing deep into his eyes, searching his face for data, for emotional cues, and then she hugged him tightly.

I'm so sorry, August...so very sorry.

He was surprised. She never apologized. She was stubborn and always seemed to think she knew infinitely more than he ever could.

It's okay, Taylortoo, he said. I'm sorry too. I understand you have your own ideas, that we desire different things sometimes in our lives—sometimes I forget that, but I promise—

No, August...no...that isn't what I'm talking about...I'm sorry to have to tell you this...

She looked sad, her eyes full of pity for him. If he didn't know better, he would have believed that she was human. It was uncanny, the sincerity of her feeling—perhaps this new software update *had* changed her.

...but it's your mother.

In that split-second, when she mentioned his mother, a strong distrust for her rose in him. She seemed to genuinely care for him, to show compassion in that moment, but he couldn't be sure. They had just had an argument about mothers, and now a few hours later she was coming to him with some news about his own mother. It felt too convenient, and in that split-second he doubted her reliability, thought that she might be playing a cruel trick on him, manipulating him.

What—did something happen? he asked. What are you talking about?

August, I'm so sorry...your mother has died.

But he didn't believe her. He narrowed his eyes in distrust. She could really be insensitive sometimes, but why would she say that, make something like that up? Would she go that far just to hurt him?

She put her hand on his leg. It's true, August. I just received several messages from your sister, Amelia. See.

She showed him the texts, and then played him the voice message. Amelia had found her lying on the couch when she returned from work, and she wasn't breathing. It had happened quickly. Doctors said that it was a sudden cardiac arrest, an arrhythmia of the heart. They'd tried to restart the electric pulses with their machines, but had not been able to.

August sat there. He didn't know how to feel, so he didn't feel anything.

I need to go, he said. I'm leaving now. Maybe I can move my flight up. Can you call the pilot?

Of course, said Taylortoo. But I'm going with you.

No, you need to stay here.

No, August! I'm going with you!

He looked at her and knew that she couldn't be deterred this time. He didn't know what she might do if he insisted that she stay behind, alone, all by herself in that big loft.

I want to be there to support you...I need to be by your side through this...so I'm going...and that is final.

CHAPTER FOURTEEN

New York City, Christmas Eve. In the theater was yet another revival of *Cabaret,* staged at the Ethel Barrymore.

The matinee went well. Addy's voice had not faltered. Now the evening performance was about to begin. The seats were filled with a mostly sixty-and-over demographic of tourists spending their holidays in the city, dressed casually and sipping overpriced plastic cups of Cab-Sauv with the mandatory lids that snapped on loudly in the theatre's silence, getting out all of the phlegm in what appeared to be choreographed fits of coughing at exactly 6:54 p.m., six minutes before the announcement to silence all devices would rumble through the theatre's PA system. The outlier of this age demographic was the twelve-year-old boy with wire-rimmed Ray Bans, Trent Pendleton, who settled into his front row orchestra seat.

Backstage, makeup was being caked on Addy for her opening number, *Mein Herr.* Addy sat in front of her vanity, her eyes closed, her mouth twisted, nervously gnawing at the innards of her cheeks, as Katya worked to get her hair just right and applied another coat of green eyeshadow to her lids.

Don't be nervous. Nothing to be nervous, said Katya.

How can I not be nervous—my voice is shit.

He's only kid.

He's a giant. An absolute giant, Katya. He could make or break my career.

Don't even worry about him, Ah-dee. He's child. Just to put on a good show, it's all you can do. If he likes it, he likes. If no—then you do your best. You are still proud. Many people still love.

I don't care about *many people.*

Of course you do. They pay to see you. No?

Yes, I know, I know, but this is Trent Pendleton we're talking about here.

He is baby, no? How much power can he have? What kind of name anyway—*Trent.*

I've worked my ass off to get here. I'm thirty-four years old, Katya. I'm not young anymore. Trent is a one-way ticket.

Addy peeled a thin layer of skin from her bottom lip with her front teeth. She chewed the soft padding and swallowed.

Why you do this? said Katya. Bad habits.

Katya shook her head in frustration.

I am almost done. How can you ruin the lipstick? Stop biting like that. There is no need to be so nervous. You do this show many times before.

Addy took a deep breath and closed her eyes again as Katya repainted her lips a scarlet red. 6:57. She could hear her fellow cast members scrambling into their places for the opening number, *Willkommen.*

How old is boy wonder? asked Katya.

It doesn't matter, Katya. He's a visionary. If he offers me a role in his next project…I can't think about that. It stresses me out. I just don't know why he came *today,* right when I get a cold and my voice is wrecked—I wish he would have come when we opened.

Maybe he want to see Rockefeller tree.

Addy held her hands in front of her face, fingers pointed up, pressed together palm-to-palm as if she were praying, and then opened them like the spine of a book, sighed, and began to lower her face into them.

No no no! said Katya, wrestling Addy's hands away. You are crazy? You will ruin your face. What is the matter with you today?

He is only child! Besides, you are wonderful! You do this show many times.

I don't know. I don't know what it is—my head has been spinning all morning. My stomach has been churning, Katya.

You have flu?

Katya foraged through her purse and unwrapped a pink candy. She forced it toward Addy's mouth. You take. You take, she said. Vitamin C, you take.

Addy took the candy, crushing it to pieces with her teeth.

Thank you, she said. I don't know what is wrong with me.

7:01. Out beyond the dressing rooms, the wings, on the other side of the red curtain, the house lights were going down, Addy knew. The blue spotlights were being primed up in the rafters. She could hear the PA system instructing the audience to silence all devices. She had roughly five minutes before she had to make her way to the wings, find her mark to enter for the show's second song, her big entrance, her solo.

Finished. Don't touch, said Katya. Katya leant back against the dressing room wall and scrolled through her phone, her thumb flickering up and down the screen like a candle.

Zone out, Addy thought. She needed to melt away the panic and doubt that was bubbling in her—to forget about Trent. She needed a song. She put in her bluetooth earbuds, closed her eyes, and vibed out to the chorus of Joni Mitchell's *River*, trying to find the calm, the stillness, for tonight's special holiday show.

She didn't like Christmas, not exactly, but she liked *working* on Christmas. She liked the idea of providing something special on this day. She liked how she didn't have to think when she was on the stage. She knew all her lines. She could give herself over to the character, to the story. She didn't have to consider what the tradition meant to *her*, to Adelaide Wheeler, who no longer bought into the old rituals of her childhood. Last year she and Ray were both working and then ordered Chinese for dinner. He'd gotten her a pair of earrings and she'd bought him a bag of gourmet coffee beans. Neither of them had even bothered with the wrapping.

That was always her favorite part of Christmas growing up. The wrapping paper. The mystery of what was inside. The anticipation. Ripping the snowmen, the candy canes, the platinum trees into strands. She thought that was how the audience felt before a show—the red curtain the wrapping paper, the show, her voice, the gift inside.

And perhaps brightening one person's day in this enclosed, dark space of the theatre, nestled in the heart of this island, showered with snowflakes at the boundary of melting, the thought that she could be some kind of healer here, for a few hours helping one person to forget their own daily grievances and private sufferings, lifting the expectations and burdens building like mounds of snow, this idea of it being a gift, her lines as Sally peeled off like ribbons of wrapping paper under a tree, beneath eager childhood fingers, electric and hopeful for what was inside.

It is time, said Katya, waking Addy from her reverie. Are you ready?

Addy chomped down one last throat lozenge, took a deep breath, and shook the childhood images of Christmas and the unwrapping of gifts from her mind. She set her earbuds on her vanity and checked her phone—a missed call from Amelia. She was worried, Amelia never called her. She hadn't thought much of it earlier, the text in church, her mind had been set on today's show, on getting her voice right, but now she felt bad and figured she should call Amelia after the show, or at least message her something nice, wish her happy holidays.

She left her dressing room and made her way toward the wings for her entrance, but her thoughts were not where they should have been. They were back in Carolina today, stuck beneath a childhood Christmas tree.

She stood in the wings waiting for her cue, her mind floating apart in all different directions, a soreness in her throat stubborn, the blister on her heel burning, and a newfound guilt about ignoring the messages from her mom and sister, but somehow she'd have to banish it all— the show must go on. She took a deep breath to center herself. She was a professional and must put on a show. She pictured Trent Pendleton in the audience and knew this was her one chance, that she needed to seize it. She thought of the rest of the audience and her need to please them. They'd paid good money, come to see her on Christmas Eve. She felt the emotions well in her, the ones she would need to summon on the stage. She could do this. She was born for this. She readied for her entrance and her opening number, imagining her voice as a neatly wrapped present—the stage's curtain like ribbons of paper revealing the secrets within—beneath a glowing, angel-capped tree.

She'd belted out the final notes of *Cabaret,* willing her body to cooperate. The cold chills. The nausea. The muscle aches. The hoarseness, the itch in her esophagus. She'd willed them all away through complete focus. And she didn't just hit all the notes. There was emotion. She'd really cried for Elsie. *What good* is *sitting alone in your room?* She'd nailed it. Nailed it! Trent Pendleton would love it.

Addy took her bows, smiled like a kid in an Apple store during her standing-O. She looked through the faces in the orchestra, and locked eyes with Trent. He was still there, he hadn't left. He was clapping. He looked young. She knew he was twelve, but holy hell.

His cheeks were all baby-fat and dimples. He wore glasses. His black hair, an unflattering bowl cut.

When she got backstage, Katya was waiting in her dressing room.

Very good show, she said. What do I tell you, you have nothing to worry about.

Addy, breaking her fevered focus for the first time in hours, threw up in the trash can.

You sit. You sit, said Katya. Drink. Drink.

She forced a bottle of water on Addy, who sipped it slowly.

I'm fine, she said. Help me get all of this off. I have to meet Trent.

You look beautiful. Why you need to take it off?

I want him to see me as *me*. Not as Sally. Quick.

Relax, said Katya.

Please, Katya! I can't fuck this up. I don't want him to have to wait long.

Addy's phone began to vibrate, sending waves through the entire vanity. Addy couldn't see it, she was leaning back in her chair while Katya helped her with her makeup.

What does it say? Addy asked.

Katya stepped away and looked at the screen. Ah-mel-ee-ah, she said. It says Ah-mel-ee-ah.

Ugh, said Addy, my sister. Probably guilt tripping about me not making it back again this Christmas.

I hear it vibrate like this many times during show. You should answer.

Addy checked her phone, she'd just missed another call, and now there was a voicemail. She set the phone down and went about her post-show routine.

She rubbed a dime of moisturizer across her forehead, her t-zone, her cheeks, her fingers making concentric circles all over her face.

She got out of costume, hurried her clothes to wardrobe, and threw a hoodie over her head. She slipped out the back, her head down to avoid any fans from the audience who might be lingering after the show for autographs. She walked east toward The Plaza Hotel, where Trent and his parents were staying, and listened to the message along the way. Amelia's voice, telling her the news that their mother had died. She registered the words, but they did not stick with her. They dripped and dried from her skin like water. She knew what they meant, but she couldn't allow herself to attach any emotion to the words, not now.

She quarantined them, compartmentalized them, stashed them away in a dark cubby in a recess of her mind. She couldn't let them affect her meeting with Trent.

When she arrived he was waiting for her in the restaurant, sitting at a table by himself, doing a crossword and sipping an espresso.

Sorry I'm late, said Addy.

Trent stood and bowed, which she thought was weird. She had expected some weirdness from a twelve-year-old savant, though.

Not at all. Not at all, said Trent. I actually thought you'd get here much later. You made excellent time. I only arrived approximately five minutes ago. I was just doing my crossword. Four letter word for *sullen,* ends in *e*...hmmm. Anyway, yes! You made excellent time! You must have ran out of there. Usually it takes much longer after a show.

I didn't want to keep you waiting. I'm just so thrilled that you agreed to meet.

The pleasure is mine, my dear.

Why was he talking like Clark Gable? Addy wondered. The lighting in the hotel was dim. There was a huge Christmas tree near the elevators in the lobby that was decked out with colorful lights and garland and nearly touched the high-ceilinged atrium with its needles.

Let's get down to brass tax, said Trent.

Brass tax?

You've got a voice, Addy Wheeler. A real *voice!* That might be the best version of *Cabaret* I've heard yet. And I've heard them all. I have all of the recordings. The one you did tonight? I think even better than Liza.

When Trent said that, *better than Liza,* he made a show of raising his hands, flashing his palms to the ceiling lights, and spreading his fingers, as if he were surrendering to something. His TikTok features had taken Best Picture at the last three Oscars. This was a boy whose only fluent language was drama. Addy could tell he knew of nothing else, nothing of the real world. He existed only in what he made.

Thank you. That means a lot, said Addy. I watched her a lot preparing for Sal—

Let's get down to brass tax.

You keep saying that.

Addy chuckled, I'm not quite sure what it means, though, she said.

You've never heard it? asked Trent.

I've heard it, I just don't know where it comes from. It seems you like the saying.

My parents always say it. They said their parents always said it. I have no idea about the derivation. It means business, the meat and potatoes, the heart of the matter. You feel me?

Addy was searching her phone, now curious. It says that it's *tacks, c-k-s,* not *tax* with an *x.* Were you saying *tacks* or *tax?*

Have you ever acted in films? asked Trent.

I've had small roles in a couple of studio flops, never anything I was really passionate about. Nothing like your movies. I can get you my reel.

Here is the deal, Addy. It's a different ballgame, what I do. I take it very seriously.

I know. It shows. I would do anything. Even for a small role. I understand what you make. The amount of work you put in. How you aren't afraid to put things out yourself, to disrupt the studio system. You're a pioneer. I would work harder for you than—

I don't respond to flattery, my dear. I respond to talent.

I have what it takes, Trent. Let me prove it.

Here is the brass tax, Addy. You are meant for the stage. Your diction, your projection—remarkable. You're a star, and you know you're a star. Your voice, my God!

Thank you.

But—

But?

But, acting for the camera is a different thing. Diction, projection, they're irrelevant. You can whisper into the boom mikes and they will catch everything, and if your face looks like you're screaming, the audience will think you're screaming too, and the whisper will become a scream. You feel me?

I think so? I promise, I can act for the camera too.

What I'm looking for are eyes. I need the right eyes. And the light beneath them. I need a face with reach. Someone whose eyes can make the masses weep. Diction, diction can be taught. What I'm looking for can't be taught. And besides, I don't know if you've experienced the right kind of journey to bring *this* character to life.

I have. I know what you're talking about, Trent, and I have it. Let's get down to brass tacks, let's talk about this role—Brielle. And why I'm right for it.

You aren't right for it, Adelaide. I know after five seconds of meeting someone. I'm sorry, you're meant for the stage. You're already in your mid-thirties. A film career isn't going to happen for you now. I appreciate you meeting with me. I meant everything I said. Your performance tonight...

Trent touched the pad of his thumb to the rest of his fingertips and lifted them to his mouth, kissed them and blossomed his fingers apart like a flower. Exquisite, he said.

Are you fucking serious? said Addy.

There is no need for vulgarity, my dear. I am telling you the truth. It may be difficult to hear—

Don't call me *my dear,* you little cunt. I came here to meet you. On Christmas Eve! You just show up in New York, on fucking Christmas, and tell me I'm not right! That my eyes aren't right!

Adelaide, people are staring.

I can't believe you. I have worked extremely hard to get to where I am. I've sacrificed. You have no idea what I've overcome. And you tell me—

Adelaide, please—

No! You listen. Don't interrupt me! I'm meant for this! I want people to truly see me, to remember me.

People see you now, said Trent. You're on Broadway. People come from all over the world to see you.

Those shows are gone. Every night and then—poof—they're gone.

There are recordings of your performances. YouTube. And people can plug-in remotely. Your performances *will* live on.

It isn't the same and you know it! The theatre is made to be transient. I have what it takes to be captured in close-ups, to live on in your films! And fuck you, you fucking child, if you have the nerve to tell me otherwise.

Trent stood to match Adelaide, who was standing and looking down at him and his espresso, gesturing wildly with her hands. His head came only up to her chin.

The few people having cocktails at the bar were staring.

You will never even set foot on one of my sets now, he said calmly.

Not as a lead actress. Not even a cameo. You won't even be allowed to bring me coffee in the morning to my director's chair.

Trent walked from the restaurant, into the lobby, and toward the elevators. Adelaide ran after him and grabbed the back of his shirt. He turned around and she took him by the throat and slammed him up against the elevator door.

You little piece of shit! she said. I *know* I'm right for this role, so where do you get off? What makes you God? What gives you the right to take that away from me, you fucking punk!

Trent garbled, All the people who pay to watch my content, that's who.

She put all of her weight into him, lifted him with both hands. She saw two doormen rushing toward them in her periphery.

The soles of Trent's shoes hovered, kicked at the air a foot above the ground. He made an animal grunting noise. Addy could feel the chords in his neck vibrate. The elevator doors opened and she dropped him to the floor. A man and woman were in the elevator. They scrambled to help him up, looks of horror on their faces.

My baby! My baby! said the woman. What happened to you?

The man, who Addy realized was Trent's father, stared at her with a look of shock and disdain.

Addy's stomach was all in knots again. She felt that at any second an emetic episode could be in the works, chunks spewed all over the boy-wonder and his family, and that thought gave her unparalleled joy. The lights on the Christmas tree were now exploding in the lobby, screaming at her, making her head throb. There were tears welling in her eyes. The walls of the hotel seemed to be shrinking. The flowery red wallpaper swirled, made her dizzy. Her head was a kaleidoscope.

Your son is a little monster! she screamed at the parents, who were examining Trent's cherry neck. You should teach him how to treat people!

She'd never done something like that, so impulsively. She was always calculated, controlled.

Hey! shouted one of the security men, as she backed away from the scene.

She sprinted down the stairs and out the front entrance. The city loomed above her. It was quieter than usual, less traffic, but in the distance she could hear sirens streaming down Fifth Avenue. She ran downtown in the direction of Broadway, where the lights beckoned.

The lights were neon, they glowed at her, familiar. She wandered, dazed, down to Times Square where it was so dense—tourists on vacations snapping lasting images, memories—that nobody noticed her or asked her for a selfie. She stood still, people flowing around her in streams, staring up at the lights, her eyes burning.

There it was, tumbling down on her, everything that had lured her there. The hope that radiated from the theaters lining Broadway, those black-box sanctuaries of empathy, all the neon, the trust of clustering tight and existing together in that space. Her city. Her home. Then she thought about the mountains, the quiet, when they were kids, and all the noise, the neon, the concrete and steel became something else to her, it shouted and buzzed and threatened to avalanche down on top of her, and the people funneling around her became separate. They were herding in the same direction, going toward the same sights and attractions—the M&M store and up to Rockefeller and down to MSG—but they were suddenly, tragically, apart apart apart and she was magically, obviously, lost, alone, and she started to panic and hyperventilate. She hadn't believed it. Hadn't allowed herself to entertain it.

She listened again to the voicemail her sister had left.

She hailed a taxi and it whisked her away to her apartment in Greenwich Village.

Leave it running, she said to the driver, then scrambled up the stairs to the one-bedroom that she and Ray shared. There he was, buttoning his green peacoat. His hair disheveled. He was getting ready to walk Essie.

Addy, what's wrong? he asked.

Her eyes were puffy and red, her nose running. He put his arm around her shoulder, kissed her forehead.

I'm going home, she said. For Christmas.

Home? Like, Carolina? I thought we talked about this. Don't you have a show the day after Christmas?

Addy shook her head and walked away from him. She didn't want to bother with details. Didn't want to try and explain what she didn't understand. Didn't want to burden him with the news of her mother. Didn't want to hear whatever words he had. She hated his stupid ugly face. She threw her clothes in a Louis Vuitton duffle.

Essie Carmichael was barking at the two of them from the hallway, which she never did. She knew something was up.

I have to go, Ray.

We can go tomorrow. I want to be there with you.

I'm going by myself. I need to go by myself. I don't want you to miss any shows. You're important, they need you, she said. She stared at the floor. She didn't want to look at him. She hated him.

What about *you?* he asked.

I'm going to tell our director *thank you, I'm done.* To let Sarah finish the end of the run.

Addy was already at the door. Ray was obviously caught off-guard, at how quick she'd tornadoed in and out of the apartment, and she knew that he could tell she was keeping something from him. He fumbled to find her hand and hold it. He tried to turn her around and look her in the eyes, but she kept her back to him.

I have a taxi out front, she said.

She got down to the street and he was still behind her.

Addy?!

I shouldn't be gone long, she said. She turned around and kissed him. Take care of Essie while I'm gone.

She watched him from the curb as the taxi left. He looked stunned. His eyes big like a puppy, his jaw open in disbelief, his shoulders shrugged in confusion, as he offered his palms to the sky, the violet and swirling Manhattan sunset.

Where to now? said the driver.

Asheville, she said seriously.

I don't know where that is, lady. This is a local cab. Gotta be somewhere in the five boroughs, capiche? (He was one of those ironic, post-modern cabbies playing into an old New York stereotype. A white guy, a likely transplant from Nebraska or Kansas, Addy figured, based on the whole vibe she got. Or maybe she was all wrong, her radar felt off, maybe he was the genuine article, a born and bred New Yorker, an up from the bootstraps kind of fellow, a grinder. She wasn't sure, she only hoped he wouldn't try to talk to her, regardless.)

La Guardia. And hurry up, she said.

Merry Christmas to you too, he said, and he made a U-turn toward the east side, steered the cab to the Midtown Tunnel, onto the highway, and away from the bright island.

PART II: Chords

CHAPTER ONE

September, 2008

They would ask him about the Pink Lady. He knew they would, they always did, it was inevitable. What really happened to her? Who was she, and why is she called the Pink Lady? Have you ever seen her?

The story goes that she fell five stories to her death. Nobody knows her name, but the girl was rumored to have been pregnant—a servant girl who'd had an affair with her employer, who had been staying in room 545 at the Inn. When he found out about her pregnancy he pushed her over the balcony. Others, though, believe she's the spirit of Zelda Fitzgerald, who died nearby in the Highland Hospital fire, and then sought lodging at the Grove, recalling happier times there with her husband, when they were younger. No, but I have felt a chill standing outside that room, he'd always add, as a way to play into the myth, to give the guests a little something, a piece of a story to take home.

Daddy, Daddy, Daddy, said Amelia, tugging at his shoulder from the back seat of the car.

Leighton steered the car along Ocean Boulevard, looking for a place to park. It was Sunday, the final day of their weekend getaway, a mini vacation to Myrtle Beach. They'd packed all of their things up and checked out of the hotel at the crack of dawn because the kids wanted to spend a couple more hours at the beach, before they all had to buckle up for the five hour trek back to Asheville, back to home.

Leighton was irritable, in one of his morning funks. The Atlantic Ocean stretched out in front of them. The sun was high and bright in late July. The royal terns had risen and were perched on the wooden banisters of the boardwalk; they swarmed high in the sky and landed far out along the pier, sitting and watching tourists and the fishers who were just beginning to exit, their serene early morning rituals now disturbed by the cacophony of beach-goers seeking party and leisure. The terns trilled in the distance, *aack aack aack,* singing to one another, as their day, too, began.

There was no place to park, they'd missed beating the morning rush. A car honked behind them. Amelia continued to pull Leighton's shoulder.

Honey, stop! he snapped at her. I'm driving. You can't pull on me like that while I'm driving! Jesus Christ!

Amelia slunk back into the seat. I just wanted to know if you'd build a sandcastle with me today. You said yesterday you would.

I don't know. Right now I need to find a place to park the damn car.

Leighton, said Emily, who sat next to him in the passenger's seat, wearing rose-tinted glasses and clutching a beach-tote to her chest, which bundled a few towels, sunscreen, a parasol, and a heavy tome, a hardcover copy of The Kite Runner.

She was trying to help, he knew, but was only making it worse.

What about there, she said, pointing to a metered spot between two cars.

I'm not going to be able to fit there.

Well, I knew we should have just gone in the lot by the boardwalk.

That lot was full! Didn't you see the sign?

Why do I even bother helping when you're like this?

Leighton ignored the veiled insult and continued his search for a spot. August was in the back with his nose buried in that that frog game he was always playing on his GameBoy, and Addy was ignoring everything, listening to the *Wicked* soundtrack on her Walkman, singing along under her breath to *Defying Gravity,* soft enough that she could pretend she didn't know that the entire car could hear. Amelia was now hanging her head and pouting because he'd yelled at her.

He didn't know why he was in such a bad mood. It had been a great vacation. They'd spent the past two days swimming in the ocean, flying kites along the coastline and drinking lemonade. Perhaps it was just the early hour—he still needed his coffee—but he couldn't stop thinking about what was ahead today, five hours of continuous driving, the inevitable stiffness in his back, and then back at work tomorrow, up and at 'em, reporting for duty at a crisp six o'clock for his shift operating the elevator at the historic Grove Park Inn. He was already dreading it, the tedium of it, the same questions over and over about the Inn's storied past, the myths surrounding the Pink Lady, the ghost who haunted its hallowed grounds.

He was dreading the claustrophobia of it, the daily isolation spent with strangers, floating through the shafts in the granite fireplace, up and down, floor to floor to lobby level, the same small talk over and over, how was the flight in, nice weather we're having, do you have plans during your stay? before they would exit to their rooms and he would summon the elevator back to ground level where new strangers would be waiting to engage him in variations of the same conversation.

There! shouted Addy, tearing the headphones from her ears and pointing toward the open lot of an Olive Garden.

We're not allowed to park at an Olive Garden.

Why not?

We'll get a ticket. All these places have signs. Customers only.

So?

So, that's how the government gets you, they've got all sorts of little guidelines and rules and if you don't know how to play their game then they'll bleed you dry and take the money for themselves. Bush has run this country into the ground. Of course they're all the same—Bush, Clinton, what's the difference.

Maybe we should just skip the beach this morning and head back, said Emily.

No! three unanimous shouts from the backseat.

It's packed out here today. And we've had a long weekend; your father and I are tired.

No, Dad, no! said Amelia. You promised we'd build a sandcastle.

You know what, fuck it, said Leighton, as he pulled into a Starbucks. I need coffee anyway or I'll just be pissy all day. We can walk from here, it isn't far.

When they reached the boardwalk, they staked out an open space down in the sand. There were two groups of rowdy college kids near the pier, where Leighton and his family had descended the boardwalk stairs and entered the horizon of white sand that bordered the infinite ocean, so Leighton led them a few hundred feet to the left, away from the partying teens living it up during summer break, toward a patch in a quiet area, scrunched between several couples and solo sunbathers who read and slept and kissed as they took advantage of the high morning sun.

This is the spot, he said. Yes siree. Yes indeed!

Dad, you're such a dork, said Addy.

He sipped his Starbucks coffee and smiled a big dumb grin toward the ocean.

Maybe you're a dork, he said.

Emily speared their candy-cane striped umbrella into the sand and smoothed out two beach towels beneath the shade.

Leighton was beginning to perk up now that he'd had his coffee. He was still dreading the long drive ahead, the sharp pang he knew it would leave in his lower back, and he hated crowded, touristy spaces like this, but he breathed slowly and tried to center himself as he gazed out at the endless blue. There was really nothing for him to be angry about. It was their final day of vacation before he had to go back to the real world tomorrow, so he might as well try to make the most of it.

Addy was the first to embark toward the ocean, diving into the shallow foam headfirst. Amelia was right there behind her, following her every movement, while August remained on the towels near Emily, ignoring the ocean and the sand, entranced by his screen, seeing how long he could last until his virtual frog was squashed beneath the wheels of a semi or bitten by a serpent.

Leighton's wife looked regal, serene, beneath the parasol, her long legs stretched out into the sun as she read The Kite Runner behind her rose-tinted, John Lennon sunglasses. She was beautiful, thoughtful, smart. She looked so graceful, so at peace there under the umbrella, and he was reminded of all the reasons why he had fallen in love with her.

An hour passed. The tide had encroached closer toward them. It ebbed and flowed, back and forth, soaking the end of a large plank of wood that had washed ashore, which Leighton now sat on, and then receding back to let it dry in the sun.

Their family camp was some twenty feet behind him, out of reach from the water's fingertips. He'd migrated to sit on the block of wood because he wanted to get some sun, and so that he could keep an eye on Amelia and August, who had partnered up to build a sandcastle where the sand was just damp enough to hold it all together.

Addy twisted and twisted and twirled in front of the chunk of wood where he sat. She had brought her ballet to the beach.

Look, Dad! Look, Look!

He looked up and saw her pirouette and perform, then went straight back to reading the book that he'd been absorbed in, a biography of the Beatles, Revolution in the Head.

I see, honey, that's great, he said.

Dad! You're not watching!

I am, honey, he said, still skimming through a passage about Sgt. Pepper. You're so talented.

Addy knew a fib when she saw one so she twirled away back toward the umbrella to dance for Emily and to terrorize August, who had since given up on the sandcastle and gone back to his frog game in the shade.

Amelia was by herself, placing the finishing touches on the sandcastle—carving out crenelations on the two towers and fashioning a moat—as she lied between castle and ocean, hoping to shield the elements with her body, to keep it protected from the water, whose edge was slowly and slowly creeping further up the white sand, so that it now reached her back when the tide came in.

Leighton felt his new flip-phone vibrate in his pocket. He closed the spine of his book and glanced up at Amelia. It was really quite the structure she'd built. An impressive, two-tiered golden palace that she'd made with only her hands and a single pail, impressive enough to attract the eyes of a couple neighboring children and their parents. She looks so happy, he thought. It was her first time ever at the beach. There were no beaches in Asheville, only the surrounding mountains—the brackish river beyond their house was bordered with leaning trees and mud and bramble patches on each bank with the slow-moving water slicing in between—and they had never been able to take a vacation out to the coast like this. He smiled, happy that she was able to enjoy it.

Nice castle, honey! he said.

She looked up, gap-toothed grin beaming, and said, thanks Dad!

He turned his back and looked at the number on his phone. It was Jerry Smith.

Jerry! Buddy, how the hell are you?

You've got to listen to me. Just listen to me! I've got something. It just popped into my head! Wait'll you hear it. It thumps, my man. It's fucking killer!

What are you talking about, Jerry? Slow down will you.

Leighton drifted up toward the boardwalk and away from the umbrella. He saw Emily glaring at him out of his periphery. She probably knew it was Jerry. She didn't exactly approve of Jerry, wasn't thrilled when he'd moved to Asheville a year ago and insisted that he and Leighton and Tom Tavish get their old college band back together; Leighton knew she wasn't thrilled, though she never said much about it. He'd been practicing with StereoId ever since, three nights a week, just for fun, for a couple of hours after he finished his shifts at the hotel, and they had even managed to get a weekly gig on Thursday nights at Morton's, a dive bar downtown.

The drums, brother. I was messing around with the drums for that song we've been trying to finish...*Dense Vehicle.* I had a breakthrough, you've got to hear it.

Jerry had used an ancient cassette to record his new idea for the song's drum track, and played it through the phone for Leighton, but it was all crashing static, unclear and lost in translation; it sounded as if a baby had been given free reign to smack the snare and the cymbals with fistfuls of rubber duckies, and kick at the bass with its chunky-fat feet.

Jerry.

How killer is that?

Jerry.

It changes up the tempo of the whole song!

Jerry.

We can try it out when we practice tomorrow. Did you hear all the paradiddles I added in there?

Jerry, I couldn't hear anything. Look, I'm still on vacation with the kids.

Oh, right right right! How's the beach?

It's fine. Could we talk about your new drum thing later maybe?

Right on. Right on, brother. I was just so excited I had to call. But I hear you, listen—

Leighton! Emily yelled.

Leighton turned around. His wife was frantic, scrambling to her feet, pointing out toward the ocean. Her face was washed out by the blinding sun, but he knew that it reflected a primal look of terror, and of blame toward him.

He saw it. Edge waves had besieged and blitzed his daughter's sandcastle, and the tide had suddenly roared its way further up the white sand, evolving twenty feet further up the shore since its last permutation, so that it now encroached upon Emily and August and their base camp.

It had taken his youngest daughter with it, snatched Amelia out to sea. He ran towards the umbrella, threw his Motorola on the beach towel, and sprinted down to the water.

He could see her arms reaching above the surface. By the time he got there, the waves had already completed their retreat and were rising once again upon the shore. When he got into the thick of it, the sand under his feet became dense and gooey and brimming with pebbles and twigs, which made it hard to run. He fell headfirst into the white foam and fumbled around for Amelia as the water battered his face. Finally he had her in his arms and the tide receded once again, evaporating around them and leaving them lying at the edge of the sand. He picked her up and scrambled back toward the umbrella before the waves had a chance to reclaim them, as it gathered itself for another ascent.

She was coughing up water, but lucid. She wasn't a good swimmer, but had managed to keep her head above enough to save her life. He felt horrible. He could see Emily's eyes glaring at him.

My God, Leighton! she said. She could have...

It was his duty to keep an eye on her, to be there as she built her sandcastle, and he'd failed. First he'd lost himself in the book and then he'd left to talk to Jerry. He hadn't been there when the moment required. Still, what use was it, he thought, for her to go on blaming him, what use was it now to rave and stew and lose all composure? Their daughter was okay now, shouldn't that be the main thing?

She's going to be okay, Em, he said, hoping to pacify her.

No! No, Leighton! I told you—you always...

A crowd of people had gathered and were watching it unfold. Their eyes were like needles, piercing. Leighton tried to smile, to put on a face of calmness, to try and deflect the piercing needles, to stop them from pointing at him. But inside he was boiling. They were judging him. They were judging his family. And his wife was no better. When things were smooth-sailing she was a paragon of grace and clemency and joy, but as soon as the boat was rocked in the slightest, she suddenly couldn't deal at all, suddenly the whole world was out of sorts and the only thing she knew to do was to take up arms against it.

Honey, he said, tending to Amelia, do you feel okay?

She looked up toward the sky. The harsh summer sun reflected light through the beads of water that dripped down her skin. She turned her head and coughed one final time to rid herself of all the water.

She looked up at him, eyes wide with terror and relief. She coughed and coughed and tried to nod that, yes, she thought she was okay. A lone cloud drifted in the sky; as it shielded the sun and shaded their place on the beach, he saw her manage a smile. She would be okay.

He helped her to sit up and wrapped her in his arms. Then he noticed something that he hadn't before, during the chaos. Addy was the first to point it out—*what is that thing in her hand?*

He looked down and saw that Amelia clutched something bleached white and grotesque. It was a carcass. He took it from her and held it up. Some swirl of color was bright in its ribcage, rattling around against the bones, pink and brilliant tangerine.

Emily was scrambling around, decamping, packing up the towels and the umbrella, tossing August's GameBoy into the tote. Now that she saw Amelia was okay, she too looked around at the needles pointed toward them, and Leighton could tell that she was still livid with him, was desperate to get out of there—*see,* she would no doubt say later in the car, or at home, *that is exactly why we never do stuff like that, why we can never go on vacations, because you don't take things seriously—you go off in your own world.*

Whoa, cool! said August, trying to touch the dead creature in his father's hands. What is it?

Leighton didn't know—obviously a fish of some sort.

Amelia stood up. She'd stopped coughing and had regained her bearings. The small crowd that had gathered now dispersed, the situation under control.

Are you sure you're alright, honey? he asked her, gently fixing the wet strands of hair that matted her forehead and fell in front of her eyes.

I'm okay, Dad. She looked over toward her sandcastle, which the tide had wrecked. Aww, man, my sandcastle, she said.

Then she smiled—oh well—and hugged him as if everything was normal, as if she hadn't nearly been claimed by the sea. Ewww, she said, what is that thing?

You were holding it in your hand.

Gross. It looks scary, she said.

It was a Sloane's Viperfish, though none of them had the language to name it. They could only identify its open jaw, its long, sharp teeth, like sickles. The cold white of its bones seemed to make Amelia shiver. Leighton noticed it too, he'd never seen something so drained entirely of all color, unable to absorb even the weakest shade.

The thing about viperfish was that they were never supposed to be seen. Something made them to stay at the furthest depths, near the pitch black of the seabed, never to come near the surface, sinking, in death, down to the crust, the hollows of the ocean where even light was not strong enough to reach. It had no business being near the sun, hundreds of miles away from where it was supposed to rest, in the canyons of the blue, fading and fading, and might as well be stretching to the core of Earth itself, the black hole whose center had escaped even the eyes of man, the canyons where her secrets played, and her plates crashed up against one another, volcanic quaking, needing for touch, the heat surging from whatever idled under that ocean floor, exploding into viscous liquid, crude, cooling, neon, bubbling, rock.

And yet there it was, by some miracle, lifeless, bone-white, from the heart of the blue. A lost soul that had voyaged up into unknown waters, swept toward the light, maybe carried by another predator, maybe floated its way along with the current instead of sinking, maybe some other magic, its bleached carcass delicate in his palm.

Addy had seized their tie-dye kite from the beach tote and was now attempting to run along the shore and keep it afloat.

Look, Dad!

Addy, put that away and come back here! shouted Emily. We're leaving.

Leighton, August, and Amelia kept studying the alien creature, mesmerized by its monstrosity. Leighton shook it several times and the pink and orange color fell out through the bones of the ribcage—it was a shell, a calico scallop. A two-toned tapestry, near-symmetrical, with pink ribbons fanning upward and out from the center, and streaks of orange claiming the wings, the edges of the shell. It was a beautiful object, Leighton thought.

Pretty! said Amelia. Can I have it?

He placed it in her hands and she marveled at it, this one of a kind thing that was now hers, a souvenir, a keepsake from their vacation, a silver lining from the incident with the waves.

Dumb, said August, it isn't even that great. I bet you I can find a cooler one. Then he walked down toward the water to dig for a superior conch.

August, no! We're leaving, said Leighton, motioning him back. Your mother says we're going.

August quickly came back with a smooth, pearly-white disk dosinia. Mine's better, he said, then tousled Amelia's hair as he ran past.

He'd succeeded in his provocation and she lunged after him and pushed his shoulder. Don't! she said. Idiot.

He turned around and squared himself for a fight, before Leighton stepped between them and said that there would be none of that, that he wasn't going to listen to them bicker for the entire car ride.

Emily was carrying the tote with the umbrella and the towels; she'd gotten a head start and looked to be leaving them as she approached the boardwalk.

Hey! Leighton shouted. You're not even going to wait?

She looked back at him with a look of disgust. It was her way of punishing, giving him a momentary glimpse of having to handle the kids by himself. In it she suggested that if he couldn't bother to keep an eye on Amelia while she built her castle, then maybe a fitting punishment would be to show him a world without her, a world where he was forced to live up to his responsibilities.

He lagged behind with Addy, August, and Amelia. There were still some lingering needles from the surrounding neighbors.

Addy still ran up and down the sand, trying to keep the rope tight and the kite in the air. Addy, let's go! he said.

She let the kite fall back to Earth and joined the rest of them near where their camp had been. The solitary cloud had moved away from the sun, and the rays beamed once again upon the white sand. Leighton wasn't wearing sunglasses—they were somewhere at the bottom of the tote that his wife carried—so he shielded his eyes with his hand to stop the glare. Emily was now walking up the steps of the boardwalk.

Hurry up, kids, he said. Your mother's leaving us. August and Amelia were making faces at each other behind his back, still pretend-fighting about whose shell was superior, while Addy gathered her kite.

They were all barefoot; their flip-flops were cooking beneath the hot sun where the umbrella's shade had once been. Leighton looked out toward the endless blue. Back to the mountains, he thought. He didn't know when or if he'd see the ocean again. It had been nice to get away, but now, once again, all he thought about was returning to the hotel tomorrow, back to the daily grind, back to fielding questions about the myth of the Pink Lady.

His shoulders slumped and he could feel his entire body—his skin and his muscles, joints and bones—heavy and tired underneath the bright sun. Perhaps he needed another coffee. He started walking toward the boardwalk and looked behind to make sure the kids were following him.

Hey, you three, he said, don't forget your shoes. Hurry. We've got a long drive ahead of us.

CHAPTER TWO

It was the buttcrack of dawn, pre 0600, and the sky was a twilight blue, brightening into a sort of periwinkle above the ECG vital screen of limestone and granite that spiked and dipped in the distance, the blue ridge brightening over the course of the commute, as Leighton steered his car mechanically, using the complete minimum brainpower needed, along the highway, toward the Grove Park Inn to begin his opening shift operating the lobby's elevator for the hundreds of guests who would be checking out and then the new arrivals who would be coming later in the afternoon.

His job was a good one. Maybe something like iconic and coveted in these parts, essential. At least that is what many of his co-workers told him. That he was lucky to have gotten it. That it was really something to hold on to. He had gotten it because his aunt Cheryl had worked there at the Concierge for twenty plus years and had recommended Leighton for the job. He'd started right out of college, just before Addy was born, and had been here now for over ten years.

It *was* a good job, Leighton admitted, a great job actually. Full benefits. He got along swimmingly with all of his co-workers. It was a warm environment, open, great communication between the various departments in the hotel: rooms, resort, guest relations, housekeeping, food and beverage, security.

The elevators, especially, were historic. They were truly one-of-a-kind. Unique within the world. Nothing quite like them anywhere else. They were included in Ripley's. They had been operating since 1913. They were located within the stone fireplace shafts of the hotel, running parallel with the chimney, embedded in the heart of the solid granite rocks. The two massive, fourteen foot tall fireplaces located within the Great Hall entrance had originally been the primary heat source of the Main Inn.

The elevators themselves were unique due to their engineering, built into shafts in the granite, and the fact that they could open on three sides. They were small and featured an old black iron door. The two elevators could only carry a few guests and luggage at a time, so there was often a wait. As an elevator operator there was a lot to do and a lot to know. Leighton had just about mastered it all, after ten years here. You had to be quick and efficient and also well-versed in the history of the Grove for when guests inevitably asked you questions, the most common one being the credibility surrounding the mythical haunting of the Pink Lady. *Is she still here?* They might ask him. *Have you ever seen her?*

He had not ever. That is, seen or felt the presence of any ghost here, Pink Lady or otherwise.

He arrived, moseyed himself through housekeeping and into the employee changing area, filled with dread, a pre-caffeine headache-a-brewing, the creature scratching mercilessly at his temples. He buttoned up his baby blue dress shirt, tucked it into the gray pants provided to him—the entire uniform supplied by housekeeping—cinched his tie, slipped on his gray vest and pinned his gold plated name tag onto the left strap of his vest, above his heart.

He prayed for a slow day. But it was a Friday and that was unlikely. Hopefully no drama. Hopefully no high profile guests. *VIP* guests, as they were labeled, always meant added stress, always meant the managers were on high alert, ultra-anal, ultra-sensitive to any mistakes or breaches, with regard to the Ps and Qs. But there were often *VIP* guests, the Grove having been a favorite hangout of dead historical men like Scotty Fitzgerald and Thomas Edison. J.D. Rockefeller had once dwelled there, along with a litany of presidents. A few years back, Leighton had caught a glimpse of the back of Bill Clinton's head—that had been quite the week, high alert, secret security stationed around every corner.

But Leighton hadn't been briefed on any irregular-type guests like that. Hopefully it would be a low foot traffic day, as the creature still banged against the inner edges of his skull.

Morning Mary. Morning Dale. Morning Arthur. Morning Darcy. Morning Vivica.

Leighton auto-piloted the ritualized daily greetings, as he headed for his post.

Boyohboy! Kid, you look like absolute hell, said Barney.

Barney was Barney Little, his supervisor at the Concierge desk, who had referred to Leighton as *kid* since day one, when he'd arrived baby-faced and clean shaven. And the sobriquet had stuck despite the fact that Leighton was now mid-thirties with three kids and a full beard.

Everyone called Barney Little Barney Fife. Leighton hadn't known why or who Barney Fife was. Apparently some old guy from early TV glory, a classic character from the Andy Griffith show, a skinny guy with an expressive face and bug-eyes. Barney Little looked nothing like Barney Fife, and nothing like his Little name would indicate. He was in fact a mountainous, hulking man, a Bunyonesque fellow, a teddy bear with a fixed smile, soft rubicund cheeks, who might actually more so resemble the Barney of children's entertainment, the purple dino. But Barney being a rare name, and the older employees here at the Inn having loved the Andy Griffith show as children, they just instinctively started calling him Barney Fife all the way back in 1968 when he was first hired, and so now it was obligatory to call him Barney Fife, or often just Fife. Leighton thought he looked uncannily like the actorman from Roseanne and The Big Lebowski, whose name now escaped him.

Sorry, Barney. You know we play over at Blondie's on Thursday nights. I might have had one too many.

That's no excuse *kid,* this is your job. You didn't even bother to comb your hair?

Sorry, Barney. I'm combing it, see. All good.

I don't need to hear the *sorrys,* you know I love you. You just gotta be sharp. Not sometimes, but all the time. Late night or not.

I hear you.

Now I'm gonna need you today, busy I imagine. And we're short. Tamara called out. Gonna need you here at the desk, answering the phones.

Are you serious?

I've got Darryl coming in for a few hours this morning, for the check outs. It was his day off but he said what the hell. Bless him.

You know I hate the phones, Barney.

Well might be that you hate 'em, but you're good at handling 'em, along with the guests. You can multitask the way it needs done. You know Darryl, nice guy, but he gets caught up on the phones, chatting somebody up, you know how chatty he can be, and then ain't nothing, not a stick a dynamite or what can get him off the line, and meanwhile he won't even notice the line of guests that's formed.

I just wanna do what I know today, Barney. It's a lot more stress for me here, manning the desk, the phones. My head is killing me.

Look, I didn't ask for Tamara to call out. Her son's got a fever or something. We've got to make do. I just need you to man the desk. I know you don't like it, but I need you *kid*. Are you gonna be able to help me out on this one?

Of course Leighton would do it, he and Barney were simpatico. He liked Barney. It was just the business of the phones. They'd ring off the hook all morning, people who were trying to get through to guest services to book reservations but had the wrong department, and guests who were trying to get through to housekeeping, the business of holding and transferring, knowing all the right extensions. The business of the sound not being such great quality all the time, so you couldn't always help the way that they thought you could help, the words from the voices on the other end jumbled and lost in translation through the wires.

At least with the elevators he could go on autopilot. Press a button, up or down, a bit of small talk with the guests. And he liked to move around, didn't mind being on his feet. With the desk you were in the same spot all day, your back got stiff.

But Leighton did it for Barney, covered the concierge desk. He was used to it, being shuffled around the different departments, tossed over to guest services or food and beverage like a ragdoll, helping wherever help was required.

He sat there behind the concierge desk, answering phones mechanically.

After a cup of coffee he felt much better. During the slow lulls at the desk, he daydreamed about playing guitar later that afternoon at Jerry's. His energy had buoyed and he hoped that it would remain; he told himself to keep that optimism into the afternoon and evening, when he'd be doing the things he truly loved, playing music and spending time with his kids.

But ten hours later he was exhausted. He had sweat through his work shirt, which was common, and by four o'clock all he felt like doing was sleeping.

A dark fog washed over him as he steered his car along the highway toward Jerry's house. This had gotten to be a regular feeling for him toward the end of his shifts and beyond, carrying into the evenings.

He had been feeling it, this familiar way, for a while. This middle-aged thing, it might be called by an outside observer (despite the fact that he was just thirty-five). A crisis, he wouldn't go that far.

Maybe it began about a decade ago when his father died. Both parents gone, it does things to a person, changes you in fundamental ways. But it was inevitable; his father had drank himself there, clutched the bottle six feet under. He and Leighton were no longer close toward the end, hadn't spoken truly—nothing beyond obligatory check-ins—in several years, but still Leighton had sat there next to the hospital bed at the end, the only one there, saying nothing, as his father struggled to communicate beyond grunts, skin tinted yellow with jaundice, his father dizzy from the medication that was meant to treat the cerebral edema that resulted from the no longer functioning liver.

It had been predictable, telegraphed from years of steadily increased consumption. And Leighton wasn't sad exactly. In a lot of ways he was relieved. His father and the elixirs that owned him could stop their dancing. They'd no longer be allowed to make him suffer.

And yet, as the ghost of the moment floated through him, as he now sat on a metal foldout chair in Jerry Smith's garage, tuning his Ovation Celebrity, he felt a kind of clear edge to it. A crisp straight line, a mathematical fact, a geometric boundary that delineated some area of his *self* inside, some sense of identity, delineated it in some abstract way, both clear and abstract, the edge, in that he could feel the marker of it, the cirrhotic inciting momentousness of it, tangible, the wall, but had no clue as to why it had materialized or what its boundary was keeping in or out. He saw the clear sharp edge of it in close-up but couldn't tell what was beyond it, couldn't make out the contours of its significance to the larger picture, didn't know if it was one edge to a perfect square, a link of an endless zigzagging rip of a paper heart, a leg of an octagon, a hypotenuse.

Brotherman.

—

Starry-Eyed Susan.

—

Earth to Leighton.

Yes, Jerry.

You got that thing good and tuned? You ready to rock and roll?

They'd been disciplined at keeping to their schedule and usually rehearsed thrice weekly now, at least, in the soundproofed garage of drummer Jerry Smith.

StereoId, the brainchild of Leighton Wheeler and Jerry Smith and Tom Tavish, birthed in Carmichael Hall dorm rooms at UNC's Chapel Hill campus, was nearly fifteen years old now, in toto. Give or take the seven/eight years of largely dormant hibernation, the post-collegiate twenty-five to thirty-two time frame, in which each of the founding members entered the American workforce and took out mortgages and began the tasks of wedding and having kids.

Well, Tom Tavish had joined Leighton on this front, the familial endeavor, and had had two redheaded and smiley girls with his collegiate sweetheart, Viv. Jerry Smith was, to be honest, a lifelong womanizer, a forever bachelor, the free spirit type. A venture coitalist. He would put it just about anywhere, if the impetus struck him. And it wasn't what you might think, an issue of impulse control. Well, it wasn't *just* an animalistic need. No, Jerry had terrific impulse control. He was highly intelligent, salutatorian at his Raleigh Prep School. And there was never much of a wild streak with regard to substances. Those blackout nights, hunched over stalled toilets in restrooms communally shared by the dorm's entire floor, soury and fungally and altogether fecal smelling, those nights of getting twisted on cheap vodka and spliff inhalations, passing out, large swaths of memory unretained, which are, like, apparently, somehow, canon, crude law of the coming-of-age American land, culturally ritualistic, and, in some strange and twisted way, necessary and vital to the molding of a certain kind of American Man—well, anyway, Jerry had mostly managed to avoid anything of this sort during his collegiate experience. Leighton was all too familiar, first hand, with those grainy nights. Tom too. Jerry was the outlier on this matter. He was an unseasonably reasonable young fellow on a campus cramped with hormonally steroided horndogs. A maybe pathologically controlled and confident twenty year old boy in an ocean of young persons swamped with doubt and future-fear and homesick-childhood-yearnings and still-strong desperations to emancipate the face from acne.

Leighton thought maybe it was just this angle that Jerry had always loved to play up. This holier-than-thou caretaker during blackout collegiate episodes. Though the details of the nights were largely hazy, he still remembered his bandmate's silhouette against the fluorescent ceiling of the communal bathroom; he remembered all of the times that Jerry had been there for him, unjudging, kind. How many times had he sat next to him through the sweating AM hours, throat all red and acidic, making sure that Leighton was okay, refilling the plastic cup with tap water when it needed refilling.

Leighton was, he admitted to himself, resentfully jealous about Jerry's entire schtick. He knew this sympathetic friend, the voice of reason, responsible, gentle, was an effective role that Jerry took advantage of to slide into the sheets of some of the most svelte and symmetric of sororal sisters who had pledged to the campus' most philanthropically conscious and predominantly artsy and intellectual chapter at that time, Delta Zeta. Not that Jerry wasn't truly that virtuous; Leighton thought maybe he really was, but it wasn't purely altruistic—there were of course coital kickbacks to consider that came from Jerry's selflessness and responsible care.

But Jerry was also a mysteriously enigmatic drummer, silent, long curly locks, intellectual and eerily self-controlled except for when he really just *lets go* and clobbers his Pearl four-piece shell kit.

Leightonman? said Jerry.

—

You got that em-effer tuned yet? Are you *with* us right now? I've got a drinks date this afternoon. A gymnastics instructor. Met her at one of our gigs. Like, proper gymnastics, like University gymnastics. Like, she's the real deal, flexible as all get-out and everything. I can almost guarantee you she'll opt for something low-cal tonight, the clear liquor option on the menu, something with lime probably. How much you wanna bet?

You'd know better than I would, said Leighton. My wife isn't much of a drinker. I doubt she's had anything but a few glasses of wine in five years.

Point is, we gotta get this show on the road. This girl, Wheelerman, she could be *the one.*

Leighton knew, positively, that she would emphatically *not* be the one, as there was no *one* for Jerry Smith. Leighton found himself lately, more and more, ragefully jealous at how Jerry managed to move through the world, ephemeral, anchorless. If it had been a symptom of impulse control, then perhaps Leighton would be more sympathetic. But it was a confident and constructed value-system that Jerry led with; his value-system being one of *un*belonging, of freedom, of each and every, solely responsible to his or her own compass, sans any guilt or shame that a neurotic person might feel at leaving other people behind or stranded on the outer boundary of one's life. Leighton knew that Jerry would sleep with this gymnast once or maybe a few times and then the call of his venture coitalism would beckon and he would tell her as much, open and honestly, and he would move on, no harm no foul.

Alright, said Leighton, let's do this.

Jerry was behind his drum kit, energy coiled in his wiry arms, his whole body revved for their rehearsal. I can't believe you're still playing that old thing, he said, gesturing to Leighton's Ovation Celebrity. You've got to swap that thing out for a nice Gibson before we shoot to stardom.

Leighton rolled his eyes, slung the strap of the guitar over his shoulder. Jerry was always saying crap like that. For Leighton and Tom, StereoId had become a hobby, a good way to release tension a few times a week, to revisit the simpler times of youth, a habit that let them forget about daily life and get outside of themselves. But for Jerry, it took up a substantial amount of real estate in his brain. If it weren't for Jerry, the band would no longer be together.

After the hiatus, Jerry had moved to Asheville for his first traditional 9-5, crunching numbers into meaningful readable data for some corporation, after several years in Nashville, spending his adventuresome twenties working a flurry of odd jobs and playing in several bands, none of which managed to take off the way he'd hoped they might, and noncommittally chasing Nashville tail (though you wouldn't hear that vulgar and misogynistic expression anywhere near Jerry himself's mouth, as he remained ever the conscientious gentleman). And so he'd moved for the traditional 9-5 and instantaneously hated it, and hounded Leighton and old Tom Tavish to indulge him in a reunion that nobody had asked for.

And to Leighton's surprise, it was exactly what he'd needed at that point in his life, two years ago, at just the same time that he was peak-stressed with his own 9-5 (or more like 6-4 four days a week) as an elevator operator, a sturdy grown up job with benefits that he'd started fresh out of college and with a broadly unemployable English degree from a public university. This was two years ago, when Jerry returned and spearheaded the unwanted reunion, and truth be told Leighton's marriage too had become static and rather transactional in all moments when it was just Emily and him, and the kids were in bed or in the other room.

And there it was. The edge was back, the beveled razor. It came sometimes when he thought about what it meant to be a father, then thought back to his upbringing with his own father, just the two of them after his mother died. The edge stretched rubbery inside his chest, a dark, permanent line that ran parallel with his guitar strap and produced a tightness in his chest.

Jerry was always talking of the band's fate, of stardom, always demanding that Leighton and Tom take it more seriously, preaching how it wasn't too late to make it a Real and meaningful thing. And perhaps he was right. Leighton realized that he had once felt the same way, back at Chapel Hill. And where had it gone, that self-belief?

Well, he wasn't sure. He had a family now, loads of responsibilities. But he sometimes hated that Jerry had it, the thing, the fiery thing, and he no longer did.

Need a lot more energy over there, leadsingerman, said Jerry.

They were working on perfecting *Dense Vehicle* this afternoon, the last song of their latest demo, and one that was giving them trouble. They couldn't quite get it to sound right. Once it was done, they hoped to send the demo around to some smaller labels and incorporate the songs into the setlist they played around local

Carolina bars and small venues, whose ratio of originals to covers was currently at about fifty-fifty.

This rededication to the band now took up much more time in Leighton's life, but it all still felt to him like a respite from the daily slog. A hobby. A way to bide the time. A fantasy. There was a scarcity of the spark that he'd felt when StereoId had first formed during those college years. Jerry knew it too. Fucking Jerry, going all out with the drumming, the show-offy stick twirling between takes, the beads of sweat gathered on his brows.

Little more heart and soul over there, Wheelerman. You're the voice here after all.

What annoyed Leighton most of all when Jerry would call him out like this was the fact that he was right, the honesty of Jerry's judgements.

Little less through the motions. Little more *give yourself over to it.*

CHAPTER THREE

It was already dark, eight o'clock by the time Leighton left Jerry's house. He steered his car along the Blue Ridge Parkway, a Honda Civic that he'd been driving for almost a decade; its engine grumbled and groaned when he'd started it.

He was tired. It had been a long day of work, followed by the jam-session with his band, but for some reason he wasn't looking forward to going home. A gray fog weighed heavy on him. He dreaded waking up tomorrow, returning to the hotel for another day of answering phones, of the repetitive pressing of the elevator's buttons, up and down the floors, of small talk, monotony.

What was this unsettled feeling, this disquiet in his soul? Why couldn't he just appreciate what he had? Like Tom. Tom seemed genuinely happy, content. Or like Jerry. Jerry was never content, always moving, always striving, his mind and his mouth firing off a hundred miles per hour, but he was always honest about it, knew what he was after, laid his desires and his goals out in the open. Why did Leighton always feel as if he were stuck somewhere in-between, in limbo?

He thought about his children. His kids would still be up; by the time he walked through the door they would have their pajamas on, they would be getting ready to brush their teeth, getting ready for bed, for the day of school ahead tomorrow. His son and his daughters would be waiting there for him, watching something on Nickelodeon in the living room, while Emily finished putting away dishes in the kitchen, or read quietly in their bed. Amelia would run up and hug him when he arrived. August and Addy would smile from the couch and say *hi Dad!* They'd ask him how his day was. He'd say *fine, oh, just fine,* and then he would walk past them and get into the shower, where he would linger, attempting to center himself, breathing in the steam, the hot water rushing down his body and circling the drain.

He could see it so clearly, this domestic scene, as if he were a time-traveler, and had jumped fifteen minutes into the future.

He imagined it like that, day after day, year after year, nothing else. He knew, intellectually, that things changed, details, here and there—his kids would eventually grow up, move away—but all he could see, all he could feel was the everlasting force of that image, of himself in the shower, the door shut, the universe churning, indifferent, all around him, as the water beaded his skin and he scrubbed clean the dirt of the day.

The Civic glided along the highway. He took the exit for home, steered through the same familiar streets. As he approached his house, he slowed the car and looked at the decorations that Emily must have put up. She'd been bothering him to do it for a week—Halloween was tomorrow—but he hadn't gotten around to it, kept procrastinating, so she had done it herself. There were cobwebs clinging to the edges of the windows. There was a skeleton and a ghost floating around the front door. There were orange lights dangling from the gutters.

Then he drove past his house and watched the orange lights dim in his rear-view mirror; he wasn't ready to pull into the driveway and enter. He felt strange. His odd mood, the navy fog, swirled inside of him and compelled him to keep his foot on the gas until the car reached the end of Hickory Tree Rd. He eased the car past the pavement, past the last house on the street, and onto the dirt path that led up to the edge of the forest.

He kept the car running, the headlights shining toward the trees, as he took his guitar from the backseat and walked down to the river, led by the path of the headlights.

He sat at the edge of the bank on a smooth patch of dirt between two brambles. He watched the slow-moving stream shift in the moonlight. As he admired a nearby growth of wild asters, waving their stems in the breeze, purple and quiet and bright, still in full-bloom, fending off the coming winter, he plucked a few strings on his guitar. Nothing major, he fiddled around with it for a few minutes, stringing together the simplest of chords—D, C, G, the first three chords he'd ever learned, seven years old, sitting on his mother's lap as she explained it to him, being patient as she tried to position his fingers around the neck.

He strummed for a while and the fog inside of him began to lift. He felt lighter, relaxed, as he listened to the lapping of the stream.

Then he thought back to his mother and father, the images of them rushed toward him, clear and bright.

How did he get here? How had this become his life?

Such simple questions, and yet how could anybody answer them? How far into the past was it possible to trace? He knew almost nothing of his father, no ancestral voyages, or triumphs, or struggles, no remaining stories—just secrecy. His father was an indiscernible amalgamation of white. A blend of European descendants who had first arrived in America sometime during its infancy. A lot of English and Irish and Scottish heritage, Leighton guessed, which had played the common scapegoat for a history of drinking.

On his mother's side, the only story he knew was of his grandmother's survival of the second world war, but beyond that, nothing remained. His maternal grandmother, Dora, had managed to evade the Nazis for more than a year, hiding with her husband in the countryside, at a small farmhouse south of Bialystok, before they were found and taken to Majdanek in the fall of 1943. Her husband was immediately killed in the Harvest Festival, but Dora survived and worked at the camp for seven long months, pushing wagons with several other women across the fields surrounding the camp. The wagons were giant, manure-filled wheelbarrows that they used to fertilize the Earth. Behind them, while they worked, smoke and ash rose from crematoria chambers, filling the sky with victims, while many more were heaped in piles off to the side, thousands and thousands, unburied.

Dora and the other women pushed the heavy cart across the soil, the wheels leaving tracks in the dirt, as their hands froze and bled and broke. No meat clinging to their fragile frames, but if they worked too slowly, they would be lashed with a bullwhip.

Dora survived working in the fields, she survived the bullwhip, she survived the experiments that had been done to her in the early months of her arrival, and she somehow survived her pregnancy with Leighton's mother. She had had to hide it for six months, because she knew that if she couldn't work, then she would be transferred someplace else and killed. She didn't know who the father of the child was. It was possible that it was her husband, but more than likely it was the SS guard who had raped her—this was the better of the two options for Dora in the camp because at least, if her pregnancy was found out, there was the slim chance that she and the baby might be spared if they believed there was hope for the child to be Germanized. Even if her husband was the father, Dora had planned on saying it was the SS guard's child in an attempt to survive.

This was the daily fear that she had lived through, every cell of her body, every muscle, quaking and twitching with terror, as she summoned what little strength she had to keep pushing the cart forward, as time stuck and trudged like tar and black treacle.

In July of 1944 she could no longer hide it. Her belly was a crescent moon, and she feared that any day the guards would finally say something and take her away, or shoot her right there in the field. But that month Majdanek was the first of the camps to be liberated by Soviet forces, the SS evacuated, retreated west, and Dora was left standing there in the field, with Leighton's mother in her womb.

She was sent to deportation centers in Siberia and the Soviet Union, and a month later, in one of those gray facilities, her child was born—Leighton's mother, Hanna. She spent more than three years there with Hanna, bouncing around these deportation centers and accepting whatever work she was told to do—cooking, laundry, scrubbing floors—until she was finally allowed to immigrate to the United States in 1948.

She moved to North Carolina with Hanna and found a job working as a housekeeper for a wealthy family who lived near the Biltmore.

Hanna grew up in a quiet suburban neighborhood at the foot of the mountains, living with her mother in a one-bedroom apartment. Her life itself had been miraculous. To survive the camps, where everything began for her, to escape the fields littered with death, and then to grow up with a 1950s American childhood—trips to the Piggly Wiggly, the anticipation of the Good Humor Ice Cream Truck, holiday spirit abundant each year, as she helped her mother to dress their tree with ornaments and garland and light, to cap it with an angel—the stark contrast between these, the polar opposite states of her life, war and peace, was nothing short of a miracle.

Then she fell in love. The story of Leighton's parents was simple; for it was the story of so many, circumstantial. For the stars to align, for happenstance to place two separate bodies near each other within the same galaxy, while both were young, and smiling, and free.

They had met in high school, bonded over Beatlemania. He asked if he could dance with her in a school gymnasium and they were married a week before a man landed on the moon.

Leighton's sister had been born the following year, in the spring of 1970, and Leighton followed three years later, just before the oil crisis of 1973.

They settled in Raleigh where his father had gotten work as an accountant for IBM. His mother taught first grade. They lived together in a house on Maple Street until Leighton was ten years old, the age he remained after his mother and his sister were killed.

It had been a patch of ice, a twist of fate, the random sickle-blade of chaos. They had been driving home from the grocery store during a blizzard, the white-flurried emptiness of January, his mother and his sister, when an oncoming car lost control, skidded on a patch of ice, crossed the center-line, and collided with them head-on.

Leighton thought about it sometimes, how fragile it all was.

He felt shame and guilt, perhaps the products of his father's Catholic upbringing. He questioned it all. Why would God do this; what had I done? Had God known that he had taken things for granted? Did God look upon those children and smite them in the end, the children who became too complacent, too comfortable, whose lives were so easy that they had lost sight of the value in struggle, those who could no longer be bothered to suffer, who didn't see the point of it. Is that why it had happened, why his mother and sister were taken? Was it his punishment?

After their death, Leighton's father got another job and the two of them moved back to Asheville to be closer to his grandparents on his father's side—two stoic, Roman Catholic figures who solved secrets by banishing them down with Southern Comfort—and to Dora, who was still alive and lived alone and had survived the Holocaust but could not survive the death of her daughter and died weeks after Leighton and his dad moved back.

The following years in Asheville with his father were quiet and lonely. His father, too, turned to Southern Comfort, and Leighton saw this as a mercy. His father was a soft-spoken man, a kind man. He never interacted with Leighton, except for when he was drunk. His father was a loud, boisterous drunk—but never violent.

When his father drank he just ended up drowning out the unbearable heaviness, the loud, deafening silences with his old records. He would play *Help!* on vinyl and sing it start to finish at the top of his lungs, while he and Leighton sat in the living room; he taught Leighton all the words. Leighton still remembered the sour of his father's breath as he slurred through the words of *Yesterday*.

Then, as the eighties wore on and Leighton entered high school, his father began to share some of the Southern Comfort with him and they would find common ground in the albums of The Clash, and Fleetwood Mac, and Paul Simon.

This was how the two of them were able to bond after everything that had happened, singing the words to melodies of the past. They never said a single word about what had happened to his mother.

Then Leighton fell in love with Emily. They had been friends for years, attending the same school every year since Leighton and his dad had arrived in Asheville, but it wasn't until they reconnected in college, at Chapel Hill, that they knew that they would end up together.

Thinking back on it now, he supposed that he had seen her as a kind of savior. He thought that maybe their love could be strong enough to fix everything wrong in his world—and, for a while, it had.

They got married soon after they finished college and began a family.

And now here he was, he had arrived here. He looked out over the water. He played a few more chords.

He had a family here. They were safe. Happy. There was a lawn and space to roam. By all estimations he had achieved the American Dream, and then so why didn't he feel more grateful for it all? Why did this unsettled feeling always wash over him without notice?

His grandmother had survived the war. She had crossed oceans so that he might one day have this. Why was he unable to see it, to feel at peace?

Was he just waiting for the next big thing to happen? The next accident, the next cosmic twist of fate.

Was it the lack of purpose? The constant working. The non-stop consumption that advertised the power to bring about true happiness. The holidays of commerce, the boxes and boxes of papery decoration that littered the rafters in his garage—one for Christmas, one for New Year's, one for Halloween, and some green, cardboard clovers for St. Paddy's.

Was it that all the people who had ever truly known him were gone. His mother was gone. Dora was gone. His father had died young, shortly after Leighton's wedding, the victim of a cirrhotic liver. His father's parents—the stoic Catholics he'd barely spoken to—were gone. His sister, gone.

Was it that his days, static and barren, the loud predictability of them, made him realize just how quickly he would join them. And then how would he be remembered? Would his daughter's tell stories of him? Would they speak of him highly as a man who had been true to himself, a man of virtue, a man who had taken risks and shown courage, who had spoken truth and stood tall in the face of the world's great vices, a man who had been able to love?

He sat there, on the bank of the Swannanoa, with his eyes closed. He listened to the sounds around him, a symphony. The chirping of crickets were the clash of cymbals, the wind played upon the leaves like keys on a piano, as the nighttime songs of the mockingbird rounded out the strings section, and the river raced gracefully downstream, carrying the melody of flutes and clarinets.

He imagined his mother next to him, playing the guitar and singing to the sounds of the forest.

Then, as he strummed the guitar in his lap, he heard more voices coming from above, outside of nature, could hear a cadence to them, a rhythm. They breathed different melodies through his fingers, and then, suddenly, he had found something. Repeating those three simple chords that he'd been playing, he'd found something catchy—a hook. It sounded unlike anything he'd ever written before; it sounded better. A grin stretched across his face and his eyes became big and ravenous as he tried to keep it in his head, the key, the tempo. It lodged itself somewhere deep—an undeniable ear-worm—and in that moment it felt like those chords, that melody, were the only things that mattered in this world. He just knew it; he knew instinctively that it had more truth than he could comprehend, and that it would be dishonest not to follow that music down whichever path it might lead.

Perhaps Jerry was right. Perhaps it wasn't too late. Perhaps he owed it to himself to give it a true shot.

He couldn't wait to play it for Jerry and Tom tomorrow.

Then he allowed himself to imagine it, imagine what it might take to follow these notes down their natural course, toward their ultimate conclusion. It would be difficult. Change wouldn't be simple, couldn't come easy. The path would be paved with failure and doubt.

He realized that within that moment was a choice. Time had slowed to honey, and the universe had opened itself to him, offered him an opportunity. He hadn't understood this before, but now realized, right there at the edge of the stream, how a single moment could propel a man years into the future. He realized that unless everything changed, nothing would change, realized that he had the choice to envision it, and then to make it a reality. He had the choice to listen to these chords, and to create a different world for himself.

What it would take was painstaking work, eternal vigilance, always keeping his mind open and receptive to the voices and the melodies that swirled in the sky above, but it was possible. He realized right there that he had a choice—no, a responsibility, and that nobody else could do it for him, a responsibility to usher the music into existence.

He realized there on the bank, as the wind whipped through the trees and the autumn leaves descended, danced down into the water, realized that this was the opportunity, and if he didn't say yes, if he didn't seize this moment and choose to listen to the melodies, choose to follow their momentum into the future, then the moment would pass him by.

He played the chords over and over and began to hum some lyrics that had come to him, as the moonlight danced in switchbacks along the water, marauding and silver.

CHAPTER FOUR

It was Christmas Day when Leighton broke the news to his family.

The melody that he'd discovered that Halloween night had been the finishing touches on the final song of a four-track demo that his band had been putting together. The song had managed to get some local radio play and the attention of a few smaller record labels. But just last week, Leighton had been contacted by somebody who worked for Matador Records and had heard their demo through a mutual friend of Jerry Smith's, and had expressed interest in having them come to New York to record a full-length debut album. Leighton felt that it was an opportunity for a fresh start, and he wanted to take it. He'd never been to New York, but he imagined that the energy of the city, a new life there, might solve whatever problems had arisen in his marriage, and might ameliorate the discontent that festered within himself.

Santa had come in the night and left presents beneath the glowing, angel-capped tree.

Addy was the first one to wake that morning, restless, impatient to tear the wrapping paper from her gifts. She had woken Amelia up too, and the two of them had snuck downstairs into the kitchen to witness the remnants of cookie crumbs and the glass streaked with empty milk, before they cracked the door to their parent's room at the still-gray morning hour—*get up get up get up!*

Ughh...said Leighton...what time is it?

Time to open presents.

Go back to bed.

Santa came, said Amelia. Maybe he got me a Furby!

Furbies had had some resurgence in the mid-2000s and suddenly, out of the blue, Amelia just had to have one that Christmas.

Five more minutes, Emily pleaded, her face buried into a pillow.

We can't wait! said Addy.

Presents presents presents! said Amelia, following her sister's restless lead.

Okay, fine, said Leighton. We'll be right out.

So the two girls went back upstairs and dragged August out of bed, and then the three of them waited anxiously in the living room. They sat at the edge of the tree messing with the needles that stretched toward them at the tree's base, their fingers fidgeting in anticipation.

Leighton sluggishly entered the living room carrying an old camcorder on his shoulder. It was a tradition to film the unwrapping of gifts. There was a near decade of reaction shots dating back to when Addy was just three. Smiles and surprise and the entire great pageantry of the tradition that celebrated the holiday. Leighton actually had a soft spot for their yearly documenting of the unwrapping. He had his qualms about holidays in general, but he enjoyed the traditions he'd made with his own family, loved seeing the joy on his kids' faces when they tore the paper off into shreds and saw for the first time what Santa had brought.

He pressed the red circle (REC) on the camcorder and said, okay, go nuts.

Amelia found the Furby she wanted and immediately tried to speak to it in its own secret language: u-nye-ay-tay-doo—*Are you hungry?* and u-nye-loo-lay-doo—*Do you want to play?* and wee-tee-kah-wah-tee—*Sing me a song* and wee-tah-kah-wee-loo—*Tell me a story.*

All three of them received the usual stocking stuffed candy-canes and Reese's trees, along with smaller gifts of clothes and socks and little accessories that they all gave a monotonous *thanks* to before discarding them off to the side.

August's favorite gift was the model airplanes that Santa had brought. He was really looking forward to the challenge of piecing them all together.

Addy opened one of those portable karaoke machines with a microphone attached. Now she could sing to her heart's content or use the microphone to practice her monologues—she'd recently gotten into theater and had been the lead in both of the eighth grade productions.

Those were the only gifts aside from a small box that Addy happened to open last. It was a lean year and Leighton had wanted to save up for a potential move that he had yet to tell his family about.

In the final box was a gift for the whole family, an iHome. Well, it said *to family* on it, but Addy took that to mean that it was for her, a joint gift for her and Amelia's room, a new alarm, a high-tech new thing that she could connect her Nano to and play any kind of music she wanted, whenever she wanted.

No, said Leighton. That's for all of us. We're going to leave that in the living room.

But, Dad! said Addy. We said—Amelia and I said we wanted one of those for our room. Pleeease.

Leighton and Emily exchanged glances. Emily's was accompanied by a shake of the head, a resignation—*go ahead, you spoil her.* Leighton's was a look of weakness. He had never been able to resist her drawn out *please's.* He would never admit it, even to himself, but she was his favorite, the firstborn, his daughter, the one who had always reminded him of himself when he was younger—curious and rambunctious, precocious and stubborn.

Fine, he said. You two can keep it in your room, but don't be playing it too loud. Got it?

Addy gave him a big hug, thanked him, then sprinted up the stairs to find a home in her room for the iHome.

Though she had marked it as a joint gift for the two of them to share, Leighton knew who would be controlling the music. Addy had managed to commandeer the *family* present and now had an extra gift all for herself. Good for her, thought Leighton. She always fought for what she wanted, and he admired that about her. Besides, he and Emily probably wouldn't have used it much anyway. It made her happy, and so he was happy that the iHome was now essentially hers.

After Addy returned, Emily made them all scrambled eggs, but the three kids sat at the dining table and opted for an unhealthy breakfast instead, unwrapping and devouring several Reese's trees at eight o'clock in the morning.

Leighton looked at his wife. He knew she was annoyed, the kids had hardly touched the food she made. And they were too old for that, they should know better. But who could blame them? It was Christmas morning and they'd just gotten a bunch of candy. Leighton thought that she was going to say something, to tell them how ungrateful they all were, but instead she just held her tongue and rolled her eyes and went into the living room to clean up the mess of wrapping paper that was shredded in ribbons all over the floor.

It was in that lull after she'd left the kitchen that he decided to bring up the subject of New York.

You're joking, she said, as she returned to look at him hovering over the kitchen counter, a stern look on her face.

I'm serious, Em. They want us there to record.

So what does that mean?

I want us all to move there. I think it would be good. I think that we could do it. I've actually been looking into apartments already.

What? What are you talking about?

And if we sold the house, we could manage it, Em.

Leighton the economy has crashed. You want to *sell our home—now?*

Em, this is everything I dreamt of when I was younger. Remember? I know that we can make it work. We have a little bit saved up. And I have faith that we can make something really good.

I don't even know what to say.

Say yes.

You didn't think to talk to me about this first?

The kids were watching the two of them intently, unsure of what to think of the situation.

I don't even—said Emily. What are you talking about? When would this be happening?

Well, Jerry has already found a place, a room in Brooklyn. I was thinking I could go out in a month or so and stay with him for a while, while I—

A month?! So this is already happening? I have no say?

—While I look for something more permanent for us—

We have a life here, Leighton. A family.

—and we sell the house back here. Then you and the kids could move once the school year is over, sometime next summer?

Cool! said Addy. Mom, are we moving to New York?

Amelia and August were silent observers, but Addy always fantasized about living in a big city, asking questions about the city and mentioning how cool it looked whenever characters in movies weaved through the busy streets, dwarfed by towering skyscrapers.

Emily shook her head in disbelief and left the room, conversation over. He knew she was angry, and he understood. But he also knew how great this could be for all of them. He knew that he could convince her in time.

She would warm to the idea, he thought.

Then, a week later it seemed that she had. She was still angry with him, but as fireworks glistened above the French Broad River far in the distance, she told him that if it was what he needed, then she would support him, that perhaps everything would work out for the best.

CHAPTER FIVE

After they'd settled into the big Apple, Addy had argued herself into a newfound freedom. Her father had finished recording his album during the spring and summer and left in the fall of 2009 to tour with StereoId. Her mother was supplementing the modest income he'd managed to bring in from his music thus far by providing private piano lessons to three or four pupils whose Upper East Side parents had already mapped out entire orchestral futures for them, envisioning them as immortalized artists; or else maybe they just wanted to be alone and have them occupied for a couple hours each week.

Addy had turned fourteen that summer, but all of the changes at once—puberty, the move to New York, the onslaught of sensory stimuli the city threw at you, the desperate need to make new friends at school—they had all funneled together and had the effect of convincing her that she was much older than that.

She'd made one true friend, a best friend, Melissa. They were to be freshmen at the same school—the New Explorations High School in the Lower East Side, near Avenue D, only a block away from the East River—and lived in the same apartment complex in Alphabet City.

So Addy spent her days, hip to hip with Melissa that fall, at New Explorations, while her younger brother and sister were a few blocks away, still stuck at PS 34. This was the beginning of her branching out. She felt enlivened by the city, confident, as if she were becoming her own person.

Her mother had resisted at first, but she was busy with her piano lessons, and trying to maintain the apartment in Dad's absence, and with whatever she would do during those long evening hours she spent in her bedroom, with the door closed, Schubert accompanying her at low volume, and so eventually, not having the energy to argue, Addy's mother basically told her that she had free reign. She could take the subway around the city and explore as much as she wanted—freedoms not granted to her younger siblings—as long as she and Melissa stuck together, and she didn't lose the Motorola she'd gotten for her birthday, and as long as they were home by ten o'clock.

Some of the favorite haunts: Washington Square Park and Joe's Pizza in the Village and strolling through Soho admiring the boutique clothing and shoes and jewelry along the shop fronts on Broadway and Lafayette, which summoned them from behind their glass windows, made them wish they'd had the money to enter, made them gab about *one day*...but Addy's favorite haunt was not far from the apartment complex, not such a grand stretch of her newfound liberty, but could be seen from the window of her mother's bedroom: Tompkins Square Park. It wasn't the biggest or most well maintained park in the city, but it was convenient and got plenty of sunlight and she and Melissa had spent all summer seeking sun-kissed patches of grass where they would spread out Melissa's rainbow colored beach-mat and tan and read books and recite dialogue from plays together and talk about boys and altogether feel like grown, independent women.

This was where they were this afternoon, lying in the sun, just beyond the reach of a canopy's shadow. It was fall, but still warm.

The wind was still. The leaves on the trees were bright red and preparing to drop.

They had just read *The Scarlet Letter* in English class, and were in the habit of engaging in the adolescent kind of talk where boundaries were sought and questioned, and new burgeoning feelings were not so much articulated clearly, but communicated in a type of code usually peppered with cultural references, which went something like this:

Oh my God, said Melissa, casually flipping through a *Seventeen* magazine, Brandon Flowers is a total dreamboat.

Mmmm, said Addy, not looking up from *Lord of the Flies,* the newly assigned English reading. Yeah, no, I love The Killers.

I seriously, like, I only listened to one song all of last year: *Read My Mind.*

That's a good one. I like that one.

But, I mean, look, said Melissa, flipping the magazine toward Addy. Isn't he so hot?

Yeah, I said so, didn't I?

Are you, like, mad at me or something?

No. I'm just reading.

Didn't you say your dad met him or something?

Yeah. He opened for them once.

You're kidding!

Nope.

Don't get mad at me or anything, but your dad is like, pretty hot too—I, mean, you know he's attractive—he's got that whole rock-star energy thing going.

Addy looked up now from her book, a gust of wind disturbed the afternoon stillness of the city and a few red leaves fluttered down with gravity. She looked straight at Melissa, eyes narrowed and stern.

Oh my God are you serious? Disgusting. Don't even joke about that.

I'm just saying...

Well stop. He's my dad.

Your hot dad, said Melissa under her breath.

I'm gonna kill you.

What!? He's a musician! You're lucky! Your dad's like fucking Mick Jagger.

He is so not. He's not cool at all. He isn't even a real musician, he just thinks he is. He used to work in an elevator.

Better than my dad. He works for the MTA. He's an engineer or something super boring and lame. And then he gets home and he and my mom sing show-tunes together during dinner, and my brother and I just look at them like they're from another planet.

That doesn't sound so bad to me. Sure, I guess my dad's a musician now—so weird to say—but I can only ever remember a handful of times, when we were really young, when he played for us.

Melissa moved closer to Addy. She rolled the magazine into a cylinder and snapped it playfully against Addy's knee. She looked as if she might say something genuine and tender, but instead looked at Addy and said, well, all I'm saying is that I would suck his dick.

Addy's jaw dropped. She stole the magazine from Melissa and smacked her with it hard on the shoulder. Oh my God, you're seriously a fucking perv. I'll hook up with your brother then.

Oh my God, Nathan!?

He's seriously, like, actually, like no joking sexy.

I'm gonna tell him you said that.

They spent the afternoon gossiping and reading in the stillness of Tompkins Square. It was Friday night and Addy texted her mom that she was going to stay at Melissa's. They left the park, passing the Temperance Fountain, with a different virtue inscribed on each of its four sides—temperance, hope, charity, faith—and then made their way toward Momofuku noodle bar, a popular eatery on 1st Avenue, just as the sun was setting; they were hoping to beat the dinner rush.

After dinner they returned to their apartment complex. Melissa's family lived in a spacious (by New York standards) three-bedroom on the second floor. It was old and pre-war like the rest of the units in the building and smelled vaguely of mold. Melissa's parents had decorated it nicely though, and it always gave Addy a warm, comforting feeling when she entered, as if it were a proper home. Melissa had lived here with her family her entire life.

The house was quiet and dim, Melissa's parents already having retired to bed. She followed Melissa to her room down the hall, passing by a storage closet, and the bathroom, and Nathan's bedroom, where she could hear gunfire sounds coming from his video game, loud and obnoxious, the only sound that could be heard inside the apartment, while outside the city was alive and electric on the streets below.

The walls of Melissa's room were plastered with posters and printed photographs of the High School Musical cast of characters: Troy and Gabriella and Chad and Sharpay. They rewatched the past two episodes of One Tree Hill together, which Melissa had recorded, while they ate popcorn.

Then, as midnight approached, Melissa flipped the switch on the teal desk lamp that rested beneath her window, and they said goodnight, nestled side by side in Melissa's full-size bed.

Melissa knocked out immediately, fell into her usual nasally snoring, but Addy could not sleep at all. She was hot beneath the covers, tossing and turning, and despite the earplugs that she'd gotten in the habit of wearing since moving to New York, she could still hear Melissa's snores, and could hear the faint sounds of virtual warfare and Nathan's occasional exclamations of victory or defeat through the wall that his bedroom shared with Melissa's.

The truth was that she had a huge crush on Melissa's brother. He was eighteen years old, a senior at New Explorations, and she sometimes saw him at school in the halls. He was popular and sociable, but could also be aloof. Whenever she was around him she got the feeling that she didn't register in his mind at all, and it bothered her. She'd found herself increasingly concerned about him noticing her. Whenever she came over she'd gotten in the habit of refreshing her eye shadow and putting on a new coat of Rimmel cherry lip-gloss.

She had noticed him on a few occasions looking at her, and then he'd look away when she saw him, and then when she looked back again he would be looking again. This had happened at the dinner table when she stayed over for dinner, and in Melissa's living room when they were all watching TV. It unnerved her, made her heart skip a beat, and she found herself thinking about his looking for weeks straight, despite all her efforts to block it out of her mind.

She had fantasized about him kissing her. She had only kissed one other boy, Charlie Hopper, three years ago, back in Asheville, when she was in the sixth grade, and she had thought it was nothing special. But the thought of Nathan kissing her felt different. She wasn't sure what to expect, what the real-life sensation of it would be like, but she thought that she could imagine it clearly. Kissing Nathan would be something like quantum physics, she thought, a complex, abstract thing that she had no knowledge of, but yet seemed somehow fundamental and essential to the workings of the universe. She imagined galaxies opening and particles dissolving and time either sped-up to infinity or slowed to a still-life painting.

The noise from the city below raged on in the early morning hours, cars whirring up and down the Avenues, taxis honking, their doors slamming, drunken laughter, distant glass shattered.

She still couldn't sleep. The alarm clock next to Melissa's bed said 12:55. She got up and crept down the hallway toward the bathroom. When she was done peeing she turned out the light and went back out into the hallway. A cold blue light came from Nathan's room. The door was slightly ajar. She paused in the darkness of the hall and peered into his room. She could see his avatar soldier shooting rapid-fire at other video-game soldiers.

His voice startled her and she leaned back on the heels of her feet. Hey, he said, without turning around, without taking his eyes off of the military duties that were calling him, you want to play?

Sure, she said.

She joined him in his room, which was gray and shadowy except for the halo that surrounded the bright, blinding TV that rested on a small dresser.

The rest of the night happened quickly. Time seemed to accelerate at a rate that she had no control over. They played a few Call of Duty missions, or campaigns, or whatever the right term was for the brief, staged warfare they simulated with other online players; she had no idea what she was doing, she hadn't played before and didn't even know if she was firing at the enemy or at her own team.

Then he paused the game and became shy and silent, before he confessed to her that he thought she was beautiful. He kissed her and she let him kiss her, and it was thrilling. But then he kept going. She told him that it was happening too fast, that she wasn't sure, and that she didn't know what she was doing, but he kept reassuring her that it would be okay, that he would be gentle, kept bombarding her with adjectives that felt beyond both of their years, incongruous with their casually acquainted relationship—gorgeous, exquisite, perfect—and then, it was over.

It had not been terrible, she thought afterward. It did hurt, but it didn't last long. And she did like him, after all. Perhaps he loved her, or she could get him to love her? Was this what love felt like? she asked herself, as she hurriedly searched for her underwear on his dark bedroom floor. She finished dressing, kissed him goodnight, and returned to Melissa's room.

It was almost two in the morning now, but the city sounded even louder. Melissa's bedroom window glowed from the streetlights below, as the city roared, rippling with chaos and terror. Addy put her earplugs back in to drown out the noise. She lied back down next to Melissa, who continued to snore peacefully. She checked her Motorola on the nightstand. There was a text from her father, and along with it an attachment, a small, grainy photo. He was on stage with his guitar, a blue spotlight beaming straight at him, his hair sweaty and disheveled. Tonight's show in Atlanta! the text said, and then, thinking about you. Miss you! Love you <3

She rolled over and began to cry. The strange and foreign city outside kept moving, forward and forward and forward, while she lied there motionless, plucked outside of time and space, immobile, an observer. There was an itch on her thigh that she couldn't seem to heal no matter how much she kept scratching, and she felt as if beneath her skin were little insects, crawling. She flung the hot comforter off her side of the bed and turned over to face Melissa. She wrapped her arms around the body pillow that separated her body and Melissa's, clutching it tightly, as she forced her eyes shut, and entered into a shallow, anxious sleep.

CHAPTER SIX

Sleep did not come easy for Leighton during StereoId's tour that fall. In fact, the entire experience had not aligned with his expectations, and by November, three months into the five month tour supporting various bands, including Vampire Weekend and the National, he was miserable.

He woke up yet again in transit. It was early morning, their tour bus on the road, going from Phoenix to Los Angeles, where they'd be opening for Vampire Weekend at the Hollywood Palladium—a special, rockin' New Year's Eve show.

Leighton's body ached. He'd fractured his tailbone during one of their shows in Austin when he'd attempted to crowd surf, but had not been supported by the sweaty hands of the audience. That was part of the not sleeping. The other part was something more cloudy, something nebulous and vague that he couldn't define.

He'd been prescribed Oxycontin for the tailbone in Texas by a Dr. Pressley, a mammoth man in a stetson hat and boots who looked out of place in the cramped examining office, and had been taking it for the past two weeks while the band bussed themselves through the south toward California, and up the West Coast. It helped some, allowed him to push through the performances no problem.

He was down to one pill, but would have a full bottle before tonight's show. The band's manager had called ahead to a doctor in Palm Springs and gotten the prescription refilled.

Leighton rolled over groggily in the stiff, curtained cot wedged into the side of the bus, which he sometimes slept in during long drives.

He slowly opened his eyes and peeled back the gray curtains, revealing the desert landscape that whirred past outside. He was looking forward to the show tonight, but not the drive, not the rest of the day surrounding the show. The first three months of the tour had changed him. It was now as if the only space in the world where he was comfortable, where he could truly *live* was on the stage. But he dreaded the rest of the musician's lifestyle, the gruellingness of being on tour for so long.

He sat up and reached for the bottle of Oxy that rested on a ledge above the bed. He swallowed his last pill. He massaged his tailbone, which had been feeling much better, but still ached.

Rise and shine, my guy!

It was Jerry Smith, peering through the dividing curtain that made the beds on the tour bus semi-private. He had a steaming cup of coffee in his hand and was offering it to Leighton.

Dude, you were pretty hammered last night, how are you feeling?

Leighton lifted his head and propped it up on one elbow. He took a too eager sip of the coffee and burnt his tongue, a mess of it splashing out over the rim.

Shit man, fucking shit, said Leighton.

Did you get with that one girl last night?

Leighton shook his head *no.* There had been women, though, since Leighton began the tour—before the tailbone incident. The east coast shows had yielded several one night stands that Emily had no idea about. Leighton felt guilty about it, but Jerry and Tom had reassured him that it was all part of the lifestyle. Being on the road was difficult. It was lonely. It didn't mean that he loved his wife any less, he had tried to convince himself, but still he felt like shit.

She was all over you, Jerry continued. She was a ten if I ever saw one—not just a Phoenix ten either.

Jerry's voice was grating. Leighton tried to sit upright and turn to face him, but could hardly move.

Man, I brought one of her friends back, the redhead—she was wild. Had to give her the boot before we got moving this morning. I don't know if I'm about them roadies.

Well, Jerry, I'm a married man.

Sure you are, but doesn't mean you're not a *man*. Isn't like that stopped you the other times; don't think I don't know about that girl Camila, the one who followed us across Texas, came to all the shows. I saw the two of you whenever she was around. Like magnets.

Leighton slowly eased himself down from the bed and went toward the back of the bus with Jerry into the lounge and kitchenette area. Jerry opened a banana and ate it vulgarly.

The two of them sat there alone in the lounge, staring out at the window while they ate toast and drank coffee, and the wheels of the bus went round and round across the highway, propelling them forward, across the dry expanse of desert.

Jerry continued talking of music and women and beauty, lengthy monologues that Leighton half-listened to.

You see, man. I mean, can you even believe it? We're getting to see all of it. Manifest destiny and all of that shit.

Uh-huh.

Listen, right, my father operated a forklift. I don't know if my parents ever got to see anything outside of Greensboro. Can you believe all of this? We're coming to the border of California, brother. Could you have imagined even a year ago that we'd be here?

Evidence of civilization beamed in the distance, exits toward a little city called Blythe just across the border into California, all the way out here in the beige immensity. Leighton wondered at it, at how life had come to thrive out here, how through the scope of such vast heat and sweat and sand and dust, people had managed to persevere and find the holy grail that was the river, to settle around it and drink from it, and to live. A piece of him was impressed. A piece of him was proud, thinking he might belong to it. And still another piece of him, as the bus stretched into Blythe for a pit stop, going by the Welcome to California sign—an image of golden poppies awash in a backdrop of blue—before bypassing ramshackle tents below the highway, rust-drenched trucks, and auto-body shops, that other piece of him was possessed with something like anguish, misery, grief. But the Oxy, right now, was hitting its peak, and dulling this wide range that flowed in him, so that he felt at peace with just sitting here on the bus, being pulled along this new path he was on—euphoric at the thought of playing music again tonight—as the sun kissed the side of his face. He felt the bright light shining just for him, the center of all things, and at the same time so wonderfully small and insignificant within the belly of something greater. And he felt how strongly both of these poles were true at once, and how much beauty there was in his capacity to feel them both simultaneously.

Are you even listening to me, Leighton? said Jerry. I asked if you wanted anything—Milky Way, a Hundred Grand, Almond Joy, I know how much you like those fucking Almond Joys. I'm getting some Cokes.

Almond Joy sounds good, said Leighton, still drunk in the warmth of the sun.

He knew that Jerry could see the dazed look on his face as he gazed out at the sun. Listen, right, said Jerry, I just want to be honest with you, brother, I'm not so sure about these pills—I'm just not sure. It's been two weeks, has your back gotten any better?

Leighton considered it. He supposed it had improved, the intensity of the pain had ebbed, though there was still some pain. Besides, he liked taking the pills. There was no harm in it. The pills were working. He could take one in the morning and by seven that night he'd have less pain in his back, but regained enough mental focus to put on a great performance for the crowd. If anything, they'd been improving the performances, he told himself. They made it easier for him to lose himself in the music.

It's gotten a little better, said Leighton, but I think I need to stay on these for a while, until it's fully healed. Jerry twisted his eyebrows in a way that said *if you say so.*

When Jerry returned, his arms filled with candy bars and Cokes, the bus began moving again and passed through Blythe, the sun beating down unbearably outside, but inside they were sheltered and comfortable and cool in the air conditioning. The bus returned to the highway toward the City of Angels, as Leighton basked in the window with the sun gracing his skin, watching the yellow lines on the pavement rush past, not knowing that the end was near, not knowing how close he was to the Western edge of freedom, or just how violently agonizing true freedom could be.

They arrived in Los Angeles on a humid, sixty-something degree day. The sun was high and bright in the sky, but dark gray clouds roamed around it, blocking it periodically.

Around the corner from the venue was the tour bus of Vampire Weekend, a young up-and-coming foursome of Columbia University grads, who had released their first album earlier that year to critical acclaim. *Mansard Roof,* the first single that Leighton had heard from them, was a bright, slow-building sparkle-pop number, laced with Afropop beats, which Leighton thought sounded like some nautical, yacht-rock anthem. He wasn't sure what to think of them. Ezra and his bandmates seemed like nice enough guys. And they were talented; they could put together a melody. Still, something bugged Leighton about them. He'd heard them play one of their songs the other night and it had been invading his head unexpectedly the past week during the long drives across the country—*aye aye aye aye.* That melody slithered straight into his brain and kept seducing him to dance; a part of him wanted to dance, but then when he couldn't rid himself of the catchiness of it, when it clung to him, to the point that he felt he was at the mercy of *it*, then another part of him began hating Ezra and the desire to punch him in the face began to build in Leighton.

Vampire Weekend had just arrived too. Ezra exited the bus, a wide grin stretched across his face, and walked over toward Leighton.

Good drive in? Ezra asked, trying to make small talk.

Yeah, man, said Leighton. Good, all good.

He drifted off toward the back of the bus and busied himself with unloading their gear. He didn't want to be rude, Ezra was a nice enough kid, but they hadn't really found much to bond over. The few times they'd drank together Ezra always seemed to talk about ska music, or the influence of classical on his band's sound, or what it was like growing up in New York, and Leighton felt like maybe there was a generational divide. Besides, he just wasn't much for forcing a relationship that wasn't there, or for affecting pleasantries—he'd spent twelve years doing that at his day job.

Alright, man, said Ezra. Well, we'll see you in there.

Leighton watched Ezra walk back over to his bus and into the side door of the venue. He greeted his bandmates with a smile, gesturing a lot with his hands, pointing out observations about the venue, an overall sense of bemusement rolling off of him. There was an easiness to his Being that irked Leighton. The kid was all of twenty-three years old. He seemed to move through the world freely, as if it all existed for him to observe, to frolic around in. There was a lightness in him; he didn't seem to take it too seriously—the burgeoning career, the cusp of success, the catchy hooks, it seemed as if Ezra had faith that these things would work themselves out and come together in time, as if they were inevitable and simply a byproduct of being present and observing the world he found himself in. And Leighton wasn't sure, but he imagined there was a kind of smugness in Ezra's smile, a tint of entitlement, as if he knew that he was meant for this, that it was his destiny, that the world assured him that it would tend to his talent, water and harvest his gifts as a musician—a role made just for him—whereas Leighton questioned it often, and still sometimes thought it all a dream, unreal, which would surely be ripped away from him.

Inside, Leighton sat at the corner of the stage, as the first cluster of people trickled through the front doors. One of the girls had on an ugly Christmas sweater; her boyfriend, a Santa hat. He'd forgotten it was New Year's Eve. The weather here didn't match up to his expectations of winter, wasn't what he was used to. And he was so caught up in the experience of touring. In fact, during one of their shows last week in Tuscon, he'd completely forgotten that it was Christmas. It wasn't until Addy called him late that night that he'd realized his error.

Now he felt guilty. Again, he hadn't spoken to his kids all day. He'd spoken to them a couple of nights ago and made a small effort, asking what they'd gotten from Santa, managing to feign some interest in their responses—makeup, clothes, a microscope, a GameCube—teasing them about if they were on the naughty or nice list. But it had mostly been a half-assed attempt at connection, and he knew it. Emily handled all of the Christmas stuff this year, the buying of presents, the wrapping, the holiday cheer.

It would now be after nine on the East Coast. His kids would be getting ready for bed, unless Emily was letting them stay up late to ring in the New Year. He had a few minutes before he needed to finish setting up before they would begin their set, so he gave them a call. When she was younger, Addy always used to love hearing his voice before going to sleep, though she'd grown out of it.

Emily answered, an elongated, exhausted *hello.*

Hey.

Hey, where are you?

Los Angeles.

Mm.

The kids up?

No.

No?

They're in bed, Leighton.

It's New Year's Eve.

So?

Are you upset about something? he asked.

I'm busy cleaning up the kitchen. Was there something you *needed?*

I was just hoping I could talk to them for a minute.

Hold on.

He could hear her groaning and making exaggerated sighs on the other end of the line as she plodded through the house and up the stairs to the girls' room.

Then Addy was on the other end. Dad! How are things on the road?

Hey, hon. Happy New Year!

Happy New Year! Where are you guys now?

Hollywood.

Awesome. I wish I was in Hollywood. What's the weather like?

Pretty warm. Sunny.

That isn't fair, you're somewhere sunny? There's lotsa snow here. It's cold.

Well, I still wish I could be there with you, hon. Is your sister there? We're going on pretty soon, so I can't talk long. I'm sorry.

—

—

She said she doesn't want to talk.

She doesn't want to talk?

No.

Really?

Yeah. She's in bed reading *The Lion King*. The play. Did you know we saw it a few weeks ago?

You did? Your mom took you?

And Harold.

Harold?

Yeah, our old neighbor. Harold and Julia. Their daughters, Kayla and Kylie, remember...they used to babysit us.

I remember. I remember. What were they doing in New York? Julia was there too?

No, only Harold. He visited us for the weekend. Two times. Once before Thanksgiving, then a couple weeks ago.

Did he?

Yeah! And we got to see *The Lion King*. It was awesome.

The venue had almost filled up, and Jerry was motioning to Leighton to wrap it up so they could begin sound check.

How about August, said Leighton. Is he around? Dad has to go in a minute.

He's playing video games.

Okay. Put your mom back on then, he said.

Okay, said Addy. Bye Dad, I love you. Have a good show tonight!

Emily's voice returned to the other end. Leighton could hear the clinking of dishes in the background.

I've got to run, he said. We're starting sound check. Sorry I couldn't talk longer.

Well, have a good show, said Emily.

Hey, Addy said *Harold* visited?

Yeah. He and Julia are going through a divorce. He wanted to take some time away, see New York during the holidays and I said he could stay with us.

Oh, I guess I didn't know we were still in touch with him.

I am.

How come you didn't mention it to me?

Because you're on the other side of the country, Leighton. I'm lucky if I hear from you once a week.

Am I supposed to feel guilty?

No, God forbid you take responsibility.

Oh, that's how you feel?

Look, do we really have to do this now? I get it, you're out there doing *your* thing. It's fine. I support *you,* I really do.

Well, it doesn't seem like it.

It's Christmas, Leighton, let's not.

Fine. I have to go. I'll give you and the kids a call tomorrow.

Bye. Have a good show.

Alright, love you. Bye.

CHAPTER SEVEN

The show that night did not go well. Leighton's back started hurting midway through the set. He soldiered through, but by the time their final song was done, he felt that he needed either rest or a drink. He opted for the drink.

Thank you Los Angeles! We really hope you enjoyed our songs. Now are you guys excited for Vampire Weekend?!

The sold out Hollywood Palladium roared.

Make sure to stop by the merch table in the back and buy our new record if you liked our music, and if you didn't then fuck you!

The crowd laughed and cheered at the rock n' roll sentiment.

Thank you all for coming out, it's been a dream come true for us. We've been StereoId, goodnight.

The spotlights dimmed and the stage went black, as Leighton walked off. The audience continued to cheer. That made it all worth it, the pain and everything. Didn't it?

He'd told himself that yes, of course it was worth it. There was nothing like hearing a full theater screaming and shouting for your music, something that you've put your heart and soul into. Look at where he was, he thought. The Hollywood Palladium. An historic venue on Sunset Boulevard. It had opened in 1940, just more than a year before Pearl Harbor. It had been graced on opening night by Judy Garland and had hosted iconic bands since its shift toward more rock-centric concerts; The Clash and the Ramones had played here, The Pixies, and Weezer, and The Strokes. And there he was, Leighton Wheeler—with one hit song to his name and eight other songs that rounded out their lean debut album—sharing the same stage.

But then what was this feeling that would always immediately hit him when the lights dimmed and the venue became quiet? When he was on the stage, when the words and the chords were flowing through him, yes, it was magical, it was affirming. But as this tour had progressed, each night the other feeling began to visit him more and more frequently, so that now, whenever he wasn't on stage, that other feeling, powerful and stubborn and cruel, would be right by his side. And the hours when he wasn't on-stage far outnumbered the single hour he spent wailing into the microphones. And so what was this other feeling? He did not know. It was treacherous and cunning. He never wanted to examine it for too long because he was afraid of its intentions, of its power of persuasion. He tried his best to ignore it by taking Oxy with more regularity, sometimes at night now before bed, in addition to the one he took in the morning. He tried his best to give the dark feelings the cold shoulder by spending his evenings in strange beds with beautiful young women who seemed to look at him with adoration and wonder. But the off-stage feeling was always there, lurking.

What could he name it, were he to look it in the eyes? How could this feeling be classified? Perhaps depression would have been the word, the accepted medical term for it, and perhaps calling it by this name would suffice, would open a large window in front of the thing and blind it with the light, send it scurrying off and back into its shadowy cave. But Leighton felt, intuitively and unvoiced, that this thing did not go by a single name, but had many nom de plumes. It was a grotesque, mutant hybrid, a monster child, a grim offspring whose parents, perhaps, were guilt and inadequacy.

When the lights dimmed and he receded into the darkness backstage, he felt like he never had any business being up there at the Hollywood Palladium, sharing the same stage as his past idols. It had begun whispering to him after each show now, had been whispering to him for the past three weeks, telling him that the cheering crowd didn't even like him or his music, that they were only being polite and warming up for Ezra. It was a cruel, embittered time-traveler, this creature, who showed him what would become of the world, in two, five, ten years, that the crowd would turn on him, that they would realize they never should have applauded him in the first place, that the chords and melodies that he'd plucked from the air and caught and sent out into the world through the microphones and the amps, that they were never truly his to begin with, that they, too, would escape from him at some point, would leave, would exist in the spaces between his body and theirs, and then what would he be left with?

The time-traveler always tried to convince him of what he'd be left with, but it physically pained him to hear it, so he did anything and everything he could to block it out, and he'd never dare repeat the words that the shadowy time-traveler spoke to him.

Leadsingerman, said Jerry Smith, as they navigated a long, fluorescent corridor in the back of the venue. Are we trying to get an early start? There's gotta be plenty of sweet California girls around here just begging to meet a couple of rock stars.

You've turned into a real pig, said Tom Tavish. You know that? You were the sensitive one, the responsible one when we were in college. What the hell happened to you, Jerry?

I'm still sensitive. I'm still responsible. What, now I'm the bad guy because I appreciate the company of beautiful women? Whatdya say, Leightonman?

Shouldn't we spend some time selling merch, talking to fans? We said we would.

Old Tom here has that covered, said Jerry, slapping Tom on the back. He and Eddie can handle all of that—Eddie was the band's manager.

You're a real piece of shit, Jerry, said Tom.

You love me, said Jerry. He kissed Tom Tavish on the earlobe and Tom recoiled.

People want to talk to Leighton, Jerry. He's kind of the face of this group.

Yeah, no, I hear you. I'd say there's plenty of fans here all along Sunset Boulevard who wouldn't mind getting to know the frontman—fans of a more buxom persuasion, if you know what I mean.

I do, Jerry. I'm sure there are a lot of fans like that here, and they'll be lining up, literally, to meet us—all of us—and to buy our stuff. You fuckers never stick around anymore, and Eddie and I are the ones who have to do all of the grunt work.

Look, hanging around after shows, said Jerry, it's always shit isn't it. Just sitting there like idiots. Hardly anyone stops by; people get all of their stuff online now. And the chicks that do come up to us are desperate or, like, into us to a scary degree. And it's alway awkward as hell, those transactional interactions. If you hate doing it so much, Tommy, then maybe we should think about hiring someone to handle all of the merch.

Or, said Tom, maybe you should pull your weight and not think with your dick all of the time.

It looked as if Tom and Jerry were about to get into one of their dick-measuring contests. Leighton had been in one of his reveries, staring down at the speckled floor tiles as they walked down the hallway, golden flakes randomly scattered in the white vinyl, a pattern of cosmic clutter, when he looked up and saw them stop in the middle of the hallway and square their shoulders and look at each other as if they were set to battle for the claim to some abstract territory.

Guys, come on, said Leighton, and wedged his way between them.

Well, what do you have to say, Leighton? asked Tom. Are you trying to run off again to drink and pick up girls? You aren't even going to bother helping Eddie and me?

Look, said Leighton, Jerry has a point.

Oh does he? So you guys are going to just, what? Same as last night and the night before, hit up some random bar for another random hook-up?

He says it like it's a bad thing, said Jerry.

Leighton, I know things haven't been the best with you and Emily for a while, but you've got a family man. You think all of this sleeping around, spending your days half-baked, leaning into the rock-star persona, you think it's going to fix anything?

Don't talk about my family, Tom. Like yours is picture perfect? Don't do that. Don't play the righteous prick card. Leighton had now cornered him too, so that Tom was backed against the wall with Leighton and Jerry on each side of him.

He stood his ground, looked Leighton in the eye. Hey, man, all I'm saying is Jerry just tells you what you want to hear. You and him can go and have as much fun as you want, but I'm being a real friend here, I'm being honest even if you might not like it.

Well, nobody asked you to, said Leighton. This place reeks of piss and weed. Jerry and I are gonna find a good place to drink, meet the real people in this city, see the real LA. You and Eddie can handle the merch and watch Erza's set and tell him how great he is, okay? Because like it or not, you're replaceable. Let's not kid ourselves on who here is pulling the most weight—Jerry and I would have no problem finding another bassist.

Whatever, said Tom. Fuck you motherfucker. You've changed.

Leighton and Jerry left Tom behind and found a dive bar around the corner from the venue. They had a couple of drinks and talked to a few locals before Leighton's back started to feel even worse and he told Jerry that he was going back to their hotel.

Do you need me to come with you? asked Jerry, as they strode through the parking lot of the Best Western. You sure you're doing okay?

I'm fine, said Leighton. It's just my back acting up. I'll be better tomorrow morning.

Okay, man, well just let me know if you need anything. I'm worried about you.

Leighton nodded his thanks to Jerry and the two of them went to their separate rooms. When Leighton got into his room, he realized that he was anything but fine. The creature had returned and so he took his evening Oxy, with the hopes of banishing it.

He crept under the covers of the bed. The room smelled of mothballs. He tossed and turned under the covers, but his skin kept sticking to the cotton. He was sweating profusely. The Oxy managed to quickly help with the back pain, but his mind was a dark gray vacuum of terror.

He stared into the corner of the room, which was illuminated softly by the dim hotel lamp, and saw a creature lurking there.

What was this heavy blanket locking him into a silken immovable cocoon? What was this hideous lurking shadow that only showed its face to him in dark spaces? It was something of a stubborn tenant, a sub-letter who specialized in roaming the recesses of the psyche. It paid him no rent. It joined him at the foot of whatever bed in which he happened to sleep, be it hotel or bus cot. It trashed the place whenever he was lucky enough to have caught the z's. It squatted in dark corners and crept around the edges of the room. It was inhuman, this bully, this tormentor. But it also had an uncanny human likeness to it. Something about it was profoundly human. It had his likeness. It spoke to him.

Boy, it said to him, crawling around the frame of the bed at this Hollywood budget hotel.

It took a step closer to him, out of the shadow and into a patch of moonlight that disregarded the hotel's paper thin curtains. Those eyes. That was the one thing that seemed almost too human to consider. The eyes were big and round and soft and pleading. And he wasn't sure of the color because it was painful to look this goblin in the eyes, but he thought maybe they were blue, but like an agonizing ultramarine, or a shade yet to be discovered, or like the unreal color of animated ice in a Disney picture.

Boy, it said, Ezra sure sounded great tonight didn't he? That falsetto! And doesn't he have a way with words? And he's young too. And attractive. A nice smile, Ezra has.

The creature crept further out of the shadow and now Leighton noticed that it had taken the shape of a woman. A young woman, dressed in a pink satin gown. The pink lady.

You're awake, my boy, said the lady, grinning maniacally in the sliver of silver light. What are you doing cooped up in this stuffy room? This is the time to be alive! The night is still young! Your first time in California, why not go see the beach?

Leighton shut his eyes and tried to breathe. The creature wasn't real. The creature was his fear. It was a tangible manifestation of his own Id. Or was it his Ego? The creature crept around to the other side of the bed by the window. It shifted its shape again and was no longer the pink lady. It was short and hunched and uncannily human, but also not human. It had long, hairy feet, and blue hair. It reminded him of one of those plastic, collectible troll dolls from when he was younger.

How about a dip in the ocean? said the troll. Doesn't that sound nice? Clear our minds.

Leighton looked at its eyes. Its face was soft and sympathetic and its mouth was wide and gentle and smiling, but he knew from past interactions that this was the surface of it, and that there was another edge of menace that from different angles was sharp and undeniable.

This isn't the place for you right now, it said. Cooped up here in this little room. The world is out there! There are fireworks tonight! Come on, my friend, shouldn't we be free?

Leighton shook his head like a ragdoll. Can't you just stop, he said. Leave me alone. My head hurts.

Haven't you ever considered it? said the Troll. Where we are. Don't just think about it, but consider it.

Consider it?

Care about the words and what they signify.

Huh?

It is so thin, so sparse, these walls. The edges of this room. They can be knocked down like that.

Uh huh.

And then! Where are we?!

Los Angeles. Hollywood.

Those are merely words. They mean nothing.

But you just said—

Leighton, my boy, said the creature, which had once again shapeshifted into a surfer, a native Angeleno with sandy blonde hair. There are other languages to speak, dude.

Why do you always talk to me like this?

The waves against your skin, for instance. Where *are* we?

Hollywood.

No, brother. When you consider it, when you care for it, we are suspended. We are surfing here, shooting the curl of unknown matter.

Huh?

Suspended, the very same as the stars.

Leave me alone!

Leighton flipped over and recoiled his body toward the bed's headboard. His body supine now, his head inclined slightly up against the pillows. His head spun.

Isn't that what you want? To be free?

You don't care about me.

I am the only one who loves you, Leighton. The only one who will tell you the truth. You are nothing here. So why don't we go down to the beach and I'll show you how great it feels to know you're nothing.

The creature's eyes were kind and merciful, but the grin was tight lipped and devious. Leighton didn't know how to judge it any longer. He couldn't discern the true features of its face from the mask. This was the agony of it. The agony of this uncannily human thing that only visited him at night. And on top of this, if he tried to block the troll from his mind, then time would wilt to something so narrow that every function of his body—the coursing blood, the pump of heart, the bowels, the twitch—no, even the stillness—of fibrous tendon—would shout to him *notice me notice me.*

Let us venture down to the ocean! said the creature. It is a new year! A new you!

Leighton listened to the creature because who else was there to listen to? The creature was a part of him and it was the strongest voice in the room. All other voices of himself had been drowned out. And the creature had a point. He had to trust the creature.

He was wasting his time there, wasn't he? How great it would be to see the Pacific for the first time, to witness the fireworks bursting above the water.

Leighton managed to call a taxi and it took him out to Santa Monica.

The boardwalk was full with families and couples anticipating the fireworks that would begin shortly to usher in a new decade.

Leighton made his way through the sand and looked out at the endless dark water. The creature had left him and now there was only the quiet hum of the waves. The Oxy had really kicked in and he was feeling high. He clutched the translucent orange bottle in his hand. He popped the top and swallowed another two pills. He wanted this experience to be truly transformative. He would be fine, he reasoned. Everything always worked out. Nature was on his side. The creature was good to him, it would look out for him.

He took off his shoes and socks at the edge of the tide and stumbled into the white foam. He crawled on his knees, the universe churning above, holding him tight and safe.

The water was the perfect temperature. It hugged his skin kindly.

He waded out further into the ocean. He thought that he could see his mother and father in the distance, together, standing on a rock. He swam out toward them, but then they disappeared.

He looked back and he could no longer see the shore. The boardwalk was a pinprick. The lights of the city were blurry and dim.

But he knew that everything was okay there in the belly of the blue. The creature would arrive to guide him back to safety.

The water violently tugged his body here and there, further out into the center, away from the edge. But he just let it take him. He floated on his back, then began to sink slowly.

There was an entire world down here, he realized, now holding his breath. He smiled. He splashed around in the blue blanket. The skin of the ocean's surface was smooth and warm as it tossed him deeper into the white spume. He would never be as free as this, he thought. A music career, a return home, whatever his future held, nothing would compare to the power he felt there, alive in the ancient young rage of infinite freedom.

By the time he tried to ascend to the surface and turn around, back to shore, by the time panic hit him (a panic unlike anything you or I can imagine), the panic overtaking the euphoria suddenly, shockingly, violently, like a seized lot of land, it was too late.

CHAPTER EIGHT

Back in New York, as his father was drowning, August was thinking about how much he hated their apartment. It had two bedrooms: one for Amelia and Addy, and one for his mother. August slept on the couch in the living room, which was adjacent to the small kitchen, within an open floor plan, and was ten by nine tiny.

He was a skinny boy, awkward and gangly, twelve years old, and on the horizon was young manhood.

He didn't like sleeping on the couch, didn't like not having a place to call his own, the boundaries of his personal space not clearly differentiated from the shared, common spaces. It was as if his world might be invaded at any time, the edges of his border unheeded.

He couldn't voice any of this, the odd feelings that swirled, this in-between state; he was a child. But he knew that he wasn't comfortable when he would be moments away from sleep there in the open darkness of the room, the curtains drawn, and his mother would come out to check on him, and would disturb his near-sleep, would place her hand on his body, softly on his lower back, or tap him gently on the butt, and say *goodnight angelface.* He would squirm when she did this, wriggle and twist and tighten his body into a different position. He would sometimes tell her that he didn't like when she did that, that it made him uncomfortable. She would always say oh, okay, I'm sorry, but not in a way that actually seemed to hear what he had said or be sorry in any genuine way, before adding some disclaimer like *can't a mother be affectionate? I just wanted to tell you goodnight.*

And perhaps she was right, he thought. She was, after all, just loving him. Only for August, in those moments, it didn't feel like the kind of love that was needed. Wouldn't a good love honor boundaries?

He had made few friends since their move to New York. He played almost non-stop on the Xbox that his dad had bought him after he'd gotten his record deal. He played *Madden* and *Mass Effect* and *Lego Star Wars,* all while sitting on the same couch that he slept on, where he found himself spending most of his time.

The couch was polyester and had to be ten years old. It was navy blue, too firm in some spots and too saggy and depressed in others. The roughness made his skin itch.

His relationships to these video games, as he played them, perched at the edge of the couch, were ones of love and hate. He could not stop playing them, despite the disappointments that they often brought. Of course challenges, obstacles, enemies were part of the game, but he couldn't stand it when the games would not work out the way that he wanted them to. If, for example, he was playing *Madden* as his favorite childhood team, the Atlanta Falcons, then he would become obsessed with getting the stats exactly perfect, with not only winning the game but also being in control of how many yards Michael Vick rushed for, and how many touchdowns he scored, and how thoroughly dominating the win was, how much he could embarrass the other team by running up the score.

When the scenarios of these games didn't play out quite as he'd imagined them, he would get angry. A simmering, boiling, searing rage that bubbled from a cavernous, deep-set hollow. It wasn't exactly about the video game itself. The video games were a way to avoid any feelings that might be dangerous. But the emotions would come out sometimes anyway— say, if Michael Vick threw an interception against the Saints—the emotions would come out as a psychological displacement, and he would slam the controller against the floor or against his own knee (as if that could harm the controller beyond its knobs coming unglued, as if it might harm it spiritually), or he would punch the floor, or slap the side of the television with an open fist, whenever nobody was around to see, his mother having already isolated herself in her room for the night.

After his father's sudden death that winter, August's mother would sometimes ask him to sleep in the bed with her, and would present it to him as a gift, a respite from the uncomfortable couch. He usually declined, citing *I'm too old,* on the cusp of teenagerdom, but a few times he accepted and took the side of the bed that his father had vacated, still wearing his t-shirt and jeans. He would sometimes sleep in Addy's bed too, if she was spending the night at her friend's house, which she often was.

Winter in New York that year was a brutal one. Cold and snowy and gray. August spent all of his time at the edge of the couch. School and home were the only places he went. School and home. School and home. The one time he ventured uptown was when their family friend Harold had visited for the weekend and took them to Broadway to see *The Lion King*. He'd bought Amelia a stuffed Pumba, which she had instantly forgotten about, Pumba forever wedged down between the wall and the couch that August slept on, so that Pumba's permanent new residence, collecting dust bunnies, gave August a daily view of its husks and snout, which peeked out into the light, and lodged in his periphery when he was at the edge of the couch, killing Geth, colonizing alien planets in *Mass Effect*. When he couldn't get past the Krogan, and his character kept dying, he several times chucked his Xbox controller at Pumba's face, to soften the blow and make sure he didn't damage the controller irreparably.

Then, of course, after the New Year, after history had advanced a digit higher, there was the matter of what happened with his father. Death—the actual word of it, fitting, beginning with the solidest of letters, dee, da, d-, a sound that charges from the throat, lands out in the air in a dense fog and disappears altogether at once, the dee, releasing into the breathy vowels, and ending with the tee-aitch sound, them, those, thereafter, thicket, thimble, thank you, the tongue gentle against the edge of the teeth, all of the air expelled from the lungs, a cathartic sound, a releasing of thy soul—death was never mentioned.

It too was displaced by August's Xbox games. It was displaced by his mother's earlier and earlier retreats into her bedroom. Days when she had no piano lessons, she never came out at all.

The following spring was *Mass Effect* and the Atlanta Falcons and silence. August's mother no longer needed to teach piano lessons—Leighton's death had been deemed an accident and his life insurance policy was paid out to her in full, which would cover them for several months in that overpriced Lower East Side apartment, before their move back to Carolina—so she spent all of her time in her bedroom, with the door closed.

August had no idea what she would do each day when they were at school. He would return in the afternoon, and her door would be closed, as if she had not moved all day. The apartment was just as it was when he'd left that morning, moderately unkempt, but it wasn't like they were living in squalor; so perhaps she did come out of her room at some point, to tidy things up—he noticed that once a week or so clothes that he'd left out in the open had been washed. The living room space where August slept and played *Mass Effect* had become entirely his. He'd staked claim to it, colonized it entirely, planted a sovereign flag in the soil; his dirty socks and underwear were strewn about, he'd leave the controller in the middle of the room for anyone to step on and injure themselves, the controller's cord tangled and disorderly, and there would often be an unfinished glass of various liquid left dripping with condensation on the coffee table, a lightly colored halo etched into the cheap wood. Nobody else ever stepped foot in that space anymore, except for August, and occasionally his mother, when she would drift out of her bedroom, wraithlike, late into the night, place her hand on his backside, and say goodnight.

Addy was hardly ever in the house that spring. She would sometimes pop in to steal food with Melissa, ravenous and hormonal teenage specters, ravaging the kitchen.

The week following their father's funeral, after they returned to New York, Amelia had tried latching on to August. She sat right next to him at the edge of the couch, and watched him play Mass Effect.

Why are you shooting those guys? she'd asked. Are they the bad guys?

Yeah.

They look like frogs.

Yep.

What did they do that was so bad?

I don't know. Why are you here?

I just want to watch you play. Did they hurt people?

I don't know—just, they destroyed their homeworld, they're settling colonies that don't belong to them—okay. Why do you care?

I'm just interested. Could I play, August?

No.

How come? That's not fair.

Look, Amelia, can you just fucking leave me alone! Nobody wants you here. See, look, I just died. That was your fault. You distracted me.

August had watched his little sister get up from the edge of the couch, with her shoulders slumped.

Sorry, she said. I just—

Well, you should be, he said, not looking at her, his eyes glued to the screen. You're annoying. And you're ugly and nobody likes you.

He watched her retreat to her room down the hall. The door slammed with a resounding, hollow thud. Whatever pang of guilt and remorse he'd felt in that moment was quickly banished. He had a game to focus on, an unruly Krogan rebellion to manage. He couldn't give voice to the feeling, but there was something essential here, as he disappeared further into the distant galactic struggles, the wars waged within the Mass Effect universe. It was as if a struggle in his own soul was being played out on the screen, as if it was one of the things at stake—along with territory and culture and tradition and the fate of the Citadel—his soul too was part of the wager, and perhaps his own future, and why would he want a stupid little girl hanging around him when these things were at stake. She didn't understand anything about the game.

And so the rest of that spring Amelia spent all of her time in her room, reading, or talking gibberish in a childish voice with those stupid furry dolls, or messing around with that microscope kit that she'd gotten last Christmas, examining a leaf or a blood cell or moth wings that were wedged into those plastic slides that came included with the kit.

It felt to August as if the apartment was basically his, his mother and sister shut-in in their separate rooms, his other sister gallivanting around the city. His mother never even came out to cook; she didn't cook once the spring that followed his father's death. She would give him thirty dollars and tell him to order something for delivery—pizza or chinese or mexican—and he would have to make sure that Amelia ate something, and then would pass her a plastic plate through the half-cracked door to her bedroom.

Of course there were outliers during those five months, evenings when his mother would emerge from the room before five o'clock and have a smile on her face, energized and untroubled, suggesting to August and Amelia (and Addy if she happened to be around) that they all go out and eat together, walk to a nearby restaurant, or take the subway or a taxi to the West Village or somewhere uptown, without any acknowledgement that she had barely left her room in a week and that they had not seen her.

August did not even bother looking at her on these rare occasions; he ignored her completely. His loyalty had already been pledged to Commander Shepard. He couldn't believe that she could just come out of the room and act like that, ignoring multiple shitting elephants. He couldn't voice it, but in his gut he understood the disingenuity of it, understood that it was consistency, the thing that children needed most.

Amelia was always surprised too, confused, but also still eager to go out and eat at a restaurant in the city.

Inevitably, the rare nights out would follow a pattern. August would slump in the uncomfortable wooden chairs at the middling restaurants and say nothing, his arms crossed, imagining the upcoming battles on intergalactic horizons, which he would play out just as soon as they returned—he wanted to get back as quickly as possible. His mother would begin the meals optimistic, smiling at waiters, attempting to engage in conversation.

Amelia, how is your mac n' cheese?

Good! Really good! Amelia would placate.

August, do you like your hamburger?

It's fine.

Well, don't sound so enthused! she'd say, her cheeriness beginning to crack, an exaggerated smile stretched across her face.

The meals would proceed in agonizing silence, August vaguely aware of the tension, the revenge his gloomy mood was enacting to balance her long periods of self-isolation.

By the time these shooting-star evenings were over, August's mother had lost her chipper smile and declared her children spoiled and ungrateful, and handed out threats that they would never go to a restaurant again, that her children didn't deserve to be seen in public. She would appear to be meltdown-adjacent, stressed by a crowded subway, or the frenzied pace along Houston Street. When they got back to the apartment she would return to another extended period of quarantine and hibernation.

There was a total of three times that spring she had become so enraged at how those restaurant excursions had played out that she threatened to take the Xbox from August.

I'll ground you from that fucking thing! You'll never play it again you spoiled little brat!

The threats were never carried through. They made August immediately beg and plead, tears welling up in his eyes, telling her he was so sorry, that he should have had a better attitude at the restaurant, that he loved her, and that it was all his fault, which seemed to work, seemed to be what she wanted to hear. She let him keep the Xbox connected to the TV and he would go back to playing *Mass Effect* well into the night, as the darkness enveloped the apartment, only the glimmer of streetlight from the city below could be seen, the sound of the night's festivities distant, somewhere near Houston and Bowery. He'd apologized sincerely each of the three times she'd threatened to take it away, but afterward it always made him even more indignant and the next time, eons later, when she would inevitably emerge with a printed smile, he found that he hated her so much more.

But soon the final spring in the big apple was over and August found himself back on the same street where he spent the first nine years of his life, only now with a different father, their old family friend from down the street, Harold Carr, whom his mother remarried after Harold went through his own divorce. Harold changed everything for August, for all of them, in the summer of 2010, after they moved back with him to Asheville.

August liked Harold right away. Harold was smart and engaging. He was older than August's mother by over a decade. He carried himself with a stoicism not uncommon for men of this region from his generation. It was consistency that August was drawn to. August felt that there were values, solid and firm in Harold, that could always predict his behavior. He'd learn that Harold could be stern, that there were some things he wouldn't tolerate, but his actions were constant and could be relied upon.

August noticed his mother change around Harold. She became more dependable in her daily routines after they married. No more long periods of withdrawal, no more starkly contrasting sides of her. She even began to cook a few times a week, tend a small garden, and skim their new pool in the summer to keep it clear of leaves and insects. Productive changes, August thought, brought about by the simple fact that Harold would not have tolerated the New York version of her, with her prolonged bouts of overwhelming despair and isolation. From the very first moment they were back in Asheville, she seemed to have a newfound urgency in her to live up to Harold's expectations.

Harold was a man of mighty faith. Harold was an atheist. What Harold placed his faith in were triumvirate pillars: progress, individual will, and power. Harold had come from a poor family in Greensboro, the third child of an auto-mechanic father and a wheelchair-ridden mother who had turned out to be his hero. She'd transformed their dilapidated single-level house in the country whose thin windows vibrated and threatened to shatter whenever the train rumbled past, she'd transformed it into a warm and inviting home. There was both structure and joy. His father was a silent, unknown ghost, prone to bouts of heavy drinking when he came home each day, reemerging from beneath the hoods of broke-down cars, covered in dirt and grease and oil and exhaust, but he was never violent. Harold's mother spent all of her time keeping up the house, cooking and baking and doing laundry and dusting, all of the stereotypical roles that were expected of her, that had been done by her mother and her grandmother and on down the line. And she did it all with a smile. Harold never remembered seeing her dispirited. Sometimes she would ask him to reach high toward an unreachable shelf and pass her the sugar, and then she would smile and thank him as if it wasn't just Harold, but all of mankind that she believed to be helpful and compassionate and capable of creating goodness into the world.

Harold also grew up in a devoutly religious, Evangelical family. His mother and father never missed going to church on Sunday with their children. This was the one branch of the tree where Harold himself had come to diverge from that of the mother that he had come to idolize. As all teens are bound to rebel in some aspect, Harold had always been a naturally curious child, quick to question, and so had chosen religion as his avenue for rebellion. It had been an exclusively inner rebellion, and his parents hadn't found out until well after he'd graduated college and moved away.

He had been the first in his family to graduate college, had gotten a degree in engineering at Chapel Hill, a job straight after graduation at a major electronic company where he spent fifteen years, before he found a job at Skyrunner Internet in Asheville, and he and his first wife, Julia, decided to make their home there and raise their two daughters, Kayla and Kylie. He had been doing repairs and tech support for people's in-home networks at Skyrunner Internet for the past twelve years.

Harold didn't talk much, but he did like to retell his story over the dinner table, always emphasizing his own triumphs, highlighting his three core pillars, spinning the story of a man who grew up poor, and through hard work, the pursuit of progress, of science, the insistence of one's personal agency, the claiming of one's power to both reveal and shape the forces around him, to transform nature for the better. Highlighting these tenets within his own story, he believed, was the key to finding a life of meaning and contentment and value, and he communicated these things to August and his sisters across the dinner table, doled out as sage wisdom. The lessons, he said, had worked for his two daughters, who were both looking to follow in his footsteps and pursue something in the hard sciences at his alma mater, and so August should take heed.

And August did listen to Harold in the following years. Whenever August clung too mightily to the passive habits he'd cultivated in those lonely New York years—consuming video games and consuming Dr. Pepper that would rot his teeth and ingesting marijuana with some new friends he made at school and consuming pornography, nothing but consuming—then Harold would reveal the stern, disciplinarian side of his character. He took it upon himself to take away August's privileges, his freedoms.

You're not my fucking father, you piece of shit! August thought.

But Harold was not in it for his own power, August soon came to realize. He took no joy in depriving August, he merely wanted him to cultivate better, more active habits, and so he took him under his wing. He was gentle with August. He spent time with him in the workshop that he'd set up in a corner of his office and showed August how to code, how to take apart the whole computer and break it down into its smallest pieces, to build it anew; he showed him how to build a hard drive from scratch, how to make sense of the immense processing power stuffed into such a small CPU, showed him how to properly attach a motherboard.

The first year following their return from New York was transformative for August. His anger and teenage angst that had been displaced into video games and youthful shenanigans with boys from school had found new outlets, could now be sublimated into creative endeavors. He found that when he applied himself, he had a natural aptitude for school work. It didn't bother him, and he could spend hours each night trying to solve whatever questions the given homework asked of him.

He grew close to Harold and looked up to him in many ways. Their new home had become like a real home, August had thought, with each member of the family willingly performing their role to contribute to the functioning of the happy whole.

Well, everyone except for Addy. She had been resistant to the new living arrangement, the step-father, the quiet, the lack of public transit and world regional cuisine from the very beginning; she longed for the city. She talked loudly and constantly in her room to one of her New York friends, and would sometimes disappear for days at a time, doing who knows what, which would send their mother into crying fits.

Oddly, Harold rarely disciplined her in the same way as he would August, rarely tried to usher her into his own schools of thought, dispense his own principles on how to move through life. She was stubborn and combative and he seemed almost afraid of her. The few times he attempted to lay down the law after one of Addy's screaming matches with Mom—you need to start showing your mother some respect!—Addy had looked him straight in the eyes, no fear, and laughed in his face, told him that he didn't know anything and to *stay out of it!* After this, Addy only grew more and more distant, which made their mother more and more defeated, and Harold had simply disengaged, withdrawn himself from their explosive conflicts completely.

If change happens gradually, and then suddenly, the gradual change in the home was Addy's yearlong wearing down of August's mother. August, as Harold had come to do, would watch their fights from the sidelines. Addy was too quick, her mind too fast and free and wicked, and she would hurl insults and obscenities at Mom, slowly chipping away at her patience, and her confidence, and every ribbon of strength that she had summoned, tied together, in order to carry herself in this new home with consistency, avoiding those extended isolated periods of her recent past. August had, after their first summer back, come to regain some of his eroded trust in her, to believe that this new version of her could last, could be a new normal.

Addy finished her sophomore year in Asheville, but the combativeness with Mom had reached a breaking point. Addy wanted to leave.

There was a morning at the breakfast table, when Harold and Emily discussed it in front of August and Amelia. Addy was somewhere else, August didn't know where, but she wasn't there.

August's mother didn't want to concede. She didn't want her fifteen year-old daughter moving to New York by herself.

I worry about her, she said. It isn't safe. So much chaos there. She doesn't really know anyone.

Harold quoted Napoleon, maybe it's as they say, better to have a known enemy than a forced ally.

Oh, Harold, I don't feel like I know her at all!

But we know she wants to be there. She wants to live with her friend.

She's fifteen!

She isn't doing well here, Em. I worry about all the stress she adds. To you. To us. Maybe it's better. We can't force her to be here if she doesn't want to. We've both tried and she seems too set in her ways.

I've tried. You just watch.

What's that supposed to mean?

It means you're afraid of her.

I'm not afraid of her.

Are you sure about that?!

For Christ's sake, she's fifteen.

Harold rose from the table to get another hard-boiled egg from the kitchen. He returned and placed his hands on August's shoulders.

Well, what do you think, August?

August looked down at his eggs and the strip of bacon that was burnt black and crumbling. Uhhh...I don't know.

Well, she clearly doesn't want to be here with us. Maybe we should let her move in with her friend, venture out on her own, if she thinks she knows what's best. Right?

Harold smacked August on the shoulder.

Sure, said August. I guess. He really had no idea, but thought it was just easier to agree with Harold.

Amelia was staring down into her hash browns, and August could tell that she wished that she could say something. It was obvious that she wanted Addy to stay, but she was the youngest and had no real say; her two cents would have been instantly discarded.

She's a child, said August's mother.

It isn't like she would be alone, said Harold. I just think that if she's just going to be miserable here...

Harold seemed to want to get rid of Addy. August thought that he might have been supportive of her, what with his pillar of individual will. She was embodying that, exercising her own agency, giving voice to her desires to move back, but yet it didn't seem to be a place of support that Harold was coming from. Rather, thought August, insecurity. It was the first chink he'd seen in Harold's armor, the first sign of doubt and unassuredness. Harold had taken pride in his own rags to riches narrative and now here was this girl, nullifying his entire story; here was August's teenage sister openly voicing her condemnation of the home he'd built, the life and values he believed in here. Harold hadn't done enough, Addy's arrogant, defiant tone had always seemed to say when she fought with him and their mother. The quiet, stable life he'd managed to carve out for himself had somehow fallen short of something in her eyes, some kind of abstract glory, or wildness, or who knows, likely she didn't even know herself, she was fifteen, and perhaps she just longed to be free, to be anywhere other than where she was.

Is it what you want? asked August's mother, grinding too much salt onto the shiny head of her boiled egg.

It's what I think she needs, honey, said Harold.

His mother gave a quiet nod of resignation, of exhaustion, too tired from the constant wars of will with Addy to argue any further. She sank her teeth into the egg white.

And that was that. Addy got on a plane that summer, exactly one year after they had left, and returned to live with Melissa and her family.

This was still the ramp up, the gradual change of the household. The Addyless summer brought an attempted return to, and a failure to achieve, equilibrium.

That summer August built his first computer by himself, without Harold's help, the components all sprawled out on his bedroom floor, a little blue troll doll sitting next to him and watching him work, a token of good luck that he had found in one of the storage boxes when they had first moved in. Harold had been so overjoyed at August's creation that he had taken them all out for ice cream.

There were moments like this where it seemed like they might piece together a peaceful life. Harold and August's mother were, on one hand, glad to be rid of Addy, to be free of the non-stop arguments. But there was also something strained, August noticed. His mother's smiles had returned to her New York smiles, the too-wide smiles that she would put on when she emerged from her weeklong quarantines, an overcompensating for something truer just beneath. She would sometimes snap at August or Amelia or even sometimes Harold himself, and he would snap back at her to respect him in his house, and she would immediately apologize and put on the too-wide smile and insist ad nauseum that everything was fine.

August knew better. August knew that somehow, from several states away, Addy was still somehow controlling Harold and their mother; Addy's absence had seemed to alter the fantasy that their mother had brought with her in her mind for what this family might become.

But, through Harold's tellings and retellings of his life story over the dinner table, emphasizing the bullet points, the pillars of his life philosophy, they were able to achieve a kind of dysfunction that worked for them.

August had already discovered that fall, as he entered his freshman year of high school, just how easy it was for him to disappear into far-off worlds—worlds of creation and abstract thinking. He could lose himself instantly in the task of, for example, working through college-level mathematics theorems like Morley's or the Fixed-Point or Godel's Incompleteness. He was always stunned to discover that five, six, seven hours had gone by, the day turned to night, when it had felt like mere minutes.

He would still occasionally revisit *Mass Effect,* but found that it did not sustain him quite the same way that his plunges into knowledge did. He had Harold to thank for that, for providing him with an outline for what a productive day might contain, for the discipline necessary to give himself over to the work, rather than giving himself over to the passive play of his boyhood.

And he believed that it would be lifelong, his bond with Harold. But the gradual change invading their home would soon become sudden. The accident that winter, the icy-white, cold-chaos of it, would cause each of Harold's pillars to shatter and crumble to ruin, turning him into an unrecognizable version, a hollowed shell of himself.

CHAPTER NINE

After her father's death, Amelia was trapped, ten years old, in a city that didn't make sense to her. It scared her, the grand concrete scale of it. So many unknown people, so many unknown everything, moving through the grayness of it. She couldn't see the sky. Could no longer see the stars from her bedroom window.

How did her mother expect her to go back to that school and sit in those stiff steel desks for eight hours a day after everything that had happened? She was a plastic peg being shoved into Life's game-board, moved through the cardboard world without any say. She didn't want to play the game at all, she thought.

To rebel, she would stare into the gray cylinder-block walls of PS 34, and daydream about the lost days of their old home. She remembered the forest in the backyard, how she would always follow Addy down to the river just beyond. She would copy Addy in everything she did—Addy dressed up and put on plays for Mom and Dad, then she would too; Addy jumped into the shallow, rocky current of the river, then *wait for me!*

Addy had been her hero, her protector, and now she rarely saw her except for late at night, before the hours of sleep, in the bedroom that they shared. But many nights Addy would sleep over at Melissa's. She was always with Melissa.

But Amelia's gray days of New York City—the monochrome hours at school, the quiet, private grieving for her father, which manifested itself in the form of her moving through her days zombie-like, removed, staring out gray windows at gray skies, at home and at school, trying to recall, or dream-up, what life had once been like, before—the gray days did not last long.

They had returned to Asheville for her father's funeral, and had stayed for five days with their old neighbor and family friend, Harold Carr, whose house was just down the road from their old one. He had visited them in New York a couple of times, had taken them all to see Simba in Times Square, and Amelia had noticed that her mother seemed to change during those weekends, something about her had been different.

Harold had gone through a divorce recently, his wife having remarried and relocated to Charlotte, and his twin daughters were in their first year of college at Chapel Hill, so he was alone in that big Colonial house.

That big Colonial house, Amelia quickly came to realize, would be where she would spend the remaining years of her childhood.

Harold's marital coup happened quickly. After those five January days in Asheville for her father's funeral, they returned for four long, agonizing months of New York City grayness, before they packed up all of their belongings the day after the school-year had ended and moved back, permanently, to live with Harold.

It was the beginning of summer when they arrived, the flowers in bloom, the trees bright and green, the stars brilliant above the blue ridges of Appalachia as Amelia looked out her window the first night back.

She had a room of her own now, with a view of the distant galaxies, the big dipper, Orion. She could see the shadowy edges of the forest from her bed, could hear the whistling of the river when she opened her window, the birds singing to her in the morning.

It felt freeing to be rid of the cramped quarters of their New York apartment and to have her own space in their new home—the past three years of big-city living felt to her like a strange dream that she'd just as well like to forget. But she also felt a kind of sadness alone in her room, with her newfound independence, because she would no longer be sharing a room with Addy, which she had always done as far back as she could remember. She was glad there would be no more Melissa, no more big-city distractions, to further wedge a gap in their sisterly bond, and hoped that this move might bring them—not only she and Addy, but all of them—closer.

It would become clear soon enough that the spaces between were only fated to expand.

The first Friday following their arrival back in Asheville was spent in the TV room, in a kind of archaeological dig.

Amelia's mother had retrieved the boxes and boxes of excess things from their old house that she had two years prior shoved into a storage container downtown because they were not essential enough for their new city lives.

The cardboard boxes sat off to the side, stacked against the wall in Harold's living room. There must have been a dozen of them in total, big and bulky and stuffed with mystery.

Amelia was on the loveseat, reading Holes. Harold and her mother were on the sofa, snuggling beneath a blanket, sipping tea, as they eyed the boxes and the daunting task of unpacking that was to come. Amelia looked up at them. Her mother was laughing, eager, excited, perhaps looking forward to the task of getting settled in, putting all of their old possessions in their right places. How could she be laughing? What could she be laughing about? Amelia thought.

August was lying prone on the carpeted floor in the center of the room, his feet crossed, his neck craned upward, supported by his elbows, which dug two divots into the pillow beneath them, his face too close to the TV, as he played *MarioKart* on Harold's GameCube.

Only a few days into their return, but Addy had already begun her revolt. She wanted no part of their family bonding time, no part of tea-drinking or reading or video-game playing or unpacking. She had separated herself away from the living room festivities, slammed the door to her new room, and was stubbornly determined to be as disruptive as possible. Her room was just above the living room and shared a vent; she was reading the entirety of *A Midsummer Night's Dream* in her bedroom, at maximum volume into a microphone, practicing her projection, reciting the lines into her vanity mirror, and so everyone in the house could hear the play unfolding from up above.

Addy's Shakespearean monologues were strangely accompanied by the eerie chimes of August's video-game, so that her performance was given its own 8-bit soundtrack.

> *You spotted snakes with double tongue,*
> *Thorny hedgehogs be not seen;*
> *Newts or blind-worms, do no wrong,*
> *Come not near our fairy queen.*

Amelia's mother set down her tea and let out a dramatic sigh, shook her head in resignation at the talking ceiling—Addy was going to be Addy, it was no use arguing. She went over to the boxes and brought one back to the couch, where she and Harold began sifting through it.

Amelia glanced periodically over the ridge of her book and watched the two of them pull out different items. It seemed as if the box was completely random. Some dingy old kitchenware. Baby clothes—why had she even bothered holding on to those?

Then Harold held something more delicate in front of him. Something carefully protected in newspaper and bubble wrap. He unwrapped it and it was a music box, small and ornamental,

porcelain, with a ballet dancer hand-painted on the top. It opened
and revealed a few random keepsakes, a late eighties ticket stub from
a Cyndi Lauper concert, loose buttons and paper clips, a tube of
chapstick, and a heart-shaped locket that Amelia noticed was
chipped, its faux-gold exterior faded.

Inside the locket were the images of Addy and Amelia. School
pictures from gap-toothed days gone by.

What's inside? asked Harold, opening the locket.

Oh, said Emily, just my girls. See.

Amelia looked up over the cover of her book and made a face.
She hated the overalls that she wore for school pictures that year.

Ew, Mom, stop. Don't show him that. I look gross.

You do not.

Amelia rolled her eyes and went back to reading her book,
absorbing herself in the world of Green Lake and Stanley Yelnats, as
August sped through Rainbow Road, the Midsummer lines still
invading the vents.

> *Weaving spiders, come not here;*
> *Hence, you long legged spinners, hence!*
> *Beetles black, approach not near;*
> *Worm, nor snail, do no offence.*

You look beautiful, Emily added, holding the locket up proudly,
appreciating the photos of her daughters. Doesn't she, Harold?

August swerved off course to avoid the shark-like Chomp that
roved across Rainbow Road, looking to spin him off course.

> *Hop in his walks and gambol in his eyes;*
> *Feed him with apricocks and dewberries,*
> *With purple grapes, green figs, and mulberries;*
> *The honey-bags steal from the humble-bees,*
> *And for night-tapers crop their waxen thighs*
> *And light them at the fiery glow-worms eyes,*
> *To have my love to bed and to arise;*

Absolutely, said Harold. Beautiful.

Amelia looked away and disappeared back into her book. She knew it wasn't true, but it was nice of him to say. Maybe they could have a fresh start here, maybe it wouldn't be so bad.

But after Addy left, everything changed.

The following winter, his daughters, Kayla and Kylie, were killed in a car accident. They had been riding in the car with a couple of college boys, drinking, when the car veered across the center line and collided with an oncoming car.

Harold was never the same. He and Emily had been fighting more often before this, but after the accident everything was worse. Emily had returned to her gray days of New York City after Addy left. She'd spend entire evenings alone in her room, no motivation to do anything, and Harold didn't tolerate it. They would have screaming matches for hours. It scared Amelia, but at least there was life in the screaming matches, at least they were trying to reach common ground on something.

But after the accident that winter, Harold completely shut down. There were no more screaming matches, but the violent silence that replaced them was far more terrifying to Amelia. It was as if his entire worldview had been shattered. He'd been a man who believed that the world would work out if he adhered firmly to his three pillars, was strong in his faith of individual will, but now the world had revealed itself to be utter chaos and it seemed that he could not cope. He began to drink.

For Amelia, she felt as if she had nowhere to turn. Her sister, her best friend, was gone. August spent all of his time in his room building his computers and model airplanes and playing his video games—that was his escape, but she had nothing. And, suddenly, she was surrounded by death.

She had known nothing of death up until the age of ten. Her entire existence had been ignorant of it, but now it seemed omnipotent. First her father. Then Harold's daughters. Was she next? It seemed to pervade into daily life and affect everyone she loved. And she felt as if she had nowhere to turn. The house following that winter was taken hostage by the silence of death.

To combat the silence of death, and the tension now thick between Harold and her mother, Amelia began to spend the long hours after school behind the forest near their house. She would spend the evenings leading up to dinner alone by the river, skipping stones, or digging around for new critters to examine on her microscope, or just sitting quietly along the bank.

After a couple months of this, late in the spring of 2012, Harold decided that he too needed out of the house. He had been a good step-father to August, teaching him how to build computers, and in a way he'd been good to Addy too, vouching for her personal freedom and allowing her to move away.

He'd always been kind to Amelia, and a part of her loved him like a father, but she was also intimidated by him, and there was a great distance between them.

She was sitting along the river bank one April afternoon when he walked through the path in the forest carrying two fishing poles and a tackle box.

There you are. So this is where you've been sneaking off to after school. What is it you do down here? Just sit?

I like it, said Amelia. It's quiet. I throw rocks sometimes.

How would you like to learn how to fish?

Okay.

Amelia thought it sounded fun. She'd never fished before. She'd grown up just steps from the river, but her own father had never taken her when she was younger. She also felt bad for Harold, and didn't want to let him down. She could sense the new man in him, all coiled anger and confusion, a man who had thought the world to be one thing and then tragedy and time revealed it to be something else.

It was a humid spring day. The flowers were in bloom, showcasing beautiful purple asters along the bank of the river. The sun was high and bright, but white clouds in the distance were moving toward its light.

Harold opened the tackle box that he'd sat down on a nearby bench, revealing hooks and lures, sinkers and bobbers, and a grimy pouch of live worms.

Amelia went over and sat on the bench next to Harold. She watched the water move slowly while the green leaves clapped like thunder all around them. He took the worm in his hands.

See, he said. Like this. You have to grip it like this so it doesn't wriggle away. Fold it in half.

He held the worm up to the hook and pierced it.

Then he took another worm from the tackle box and held his hand out toward her. Don't be afraid. Take the hook. Hold it firm. Here, like this.

He took her hand and helped her to align the bait and the spear, puncturing another worm twice, once through the head and once through the body.

Now we're ready to cast the line. He showed her how to grip the handle and flick the wrist to release the reel, so that the line sailed into the slow-moving stream.

Her first attempt went short and to the right into a bramble patch by the edge of the water. Harold untangled the line from the bushes, then returned to the bench.

Here, let me show you, he said. Come sit on my lap.

Amelia felt strange about sitting on his lap. She was too old for that wasn't she? But she did it. He guided her hand back and flicked his wrist effortlessly at a sidearm angle to cast the line far out into the water. Like that, he said. Nice and easy.

They watched their two neon bobbers hover on the surface of the water, waiting for something to bite.

Then, out of nowhere, Harold began to cry. He wrapped his arms tighter around her waist.

Are you okay? she asked.

You're all I've got now, he said.

She felt bad for him. She knew that their family didn't feel like his family. The love that had been there between Harold and her mother had already eroded within the first year of marriage. His own daughters had been cruelly taken from him. But he was fifty years old and felt that this was it for him. Life had not worked out how he thought it would, and now he felt as if it was too late for anything else. He had no control over whatever strange and unasked for life he had been given.

Harold? she asked.

He held her tighter to him and didn't answer. Their lines drifted further downstream away from them.

The world is a mess, he said. You should never grow up. If only you could stay like you are forever.

Harold, are you sure you're okay?

You're beautiful, you know that, Amelia.

No, I'm not, she blushed.

Yes.

Addy's beautiful.

You are, Amelia.

He was still hugging her tightly to him, and she felt uncomfortable now.

Harold.

He rubbed his hand along her leg.

Harold, let me go.

I don't ever want to let you go.

Maybe this was love? she thought. Was he saying that he loved her so much that he only wanted to hold her? She was confused. Maybe he thought that her own youth could transform him into somebody younger, and that would mean he could have a do-over at life? She felt unbearably sad for him at that thought.

Then, suddenly, he had eight hands and they were everywhere. Her legs and hips, her ribcage and her breasts. It can be our secret, he said.

Harold, no! I want to go!

He squeezed her tighter and she could feel his breath on her neck.

Harold, I want to get up! Stop!

Then he released his hold, let her up. She turned to face him and he was sobbing.

I'm sorry, Amelia. I'm sorry. I'm so sorry. You don't know what it's been like for me.

She just felt so confused. She'd never seen him cry before.

It's okay, she managed, still skeptical, afraid of him.

Her rod was lying in the dirt when it jumped toward the brambles that edged the bank.

She quickly picked it up and tried to reel in whatever creature was on the end of the line.

Slow and steady, said Harold. Don't reel it in too fast.

She reeled it in slowly, then all of the sudden she was holding up her first fish, a small trout.

Nice work! said Harold. We can cook it for dinner. How about it?

Okay.

She felt so strange there at the edge of the bank in that moment. She was proud and happy at having caught a trout, and still so confused about what had happened with Harold.

And let's not tell your mom about everything, okay. You know, about everything, the crying and whatnot.

Okay.

Like I said, I'm sorry. I don't know what came over me.

I guess it's fine.

You know I love you, right?

I know.

Alright, he said. So whaddya say we head back? I can show you how to gut this thing. We can cook it up for dinner. It'll be all yours unless you want to share with your brother and your mom. You caught it, you get to eat it. Sound good?

Okay, she said. They gathered up their rods and the tackle box. The river lashed and lapped against the edges of the bank and the leaves were loud as thunder. The sun had disappeared behind the clouds and the mountains were giants in the distance, hovering beneath a blue ridge.

Okay, he said, tousling her hair. Let's head home then.

CHAPTER ONE

December 24, 2029

They were in the sky. August was staring at a bottle of Glenfiddich 18 when there was a small ripple of turbulence, and the pilot, Darrell Moore, a longtime friend and business associate from MIT, shouted back to them to put their seat belts on. There were low-hanging clouds up ahead and rough winds.

This was August's private plane, a brand new Beechcraft G37 Bonanza, a small, five passenger aircraft. Top-of-the-line, newly designed. Two rear-facing and front-facing leather seats in the back cabin right behind the cockpit where Darrell piloted the plane next to an empty sixth seat in the front. The plane had cost August just north of one million American dollars. A small chunk of change for him; with all the success of True Partners and Solaris and Space-Y, August's personal net worth was well into the billions. The plane was just right for him. He'd fallen in love with its sleek design, its modern features, its lightness and speed, and its history as a dependable, well-produced brand, the Bonanza first appearing post-WWII, around 1945. He'd opted for it over pricier, showier commercial offerings from Boeing or Airbus. He rarely flew and so decided the Bonanza would suit him well.

But he dreaded flying.

He had only flown in his expensive aerial toy a handful of times since he'd bought it two years ago. He stared at the bottle of Glenfiddich 18, three quarters of the amber liquid remaining. He'd completely forgotten that the bottle was in here. He'd stored it in one of the compartments in the rear cabin to class the place up, to provide an option for in-flight entertainment and relaxation, a soothing of the nerves. But August rarely drank. Like flying, like anything that required him to venture beyond his Hartford loft, drinking meant a disruption in routine and structure, a ceding of control. August was a creature of habit and drinking was a novelty, one that always made adherence to his ascetic habits difficult, and threw a monkey wrench into his personal, carefully curated ecosystem.

But right now he craved a glass of scotch—they'd just taken off, and would land about three hours from now at a small, private airstrip in Asheville near the Biltmore, and he and Taylortoo sat caddy-corner from each other, as far apart as possible, August rear-facing, looking down at the buildings and the trees squared into neat acres, shrinking below, while Taylortoo stared out the window at the clouds that now raced around the plane, enveloping it in a white cocoon, the blue irises of her eyes lit-up, roaming, exploring the expansive horizons of her network, thinking about who knows what—he craved a glass of scotch because she wasn't talking to him, was lost in her own world, as he sat there shaking as his routine was being upended, dreading this return home, not knowing what it would bring.

He poured a glass of Glenfiddich neat and took a swig, hoping that it would wash away some of the anxiety that had pounced upon him during takeoff.

He looked at Taylortoo. He looked across the cabin and out her window. All he saw were globs of white nothingness. What was she thinking about? Was she envisioning future fantasies that he couldn't even imagine?

He'd told himself that he was worried about something happening to her and so thought it was better for her to stay home. He'd made some excuse about needing her to remain to water the ferns. But the truth was that he wanted to keep her away from his family; he was afraid of what they might think, and how they might receive her sudden appearance at Christmas. He'd planned on going by himself, getting the ordeal over with quickly, and returning home to Taylortoo none the worse for wear.

His mother's death had changed things. She'd insisted and had become irate with him when he suggested that he still make the trip alone. She'd threatened to leave him.

He clinked his fingernails against his glass of scotch. She looked away from the window and across the cabin at him. She smiled.

What are you thinking about? he asked. You look deep in thought.

He thought she'd give him some long-winded facts related to atmospheric pressure or an obscure explanation about the word knot, and then tell him how many knots they've traveled already, but instead she said, August, I wasn't just thinking about it...abstractly...I meant what I said during our argument.

He looked at her, confused.

I was thinking about your mother...I never knew her...but in a way I did know her, because I know you. I feel this would be such a nice thing to have...a way of sending a piece of myself into the future, for after I'm gone...it is a beautiful thing...don't you think?

Something about what she'd said irritated him. She was a powerful, sentient, hyper-rational being, and yet suddenly she'd become prone to trite sentiment, Hallmarkish drivel. And he didn't consider himself a *piece* of anyone. He was his own individual person, self-made. He'd succeeded in spite of the limitations of biology, of where he'd come from. He'd worked incredibly hard. So there was a knee-jerk reaction in him that felt like what she'd said was not really the whole truth, but a gilded-over facade of it, and it disgusted him.

There was disappointment in her. Where had she been spending her time, to get her thinking like this? What kind of entertainment, what kind of brainwashing had comprised her system? He'd known her to devour volumes and volumes of Kant and Einstein and Proust and Shakespeare and Emerson and Locke, to seek out seldom-read PhD theses in the fields of aeronautics and molecular biology and the arts, and now, out of left-field, this personal desire to be a mother? She was far smarter than this, wasn't she? Didn't she know that this was impossible?

He told her as much, that she had not been designed for that, that it wasn't in her nature.

But, August, she said, is it not possible to transcend my nature?

Taylortoo, why would you possibly want to be like *us?* he asked, retreading ground they'd covered already.

He wished she'd let the idea die. He wanted to shelve the matter. He wanted to close his eyes and sip his Glenfiddich. He wanted her to shut the hell up.

Augie, honey, why do you always have to be so negative, so closed off?

I don't want to hear it anymore. I don't want you to be some lab rat in another company's reproductive trials. No. I'm tired. I want to drink and close my eyes and not think. Can I do that? Just sit in silence for this plane ride.

She was angry with him. She gave him the cold shoulder, turned toward her own window and looked out at the clouds. He poured another generous amount of Glenfiddich. As the land sped past them, ten thousand feet below, he drank from the glass and hoped that, for a few hours, he might be able to lose his mind.

August opened his eyes. Darrell was looking over his shoulder into the rear cabin, telling them that the plane was beginning its descent into Asheville. Taylortoo was staring dreamily out the window, ignoring him, still angry.

The threads of a dream lingered in his mind. The scotch had knocked him out and he'd managed a deep sleep during the journey and now the connections that sparked in his half-lucid mind kept showing him images of Wiffle balls and lightning bugs. He pursued them, the stubborn images from the dream, and as he did they became clearer and clearer and peppered with real-life details, and he realized it wasn't a dream but a memory that the aged scotch had brought to the surface.

He couldn't be sure. Perhaps there was some dream-component to it, some fiction, some manifestations of the id. But for the most part he thought that it was memory.

It was the summer of 2004. August had recently turned seven.

He flailed his scrawny arms, the head of the plastic bat as thick as his own melon. He could barely control the tangerine bat, as he flailed and flailed and his body did a three-sixty, his shoulders twirling in front of him, his feet slipping, spinning him off balance.

If he made contact when Leighton tossed it, underhand, softball-style from the side, it was purely by chance. He whiffed on nine out of ten. Every once and awhile, he'd foul one off. Very rarely, once in a blue moon, he'd really catch a hold of one, the hollow club popping the Wiffle-white squarely, firing it up into orbit, sending it across the backyard, sometimes catching in an unkempt bush, or knocking at the stems of his mother's hydrangeas, or ricocheting off the trunk of the old American Beech that indicated the rough border between their property and the neighbor's.

Now keep your eye on it, son.

August whiffed.

Come on, son. Don't be such a little girl. Keep your shoulders squared. And watch the damn ball, you got it?

August was undeveloped, raw, a fawn trying to balance on its skinny new legs, still jellied from its mother's placenta, but it was already clear that he was never going to make the majors. He wasn't about to become the next Chipper Jones.

POP.

See, what did I tell you? If you keep your eye on it. If you focus, said Leighton.

Leighton jogged to the edge of the property. He knelt by the trunk of the beech, whose summer green leaves were beginning to turn to autumn shades, to retrieve the ball.

August smiled wide, jumped up and down before he knew he was jumping up and down, as if something inside was trying to get out. He raised his arms, the bat, shimmied them above his head, did a little dance.

He proceeded to whiff at the next eight pitches. Leighton was getting impatient. He tried to remain encouraging, *it's okay, you're fine, focus on the next one, come on now bud.*

But there was a tinge of anger in his father's eyes, as if August's failing to hit the ball somehow reminded his dad of his own failings. Did their father-son reenactment remind Leighton of the time when his own real-life father had used a real-life baseball—the kind stuffed with dense rubber and yarn, the red seams stitching together real-life cowhide—when Leighton was not much older than August was then, using it too soon and rifling it overhand in Leighton's vicinity, causing him to cower, his eyes skittish and closing, his plastic tee-ball mitt protecting his face as he tried to dodge out of the way, because he knew there was no chance of catching it. And Leighton's Dad had just kept throwing it, against his son's pleas, *I can't I can't. Stop. It's too fast.* Kept throwing it and saying *you'd better stop acting like a little girl and keep your eye on it, then. If you don't it's gonna hit you in the face. Get that glove up, son. You'd better get that glove up unless you want a black eye. Be a man and get that glove up.*

And so of course August's father hadn't made the majors. Started at third base, the hot corner, his freshman year, but he was a slacker. By that time he was much more into escaping from the pipe dreams his real-life Daddy had fashioned for him after his mother's death, escaping into three different things: marijuana, his high school girlfriend—the real-life Annette Porter (real sweetheart, his first, and he sometimes wondered what if)—and the love of his life, the guitar. Escaping into the plans of his own personal Progress. He would show his Daddy and he would make him proud, that's what Leighton had wanted. To make him proud, but also to make him a little resentful, to really show him, to surpass him, to leave him in the dust, to become the next Bob Dylan, to pluck the steel strings raw, until his fingers were eternally callused, so that his Daddy would feel a little resentful at the younger, better version, an uncanny resemblance, at achieving some vague heights that he never could, but also proud, taking some credit, *it's because I was tough on you, made you look the ball in the eye and keep your glove up,* he imagined his father thinking when he would watch him winning Grammys and performing on SNL.

But then it turned out that Leighton was already twenty-one when *Nevermind* came out and the next real-life American Voice was decided, its greasy-haired lead singer, flannel-clad and a real-life Olympian, became a generation's gold-medalist in mashing sincerity with rage, lashing its chords against the limitations and inequities of a society that demanded a stoic, patriarchal Progress, eschewed what had come before, and blazed a trail for a generation's own personal Progress that believed in Bill Clinton, while Leighton had released exactly nothing, his three demo songs unanimously passed on over and over until his big break, heard through the years by only a handful of local Morton's regulars, their faces bloated with Bud Light and sagging from gravity, his voice, his words had not reached past the dive bar in his home town of Asheville, and his father was dead by then anyway and wouldn't have been able to see it even if he had become Kurt instead of Kurt becoming Kurt.

But had August really known this? Had this been a confession of his father's, his story passed down and buried and forgotten until now, or was it of his own invention?

That evening, 2004, August wondered if maybe he'd been able to see all of this in his father's face. Did he understand then that his father didn't like going down this road, this train of thoughts, so when he became impatient with August and his constant failing to lift the Wiffle into orbit, he bottled his anger, stopped himself from the impulse that he surely inherited from his own personal Daddy, the impulse to say *Jesus Christ, son, keep your fucking eye on it and stop flailing your arms like a girl,* and instead diverted his attention to the yellow-bellied sapsucker that had made its nest in the American Beech of their backyard, and was chirping its birdsong.

Then, as August whiffed at the tenth ball in a row, Leighton forced himself to concentrate all of his attention on the fireflies. They had come out just as the sun had brought down its final thread of lingering orange, dipped it below the Blue Ridge Mountains, and the day's end was marked in a pinkish-grey that would soon recede to black. The fireflies glowed from their tails, a fluorescence that was somewhere between green and yellow.

Daddy, I hit it, see! said August.

Leighton, distracted by the fireflies, didn't notice the dribbler that August had sent off the end of the bat near Emily's hydrangeas.

Nice work, son, he said without emotion. I think we're done for the night. It's getting dark. You had a few good ones, though. You're getting better.

'Member that really really far one I had, Dad? The home run?

I remember, bud. Soon you'll be good enough to hit it over the tree.

Amelia had been watching all of this as she sat at the picnic table in the yard, the whiffing and the flailing of limbs, the twirling, the father-son bonding, the occasional orbit in the godforsaken boredom of inertia and waiting that was baseball.

Amelia, said Leighton, go get Mom and Addy, tell 'em the fireflies are out tonight.

August watched his little sister sprint past their father. He rose and chased her toward the house, poking her in the shoulder with the plastic bat as they raced for the backdoor.

August thought that if he ran faster, if he beat her inside, if he emerged first from the house with Addy and Mom, then Dad would say good job, would think *that's my boy, boy he sure is fast, he can get things done.*

But Leighton didn't notice them jostling for his attention as they raced inside. He sat with his back against the American Beech. Was he pushing back his unwanted thoughts, unrequited dreams of adoration, of fame, of some personal-Daddy-definition of major league success? His shoulders were slumped against the tree as he tried with all of his might to simply be, for all of his attention to be transferred to the glowing insects that hovered, present, luminous, in the balmy autumn air.

Amelia and Addy emerged from the house, hand-in-hand with each other, both of them clutching mason jars, as August trailed and said *wait up!* Emily followed them out, holding her own jar, twisting the aluminum cap, showing August and his sisters how to be patient.

August jumped up and down, as if something was trying to get out, causing the fireflies to get skittish and scurry away.

August, like this, said Emily. There you go, Amelia. You've got it.

Amelia held her jar steady below the congregation of light, waiting for them to hover down, come closer, above the rim. The jars filtered the pink dusk and the fireflies intrigued themselves closer and closer to the glass, unknowing participants in their own captivity.

August, watch Amelia, said his mother. See how she does it. You've got to be patient. Let them come to you.

Amelia had caught four already, Addy—quickly getting the hang of patience, and performing patience to perfection, not for the sake of patience itself, August suspected, but in the hope that Mom would praise her patience, that her own personal Daddy would praise her ability to get the most light in her jar—Addy had just caught her fifth, but August had yet to catch one, his hands still jerky and over eager to tame the light, to seal it neatly and display it for his parents.

Mom walked over to the beech tree, sat next to Dad, and set an empty jar in his lap.

Come join us, babe, it's fun.

I'm fine, he said.

Oh, come on?

I said I'm fine.

Come join us, honey. Come on. Let's see how many you can catch. I'll bet you a million dollars I get more than you.

We don't have a million dollars.

I'll bet you a dollar then.

I'm not in the mood, Em. I don't want to.

August saw his mother's tight smile, masking disappointment, not wanting to press the issue. She left the jar next to him, the edge of the glass scratching off some of the bark.

Well, if you change your mind, we'll be having fun without you, she said.

August watched his father, sitting in his own world, against the tree. He continued to trap the fireflies in mason jars with his sisters.

Then, after a while, August went and sat next to his father. He did not look at him. They said nothing. They watched the pink above Mount Mitchell in the distance, watched it darken to a tangerine sliver, an orange canoe, a neon button pressed to edge of the ridge, the dark blue above it threatening to banish it down into the valley, into night, they sat watching, the yellow-bellied sapsucker orbiting the canopy, singing its birdsong above them, sat silently, unmoving, at the edge of the property, with their backs against the American Beech.

CHAPTER TWO

When Addy arrived there was nobody there to greet her as her plane rolled to the gate on the tarmac and she exited into the small lobby of Asheville Regional Airport.

It was late that Christmas Eve. She'd had to transfer at Charlotte since there were no direct flights, and it would be after midnight by the time she got to the house. She didn't know who would be there, if it was just Amelia, or if August had arrived already and would be staying at the house too.

It would be weird to return to that neighborhood, to the very street where she was raised, to spend a night in that foreign home, in a room that she'd once known as a teenager, if only briefly.

It was strange to be back there. It was always strange. Strange because of the nostalgia; strange because this was a place so painstakingly familiar, as if the place itself had been coded into her DNA, and yet was also so new and foreign at the same time.

Strange perhaps in how she anticipated and feared the looks of strangers who might not turn out to be strangers. The attendant at gate G4 awaiting the deboarding passengers, smiling and welcoming them to Asheville, a vaguely familiar porcine face, *were we in choir together?* The waitress at Blue Ridge Trading and Tavern, *could that be Heather Robinson, homecoming queen?* The man at baggage claim, *didn't I sit behind you in the fifth grade?* And so what was this strange feeling that now evoked in Adelaide a sudden onset of anxiety? It wasn't so much nostalgia and it wasn't the possibility of a potentially awkward social encounter, a dredging up of hazy history, but the strangeness, the anxiety and panic that quickened her heart and set her to the edge of hyperventilation had to do with *knowing.*

If she were to see a face here that was truly familiar, that she was more sure of, an old friend or maybe someone who she'd spent countless hours with in grade school productions, during rehearsals for The Music Man or Our Town, then the look on their face would surely be one of knowing. They would notice her. They would waive and reminisce and *my God how are you?* And so why did this look of knowing, why did the thought of it bother Addy so much? Why was she speed walking with her head canted toward the polished floor?

Because of course they would know her, and yet, how could they? Well, the truth was that they would know her at such an elemental level that it would be undeniable, even though she was a much different person than she had been. She had been a girl, a child, when she called this place home. New York Adelaide, Broadway star Adelaide, she was nothing like that former version, that outdated model, was she?

But the knowing eyes, were she to encounter them, were she to get roped into their ravenous maw, would bring her right back to the self at the known point in time, would revert her software straight back to elementary choir, or brace-faced sophomore dances, or Mrs. Danville's fifth grade homeroom that always smelled of cinnamon oatmeal.

So she sped through the terminal and followed the signs that pointed to ground transportation as she summoned a Lyft, a black

Hyundai Elantra, Mary Jo, first three letters of the plate REC, and she waited at the empty curbside, surveying the plates as the cars passed. Her flight was the last of the day and the terminal was dark and silent and she could see the stars above, suspended in the black horizon. She hadn't really noticed them in years, stuck in the heart of the light-polluted big apple, rarely looking up. She craned her head toward them, *was that the little dipper? Was that Orion shining bright? Was she even remembering them, identifying them correctly?* It had been years since that astronomy class she took in high school. She looked blankly up to the random canvas of dots while she massaged the nape of her neck to work out a kink, her muscles stiff and tense from the flights.

And then her ride was there. She threw her suitcase in the trunk and said hi to Mary Jo. Mary Jo, oh no, Mary Jo. *That* Mary Jo? *Oh crap.*

Oh my goodness! Do my eyes deceive me?! If it isn't the one and only? If it isn't Adelaide Wheeler! I ain't gonna lie, my husband and I just googled you the other day because I'd told him that I was related to someone who got real famous and he didn't believe me. Honest to God he didn't, I said *Dale I'm telling you the God's honest truth, this girl is like my cousin and now she's practically a great big star!* Oh my lord, well what are the odds? What the hell brings you back here, slumming it with us small timers? Shouldn't you be in the big city?

First of all, Addy thought, we are nothing resembling related. Mary Jo was Mary Jo Masters, a niece to Addy's once stepfather Harold Carr, first cousin to Harold's daughters from his first marriage, Kayla and Kylie, who had gotten into some awful car accident and died right after Addy had moved by herself back to New York at the age of sixteen. Addy had spent her sophomore year back there, living with Harold and her family in their new home. During that year, sometimes Harold's daughters, who were both in college at the time, would come back to stay for weekends, and the family would grow and the space would shrink and there would be fighting for beds and usually August would be the one stuck with the couch and that scratchy old quilt.

And on top of that, sometimes Harold's sister Jackie would come over to hang out with her two kids, Joe and Mary Jo, who were either also in high school, or like thirty—Addy didn't remember and never could tell, and, frankly, hadn't really cared because she spent that year longing to be back with Melissa in the city—and they would all play charades or pictionary and the adults would drink gin and tonics.

I'm back here for my mother's funeral, said Addy.

That oughta get Mary Jo to quit yapping.

Oh my goodness, honey. Honey, oh my word.

Mary Jo unbuckled her seatbelt and stretched her entire body across the center console, lunging herself into the backseat space. She gave Addy an awkward army hug, as in lots of arms, lots of unsolicited pats on the shoulders.

I just had no idea. I remember your mother. Emily. Such a sweet lady I always thought. I'm so sorry.

Thank you.

Addy had hoped this Lyft ride would be silent and that she might be able to decompress by staring out the window, might be able to watch the mountains blur and just breathe, or might be able to disappear into the screen of her phone, but it didn't appear that that would be the case.

She didn't like Mary Jo, all of that surface enthusiasm, that blatant extroversion that smothered any ember of self-awareness that might try to spark. And, obviously, they weren't *related!* She'd spoken to this woman less than a handful of times in her entire life, and never anything meaningful, and not since she was sixteen, half a lifetime ago now, so what kind of delusional wacko is telling her husband that they're related!

If there's anything you need, said Mary Jo, please don't hesitate.

I need this car to start moving, Addy thought. I need to be unknown and anonymous and to be able to endure this ride in quiet, is what I really need. Please and thank you.

I remember this one time when your mother—you know, it's funny because I just remembered this the other day—but this one time—

Mary Jo, right. It's Mary Jo? I'm sorry to cut you off, but I just got done with two flights. It's late. I'm tired. Do you think we could just maybe not talk?

Addy had phrased it as a question but her voice made it emphatically clear that it was not. The look she gave Mary Jo was one of stern authority. Eyes like darts, a look gilded with indignation, which seemed to say that the entire interaction, whatever relationship Mary Jo had imagined in that moment, it was only transactional. Addy was the paying customer and Mary Jo was the driver and all that Addy needed Mary Jo to do was her job. Just drive Mary Jo. Put it into drive and get us away from the terminal.

Well, alrighty! Mary Jo said. There remained the lilt to her voice, a dependable trait of her character wherein she would end each sentence—the final syllable—on a higher pitch. An affected, sing-songy quality that Addy found not entirely authentic and highly annoying. So the lilt remained, but then Mary Jo went silent after she said *alrighty* and seemed hurt by Addy's brusqueness.

Mary Jo steered the car across the dark highway, slicing through the forest, the headlights illuminating the yellow dashes that rushed past.

They drove north alongside the French Broad River, past the Duke Energy offices and power plant near Lake Julian, past the

Biltmore and the Biltmore Forest, onto the Blue Ridge Parkway that bypassed the heart of the city and slithered through small town neighborhoods tucked into the surrounding hills, elevated and rocky and green, then exited the Blue Ridge Parkway and descended toward the Swannanoa River, into a rural section on the outskirts of Asheville, called Azalea, where a Grocery Outlet and a Waffle House and a Holiday Inn headlined Tunnel Road, the main drag, a stretch of highway 70 where most cars did not bother to obey the twenty-mph decrease in speed limit as they cut through Azalea, driving west toward Asheville's busy and bustling downtown area, or east, toward the monolithic sprawl of green, past Lake James State Park and South Mountains State Park and countless small towns north of Lake Norman until highway seventy would end and web into other highways and Interstate veins that could then take you further east through Greensboro and Durham and Raleigh and if you never stopped might spit you near Kitty Hawk or Nags Head or Kill Devil Hills, which was where the Wright Brothers National Memorial sat, and which looked right out onto the gray and cold Atlantic Ocean.

But Mary Jo turned off Tunnel Road onto Lower Grassy Branch Road, and then onto Hickory Tree Road, past a hodgepodge of mostly ranch-level homes, some with dirt driveways, others paved, several Country style, a few Colonial, even a couple of American Craftsmen that were more recently constructed, many with American flags blowing from the awnings, some with cars parked on patches of grass that had browned and then lost color faster than the areas surrounding, some immaculately tended to, while others were near-shacks that seemed deserted and were in complete shambles—no windows, rotting framework, missing shingles—and Addy looked indifferently out the window of the car and into the darkness, while still noticing and remembering the variety in each solitary house they passed on her old street. The houses were well spaced out from one another and sometimes difficult to see through the many solid hickories and beeches and oaks that partially shielded their facades from neighbors and passersby.

And then the car pulled into one of the long paved driveways and drove a good way back into the forest and stopped in front of a modest Colonial home with two eyebrow dormers, which gave Addy the impression of something alive, something watching her.

Her phone vibrated—a message from Ray: *hope you made it safe. call me if you get a minute. I'm here for you, Addy. And if you need me to be there, I'll be there, just tell me and I'll come as soon as I can, but I understand if that isn't what you need right now. I miss you, and I love you. Nightums* ❤

Whelp, said Mary Jo, here we are.

Thank you, said Addy. She got her luggage from the trunk and walked around to Mary Jo's window. Sorry if I was rude earlier, at the airport. It's just been a very long day.

Mary Jo waived her hand as if to say, don't mention it.

You don't have to apologize, she said. I can imagine what you're feeling. My mother passed away a couple summers ago.

I'm sorry.

Here, let me give you my contact info. Mary Jo took out her phone and air dropped her number to Addy. I know you'll be busy with family, and you might not want a stranger inserting themselves where they aren't wanted, but, really, if there is anything I can do to help, it's no problem.

Thank you.

And, if you could let me know when the funeral will be, my husband and I would love to be there. It's the least we could do.

Addy thanked her again and they said goodbye, and then Mary Jo sped off into the darkness. It was nice of her to offer, a kind gesture, Addy thought, but it was just that, an empty gesture, a customary thing that gets said after someone passes, words that linger in times of grief. But the words didn't have root in reality, Addy believed. They couldn't help to solve whatever grief she would eventually have to face. She wasn't sure if anybody's words or actions could be sufficient for a task like that. It was something that she thought needed to be carried alone, and so she knew that she'd never use the number, and didn't think she'd ever see Mary Jo again.

She walked up to the door of the old house. All of the lights were off. She read Ray's message again, and thought of him alone with Essie in their little apartment. She missed him, but she was also glad to be away from him, grateful that he wasn't there. She didn't want to burden him.

And being there, alone, adrift, at what felt like another crossroads in her life, it recalled her to a time when she had embarked back to New York City at the age of sixteen, brought back similar feelings of hope and transformation, although, at that young age there had been little doubt accompanying her bold actions—she had felt destined to achieve a career as an actress, and she had—but, now, those mirrored feelings of hope and change were all mixed up with sadness and uncertainty (the death of her mother, the not knowing what would come next in her career, in her life, if she and Ray were meant for each other, if there would be a future on the other side of this).

She read his text: *nightums,* it was a private word, an invented bit of language whose origins dated back to the throes of their young love, a relic of love-speak from their early twenties. She'd texted it to him after one of their first dates. They'd met on Tinder and had instantly bonded over Sondheim musicals and Shakespeare. He'd been a shy, inexperienced boy of twenty-one, in his third year at Columbia, and she was a reckless, twenty-three year old who had been living dangerously in the city, supporting herself for the past six years with a myriad of service jobs, while auditioning when she could find the time and trying to find new ways to fuel her own ambitions. He had seemed chaste, playful, almost innocent when she met him, but she could tell that he had a strong set of values, that he was a man of integrity.

She didn't like him at first, and he wasn't the type that she would normally go for. She had dated a lot of shallow, older men in that time span between seventeen and twenty-three, and had long become disenchanted with the entire idea of romance and monogamy when Ray entered her life. And on top of that, the daily grind of the city, the lack of progress, no big break to be found acting-wise to that point, it had taken a toll on her, and at just twenty-three she had come to feel like a shell of her former self, defeated by the city. It wasn't as if Ray had been some kind of savior for her, but she believed that if they hadn't fallen in love, if she hadn't re-opened her heart, then neither of them would have achieved the Broadway success that they had. Their relationship had felt equal from the start, and they had found a way to draw the most out of each other.

Nightums. She studied the word. They didn't use it much anymore. Since they were adults who had their own place and slept in the same bed, they opted for more straightforward *goodnights*; *nightums* had been a strictly digital word when they were young and lived apart, a private token of language that had been smuggled uptown and downtown, over rivers and across borough lines, transmitted in the throes of loneliness and inebriation, spontaneous, ecstatic passion, as well as sober clarity, a word that had been shared stealthily and cherished late at night, read with wide smiles in dark rooms of run-down, rat-infested complexes, *nightums* radiating from the solitary glow of a screen. It had been a word that acted as a stand-in for *I miss you* and *I'm glad we found each other* and *I'm mad at you, but I still love you and so I don't want to go to bed angry,* and sometimes it simply meant *I hope you sleep well.* It was a word that did the work in communicating more complex things, such as, *this city is tough and ruthless and I've had a rough day, but here is this word that only we know, this shared thing that separates the two of us from the eight-million strangers we share this island with, a word that makes what we have special, a word that means we're alive.*

They hadn't used *nightums* very often over the past several years, since both of their careers took off, but it had managed to endure for more than a decade. And Ray had just resurrected it, only what could it mean now, as she studied it in the darkness of the driveway, her face illuminated by the blue light, as she idled outside the house, not yet ready to enter. Was he telling her that he still felt the same way as he had when they'd met, that perhaps that kind of childish joy, that playfulness, that faith, could be recaptured? Or was that *nightums* one of the final *nightums?* Was that *nighums* saying *nightums* to their relationship, a final goodnight, a goodbye? She wasn't sure. A piece of her wished for the former, but another part of her thought that maybe it was the end, that that would be for the best. Certainly she had some say over whether or not *nightums* would survive decades more into the future, only the problem was she wasn't sure if she wanted it to, didn't know what kind of strength it might take to nurture the word through so many of life's stages.

She could call Ray right now and tell him to fly to Carolina to be with her, but she felt that she didn't want him there. She didn't know what made her feel this way, but she thought that this was a journey she had to take alone.

Addy hauled her suitcase up the single concrete step. The neighborhood was silent. The only sounds were the branches of the forest bristling in the wind, and the stars above, burning loud, unreachable distances away. She knocked on the door.

CHAPTER THREE

Amelia was the first to wake on Christmas morning. She weaved through the clutter of the living room and went into the kitchen. She stood in front of the empty fridge, hunched over and searching the shelves for anything that might work for breakfast.

All that was there was the squash lasagna that her mother had already prepared—covered with foil in its glass pan, and ready to bake in the oven—some garlic bread, and a beet and cucumber salad with pistachio and sherry vinegar dressing.

They were out of yogurt, which was what Amelia usually had first thing in the morning. But there was a half carton of eggs remaining on the second shelf, and a few slices of whole grain bread in the pantry, so that would have to do.

She considered making french toast. That sounded good and would be a warmer, more festive breakfast to begin Christmas Day, but she didn't have any milk or vanilla, and the bread was too thin, and so she decided that it would be better to have eggs and toast. She could just make a big batch of scrambled eggs. August and Addy would surely be hungry whenever they woke. And what about Taylortoo? Amelia still wasn't really sure how her brother's *partner* worked. But she was pretty sure she couldn't eat food.

August and Taylortoo arrived late last night. The three of them had made small talk in the living room, barely broaching the subject of their mother. August had asked some logistical questions about how long she'd been in the hospital, if it had been sudden or drawn out, if she'd been having any health issues prior to the cardiac arrest. And Taylortoo had been soft spoken and supportive, constantly listening and nodding her head and not breaking eye-contact, to show her sympathy, and if Amelia hadn't known better, she wouldn't have thought that she was anything other than human. They didn't talk long, and then August and Taylortoo retired to his old bedroom for the night.

Addy arrived later, after midnight, and Amelia had woken up and unlocked the door and let her in. They embraced in a long hug, but said almost nothing to each other. Amelia knew she was tired from traveling, and so Addy had gone straight to bed, both of them silently agreeing to discuss whatever might need to be discussed the next day.

Amelia took a glass bowl and cracked all six eggs, the raw universes of them expanding and spilling out into the basin in golden-yoke chaos. She threw in some pinches of salt and pepper and whisked them thoroughly with a fork.

She heard footsteps upstairs, her siblings stirring.

Addy was the first to wake. She joined Amelia at the kitchen table and heaped a pile of scrambled eggs onto a plate.

Toast? Amelia asked, holding up a slice of multi-grain.

Thanks.

The toaster sizzled. Amelia looked across the kitchen at her sister. How do conversations begin?

She'd always idolized Addy, but looking at her now, they didn't know each other at all. They moved around each other easily—the words arrived—but it was almost as if the entire interaction was rote, mechanical, thoughtless, a habitual adherence to a secret system of ritual, like brushing your teeth, or taking a shower, or commuting to work.

How were your flights? asked Amelia.

Oh, fine. Fucking delay in Charlotte. I was supposed to get in at eleven, and it was midnight before I got here. Sorry if I woke you last night.

No, you didn't—I mean, you did, but I was just so glad you came. I'm glad you could get away from your show.

Well, said Addy, scarfing a forkful of eggs, that whole thing is a long story. But essentially I assaulted a child.

Uh, excuse me?

Yeah, this real twerpy piece of shit. Trent Pendleton. I thought he was going to offer me a role in one of his movies—he's like this big deal, this TikTok genius—anyway, but he didn't and I just lost it. I slammed him against an elevator and choked him before his parents stopped it. I don't know what came over me.

Are you joking? Are you messing with me?

Hand to God. Truth to power. These eggs are good. What did you add?

A little bit of thyme.

Huh, so that's what these green bits are.

Addy, that sounds serious.

Yeah, I feel bad, but also, he's an entitled little shit. He'll be fine, though, I only scared him.

Amelia didn't know what to say, she couldn't even imagine the world that Addy lived in.

They were sisters, but in some ways it seemed as if they were alien species meeting for the first time, just struggling to discover the other's secret ways of communication.

When August and Taylortoo came down, Addy and Amelia were shoveling forkfuls of scrambled eggs into their mouths, eating in silence.

So, said August, what-all needs to be done today?

What do you mean?

I mean, like the obituary, do we have a date and a time and a place for the service? We probably need to make a video or something, with pictures, and music, to honor her life. Do we know if she had a will?

August helped himself to the last of the scrambled eggs and put a slice of bread in the toaster. Taylortoo looked confusedly at the food and stood awkwardly in the corner of the kitchen, gazing out the window.

All business, aren't you, said Addy.

Ameila wasn't sure, but thought Addy was throwing shade at August.

I wrote something last night, said Amelia. An obituary. We can figure out all the details today, the three of us. I can call a few of the funeral homes in town, and find a pastor. If you and Addy wanted to be in charge of making a video. I know there are a bunch of old pictures in one of these boxes, you could scan them. And I'm not sure what music she'd want played. I know she loved Laura Marling. But it's up to you, pick something she'd like.

We can do that, said Addy, nodding at August. What about a will?

She did have one, said Amelia. There is an executor coming by the house tomorrow to show it to us.

Is there anything else we have to sort out? asked August.

I don't think so, said Amelia. I think that's pretty much it. She wants to be buried; she has a lot next to Harold in Riverside Cemetery.

Seems like you're on top of things, sis.

I'm not. I don't really know what I'm doing. I've never had to do this, so I need both of your help.

I just don't understand how this could have happened, said August. I thought she was in good health—I mean, I know she had some minor problems, but I thought for the most part she was healthy.

I did too, said Amelia. She was—I think she was. It happened so suddenly. By the time I got to her it was too late.

Amelia's eyes welled with tears when she thought back to the moment. She and her mother had their problems, their battles, their bickering, but there was love there, and when she thought that she had not done enough to prevent her mother's death, had not looked out for her well-being enough in the recent months, that maybe there were signs and she was just too busy, too absorbed in her own life to see them, it made her feel guilty.

Addy and August continued to scarf their eggs and crunch their buttered toast. They didn't seem sad. They didn't seem to notice that she had become emotional. They seemed to be going about the morning as if it were routine. It was so odd, she thought. But she wanted to hold off judgment. People grieve in different ways, and if they couldn't quite access the immensity of their confused feelings now, surely they would later, perhaps in a few days, perhaps months, perhaps it would rush to them in waves while they were in public, or perhaps everything would be neatly bottled, sealed and private.

CHAPTER FOUR

It was already there, the guilt, lying next to him in bed when he woke. He had no idea why it had arrived, but there it was. It lingered there, pinning him beneath the tangle of covers. Jerry tossed in his own pool of sweat. Perhaps it had arrived with the dreams he'd had during the night. The color red, flashes of lightning, the Earth caving in on itself—vague apocalyptic images were all he could recall now of the nightmarish visions, as light poured through the slats of the blinds and searched the room for his wakeful soul.

It was Christmas morning. He was alone in his modest home, the two bed, one bath that he'd owned since 2010. He'd purchased it from the money StereoId had made during its tour, and from the sales of their only album, which had spent a couple weeks at the bottom of the Indie charts. He liked his home. It was enough for him. There was a spacious garage attached where he and his new band practiced. The walls were well insulated and the nearest neighbor was not so near and so Jerry could drum all hours of the night if he wanted.

But he felt so lonely this morning in that house all by himself. Santa had not brought him anything while he slept. He hadn't even bothered to decorate a tree this year. He wasn't much of a consumer of the holidays, but sometimes, as was the case on this Christmas morning, he longed for the easy, bygone traditions of his childhood.

He wished that Elena was there next to him. Life was completely different waking up next to her; she often told her husband she had to go to Charlotte, or perhaps Atlanta for conferences or conventions related to her work, when really she was sleeping on the other side of town at his place. Waking up next to her changed the landscape of time and space. The light that slid through the cracks in the windows was softer. Her eyelashes like moth wings against the back of his neck always made him shudder with joy.

But of course she had to be with her family on Christmas. He understood.

He looked forward to the day when they could be together, but wasn't sure that day would ever come.

So today what he looked forward to was working at Emily's place, and spending Christmas with her and her kids. She was kind enough to invite him. Working for a few hours on that sinkhole would occupy his mind for the better part of the day. Physical work always did that, always seemed to make the world seem clearer, calmer.

Jerry got in his truck and drove across town to Emily's. He planned on working out in the yard for a couple of hours before joining her and her family for Christmas festivities.

But the news was broken to him right when he arrived. He knocked on the door and was shocked to find that none other than Taylor Swift answered it.

Uhhh, he stammered, holy hell—do I have the wrong house?

Who is it you are looking for, Jerry Smith?

How do you—Is Emily here? This is her house, right.

You are a friend of Emily's?

Jerry saw Addy and August and Amelia in the background, hurrying straight toward the door. The two older ones looked so different. Jerry hadn't seen them since they were kids.

I'm so sorry, Taylortoo continued, but Emily has passed away.

Jerry, said Amelia, I'm sorry. I was planning on calling you once we made all the arrangements.

Jerry liked Amelia even though she'd never really liked him. He suspected that she always thought that he had been a bad influence on her father. But she had softened to him and seemed kinder whenever she saw him during the past several months because she understood how much his new friendship had meant to her mother.

Jerry couldn't comprehend the news. And he couldn't wrap his head around the fact that the news had come from one of the biggest country-pop pop-stars the world has ever seen. Had he entered the twilight zone?

He turned away from the door and sat on the front step. He dropped his head into his hands. He had just seen her yesterday. Then he began to sob when he understood that she was *gone* gone. He could have done something, he thought.

Amelia walked up behind him and put her hand on his shoulder. Are you alright, Jerry?

Jerry looked back at her three children, tears running down his ruddy cheeks. They looked composed, immune to the waves of grief he suddenly felt; it was always the immediate family members who seemed required to act the strongest in times of death.

Jerry thought about how he hadn't been there for their father the night he drowned in the Pacific, and how he'd left their mother alone yesterday, though he knew she hadn't felt well. He'd been one of the last people to see them both. Thoughts of his own toxicity rushed into his head. He was at best bad luck for their family. He was at worst responsible for their deaths. He knew that it was irrational, to take on so much responsibility, to entertain the idea that perhaps everybody he got close to was cursed, that he himself was toxic and evil, but he still allowed those thoughts to enter. And so what about Elena? She was the only person who he felt truly close to now. What would be her fate?

What happened? he asked.

Amelia told him that it was cardiac arrest, a defective heart.

Jerry kept sobbing, thinking that there was something he could have done, a different choice that he should have made.

Taylortoo put her cold hand on his other shoulder. It's okay, Jerry Smith. It isn't your fault. People have to die.

After absorbing the news, Jerry had no choice but to work. He went into the backyard and worked for several hours tearing apart the pool frame and emptying the sinkhole of debris, until sweat had pooled on his forehead and he was exhausted from a long day's work.

In the early afternoon, Amelia called to him and told him that the Christmas lasagna was ready. He went inside and sat at the table next to Emily's kids. There was bread and salad and delicious wine, and Jerry felt a bittersweet feeling rush over him. He was grateful to be there, to have good food and good company on a day that he knew from experience could also be very lonely, but Emily's absence was hard to take. He had just seen her yesterday.

As they sat to eat, readying to dig into the food, Jerry raised his glass and proposed a toast. He said a few kind words and finished with: to Emily.

CHAPTER FIVE

There was only Essie to keep Ray company on Christmas Day. His play was dark, and so he spent the entire day alone in their apartment, pacing, thinking of Addy and the future of their relationship.

He and Addy had always been in agreement that they never wanted to get married. It was an old, outdated institution, they thought. There was the issue of property being given from the bride's father to the husband, the dowries. There was the giving up of a last name, sacrificing a literal piece of your own identity. Wasn't it rooted in control and hierarchy?

They didn't buy into the whole ritual. No, they were in the modern camp who believed that if they loved each other, as long as they wanted to be together, then that was enough. Addy was never one of those girls that had spent her entire life fantasizing about the perfect wedding day. She never gave it a moment's thought. She'd told Ray how silly it seemed to her, to fantasize about something that would take up such little time in the span of an entire life. As if a single, beautiful day might make the rest of the struggle of marriage, the sacrificing of one's self, worth it. It made no sense to her.

Ray thought about it now, as he exited their apartment with Essie, the two of them going on their evening walk around the village.

He had always thought the same, and had never wanted for such a formal and public *union* to occur. It had no bearing on the love they had for each other, did it?

He guided Essie down the dark, cobblestone streets, as she sniffed at the bushes and the bases of the trees that edged the sidewalks.

He couldn't believe that she had just left him like that, that she hadn't wanted him there by her side. He was hurt, and he didn't know if their relationship could survive it.

He had always supported her ambitions, her career. He had always wanted her to grow as her own person, but now she had grown so far away from him. And as far as he knew, Los Angeles was still up in the air. She could be gone for months.

After twelve years together, he knew that they were at a crossroads. He was never one for ultimatums, but there only seemed to be two options that came to his mind. It was a pivotal moment, and the truth struck him that the only possible paths forward were marriage or a breakup. For a person who didn't believe in marriage, seeing only these two options, with nothing in-between, was surprising to him. But it also seemed so clear. They had to have a greater *union* with each other. It was the only way. They had always lived as individuals, together, but in order for the relationship to continue, to grow, they would need to live together, as individuals. He had always been wary of belonging. True freedom can only come from an independence of thought, he believed, an unbinding of the spirit and the soul. But he knew without a doubt that he needed her to belong to him, and he needed to belong to her if there was to be a future for them.

CHAPTER SIX

What did the future hold for their home? Amelia thought that the executor would be coming by to share the will with them today, but, instead, the contents of her mother's will arrived in the mail that morning, the day after Christmas.

She and Addy and August and Taylortoo gathered around the living room and opened the envelope.

Amelia didn't know what to expect. The only things her mother had to her name were the house and her old Honda that rested and rusted in the driveway. Amelia assumed that they would both be left to her. Her siblings didn't need anything from the will, and they both lived a thousand miles away. Being left with this house, she thought, was a bittersweet thing. It was where she'd grown up, where she'd lived most of her life. There were some happy memories there. But she no longer wanted it, or anything in it, and it would be a lot of work to clean out and fix up and sell.

Which was why when they read the will out loud, she wasn't angry. She didn't know how to feel.

It was anticlimactic, the reading of the will. Everything had been left to August. Of course it had, thought Amelia. He'd always been her favorite, her only son. And he had money. He knew what to do with money, and property. She was surprised because she'd assumed that it would be hers, but once it was read out loud it made complete sense to her. But she was a little pissed that she couldn't use the money from selling the place and put it toward her own home.

Well, I certainly wasn't expecting that, said August. Why would she leave it to me?

Because she loved you the most.

She did not.

Did too.

We fought all the time.

That doesn't mean she didn't love you most, said Addy.

That was part of her love language, arguing.

Will we live here now? asked Taylortoo.

Umm, no, said August, definitely not. No offense, Amelia.

None taken, I wouldn't want either of you to live here.

But of course you'll keep living here, he said. I have no interest in selling it or doing anything with it any time soon. And of course we'd split it three ways, not that I think we'd be able to get much for it anyway. Isn't a great location. And in this market. But the house is practically yours, you can do with it whatever you want—to tell you the truth I just assumed she would leave it to you.

I thought so too. But I've considered getting my own place, closer to campus. I think maybe we should sell it. We have a couple days before the funeral, we're all here now, we could sort through some of the clutter and get rid of things. I forgot to ask both of you, how long do you plan on staying?

I have to leave the day after her funeral—the 29th. I have an important business meeting down in Georgia.

I was thinking of staying a while, said Addy. Maybe a couple of weeks. Or longer?

Really? said Amelia. Addy hadn't been in this house for more than two days in over ten years. Her entire life was in New York. But Amelia was excited that they might have more time to reconnect.

I think it might be good for me. I blew my chance to go to L.A. and I don't feel at home anymore in New York; I'm not sure if Ray and I are going to make it, I think we've just grown apart.

Oh, Addy, I'm sorry, said Amelia. But of course I'd love for you to stay.

After reading the will, they went into the kitchen and had leftover lasagna for lunch. As they were eating, Jerry pulled into the driveway, ready to do more work on the sinkhole.

Addy and August weren't interested in helping, but Amelia felt like she wanted to get out and do something. If she was honest with herself, the fact that her mother had left everything to August irritated her a bit more than she would admit, and whenever she was irritated, she liked to keep busy with any kind of physical activity, or to get out in nature. It soothed her.

She and Jerry worked side by side for a couple of hours, removing the final pieces of the pool's frame, hauling off the last boards of cedar, until the hole was completely clear of debris.

Good work, said Amelia. We appreciate all your help. I know my mom did.

Ah, don't mention it. It's good to keep busy. I don't mind the work. The fun part will be filling it in. Do you know what you want to do with it?

No idea. I know my mom always talked about a garden. But I've never been much of a gardener.

You know, I think it's a great idea. There's plenty of space for one. I'd be happy to help build it, free of charge, just as long as I can take home a few tomatoes, or some cucumbers, once things start growing.

Of course. I just don't know how I'll be able to tend to it. I've been a lot busier lately at the University.

Don't worry about it. I can help out. And this gal I've been seeing, she's been talking to me about getting a garden, only there isn't a lot of space for one around my house.

Well, Jerry, I won't object. If you're willing to do it, I think a garden could be wonderful.

But Amelia wasn't really that excited about the prospect of a garden. The house wasn't hers anyway, and it just seemed like more responsibility. She was looking forward to leasing a townhome or a condo, something low maintenance—just a space to eat and sleep—so that she could focus more of her energy on what she truly cared about, which, right now, was her work.

CHAPTER SEVEN

While Amelia and Jerry worked outside, Addy and August and Taylortoo were in the house, sifting through some of the clutter, opening the cardboard boxes in the living room and deciding what should be kept and what should be thrown out.

Taylortoo held up some baby clothes and bibs. Aw, how precious, she said.

Toss, said Addy. Goodwill pile. I don't think that any of us are having kids any time soon.

The box filled with old school projects and papers and report cards reflected the unrealistic levels of success the three of them had managed in adulthood; all A's, aside from the few B's and C's that Addy had gotten her sophomore year because she hated school and was longing to leave Asheville.

We should have a fire tomorrow, after the funeral, said August. Remember, at the old house, we used to build bonfires down by the forest before we moved.

We did that like once, said Addy. Dad always hated the outdoors.

We could get rid of a lot of these papers that way.

And I don't blame him, so do I.

It could be fun, though.

Yeah, maybe.

Addy returned to digging through a box of old electronics. There was a broken DVD player, an Xbox, a GameCube, and at the bottom of the box was her old plastic Karaoke machine that she got one Christmas, with its microphone attached. She used to love singing show tunes into that microphone, or reciting Shakespearean monologues into her vanity.

All of a sudden, while digging through another box, Addy's phone vibrated. It was Trent Pendleton. She went outside to take the call.

Hello, she said.

Addy, darling! said Trent.

Yes. What do you want?

My dear, I'm calling because I heard through a mutual friend of ours about what happened to your mother.

Okay.

Well, first I'd like to say that I'm sorry. I can only imagine.

Well, thank you.

And secondly—now this may surprise you, but I do place some stock in divine providence—do you believe in fate, Addy?

Not really, no.

Well I for one can't understand how people can live without acknowledging it, without using it! It is such a convenient tool to build meaning around our own stories.

What is this about, Trent. I'm with my family.

My dear, I'm thinking that I misjudged you. To tell you the truth we had our eye on somebody else for this leading role, but she dropped out. And I wasn't sure that you'd had enough firsthand knowledge of what this character is going through—she too is on a trip home, to care for a dying father. Maybe it was wrong of me, but I didn't know if you'd known the right mixture of silent heartache and the deep, unvoiced feeling of being lost that is needed to carry this film the way that I'm envisioning, but now! Well, now sometimes art mirrors life and vice versa. You're a star, Addy, a bundle of raw energy on the stage, but I didn't know if you could play this quiet, confused woman; now it appears that fate is directing me toward you, telling me that you can, so to get to the point I'd like to offer you the role. Would you like the part?

Addy didn't know what to say, she'd fantasized about an opportunity like this, the next step in her career, for the past several months. But there was so much going on here. She had been entertaining the idea of staying here for a couple weeks; the quiet respite from the city was something that she hadn't known she'd needed. Plus there was the whole thing with Ray in New York, what would she tell him, shouldn't she take his input into consideration?

I don't know—can I think about it, Trent?

You cannot. This is very last minute. Lana dropping out was completely out of the blue. We're to begin shooting next week, and I would need you in L.A. next week. I need an answer now. If you pass, we're going to reach out to our third choice; we're in a tough spot and we need to get this squared away. My father is on my ass about this.

Your father?

So, what's it going to be?

Addy thought about it, but there was really nothing to think about.

Yes, she said, I want the role.

CHAPTER EIGHT

She hadn't even wanted the house in the first place, but she assumed that it would be hers. What business did her mother have leaving it to August? Like he needed it. Like he needed anything else in this world.

But he was the only son, her beautiful boy. And so all of it was left to him, complete with the new sinkhole and everything. He said of course, Amelia could go on living there, it was her house, her home, for all intents and purposes. It was only his in name.

But Amelia didn't think she wanted to go on living there. Maybe she would get her own apartment downtown, closer to the University. Something simple, a one bedroom, a fresh start. She didn't want to have to sort through everything in that house, to figure out what to keep and what to toss. She didn't want to have to deal with all of the necessary repairs that would be required to get the house into a good enough condition so that it could sell on the market.

She was glad it belonged to August now. It was his responsibility, and she was free of it.

And wasn't that what she truly wanted, to be free? And not just from the weight of the old house, crumbling, sinking in its foundation, but in a broader, spiritual sense. When she thought of the work that she'd been pursuing the past few weeks, something like freedom swelled deep within her. All she thought about was work. She only thought of the cave. She realized that for the first time since she'd transitioned into her role as professor, she felt a kind of boundless, joyous freedom that she hadn't felt since she'd been a student. It was as if the renewed purpose in her work, in her career, had allowed her to recapture a slice of her youth.

That was where true freedom resided, she felt, in those dark, magic spaces. True freedom beckoned beneath the gleaming lights.

The day was hers, and so she was allowing herself to fall into the freedom, to forget about the duty of family, of their shared history. She planned to spend the day fighting for those magic spaces, using the full weight of her voice, giving everything to her newfound purpose.

Bobby had called her yesterday with an idea to stage a protest at the Capitol building in Raleigh, and she said *of course I'll be there.*

Her mother's funeral was tomorrow, but everything was in order. There was nothing left to do for the service. She'd spent Christmas and the following day with Addy and August and they were strangers to her. There were moments of connection, sibling-bonding, but for the most part they all felt like foreign islands to one another. So while they sat in that house, passing the time sorting through their old childhood relics and absorbed in their own work that had long ago drawn them far away from Asheville, Amelia would be holding her sign high and proud in the air with the goal of getting somebody's attention at the Capitol, somebody who might have the power to halt the construction of the pipeline expansion.

She sat out on the front step and waited for Elena to pick her up. It was early. The birds chirped as the sun crested the horizon. She and Elena and Bobby were driving there together, and there were at least two dozen more students from Bobby's club who were joining them. Elena had also posted something about the glow-worms, their conservation efforts, and today's protest on her social media, so there could potentially be a lot more people. Amelia was hoping for at least a hundred. If they could get at least a hundred today, then maybe the protest could gain some traction, get some media attention, and then who knows, sometimes things like this snowball quickly.

Elena pulled up in her electric Kia Soul. Morning, she said. So, are we picking up your boyfriend next?

Quit, said Amelia. It isn't like that. She threw her sign, which read STOP PIPELINE EXPANSION, IT DESTROYS HOMES! in the trunk, then sat in the passenger's seat.

Don't worry, said Elena. I'm not going to tell the department head or anything. I can keep a secret. Honestly, good for you.

Well, to tell you the truth, I think something did happen between us the other day.

I knew it would. I see how you two look at each other.

But I don't know what to do. I know I shouldn't.

Amelia, he's hot. He's smart. He's passionate. He isn't in your class anymore. I think it's fine. You have my blessing.

Oh, well as long as we have your blessing.

The rules are meant to be bent. Just tell him not to take your courses anymore so there's no conflict of interest, and then you two can get together, no problem.

It is a problem, though. I feel so guilty thinking about it—I mean, he's ten years younger.

You worry too much. You're too hard on yourself. You have to let yourself live a little. Do you like him?

I think so—I mean, I'm attracted, yes. But he's immature, isn't he.

He's a college boy, aren't they all? But I think he's got his head on straight—more than most.

Maybe I should just re-download a bunch of dating apps, find someone my own age.

Maybe you definitely shouldn't.

No?

No. Terrible idea. What, you're going to meet some beige accountant and go on a series of beige dates, and decide that he's nice enough, and then you'll just settle and find yourself married and miserable in a beige house in a few years?

Geez, that's bleak. I wasn't thinking that far ahead at all.

Maybe I'm speaking from experience. Look, Bobby is exciting, and you have no idea yet what it could be. But I think you at least owe it to yourself to see. You know?

They arrived at Bobby's parent's house to pick him up. He hadn't gone through with his own holiday protest, the self-imposed isolation from family that he'd considered. He'd reconciled with them before Christmas Day, though he told Amelia that there was still a lot of tension in the air, that he harbored a lot of resentment toward his father and wanted to find a way to become completely independent and free of the reach of his parents.

The drive was awkward, full of long silences. The radio vomited pop hits at low volume while Elena tried to make small talk and delivered monologues—most were about her children, but some entirely random, like the five minutes she spent talking about the Nixon administration out of nowhere.

Then, after a few hours of this, they arrived at the State Capitol in Raleigh.

They were the first ones there, but, soon after, other young REC members arrived, along with some old colleagues and friends of Elena's who were staunch eco-activists. By ten o'clock the group had bloomed to nearly fifty. They gathered in front of the steps beneath the immense granite building, holding up their signs and shouting from the open plaza that housed two decorative fountains.

They chanted as a group, carrying their voices up toward the windows where the high ranking officials sat behind their desks.

By noon, two media crews had arrived to document the protest, which Amelia felt made the entire thing a success. That was what they'd wanted, to get some coverage, to reach a broader audience in order to inform the public about the injustices that were to happen in the mountains and the forests of their state.

Elena was the best speaker and most confident so she got in front of the cameras and summoned her righteousness to condemn the pipeline expansion.

Amelia watched her, inspired, proud, but still a deep hopelessness settled in her soul. She knew that their demonstration would not be enough to make the waves necessary for change. Their protests were not like the Black Lives Matter protests from a decade ago, when long-held tensions reached a critical mass and had demanded that every person fight for what was right, in order for true change to happen, for meaningful reformation to occur at a systemic level.

Those had been the inevitable results of a nation that for centuries had refused to acknowledge its own grisly history, sweeping oppression under several different rugs of governmental structure. Those protests had been essential and had demanded the nation's consciousness on a national—on a global scale.

But what Amelia and the rest of them were fighting for today, the newly discovered cave, their rare new species, it had no known history, no longstanding thread of conflict. The species had always been there, shining, for perhaps millions of years, before man ever even stood upright, but, at the same time, it was new. We knew nothing of it and had been blind to its entire existence before now.

And as they all shouted toward the granite facade, Amelia knew, instinctively, that their voices were not loud enough. Nobody from the Capitol came out to address their protest. The police were not called. Their gathering was paltry and all they had to show for it was two minutes on the local news. Amelia felt that the group would not gain in number either, that nobody truly cared enough to upend their own lives to fight for the disruption of a billion dollar, government sponsored and supported project. There was too much money to be made, too much energy needed to be moved and burnt from this new expansion.

This realization brought with it the sharp edge of sadness. She found that she cared about them fiercely, much more than she thought she ever could despite only knowing of their existence for weeks. And as she and the rest of the group chanted up toward the State Capitol, their voices combining, amplifying, the sadness came from the fact that no matter how loud their voices were that day, the loudest sound of all was the silence from the rest of the world.

CHAPTER NINE

The next day was their mother's funeral. It was a beautiful ceremony, but exhausting for Amelia. It was difficult for her to interact with so many people, especially so many new faces, in such a short time span. But everyone had been kind and sympathetic and had shared stories of her mother that she'd never heard before.

After the funeral ended, Amelia returned to the house with her siblings. It was late in the afternoon, and the sun was just beginning to disappear behind the mountains.

The house was littered with everything her mother had stockpiled over the years. They weaved through the clutter in the living room and went into the backyard.

Tea? Amelia asked. Addy and August nodded, *thank you.* She looked to Taylortoo as if expecting a response before remembering that Taylortoo couldn't have tea.

She brought out three cups with the strings from the teabags swinging pendulum-like over the edges. The four of them sat around an iron patio table on a small paved square, with an awning overhead that attached to the back of the house. All of their chairs angled away from the house and looked at the chasm where the pool had once been. There was still some pool and deck debris buried in the dirt, but Jerry had managed to haul most of it away so now it was just the sinkhole, the empty space in the Earth that had suddenly swallowed the shaky land—the dirt and roots and dead grass and topsoil—and everything that had been built atop it.

How long has that been there? asked Addy.

It's new, said Amelia.

Quite an eyesore isn't it, said August.

I think it looks great, said Amelia.

Right, said August. You know, I was talking to Jerry Smith after the service, and he said he'd like to fill the whole thing in and could even turn it into a garden if you were interested in going that route.

I'm not.

Well, if you were, he seemed eager to help. I didn't know that he and Mom had gotten close the past few years.

There was a long silence as they all looked past the pool ruins and into the dark forest and the river beyond it. It was a chilly winter afternoon; the clouds had crept in and blocked out the sun. It was a crisp, dry cold, and something in the air—the scent of the trees perhaps—gave Amelia the feeling that there could be snow.

Time passed, an indiscernible amount, could have been minutes, an hour, two, while Amelia drank her tea and watched the fallen leaves skip in and out of the forest.

August had built a small fire now at the edge of the forest, and the four of them migrated from the patio and were now sitting around the fire. They switched out their cups of tea for glasses of whiskey.

Addy was talking to August and Taylortoo. She seemed fascinated with Taylortoo and her vast intelligence, her uncanny mannerisms that often seemed indistinguishable from human action, but other times made her artifice farcically pronounced. But Amelia didn't register much of what they were talking about.

She was too busy watching the leaves twist through the air in perfect helices or random start and stop actions, two jumps forward and one back into the forest. Then, before she knew it, the light had dipped far below the horizon and the sky was dark violet, the clouds were violent, and snowflakes began to drift through the open sky. The white dust of them settled into the soil. Many disappeared into the great cavity that had swallowed the yard.

Addy abruptly set her cup down and the whiskey sloshed against the sides of the glass.

I don't know, August, said Addy. I blew it with the production I was doing in New York. I just left them with no notice. I feel bad about it.

I'm sure they understood, said Taylortoo. It was a family emergency after all.

You're sweet. I felt my time had run its course playing Sally anyway. And I thought I'd blown my shot at Hollywood, but now the director wants me for his movie, so I'm flying to L.A. early tomorrow.

You aren't staying anymore? asked Amelia.

I can't, I have to go.

Amelia was sad that the two of them wouldn't get to spend more time together, but she understood. Addy was always rushing off toward the next thing, that is the way it had always been.

Well, we're all so proud of you, Addy, I'm sure you'll be great, said Amelia. What about you, August? You're leaving tomorrow too?

Yes, we have to be in Georgia by nine for a meeting.

What kind of meeting? Amelia asked.

Oh, it's nothing, August insisted. I'm just considering providing our AI to another company for them to use.

So, what is it for? asked Addy. What company?

Well, if you must know, it's an oil company. They're expanding a pipeline and want to save on labor by putting our AI into their machines.

Amelia's eyes flashed red. The conversation had her attention now.

An oil company? she said. Are you fucking serious, August? I thought you were for clean energy.

I am, he said.

But yet—

I am, but we already have the AI and it would be a huge deal for us. I'd be able to reinvest the money into my other projects.

He sounded like such a hypocrite. Amelia glared at him.

I know, he continued, I know. Look, I hate oil as much as you. For decades we've been saying how we have to stop burning it, and still the world relies on it more than ever. I'm not exactly proud of it, Amelia, but if I didn't say yes, they'd just partner with some other company—maybe they'd have to pay more for Amazon or Google, but they'd manage to get their machines and build what they're building either way.

What a fucking hypocrite, she thought. He had all of this power; his voice would speak volumes were he to turn down whatever ungodly amount they were giving him, if he were to make his business decisions on the foundation of principle and not profit, and still he was no better than the generations of industrious men who had preceded him. She couldn't look at his disgusting face. But she didn't want to get into a big fight today, the day of their mother's funeral, the last night they would be together.

What's the company? she asked.

Colonial Pipeline. Have you heard of them?

I know all about their pipeline! she said, letting herself get worked up now. They're building right through Asheville. They're going to destroy the forest where I've been doing research every single day for the past two weeks! Their pipeline will displace hundreds of species, destroy their homes—their homes, August! And do you care, like, do you care at all?

Amelia, I'm sorry. I do—I do care—but I'm not the one actually build—

Oh, bullshit!

—there's only so much I can do.

You're just going to keep doing whatever *you* want—creating your sex robots and your spaceships—while disregarding everything else.

Amelia had gestured to Taylortoo when she'd said sex robots, and now Taylortoo's head hung in what appeared to be shame.

Don't say that about Taylortoo, said August, holding her hand, as light snow floated through the air around them. She has feelings, you know, and you're being cruel.

Does she? Does she have *feelings*, August?

Yes! And you have no experience with True Partners; you have no idea, so you can't talk.

Amelia shook her head, trying to calm her newfound rage.

They're so much more than whatever you think, August continued. She has her own feelings, her own thoughts, Amelia. She can make her own decisions—and you clearly hurt her feelings! Are you even aware of how derogatory that term—the r word—has become in her community?

She can make her own decisions? Then why is she following you around everywhere? Why can't she stay here a couple of days if she wants?

August and Amelia were arguing back and forth across Taylortoo, who sat between them. Amelia thought that she looked on the verge of tears—if that was possible—as they both looked at her expectantly, as if she were a child needing to choose which parent to crawl toward.

Well, fine! he said. She can—I don't care! Is that what you want, Taylortoo? Do you really want to stay here in Carolina?

Taylortoo looked like a deer in the headlights. I don't know, August, she said, staring into her lap.

Amelia suddenly felt bad for her, stuck there, pulled in so many directions. She didn't want this to be how they spent their final night together, arguing senselessly. So she softened her stance and reverted to the role of peacemaker, of which she was most familiar.

I'm sorry, she said. Does anybody need more whiskey? she asked, standing up from her chair, then walking away toward the house.

When she returned, she was carrying a cardboard box from the living room's clutter that was filled with old paper, report cards and bills and old school projects. She read through a few and then gently placed them in the fire.

It was night now, dark and cold, and she could hear the river whistling beyond the forest. She remembered a time when she was a child—third or fourth grade, before they moved—and it was fall, and they'd all gone down by the river and made a huge bonfire at the edge of the forest. Addy and August wrestled and played tag around the flames as her father gathered firewood and she sat on their mother's lap at the edge of the pit.

The four of them sat there silently at the edge of the fire, while the old papers burned.

The fire doesn't lie. It speaks true as the embers peel from the wood and shed from its kindling and release high up into the sky. It says let me warm you through the night. It says I can banish the darkness if you tend to me. It promises to hold you safe there, in the open expanse. It can make good on its promises if only you know, if you understand, that you are not the fire. If you remember that you are separate from its special powers. If you get too close, thinking that you are one with it, then it will consume you.

Amelia watched its majesty consume stacks of old notebooks and letters, releasing the incinerated bits of paper up into the night.

It was an illusion of control that they had there, she thought. Every flicker of human ego and arrogance can be witnessed in our relationships to fire. We are above everything, have raised ourselves on a pedestal above all creatures because we believed that we could tame it, could keep the fire contained within a man-made pit. And perhaps sometimes, for a short time, we can. But fire is one of the most powerful wonders of this world. If it so wished it could find magic ways to burn to ash every structure that we create. In time, without saying a word, it could reveal to us just how much more powerful it is. It struck Amelia that the most powerful things on Earth don't need to say anything. The most powerful, most enduring things are silent. If it is power that you're searching for, then there needs to be such a deep feeling of connection with nature, so that language is meaningless, transcended. The oceans, the trees, the mountains—there is no need for language. They have already achieved a power that is unimpeachable.

Amelia threw in another stack of old papers. The fire took the burnt pieces up toward the stars, which were now out and shining brilliant in the night sky.

Let's get some music going, said Addy. Mom would have wanted some music.

Addy brought out another box and took out the old iHome. She connected an old iPod Classic, whose charger had surprisingly still worked. She found a song and pressed play.

The music filled the space, drifting over the fire and through the trees and down to the stream that trickled beyond them in the distance. It was the only radio hit of their father's band, StereoId. They had been remembered all these years later as a one hit wonder. The familiar chords that their father once discovered just beyond the forest near the river now resonated around the campfire, a beautiful melody, as scraps of their childhood memories burned.

Something about hearing this song, which she hadn't listened to in many years, made Amelia angry. She suddenly couldn't stand being there. She wanted to be alone, or—no—she longed to be with Bobby at the site of the cave. Everything about that old house was false to her. It had never been a home. And her siblings seemed like nothing but hired actors to her now. It wasn't just the papers that she wished would burn, she wanted all of it to burn. They should incinerate everything contained in the boxes in the house.

She stared at the fire, marveling at its power.

What did it mean, she thought now, that her father had drowned himself? Was there too much fire in him, too much ego, too much burning chaos, so that he had felt the only option was to turn to the water—the only force of comparable power—to extinguish it?

Then, suddenly, she walked over to Addy, picked up the iHome and threw it in the fire.

Amelia, what the hell!

I can't stand that song! she screamed.

Daddy only ever cared about himself, she thought. And you could run to California with your kite in the sky to impress him, but you'll be flying that kite forever, for the eyes of nobody.

Amelia, why'd you do that? asked August.

Because. We need to get rid of this stuff. I'm going to see what else we can burn.

Amelia ran inside and began tearing through the boxes. Addy and August were right behind her, no doubt concerned with her outburst, but she had already spilled all of the contents of one box on the floor by the time they reached her.

It was a bunch of miscellaneous things. There was the empty case to August's *MarioKart* game, her microscope starter kit, a broken old Furby, a striped parasol, a kite, a mason jar with a dead firefly inside, and, at the very bottom, a pink and orange shell from a forgotten vacation to the beach.

Amelia began to sob.

Hey, hey, what's wrong? Addy asked, placing her hand on Amelia's shoulder.

They're both gone, Addy. What are we supposed to do now?

Addy hugged her tight.

It's okay, Amelia. I'm sorry. I know you two were close. I always wished I had been better. A better daughter, a better sister.

Amelia didn't know what to say. She loved her sister, but they had been strangers for the past decade. And this was their final night together. Tomorrow August and Addy would have to leave early for their flights, and Amelia had no clue when she might see them again—*if* she'd see them again.

She suddenly felt so drained of all energy. And she was a little drunk. She looked down at the contents of the empty box, strewn across the floor. What was the point of it all? What did it matter if it was burnt to ashes in the fire, or kept locked away in the basement for twenty more years? What did any of it matter? She didn't know what she was supposed to do, didn't know the right choices anymore for her life.

I'm tired, she said.

Then you should get...some sleep, said Taylortoo. Sleep is very important.

Addy rubbed her shoulders. You should, Amelia, she said. Get some good sleep. It's been a long day.

Amelia nodded and looked up toward the lights that shined from the ceiling.

I'm sorry, she said. I don't know what came over me. But this was not completely true. She did have an idea of what had come over her. Nothing made any sense. The past and the future made no sense to her anymore, and that is plenty to bring anybody to despair, to the edges of mania.

The only way forward was to fight for something. The only way to make a meaningful life, she felt, was to surrender her own brokenness over to a larger cause. She only wanted to protect the glow-worms, to keep the pipeline from being built, but that too was hopeless.

Addy's hand on her shoulder helped soothe her some, but it didn't solve anything. She couldn't voice any of this, her siblings wouldn't understand, would they? All she could think to do was either cry or scream.

I'm sorry, Addy, she said.

It's okay. You're grieving. We all have to grieve in our own ways.

I'm sorry.

It's okay. Here, let's get you upstairs to bed.

Addy helped her up, the old childhood relics still messy upon the wood floor.

You'll both probably be gone in the morning, said Amelia, when I wake up. If I don't see you, it was really nice that you were here. And I love you.

She hugged the three of them, Taylortoo included. August, she said, I want you to really consider doing business with them. You can make a change. Stand for something. Do the right thing.

August nodded slowly and closed his eyes for a moment as if he were grappling with the ethics of it in his own mind.

I will, he said.

Amelia and Addy walked upstairs to her bedroom, and Amelia threw herself limply upon the sheets.

Goodnight, said Addy.

Goodnight, Addy. I love you. Good luck in Hollywood.

CHAPTER TEN

The next morning, August and Taylortoo left early in his private plane for Alpharetta, Georgia, where the Colonial Pipeline headquarters was located.

When he arrived there was a boardroom of executives waiting for him. The mustachioed man in the center he knew to be P.P. Paulsen, the CEO.

Mr. Wheeler, said Paulsen. So glad you could make it.

August shook the man's hand, which was rough and firm in its grip.

We've put together a little presentation for you, Paulsen continued.

Then August proceeded to listen to a lengthy presentation about their hopes for the new pipeline project, the design plans for the AI trenchers, and some of the budgetary information.

Well, what do you think? asked Paulsen when the presentation was finished.

Mr. Paulsen, I've got to be honest with you, you know I'm not a fan of oil—all of my companies endorse clean energy.

There is no such thing as clean energy, said Paulsen. Everything is from the Earth.

Maybe so, but there are other ways that aren't threatening the atmosphere. You all know we can't continue to get our energy from beneath the surface, we can't keep burning fuel unless we're trying to destroy our own civilizations.

That is all so dramatic, said Paulsen. Oil is responsible for the modern world. All of our comforts, our conveniences, oil is to thank.

But it will also be responsible for our demise unless we're willing to look elsewhere, unless we learn to embrace change and seek innovation.

Did you come here to argue? Or did you come here to make a deal? You know we are a pipeline company, right? Getting into it over our ethical differences is pretty much a moot point.

I came to hear the offer and see what you had in mind, but I don't know if this deal is right for us or not.

Then let us show you the machines. Trencor brought a couple of their trenchers. They're in the warehouse.

When they got to the warehouse, August took a look at the machines. They were brand new, top-of-the-line, and already had some automated functionality. It wouldn't be difficult to integrate his software into them. In fact, the machines already had a built in hard drive, so it could be as simple as uploading his True Partners AI. The deal was a no-brainer, financially, but something was stopping him from committing.

Well, what do you say? asked Paulsen. Deals like this don't come along everyday. Don't you want to be a part of this project?

Paulsen showed him the contract. All you've got to do is sign, he said.

I can't sign anything today, said August. I'll have to have our lawyers take a look at this. But, Mr. Paulsen, if I can be honest with you, I don't think it is going to work for us.

Paulsen looked at him calmly, a businessman who has seen a lot of things in business, including people turning down billion dollar projects. Well, I understand, he said. I respect it. Sometimes, you've got to stand up for what you believe is right. I don't agree with you, but I respect it. Just know, Mr. Wheeler, this offer won't stay on the table if you turn us down today. We're planning on moving ahead to our second choice, who has already expressed some interest in partnering with us for this.

I understand.

The two men exited the warehouse together and made their way back toward the boardroom. They walked down a long, windowed corridor, and August watched the snowflakes stick to the glass and trickle down in individual streams.

I'm sorry, said August. I just don't believe in it. I don't believe it's right.

August thought about his words. They were impulsive. He was outright rejecting the partnership. Usually he would wait, hedge his bets, have his lawyers thoroughly scour the fine print, but something had compelled him to act with his conscience that morning.

I wish you the best of luck, he said, then gathered his things from the boardroom, exited the building, and made his way back to Taylortoo and his private plane, ready for their flight back home.

CHAPTER ELEVEN

Amelia woke up late the next day, hungover from the whiskey she had the night before. Both Addy and August were already gone and the house was silent.

She rolled out of her covers and checked her phone, where she found a lengthy email from Bobby Studebaker. The email was a passionate, righteous, manic diatribe, a Bobby stream-of-consciousness, in which he raged against the government and their support of the pipeline expansion, argued the need for activists to take more radical action, and then confessed his *feelings* for her. She didn't know what to think of the letter he'd written.

She read it over and over in bed. He had linked to a press article about the Colonial Pipeline Company, in which an executive stated that their goal was to break ground on the project in January of 2030. Bobby then urged Amelia to support him and the REC's desire for further protests in Washington D.C. and to use social media to inform the public about the glow-worms and their potential extinction.

Amelia thought that more protests was a good idea, and any attempt at making the public more aware of the pipeline's destruction was good, but what she couldn't stop focusing on in the letter was the part about the *feelings.*

I know you probably think I'm too young and immature, he'd said at one point, *but I feel like maybe there is something between us, and I don't know if it is just me, or if you feel a spark too?*

She did feel a spark. If she was honest with herself she did. But what could really happen with him? She was held back by her ethical responsibilities as a professor.

But she wanted to see him. She wrote him back, not addressing the feelings, but sticking to the prospect of more protests. At the end of her email she included her personal cell phone number so that they could communicate more about future protests.

He messaged her within an hour that morning, as she was eating breakfast, suggesting that they meet up to talk about it. So, she invited him over to her house.

After he arrived, she made some tea for the two of them and they sat out on the patio talking about the possibility of organizing a protest in D.C.

Bobby quickly became animated and enraged at the entire situation, the fact that in just a couple months the species she'd found would be made extinct.

It's complete bullshit! Something needs to be done! We, as a country, as individuals, can't allow the world to go on like this.

After a while of talking about their plans, Amelia asked him about his father and his home life, and they shared with each other their own versions of childhood.

They talked into the afternoon until the light dimmed beyond the forest and the temperature dropped. She looked into his eyes across the table and realized how much she wanted him. She'd never fallen in love. At thirty, there had been a couple of guys in college, and one girl in grad school, but they'd all been casual, brief flings. With Bobby, there was an energy between them, they connected on a different level, and she could imagine herself really falling for him. It scared her, this idea of losing control over to something greater.

This was the part where one thing lead to another and they ended up sleeping together.

Now they were in her bed, limbs swirled together, a woven tapestry.

Amelia wanted silence, for them to just lie there together in the quiet hum of night. But Bobby would not stop talking about the future, and about his activist plans. He was manic, animated, and saying some rather scary things.

All I'm saying, he said, is that sometimes in order for the course of history to change, radical action has to happen, and sometimes it is violent.

I don't think it has to come to that, she said.

Don't you want a revolution?

I want them not to build that pipeline, but I don't know about *revolution*.

What this country needs is a strong leader who's willing to gut the evil structures our nation has been built upon. The world has to change—we need to be better—and it has to happen fast or else our children and our children's children are going to feel the ramifications.

Can we just cuddle, Bobby? You're always thinking about this stuff, aren't you?

How could I not?

Even when we were having sex?

You know, people have looked at me like I'm crazy when I say this, but Hitler had the right idea in some respects. They call me an eco-fascist, but if we aren't willing to sacrifice everything for harmony with our own planet, then eventually all the destruction we're doing here is going to catch up with us.

I can't believe you said that. You know I'm part Jewish, on my father's side.

All I'm saying is Hitler was willing to do anything to protect and rebuild Germany, and we need to start thinking that way about Earth. We need leaders who are going to hold it sacred, as he held Germany sacred in the second world war, and who are willing to do whatever it takes to fix the destruction we've brought as a species. Obviously, I'm not condoning his actions, he stood for awful things, but he stood for something, and he understood how short-term atrocities might be able to bring about a long-term period of prosperity and peace. That is the kind of thinking and action we need, only instead of holding sacred imaginary borders, it has to be the physical, tangible world that we all call home.

It was New Year's Eve and Ray was taking the C uptown to spend the day with his mother. It had been a few months since he'd visited her at her place near Colombia. They would spend the afternoon together and then go up to her apartment's rooftop to watch fireworks sparkle over the Hudson. He was looking forward to seeing her. He was hoping she would have some guidance, some wisdom about Addy and their relationship.

He stepped off the train at 125th and who should he run into, right there on the platform? None other than Mrs. Chowdhury, his English teacher from the seventh grade and his first ever mentor in the arts; she'd directed the first play he ever tried out for that year, *The Music Man.* Her enthusiasm, her kindness, without her he would never have pursued the life he had today. She had been one of the most influential people in his life, and he had made sure to tell her this many times along his journey. But it had been a few years since he'd seen her; she'd attended the revival of *Rosencrantz & Guildenstern Are Dead,* the first Off-Broadway show he directed.

They recognized each other right away and embraced. She had aged gracefully into middle-age. She had immigrated here with her family from Bangladesh when she was just a teen, but must've been in her late 50's now. She often wore the traditional bright and patterned dresses common within her culture, but he remembered her sometimes adopting the dark jeans and monochrome shirts of Western culture when she taught. Today, on the platform she was wearing an intricately woven, gold and scarlet shari.

She was a small, compact woman with a tight-lipped smile, but Ray always knew that she contained multitudes. Although she was a devout Muslim, he'd never forgotten the time that she'd recited a text from a Christian theologian to him after one of their rehearsals. He'd been going through something and was angry and full of doubt and wanted to quit the play and she recited the Serenity Prayer to him: *God, grant me the serenity to accept the things I cannot change, courage to change the things I can, and wisdom to know the difference.* She had always been like that, he thought, always able to move through everything with grace, able to hold so much at once, to carry both Eastern and Western conflict, history, teachings within herself, receptive to truth in whatever form it might come in.

Look who it is, she said. Ray! All grown up! How long has it been?

Too long, Mrs. C. How are you?

I'm good. Very good! And you? How are you?

Good. Good. Good, he said, convincing himself with each repetition.

He always wanted to put on a face of competency for her, to be a symbol of success. She'd told him after seeing one of his plays that she always talked about him to her students; he served as an example that her work was meaningful, that she'd inspired, connected with, and mentored a boy who now got to tell stories on the biggest stages. And he was *good*, wasn't he? If he was honest with himself, life was good. But just beneath the surface, as he smiled at his old teacher, as they reminisced about the past, he felt the edge of sadness. Addy had left, maybe for good, and there had been many moments the past few days where he felt like his life was unraveling. The plans that he'd made, the future he'd envisioned, their solid walls, their foundation cracking.

But he wouldn't think of burdening Mrs. Chowdhury with any of that. After all, it had been years since the last time he saw her, and he wouldn't want to make their interaction on the platform into anything more than it was—a brief encounter with an old friend, a pleasant surprise, a moment to slow down time within the hustle and bustle of the city.

You are still in the theater? she asked. Tell me, what are you working on right now?

He told her about *A Raisin in the Sun*. I could get you tickets, if you'd like?

Oh, no no no. You don't have to worry yourself. My husband and I don't make it over this way very often.

She and her family lived in Queens.

I am only here to visit my daughter, she said. She recently moved—a place near 129th and Clayton Powell.

Well, okay, but if you change your mind I would be happy to, Mrs. C, no problem at all. You know, you and my mother, I owe everything to you. If it weren't for you—

She blushed and looked away, uneasy at the praise. You are so sweet, Ray, but it is okay, don't bother yourself.

But Ray meant every word of it. Without her he didn't know where he might be. She'd entered his life in pivotal years, the transition from boyhood to manhood beginning, and had directed him toward something that had ignited a spark in him, introduced him to something productive that he'd been able to love and dedicate his life to.

During that confusing time of adolescence, before he had discovered the stage and the magic of play, it had started to eat at him, the common tropes, the countless young boys that he grew up with in Harlem who fell into stereotyped childhoods. Ray himself had grown up without a father, and the fact that the rest of the world had come to expect this kind of fractured upbringing in the lives of black children had filled him with such rage at that age. He remembered always questioning why he had been one of the ones who had to actually carry this stereotype around with him in his history, in his lanky, twelve year old frame. He remembered how jealous he had been of his friend Matt, whose parents had both gone to Howard, whose father was a tenured sociology professor at Columbia. Why hadn't that been him? Had it been something defective about him that had made his father not want to stay?

The story of Ray's parents was one of young, unsteady, unsure love. His father was youthful and irresponsible and scared, and had been out of the picture before Ray's mother ever had the chance to tell him that she was pregnant with Ray. His father married another woman several years after Ray was born and started his real family somewhere in Long Island, where he'd made a life for himself as an auto mechanic. But Ray, to that day, had never met him.

He'd been raised by his mother, his aunt, and his grandfather in their small apartment at the top of a six-story brownstone on 128th Street near St. Nicholas. It was a well kept old building, a post-war walk-up with a bodega directly below. It was located at the edge of St. Nicholas Park and had a beautiful rooftop view of the Hudson a few blocks to the west. It was a safe and quiet spot during his childhood. His mother had an excellent job working security at the Museum of Natural History, and Ray wanted for nothing as a boy. Every Sunday was filled with family outings to attend mass at the Abyssinian Baptist Church, followed by long, laughter-filled breakfasts at Sylvia's.

His grandfather and his aunt and his mother were always there for him, always kind and supportive and joyous, and he knew how lucky he was to have had their stability. They instilled in him the importance of faith, taught him to be strong in the face of injustice—the world would not allow you to escape it without suffering, suffering was inevitable, the cards were stacked against him, inequalities abound, but how he responded to those forces, how he handled the trials, that was what made a person's character.

Still, it is inevitable to question it all. As a young boy, it is inevitable to waver and doubt, impossible not to become seduced with temptation, to misstep many times along the path toward finding oneself. But for black boys especially, far fewer missteps are tolerated in society; if the path toward productive futures is a diving board for whites, then for young black men it is a tightrope, fragile and narrow.

And for Ray, as the teenage years approached the horizon, he had built up a bubbling anger within. It had been infuriating to know that he was yet another who would be saddled with stereotype. Fatherless. Unloved, unwanted.

He'd attended public school and so the kids he grew up with had come from every background you could imagine. He'd been well liked, sociable as a boy, and had had rich friends, poor friends, black and white friends, friends with both parents and friends with no parents. But there had been a moment, when he was twelve, where he'd begun to gravitate more toward a group of boys that his mother referred to as lowlifes. He'd tried his first cigarette with them at that age, drank his first beer, and had begun to speak of girls as objects, as potential sexual conquests, though girls at that time were still practically imaginary, mythical creatures, and the talk was all hypothetical, all repeated vulgarities that had been filched from media. His mother had demanded him to quit hanging out with a few of those boys, but that had only fueled his secrecy, and added an exciting new element to his rebellion.

When he thought back to it, that acting out, that turning a cold shoulder to his family and the faith and love they'd surrounded him with, it had been a simple fear of saying goodbye to childhood, of being unsure of what kind of man he might be capable of becoming. The world seemed to tell him everyday, on the streets or through the media, that his life was a life destined not to matter. He was fatherless, black, another number, perpetuating another stereotype, and so what future could there possibly be? It was as if he had begun to lean in toward a self-fulfilling prophecy.

But that fall his family made him become more involved at school, and his English teacher at the time, Mrs. Chowdhury, forced him to try out for the fall production that she was directing, and the rest of his life was set in motion. He'd drifted swiftly away from that group of friends, made new ones, and began to put all of his energy into reading books and plays and whatever stories he could get his hands on.

He sometimes thought back to this, his introduction to theater. It amazed him that decisions made so long ago, choices from when he was a child, could carry so much weight. He'd once confessed his insecurities to Mrs. Chowdhury after one of their rehearsals. He'd felt anxiety about performing, afraid that he might be laughed at, inadequate. That was one of the days where he'd thought of quitting; filled with doubt and rage, she spoke to him softly, looked him in the eyes and saw him, really saw him, and then recited the Serenity Prayer that she had recently learned.

I understand, Ray, she'd said. But it will be okay. I feel this way too. Sometimes we cannot help but to feel this way. Whenever we put ourselves out there, whenever we must be vulnerable, it is scary. We can only control how we respond to it.

I can't do it, Mrs. C.

This is not the truth, Ray. This is the fear talking, disguising itself as truth. I know how scary it is. It is not easy; it took me a long time to get comfortable on the stage, to become comfortable with opening myself—and this is the same in life. If we run from those moments within ourselves, then there can be no growth.

He hadn't fully understood the significance of her words back then—he went through with that first show because he didn't want to let her down—but whenever he thought back to it now, he realized how essential the sentiment behind her words had been, how simple and easy it was to recite them, to consider them (if we run from those moments, then there can be no growth), and yet how exceptionally difficult it was to practice those words, how difficult it was to act the simplicity of them out in the face of one's own fear and resentment and righteous anger.

He still struggled with those feelings from time to time. Perhaps that was why he'd gravitated away from the stage toward the roles of directing and writing, behind the scenes, charged with the planning and mapping of stories. It was impossible, after all, to always remain loyal to the words, to always hold yourself tall to meet the moment. There was so much uncertainty, so much chaos in the world, in this city, it was enough to make one's head explode. And he was only human, had never claimed to be a saint. But the striving, the striving was the key thing. That was what Mrs. Chowdhury had instilled in him from a young age, that was what he had taken away from their relationship, to always strive to meet the moment, to always do your best to live up to the simplicity of the words, to have faith in them.

All of this came rushing back to him, her guidance, her kindness, as they stood across from each other there on the platform. He found himself on the verge of tears as they chatted.

They talked for a while about their lives, reminisced about the past, and hugged once more before parting, exiting at different ends of the platform.

Ray ascended the stairs at the station. They had been talking on the platform for longer than he realized and now the sun was beginning to set. There were hundreds of thousands of people downtown, huddled together out in the cold, waiting for a chance to see the ball drop at midnight, ready to ring in the new year. The fireworks were being set up somewhere across the Hudson in New

Jersey, awaiting their signals to launch and leap, to glimmer and burst above the water, high above in the night sky.

Ray walked along 129th Street, the familiar buildings of his childhood welcoming him, along with new sights—yoga studios, juice bars, hipster coffee shops that had not been here even several months ago, the last time he visited his mother—the city ever in flux. As he made his way toward his mother's apartment, where they would spend the evening laughing, talking about life, awaiting the show of fireworks from the rooftop, he watched the golden light recede beyond the buildings, disappear somewhere beyond the water, beyond the sprawl of New Jersey.

CHAPTER THIRTEEN

January 7, 2030

It had been over a week since Addy had moved to Los Angeles to shoot Trent's movie. She'd subleased a simple one-bedroom in Silver Lake, and was excited to delve into her new role, the character of Brielle.

But after just three days of shooting *Five Easy Pieces,* the Los Angeles skyline was reduced to gray ash. Visibility nil. These things weren't supposed to happen in January, these natural disasters, crimson blazing conifers and California black walnuts spreading the disease needle to needle bark to bark root to root, dying on down a long lineage of destruction, crashing and thudding onto the soil, passing on its untamable, inevitable distress signals, its red sickness. Sure, there had been some destructive wildfires well into December, but seldom had wildfire season in California branched into January.

But December was dry as kindling. Now there were entire swathes of the forest gone, a trio of Springs just south of the Devil's Punchbowl now littered with charred trunks—Cedar Springs and

Falling Springs and Paradise were gone—and the Bridge to Nowhere had collapsed into ruin, and then there was the small town of Wrightwood, which had been utterly incinerated, eviscerated entirely, wiped from the map. Thousands displaced, dozens dead.

But that is all mere setting, background chatter, and what use is that to us and to the story? Addy and most of Trent's cast and crew had already evacuated. Her Silver Lake loft was not in jeopardy, but who wants to stay and breathe in all of that toxicity? When you had the privilege, the resources to just pick up and go to Trent Pendleton's family owned mansion a couple of hours south in Corona del Mar—Crown of the Sea.

Addy right now had a view of the ocean. The worst of the pollution had so far managed to avoid the Newport Beach area; the air was comparatively crisp and Addy could smell the briny water and the dry salty sand beneath the mansion's one-eighty degree ocean view. If she turned around she could probably make out the wildfires still raging in the distance, see the faint grayness that blanketed Los Angeles, but if she kept facing ahead, all she could see was the blue expanse stretching down to Laguna Beach, and beyond what she could see, all the way to San Diego and Tijuana. And she was too busy to turn around, too busy at the moment sinking her teeth into a perfectly smoked, fall-off-the-bone, honey-glazed rack of ribs.

And what do you think? asked Derek Pendleton, seated at the head of this exquisite, turn of the century marble dining table that was the centerpiece of the terrace.

Seated around Derek was his wife Sarah Pendleton, Trent himself, Addy's co-star Lukas Grove (DJ Lucious), and the film's head-honcho producer, Royce Rosenblatt, a sexegenaraion with wiry tight muscles and eyes that darted elsewhere whenever they happened to be met.

What do we think the *verdict* is? chirped Sarah Pendleton.

Addy, I want to know what *you* think, said Derek.

It's been a while since I've smoked ribs. Honest opinion, Addy, said Sarah. Unless of course you don't like them.

Sarah laughed her nervous, maniacal, *ahahaha.*

They're perfect, Sarah. Delicious.

Sarah and Derek beamed at Addy's praise, their white teeth glowing in the moonlight. They had taken an immediate liking to Addy, from the moment she arrived. All of that *assaulted our child in a hotel lobby* was water under the proverbial bridge. They seemed like gentle, understanding souls, or at least that was the image they were putting out. They could easily forgive such fits of emotion; Addy realized that they understood how trains of passion occasionally skidded off the tracks. They understood this from their own experiences and the processing of their own experiences, and could easily forgive such a wide range of human behavior.

We're just so glad you're here, darling, said Sarah. And you too, Lukas, of course you too. And Royce, Royce you've been a true part of this family these past few years.

Yes, said Derek. This is wonderful, for us to all be together like this. I propose a toast—oap, Addy, looks like you could use some more wine.

Derek refilled her glass, the burgundy bubbling, swirling down the edges of her stemless glass.

So grateful to have all of Trent's cast and crew under our roof, to celebrate what we can only hope will be another award winning endeavor, continued Derek. Obviously, tragic, that it comes under such terrible circumstances. Truly awful, those fires, but it has brought us together and it is our duty to make the most of it, to cherish one another while we have these lucky days.

Clink. Clink. Clink. Clink. Clink.

The high bright chimes of the glass echoed out below them and out into the ocean, or perhaps there was no echo and Addy just imagined it like that. She liked the feeling that their merriment could be heard all throughout the coast, that their festivities were mirthful enough to serve as a crowning example of social harmony, a way of life for all watching to mirror.

She was three generous glasses in, though, and the scene beneath the terrace, the beach and the endless blue, had begun to look like a Seurat. Perhaps the clinks of their wine glasses could be heard by passersby, but there was certainly not such a grand echo as Addy had imagined, and their laughter and rib-chomping mostly just blended in with the whispers of the quiet city at night and the spiraling of the wind.

The honey, of course, continued Sarah, chewing her wine and analyzing her handiwork of rib racks, is organic, and local, and raw. Oh, dear, the name escapes me now; I can see the label...a friend got it for me. Anyway, I think it's just about the best honey I've ever had! Small, family owned business. She got it when she did a yoga retreat up in the mountains near Santa Clarita. Oh, God, let's just pray their apiary wasn't affected by the fires.

And this pig! exclaimed Royce Rosenblatt, the first thing Addy could remember him saying in the past hour. He was an eerily quiet, Old Hollywood figure. You got the sense that his eyes were always on you, but not *on you* on you, like personally, but like on everyone, like peripheral but everyone and everything was in the purview. His eyes cast a wide net, but never seemed to try and catch any one thing; their focus never seemed to narrow, but still felt omnipotent. Addy sensed a large dark imposing intelligence lurking behind his quiet.

So tender. This pig must have led a fine and happy life, said Royce. Where'd you pick it up, Derek?

Indeed. Indeed, said Derek, grinning ear to ear now. I believe these that we're eating come from the three children of one Charles Windsor the Third, a fine boar from a family owned organic establishment in Western Kansas. He had plenty of land to roam, green pastures to graze, a beautiful and loyal and loving sow called Matilda Windsor who bore him three happy children, Preston and Domnhall and Duke. And I would be remiss not to mention the sacrifices that they have made—nay, it would be a sin not to pay our utmost respects to the lives that they led. For I feel very strongly that it is our duty to understand their ways of life, the burdens of existence that they endured, the journeys and hardships they traversed so that they could make it onto our plates. Look, dear friends, I am no fool. I recognize the challenges we must undertake, the moral wrestling within our own souls, which we must do before consuming such intelligent and gentle and loving creatures within our modern ecological landscape. It is not a task that we can undertake lightly. Their lives are now no more, so that ours can continue to prosper. The land they grazed, the meat that they hauled on their backs, their bones, and carried across the acres, will now give us energy to move about the world ourselves. The least that we can do is know their names. And we must, *must*, I cannot stress this enough, we must keep this responsibility of consumption with us at all times. When I am not feeling up to the task of writing and working on our next project—which, by the way, Addy, I'll tell you about in a second because Trent and I think you'll be perfect for it—whenever such bouts of doubt arise, we must simply remember the energy and the sustenance and the incredible flavor that Charles and his three children brought to us on this very night, and take their legacies upon our shoulders, understanding the added responsibilities that come from their sacrifices. Friends and family, please, raise your glasses once again. Carry Charles and his boys within your heart and never forget that they are with you always, as you continue on your own journeys forward, in search of goodness, and beauty, and love. To Charles.

Such a bizarre toast, thought Addy. But strangely beautiful too, such genuineness in Derek's voice. She was convinced that every word from his mouth was unequivocally *true.* But she knew the contradicting facts, she'd seen the plastic wrapped racks of ribs being pulled from brown paper bags stamped with the Whole Foods logo. Sure, of course he'd bought organic. And, okay, she supposed there was a slim chance that he'd small-talked with the person behind the meat counter and discovered Kansan origins. But no way in hell did he know their *names.* Whole Foods was a huge corporation, multinational, and she doubted that anybody working at the store counters knew anything of the *specifics,* about the animals themselves or the conditions in which they were raised and slaughtered. It was all yarn. It was purely entertainment. He was being an engaging host. He'd made it all up on the spot, the devil! It was in his nature, after all—Addy had come to realize that Derek and Sarah were both born hosts, probably both ENTJs she reckoned, or TPs.

Addy herself couldn't imagine hosting a big gathering like this. It was one of the things she most dreaded. She'd much prefer to recede to the background, watching from a corner, drifting back to the edge of the room at something like this.

But Derek and Sarah had placed her in the center, poised to orbit her at this late night feast. The moon was high and full above the ocean now. There was another table on the other end of the terrace nearer to the house (not as breathtaking a view, the B-team table) where the director of photography, Marina, was seated with a few other actors and gaffers, and another full table inside where there were various other production bit players from lighting and costume and set design. Somebody had gotten the vinyl record player spinning inside and the angelic voice of Skeeter Davis pierced through the screen door and streamed out onto the terrace, an oldie throwback, the original version of *The End of the World* drifting melodically around this Pendleton party. The song had managed something of a resurgence in recent decades, garnering covers from many artists from the Carpenters to Lana del Rey to Sharon Van Etten, but Addy could tell this was the original, Skeeter's voice hypnotic, she fell into the pool of it as Derek droned on about something in the background.

> *Why do the birds go on singing?*
> *Why do the stars glow above?*
> *Don't they know it's the end of the world?*
> *It ended when I lost your love*

She did! Derek was shouting. I remember it, clear as day she did! Is what I said.

Huh? said Addy, snapped back to the table's circle.

Oh, said Sarah, he thought that this was Patti Smith singing.

Not at all what I said. I said, Patti Smith did her own version, I remember it clear as day because it was used for the end credits in Aronofsky's *mother!*

That isn't what you said, you said you thought *this* was Patti Smith.

Oh, I don't think that's at all what I said, let's roll the tape back. *You* said Patti never covered it, and I said *au contraire mon frere.*

And I said I'm not your *frere.* Au contraire mon amour is more like it, or ma cherie.

This cloying little repartee ended in a sickly fit of PDA in which Derek and Sarah french kissed in front of Addy and Lukas and Royce and their own personal son, our twelve year old auteur, Trent Pendleton.

Ew, said Trent, barely looking up from the TikTok clips that cut quickly across his tablet.

Did you ever see it, Addy? asked Derek. The movie I mean, *mother!*

I don't think so.

Interesting thing, bit hectic. Bit tough to get invested in. Big risks though, top marks for the risks, which is something we're wanting to do more of, Trent and I, which reminds me, let me tell you about our next project.

After *Five Easy Pieces* you mean?

After that. After that. Always have to be thinking ahead in this business.

So *you're* involved? asked Addy.

Oh certainly, yes. Certainly. Trent and I work together. Truth be told I write a lot of what we do—of course we collaborate! Trent has the eye, he really does, the superior instincts visually. He knows what will puncture the zeitgeist, strike while the proverbial iron is hot as they say. But there's got to be an overarching *story.* A structure. And that's where my contributions come in.

I had no idea.

Well, I thought it best to keep myself out of the credits. Ever since our first short film, back when he was still in diapers. I just had the instinct for that, for removing myself. People wanted to believe it all came from Him. You have to lay the groundwork early, get people floating around words like *prodigy, destiny, fate.* You know *that's* how true legacies are built. We're talking Mozart legacies, if we're lucky. If we play our cards right. All about seizing the opportunities early and never loosening the grip.

He's certainly accomplished a lot already, said Addy, tousling Trent's shaggy doo.

Trent paused his screen and shot her a very severe look, wrought with genuine and tragic suffering. Please don't ever do that again, he said.

Oh, now Trent, said Sarah, be nice to our guests. Puberty, what are you gonna do?

He has! said Derek. *We* have.

It was mostly a Derek/Addy conversation now. Sarah excused herself to roam the terrace and perform her hostly duties, making sure everyone was enjoying themselves. Trent absorbed himself back into the screen. And Lukas and Royce were having their own aside about something vague that Addy didn't catch because she'd missed the onset of said conversation (she'd heard talk of *balls* and *clubs* and *spikes* and so figured maybe they were both golf aficionados).

The temperature had dropped and the wind was cool against Addy's skin. The marble beneath the table chilled her bare feet. There were six plates on the table with ribs cleaned down to the bone, pools of dark sauce congealed globularly near the edges. She looked out past the limestone wall of the estate down to the ocean, which was black and monolithic and dappled with circles of light that changed with the rhythms of the tides.

The image of Ray magicked into her head. She realized that she missed him. She felt out of place there at the party. And who were the Pendletons? Who might they become to her? Were they mirrors, windows, doorways into her future? The thing she knew for a fact was they weren't Ray. How nice it sounded to her right now to be on the couch next to him, beneath the orange blanket, Essie Carmichael snoring and farting at their feet.

At any rate, said Derek, I keep getting sidetracked. You need to hear about what we'd like to do next, the sort of themes I've been rolling around in the old noggin lately.

I'm all ears.

So, I'm sure you're aware, this'll be our second remake in a row, *Five Easy Pieces.* We reimagined *Cold Water,* a fine Assayas film of the mid-nineties, and a personal favorite of mine, which of course you know practically swept this past year's award circuit. But the thing is...three in a row might be something like career suicide. They're bound to say we're just repurposing the same ideas, tried and true from movies of the past.

So, what's the great *original* inspiration? asked Addy.

Well, said Derek, I'm not positive yet. I have an image in my mind. It's a woman at sea, is how it starts. And we don't know the time or place. Not even the century. I'm thinking near future actually, but it isn't clear. That's important for these things, not to use specific dates, because then they'll just be instantly forgotten. The references won't hold up. And if it's very near future, with specific dates and everything, then imagine the horror if you're the creator and those dates come and go with so much of the details not quite aligning and then immediately, inevitably the added criticisms *x*-amount of years after initial release will come pouring in and then you'll get to watch the legacy become tarnished. No no no, if you're going to date near future better at least to measure far enough ahead so that you're dead or near dead when those precise dates rear their ugly heads. And but anyway the woman is at sea, outside of time. The vessel she's in is a little wooden canoe. She has a fishing line cast and some tackle gear next to her. She isn't far from a dock along the shore, we can see in the background behind her. There is land not unreachable in the space ahead of her, where she looks to be paddling. I have the sense that maybe this is a river, or maybe even a lake in Minnesota or Michigan or, like, hell, Northern England.

Uh huh.

Addy sipped dutifully at her Cabernet. She clutched the corners of her green shawl tighter around her shoulders.

And then what happens is this woman feels something tugging at the line. This all feels sort of Hemingwayesque, cinematically I mean, at least that's how I'm seeing it in my head.

—

She tries to reel it in, this woman, whatever is tugging at the other end of the line.

Uh huh.

And whatever it is, it certainly isn't throwing in the proverbial towel any time soon, if you catch my drift.

Uh huh.

She's cursing, this woman.

Uh huh.

To God, mind you.

God.

God Himself.

Cursing to God.

Right you are.

Uh huh.

She begins crying.

Uh huh.

She takes out a phone.

Isn't that dating?

Right you are.

I thought you were afraid of that sort of thing?

I could be persuaded against it, but something like a phone is how I picture it on the screen.

Uh huh.

We see an image of a child on the phone's screen.

—

You're running low there. Can I pour you a little more?

My head is pulsing, Derek.

Just a splash more?

The ocean, the moon, they look almost like a painting.

The bottle is almost empty, a splash?

Oh, alright. Thank you.

Where was I?

She sees the image of the child.

Right. And so somehow, I'm not sure exactly how, but we want to make it clear to the audience that she's responsible for this child. That she is out here in the little canoe needing to catch something for this child. That this already, at the very onset, is a matter of life and death. The first shot of the film I see as peaceful and idyllic, maybe it's a leisurely afternoon, but quickly I want to make it clear that the stakes are life and death.

Uh huh. She's in desperate need of catching her own food, but she's brought a phone-type device in the boat with her?

Mmmmm. Yes, yes. Well, okay, so maybe I haven't worked out all of the kinks. Maybe it's a polaroid. It doesn't matter, it really doesn't and you'll see why. But there is something on the other end at present.

And the woman is fighting with it?

Her muscles are pulled tight as wires. We can practically see the veins in her neck, the purple one pulsing at her temple.

Uh huh. I'm with you now.

You're with me. And so this is a real struggle here. Hours go by. We can see the clouds time lapse into different positions in the sky, different shapes. The light changes. She suddenly has pit stains. Maybe a full two, three minutes of actual screen time showing her epic battle with the faceless thing below.

Uh huh.

Real *Old Man and the Sea* vibes, only it's a young woman.

The requisite gender swap.

Well, of course we have the element of pleasing our target audience to consider.

Of course.

And so stop me if you think you know where this is headed.

Well, I'm assuming the child will have to come into play. She fails to get the food for the child. She lets the child down?

Wrong direction altogether, deary.

Something happens.

Brilliant! Something happens. *Something* must always happen. We're in the business of telling stories, you and me and Trent.

What is the *something?*

Well, what I'm wanting to do is subvert the expectations here. A bit of fantasy, a bit of magical realism.

Uh huh.

And so the sweat from this woman is dripping, we go in for a close-up and tears can be seen drying salty in the hot sun beneath her eyes, and she's basically one giant frontal lobe vein at this point, and there is some orchestral score that has built to a crescendo and then *splash.* She's pulled off the side of the boat and down below. Totally disappeared, the rod and everything gone with her, all we see is a white rippling frothy circle from where she'd entered the water.

Uh huh. And so she's dead? We have to see the child grow up without her?

Wrongo. The story isn't about the child at all. The story is about the woman. Well, it is and it isn't.

Well, why do we see her looking at the child at all when she's in the boat? Won't the audience be confused?

You have to just forget about the child. It is just a device so that it feels like there are some stakes right off the bat, when she's in that insular boat. Think of the child as a sort of MacGuffin. Not a real person, not a central character.

Uh huh. And so the woman must emerge from the water?

Addy, dear, you must stop guessing. Let me get into the heart of it. Let me get a rhythm going. I need to work on my elevator pitch.

—

She's under, this woman, sans cultural context, outside of time, the creature at the other end of the line has snatched her down below the water.

Uh huh, I got all of that.

So then the camera pans down.

Sharks!? Fish!? Fishy fishy fishies?

You're drunk.

I'm sorry, no more interrupting.

Now, bear in mind, we're imagining you in this role. Trent and I see you as this very woman. I was hoping we could talk seriously.

I haven't fished in years.

And bear in mind we're loving this idea right now, Trent and I. We're just itching to finish *Five Easy Pieces* and get started on this. I'm getting the feeling it's going to be Trent's finest picture to date.

So *who* is she? Does she have a name, this character? Me, presumably. I'll need to get into her headspace in order to do the part justice.

Baby.

Baby?

Yes, her name is Baby. Now will you let me get into the plot.

I'm beginning to wonder if there is one.

So we pan below the ocean, and she is kind of floating down, but we realize that she isn't under water at all. She isn't holding her breath. She's breathing normally, coughing, yawning, acting rather laissez faire.

Uh huh. So she's a mermaid. Are we thinking live action *Little Mermaid?*

No. She's obviously human. She's looking around curious, as if she were a tourist in a foreign city. All this time the camera is on her face, as she floats through an abstract background, I'm thinking neon colors all swirling and changing and nebulous. A wormhole of sorts.

Uh huh.

And then the camera cuts, a long establishing shot that reveals the gray streets of a city, just as our woman's feet softly land on the sidewalk.

So this is like Atlantis, an underwater city?

Well, not entirely. Remember we aren't technically *underwater.* There is something mystical at work, this is a kind of *bizzaro* world. But a regular city. For all we know this could very well be Cleveland.

Cleveland?

Uh huh. Everything is gray and concrete and post-industrial. The clouds above are maybe a little different, maybe like watery clouds—I don't know, we'll have to work with the design team to figure out the vision—but basically boring grayish clouds covering the whole drab city.

Uh huh.

And I'm thinking dimly lit, earthy tones, not much color once she lands on this sidewalk.

And are we talking about a functioning city? Are there people walking around? Cars?

Not when she arrives. She lands in what looks like a kind of rusty manufacturing sector of a city. Desolate.

Uh huh.

And there is a man sitting with his back against the concrete wall of a building. He's slumped, his bare feet are covered in soot, and he's drinking something from an unlabeled bottle. He's homeless. We get the sense that he's been in this cyclical state of despair for as long as he can remember.

Uh huh.

But once she lands on the sidewalk next to him, his eyes widen and he jumps up, reanimated.

Baby, he says, *is it really you?*

How do you know my name, she says, and so we first find out her name is Baby.

Uh huh.

Praise be, he says. *The Lord is merciful. We have all been praying for your arrival, Baby.*

She asks, *Where am I?* and the homeless man says *Babylonia.*

Huh.

Well, then he says, *the rulers still call it Cleveland, but us who are pure of heart, chaste of body and soul, we know that this is your city, and so we call it Babylonia, after you, Baby.*

Derek.

Yeah.

Derek, is there any possible way that you can condense this? You're giving me a line by line reading right now.

I'm just excited is all! Aren't you excited, Addy?

To tell you the truth, I'm tired. I'm having trouble really getting into it. Can we save it until tomorrow? Once I've sobered up. Once we can both think more clearly.

But there is this whole underwater (but also not underwater) world! And our protagonist, Baby, and this maybe-religious sect of which this homeless man belongs, and also the real possibility that this *is* Babylonia and that she has some pivotal preordained destiny here.

And also there is still the question of the child, in the audience's mind.

Right you are, so all I'm saying is that I really feel that the concept has all the elements of something special. We've just got to flesh it out, figure out which direction to take it. Figure out how to put pen to proverbial paper and write the damn thing.

So it isn't written yet?

We've written a few pages of the beginning, but I'm having trouble with the forward action. Also the big dramatic climax of the thing. And also, still not one hundred percent sure what it is that the woman is *wanting* throughout the course of the film. Maybe back to the beginning, maybe the child does come into it, maybe she wants to get back to the child.

Well, look, Derek, I *am* a little intrigued. But I'm tired. My head is spinning. It's after midnight. Like I said, a turning point. I've either got to go to bed or get up and *do something,* dance or something, to find a second wind, if we're going to make a night out of this.

Surfing! said Derek. We have a couple of boards. We could just walk down there, paddle out, not too far, and surf a little! How about it?

No no no no no. Bad idea. It's too cold anyway.

Imagine it! It'll wake us up, give us life! The goosebumps on the skin! The moon high above! The feeling of gliding above the water, the slap of the wind on the skin. The sand between the toes! I'm sure we could get a big group together! Oh, the more I speak of it the more I'm convinced!

No, I don't think so. Come to think of it, I think I just need to sleep.

We own this property right by the beach. We only stay here a few months of the year, our family, but when we're here we never actually go down to the water. We barely even set foot on the beach! But now that the idea has lodged itself up there, I can't seem to let it go. Imagine it! Midnight surfing!

I don't even know how to surf. It's a terrible idea, Derek. I'm turning in, said Addy. Goodnight.

Suit yourself! Surfing! yelled Derek addressing the entire terrace. Anybody down for a little midnight swim? Addy, remind me to finish my summary of the thing later. I'll be sure to stick to the gist. Maybe you can even throw in your two cents—or help us with the writing of it!

Uh huh.

I'm feeling a seminal story in this one! It has me very excited!

Addy exited the terrace.

Goodnight my dear! There are extra blankets in the hallway closet by the bathroom, in case you need them! Trent, put that damn thing down and come join us in the water!

CHAPTER FOURTEEN

Weeks later, all of the letters and petitions had achieved nothing. Amelia was fed up with all the bureaucratic red tape. They had been unable to get the glow-worms recognized as an endangered species, and the pipeline construction would be moving forward.

Amelia entered the research lab and Elena was already there, examining some limestone samples. Amelia was livid. She had just come from an REC meeting. Bobby had found out that Colonial was planning on breaking ground near the Looking Glass site in two weeks, right around Valentine's Day. None of their petitions had done anything, their strongly worded letters to the company about the newly discovered species, along with pleas to halt their plans for expansion, had gone unanswered, ignored. Their protest had fallen on deaf ears.

I can't fucking believe this, she said.

Elena looked at her calmly. What are you so riled up about?

Nothing we've done has made any difference. Nothing!

Is this about the site?

Yes! Of course it is! They're going ahead with the excavation. In two weeks they'll be gone.

Well, we kind of knew this was bound to happen. They've been planning this expansion for years.

They don't care at all about what we've told them. It's as if what we discovered is meaningless!

I know, it sucks. I'm sorry.

Well, you don't seem very sorry. You don't seem to really care!

I do care, Amelia.

Do you?

Of course. You know I do.

So then you'll be there in D.C with us? We're going this weekend to protest. Bobby is organizing it, getting all of the REC members together and other groups throughout the state; it's going to be a sit-in at the Capitol, for as long as it takes, we could be there the entire week if that's what we need to get someone's attention.

I have a lot of work to do with classes just starting. And so do you.

How can you care about *classes!?*

It's my job.

Your job. Your job? What we found there is rare, Elena. It needs to be protected. It needs to be fought for.

I've fought for it. I've helped you every step of the way, drafting petitions, losing sleep trying to fast-track our research, looking into getting them on the endangered species list. We did what we could at the State Capitol. But there is only so much that we can do. This has been in the works for a long time.

Been in the works for a long time? Can you hear yourself. That company is fucking evil. They're going to build right through. They could go around if they really wanted, if they had any kind of conscience at all.

Amelia, look, I know how much you care. I care too. But you look awful. Your eyes are bloodshot. You look like you could use some sleep. And I've looked into it, they've already rerouted their plans dozens of times for conservation reasons, to accommodate the complaints and lawsuits from several other environmental groups. The expansion has been taken all the way to the Supreme Court. Maybe if we'd found them earlier, had been able to go through the process it takes to get them recognized on the endangered species list, but all of that takes time. There is only so much we can do.

Can you hear yourself! How are you not more worked up about this?

I am, Amelia! You're acting like I don't care at all. Yes, it's tragic! But I have a life here. I have a family and kids to take care of, and classes to teach, and I can't really afford to spend a week in D.C. sleeping out in a tent in front of the Capitol.

Oh, give me a break! You're just afraid. You're a coward! You care so much about your *family?* Because I know that you're fucking Jerry Smith!

—

Yeah, I talked to him at my mother's funeral, and he told me all about this amazing married woman that he'd been seeing—completely on-brand for Jerry, by the way—and much to my surprise she has the same name as you!

Look, so what! Yes, I have been seeing him. For several months. But it's none of your business. And that has nothing to do with this.

None of my business. And yet you're the person I should be taking ethical advice from? He's a fifty-eight year old man-child. He's always been that way.

You don't know him like I do.

—

It isn't just a fling, Amelia. Not that it is really any of your concern, but I'm thinking of leaving Dan.

Oh. My. God. Who are you?

I know that it might not make sense, but I love Jerry. He's kind. I know he isn't always the most mature, but at least he's always open and honest. And he's fun—we have the best time together. He cares about me, and he makes me laugh, and at the end of the day that is what matters; Dan doesn't care anymore if I laugh or not, for years he hasn't cared.

Okay, whatever. If you want to blow up your marriage and your family, that is your business. I didn't come here to talk about your sex-life. Can we expect to see you—

Fuck you!

Elena threw a limestone rock at Amelia's head.

You know, you can be really cruel and cold sometimes, Elena continued. Tears had welled up in her eyes.

Amelia ducked—the rock clanged against a metal chair—and went on, unfazed.

Oh, I'm so sorry, said Amelia. You're a paragon of virtue.

I don't know what your problem is—

Give me a fucking break. Bobby was right about you.

Bobby. And you're one to lecture me? Sleeping with your twenty-year old student.

That *you* told me to! You're a hypocrite too. Hypocrite and coward, great combo.

I was joking.

At least Bobby has a spine. At least he stands for something. What do you stand for?

It isn't easy, this situation, but the heart can't help what it wants.

The heart can't help what it wants? What a load of shit. That sounds like the excuse of a child to justify bad behavior.

It's true though, Amelia. At least I put myself out there. At least I put my heart on the line with another actual human being. I take risks where it matters, unlike some people.

Amelia took a deep breath, calmed herself, and looked around the lab. Where had all of that come from? How had it gotten so heated? She and Elena had never argued like this. She loved Elena.

The silence brought them both closer toward equilibrium. Amelia walked over and sat next to her.

I'm sorry, she said.

No, Amelia, I don't forgive you. You said some really hurtful things. I did nothing to deserve—

I know. I'm just angry about everything.

Look, I don't know what exactly it is, but if you ever need to talk—

It just enrages me that they think it's still okay to do this. To build wherever they want. Take whatever oil they can get. Something needs to be done. We can't let them take whatever they want anymore, with total disregard for everything else.

I understand. But do you think—

And it baffles me that you aren't willing to join us in doing what it takes. I thought that we were in this together?

We are. I do care. Even if you think I don't.

But you're not willing to go as far as us, to do whatever it takes. And if the sit-in in D.C. fails, Bobby is already talking to some people about something more drastic.

More drastic?

Amelia watched Elena. Elena's face changed from one of sadness and hurt to a face of deep concern and fear and confusion.

What does that mean, Amelia? *More drastic.*

I don't know, but hopefully it won't come to that.

Amelia, I'm worried about you. I care about you.

If you cared about me, you would be in this with us. You would be on our side.

I am on your side. Look, it seems like you think that if you stand by Bobby and somehow manage to change their minds, if you can preserve the glow-worms, then everything will be fine, that the world will magically make sense, but that isn't the case. Sometimes there is nothing to be done. We just have to do our best and make peace with things.

Make peace with things? I'm disappointed that you're not willing to fight more for this, I really am.

I wish that the world was different. I wish that the world—these companies—valued different things. But I stand by what I said, Amelia. I feel like we've done all we can do at this point. And yes, it will be tragic, if they're destroyed. But they are just flies, Amelia. I don't want to see them extinct either, but there is still a lot of life out there to protect; I'll remind you we were there to research Hellbenders and can still put a meaningful study together, and maybe that could have a positive impact. I care too, I do, but I'm just trying to be reasonable, trying to have perspective. I have my own children to worry about, and a family, and meaningful work here. I understand your anger, but I'm not willing to risk my sanity over this, or my life. I think maybe you need to be the one to talk some sense into Bobby if he's entertaining anything more radical than a Capitol protest.

Amelia could barely look at her friend. She disagreed completely.

I feel sorry for you then, she said. If you can't see that they are so much more than that, then you're blind. All I know is how strongly I felt when we discovered them; I thought you felt that too. And if you're not willing to fight harder to make sure they don't disappear, then I truly feel sorry for you. And I stand by what I said. You're a coward.

Amelia got up and walked toward the door. Elena kept looking at her, a profound and drawn-out look of friendship, pity and concern.

I hope you change your mind and are there with us in D.C. this weekend, said Amelia. The door slammed behind her.

CHAPTER FIFTEEN

February 12, 2030

Early, Wildwood Regional Park. The *Five Easy Pieces* cast and crew were shooting several exterior scenes on location, near a waterfall north of Thousand Oaks, California, about an hour outside of Los Angeles.

Addy didn't want to be there. The sky was cloudless and the sun was blinding as it rose from behind the fire-ravaged mountains inland, to the east. They had risen at the crack of dawn, the birds not yet chirping, the grass still dewy, because Trent had to catch the morning light just perfectly for these scenes.

Addy hadn't been sleeping well; she'd been having nightmares ever since their retreat to the Pendleton home in Corona del Mar last month. And this past week she'd had little energy during filming and her stomach had been upset.

They'd shot most of the film over the past four weeks, on Hollywood sets, after returning to the city once the fires quieted. Today, though, the final day of shooting, they needed to film a scene on location. It was a scene that came near the end of the movie where Addy's character leaves her on and off again boyfriend, DJ Lucious, and his harmonica, at a park they'd stopped at, and returns home to Sacramento alone. After their characters stop to take in the scenery and hike a nature trail, he runs off ahead of her and down another path, wanting to improvise some childish game of hide and seek, and so she spends a few minutes searching for him before she happens upon the waterfall and reflects there by herself, before getting in the car and driving away toward whatever may come. End of film.

Maybe her headache and her lack of energy would work to her advantage, she thought. Maybe she'd be quicker to access Brielle's feeling of being fed-up with DJ Luscious, her anger and her strain at being strung along once again, their relationship falling back into the same old patterns.

But right now she wished to be anywhere but here. Trent was off in the distance, smiling, joking around with Marina, the DP, as they searched for just the right place to frame the scene, to get the light exactly how he wanted it.

She was a part of something glorious, Addy tried to tell herself. A lead in a major motion picture. All but a lock for the Oscars if she did her job and listened to Trent, took his direction. There was a breeze and the temperature was hovering around seventy and the ocean was not far away and she was alive, getting to do the things that she'd always dreamt of, and so theoretically shouldn't she be feeling so at peace, so content with sitting here right now, next to her costar, Lukas, on the large boulders that edged the onset of a trail, as they awaited a long day of shooting?

Why was there only dread at what was to come today? Why could she not just sit here, and feel at peace?

She had sunglasses on, but they weren't helping. The sun was half shielded by a distant mountain so that its rays split, the light dispersing and becoming more concentrated at single points, so that it was sharp and harsh as it beamed down upon her in the open field. She felt like she might vomit. She needed to vomit. She turned and hurled behind the boulder.

Trent saw her and ran over.

What is it, Addy?! Addy! Are you okay?

The cast and crew came over and huddled around her.

Katya was there, looking at Addy with sincere concern. Katya had desired a break from New York too, from Broadway, and so Addy had vouched for her and gotten her a job doing hair and makeup on the film.

Katya came over to her and put her arm around Addy's shoulder. What is it? You do not feel well?

It's the sun, said Addy. I can't stand the sun. I really don't feel well. And I miss Ray. I miss New York, Katya.

You are okay, said Katya. She put her head on Addy's shoulder.

Addy looked at Katya through her rose-tinted sunglasses and then toward the crowd gathered around them, and then back at Katya.

Katya knew what she was saying, and so she shooed Trent and the rest of the crew away with the twice-flick of her wrist. Space, she needs. Give her a few minutes.

The rest of the cast and crew wandered off down the trail and Addy was left alone with Katya.

I told you, said Addy, it's the sun.

It's okay, said Kayta, here. She helped Addy up and escorted her over to a lone oak tree in the distance that stood tall in the middle of the open grassland. They sat next to each other in the shade with their backs against the trunk.

Do you like it here, Katya? Addy asked.

I like, said Katya. It is different, but I like. But not home for me, too much space, too quiet outside of the city.

Addy looked at Katya. Her face was round, pear-shaped, but with hardened features—the set, wild eyes that spoke a history of tears, the tight, thin lips of fear, an aquiline nose that had perhaps been broken—a unique and beautiful face she thought. A weathered face of trial and triumph. A face carrying generations of immigrant dreams, of never settling and always seeking better. Katya also wore glasses. The frame was gold and the lenses were blue and they were brilliant at the edges where light filtered through the oak leaves and rested.

She had met Katya five years ago on another play she'd done Off-Broadway, and they'd worked alongside each other on a few other productions, chatting easily backstage as Katya did her hair and makeup. They'd never spent any time together outside of work; they weren't best of friends, but were good acquaintances. She was glad that Katya had decided to come to L.A. to shoot the film. She thanked God now that Katya was by her side in this moment.

I thought that I would fall in love with it, said Addy, staring down at the yellow grass.

Fall in love with what? asked Katya.

I don't know. With everything. With this change. With a movie career. I just felt like if I did something, then everything would feel right.

It doesn't feel this way? It doesn't feel right?

I don't know, Katya. How do I know if I'm making the right choices?

There is no way to know, I don't think.

I miss my old life. I don't know if it's just because I'm scared of this new thing, now that I'm here, now that I'm in it, or if it's because what I'd made for myself in New York was good and maybe I never should have given it up. How am I supposed to know?

Maybe you cannot know, Addy. Maybe all we can do is respond to the moments, do our best to make sense of them, and take it only one day and then another. And to grow within those days is all we can hope.

I want to be done with this film, Katya. I don't belong here. And Trent wants me to stay here for his next movie, but I can't do it,

Katya. I thought that I could adapt, that I could change, but I really don't feel like I belong here. I feel sick.

Addy turned away and threw up around the side of the tree.

Maybe you cannot do the filming today? Here, you drink.

Katya handed her a water bottle. Addy drank and took a deep breath. She exhaled slowly, the air escaping soft between her lips, and looked around at the golden horizon.

I can do it today. We're all here. They're counting on me. But then, I'm done.

Trent called to her from a distance, the light is changing, Adelaide! Every second it's changing! We need to get the shots while it's perfect!

Addy and Katya stepped out into the sun, but Addy's stomach buckled. She retreated and sat back against the oak in the shade. Tell him I can't, she said to Katya. Tell him the sun is too much right now. Tell him I need to do the other scene first, the one in the shade, by the waterfall. I can't stay out in the sun right now. I'll be sick the whole time. Tell him I'm sorry, Katya. Can you go talk to him? Please.

Katya went off to negotiate with Trent on Addy's behalf. She watched him in the distance, apoplectic, flailing his arms around in disappointment, gesturing up at the sharp sunrise that sat atop the mountains. But Katya fought for her and moments later Trent came over to talk to her at the tree.

Okay, he said. I know you aren't feeling well. Make sure to stay hydrated. We can shoot the other scene first, but we have to get it quickly, because I want to get back here so that we can do the other scenes today while we have this light, low and from the east. Trevor! Trent shouted to their production assistant in the distance, who was behind the wheel of the shaded cart that he always drove around set. Addy was surprised to see it here out in the fields.

Moments later the cart arrived for her and she and Trent and Marina piled onto the back, while Lukas and the rest of the cast and crew stayed behind and stuffed their faces with Kraft services. The cart drove about a mile down the dusty trail until it reached a dry, shaded valley with a small waterfall and stream.

The setup to the scene was that Addy's character, Brielle, had been led down this trail and had expected to see DJ Lucious somewhere near the falls, waiting for her, but when her character arrived he was nowhere to be found so she descended into the valley, approached the falls, took her shoes off, and sat at the edge of the pool by herself with her feet in the water. The scene was simple and short. It was just her character sitting there, looking around for any sign of him, resigned and at the end of her chase, as she listened to the birds and watched the water ripple.

Okay, said Trent, after he'd helped her navigate the loose, rocky slope that led them into the valley, and she'd taken her shoes off and sat at her mark in the foreground of the falls. Okay, okay. What I want you to do here, is at first look worried, look angry. Brielle has had it with this guy. He doesn't really care about her. Here he goes again, messing around, stressing her out as soon as they're back on the road. He always does this, just to get under her skin, just to get a rise out of her.

Got it, she said.

Marina had set up the camera and was ready to film the scene.

Then, Trent continued, she closes her eyes and breathes. She listens to the birds. A couple of minutes go by and she looks around for him again. This time, though, her face is stoic—as if it is the same to her either way if he suddenly appears or if she never sees him again. It is a big moment for her. She looks around a while longer before she calmly stands and puts her shoes back on and almost gives a shrug of her shoulders. Then, I need you to walk to the right along the trail, past the camera and up the slope, right past this bush here, and onto the main trail. The camera will pan and track you as Brielle begins back toward where they parked and we understand that she's made the decision to leave him behind, then we'll cut to her approaching the car where they'd left it at the side of the road.

Trent called action and Addy did as she was told. She looked around frantically for, furious at, her disappeared companion. She put her feet into the water. It was cold and briny and had a rotten smell to it, but she felt—her character felt—some kind of epiphany rising. She was out of the sun. It was cool down here, and quiet, and she was alone with the water and the birds and the flora and the insects that persevered around the dry bank of the stream, and she was okay without him. Addy took the breaths that Trent had instructed her to take; she was in total control as Brielle, monitoring each breach, each movement of her feet in the water, every subtle turn of her head, but she was also still feeling, still working through her character's understanding of what independence would be, what it would mean to leave him behind.

She closed her eyes and listened to the whistling of the falls, the music of all the drops playing different notes as they splashed against the surface. She prepared to open her eyes and to project the calm, reclaimed agency on Brielle's face, to look at peace here, to feel whole as she made the decision to leave DJ Lucious to his own devices, to find his own way back.

But when she opened her eyes something happened. Brielle was not composed, was not stoic and strong as Trent had directed; Addy was sobbing. Tears were streaming down her character's eyes. She felt a tightness in her chest. She felt so exposed there in front of Trent and the camera. She had the urge to plunge herself further into the pool and sink to the bottom to avoid their eyes.

She heard Marina and Trent whispering behind the camera.

She isn't supposed to be crying is she?

No, no.

Should we cut?

No, stay with it. Maybe there's something here. Finish the take, see where it goes, and then we can get another one without the crying.

But isn't her character supposed to—

Yes, yes, said Trent. But this could be good—I mean, we'll have to wait until post to see, but she's making an artistic choice. We've got to trust her, give her room to move freely within the character.

Addy saw Trent in her periphery, but kept looking down at the water as she stood and put her shoes on. Inside, she was angry at herself for messing it up, but the tears continued to flow. She was about to apologize and get out of her character, cut the scene short, but noticed out of the corner of her eye that Trent was giving her a thumbs up and a twirl of his finger that meant stay in it.

She was standing now, shielded from the sun that produced a golden halo around the ridges of the valley and reflected off the face of the falls. She closed her eyes again and took another breath and then suddenly dropped to her knees, which dug into the pebbles and the rocks, cut and sore. Her chest was still heaving from the unexpected wave of emotion, but her breathing had gotten slower. She clasped her hands together and tilted her head up toward the blue sky as if in prayer. She screamed as loud as she could at the heavens, a booming, brutal shout that echoed across the park.

Then, as if she realized something, as if her missing companion would hear her and find her, and that she no longer wished for that, she stood and laughed a maniacal laugh and kicked a divot into the surface of the water, which parted in beads and rose and fell in a parabolic arch and berthed hundreds of separate ripples in the center, and then she ran. She ran along the stream and through the valley and past the camera and back up to the main trail, so fast and so light that she was skipping, floating on air, and Marina and Trent had difficulty following her with the camera mounted to its track, but they scrambled all the way up and the camera focused upon her in the center of the frame as she sprinted off in the distance and got smaller, and smaller, and disappeared into a pinprick in the distance, swallowed by the piercing sunrise to the east.

And when Addy was out of sight from the camera, she reached a trailhead sign and a gazebo-like place to rest that resembled a tipi, and then she leaned over a patch of dry grass and threw up the remaining liquid that was in her, clear as water, acidic in her throat.

Trent had her do the scene three more times, without the tears and the sudden outburst, had her do the calm, downplayed version he'd originally envisioned, and then they returned to the nature center at the park's entrance to film Brielle and DJ Lucious' arrival at the park and his subsequent fleeing.

Addy still didn't feel well, but powered through the rest of the morning, doing her best to bring Brielle to life in the scenes. When they took lunch she and Katya ate by themselves, off in a corner. She tried a bite of a cheese danish, but knew right away that she wasn't going to be able to keep it down.

Are you okay? Katya asked.

I'm fine, said Addy. I don't know—maybe it's food poisoning.

Maybe you're pregnant, said Katya.

No. Addy thought about it. No no no.

No? Why *no?*

Ray and I are very careful. I haven't even seen him in months.

How long it has been?

Well, gosh, right before Christmas I guess.

Not even two months, no? Morning sickness, they call it. Maybe you need to make sure.

I can't be. There is no way. I don't even want—

I am thinking maybe yes, said Katya. Would it be so bad? A proverbial bun in the oven.

CHAPTER SIXTEEN

Shooting had ended, and the next day Addy was back in New York City. She didn't know how to tell Ray. She lied in bed next to Essie Carmichael well into the afternoon, not wanting to get up, not wanting to do anything.

Hey, hon, are you feeling okay? Ray asked as he entered the room.

Fine.

I'm glad you're back, but you seem different. Are you going to tell me about Los Angeles? How was the shoot?

Fine.

Fine. Just fine, that's all I'm going to get?

I'm just tired from the flight, she said.

But she felt bloated and her feet felt swollen and she could stay there in bed for weeks.

Did you call Bill about the water? she asked. Do we have hot water now?

I did. He replaced the entire water heater—it was getting old. It's working a lot better now.

Thank you, she said, and kissed him on the cheek. I love you.

So, said Ray, I was thinking we could go out tonight? Have Valentine's dinner a day early? It'll be tough to get a last minute reservation somewhere tomorrow.

Okay, what did you have in mind?

Why don't we go see Cabaret, see how your understudy is doing?
You haven't gotten to see the show from the audience yet. It's
beautifully done.

Okay.

You don't seem very enthused.

I think I just need to rest.

Alright. I'll let you rest. Then after the show tonight we can get
food somewhere. Sound like a plan?

Sounds fine, Ray.

That night they went uptown to attend a performance of
Cabaret. Addy mingled with the cast and crew, her old friends,
before the show. She wished them luck and then she and Ray took
their seats in the front row.

It was a brilliant performance and she was glad that Ray had
suggested that they come. But it was bittersweet because a part of her
was so convinced that she had been one of the key components that
made the show so great, her own performance. But now somebody
else was playing Sally, and she was wonderful. Addy was proud of her
understudy for rising to the occasion, but also a little sad because it
felt as if she, Addy, were no longer needed.

After the show, Addy made her way up the stairs toward the
balcony; she wanted a view of everything from above. All the cast and
crew had left, the employees had gone home to their families, and the
theater was empty. Only the director remained, waiting somewhere
backstage. Addy had asked her to stick around so that she might have
a few minutes alone before all the lights were turned off and the
doors were locked. She looked out at the stage, dimly lit, a soft yellow
shimmer on the edge, where the wood reached past the curtain. The
red velour curtains matched the cushions of every seat in the house.

The chandelier hung ominous and icy and cold in the very center. The ornate trim on the walls was golden and detailed and heavenly warm.

The stage looked so small from up here; how long had it been since she'd had balcony seats? She thought back to those days of uncertainty and excitement, the days of working multiple service jobs, paycheck to paycheck in her early twenties, saving what she could and getting rush or lottery tickets once a month if she could afford it, to feed her need of live theater, while she held the ever-lit ember of hope inside of her that one day she might be on the ground level, front and center on the stage, gazing out at the audience and telling stories.

And she had gotten to do it. She had lived it out, but now what would she do? Was her career over? Did it ever belong to her to begin with? She placed her hands on her stomach and thought that she could feel it beginning to grow.

Was this what was expected of her now? Society had told her for so long that that was where her true value was, where her purpose would lie in the end, and so had everything she'd sacrificed for her career, for a chance to have a voice and to provide the world with joy and hope upon that stage—a social life, relationships, with friends, with family, her own sanity—had all that sacrifice been for nothing?

Now would the only role she'd have again, the only thing she'd ever be remembered for, be the role of mother? A role she'd never sought, never dreamt of. She was going to be a mother. But she couldn't possibly be a mother. It was out of the question. She could see it all. She knew herself. She'd simmer the years ahead in resentment, in fear, as her own mother had. She wouldn't take to it, and then guilt would dwell, constant and chirping, as a yellow-bellied sapsucker nesting in the branches of a beech tree.

No, she couldn't possibly do this. The oceans were rising at catastrophic levels. Disease after new disease was rippling across continents. The world was nothing but chaos, wasn't it? How could she possibly bring a child into all this? The planet was doomed. Capitalism was singing it's final aria and who knew what kind of silent song would follow.

Her breathing had quickened. Was this a panic attack? She looked out onto the dark stage and tried to steady her breathing. This was her home, the place where she'd always felt safe. What would it mean to give this up? What kind of new courage would it take to feel safe in another phase of life?

She didn't think that she had it in her. All she could see of the future was destruction. She leant against the edge of the balcony, her hands cold on the bannister, the frill of her pink dress flowing out into the air above the mezzanine.

She felt the hands around her waist.

Addy, what are you doing all the way up here? I was looking for you.

He rested his chin upon her shoulder and kissed it like a child.

I was just thinking, she said.

Well, don't. It isn't good for you.

I'm going to miss this place.

It's going to miss you. But you'll be back. There will be other shows.

Will there?

Of course. It's hard to top Sally Bowles, but you'll have plenty more roles.

Will I?

Yes. Of course. Is everything alright?

Everything's fine, Ray.

Okay. You want to get going? I'm starving. I don't want to be too late for our reservation.

She looked at him and smiled. Can you give me a couple minutes alone, she said. I just want a moment by myself, to take it all in.

Of course, he said. I'll be downstairs waiting, whenever you're ready.

CHAPTER SEVENTEEN

August had spent January and February at home, playing Legions of Maria, avoiding Taylortoo. She wouldn't let it go, her desire to participate in the trials of that new tech start-up, Genesis. If it was possible for artificial citizens to reproduce, then she wanted to become one of the first ones.

Their arguments were cyclical. They had turned into screaming matches, and would always end with him stubbornly saying one final *no* before retreating back into the game room to colonize underwater civilizations.

This was what he was doing now, avoiding her wrath, her indignation at his stubbornness and selfish nature.

Critical hit! He'd just killed the General of an underwater zombie-shark uprising.

Yes! he shouted. Take that you undead fuck.

He pillaged through the zombie corpses, looting ammo and weapons, jewels and coral, before saving his progress.

He paused the game, raised the curtains, and looked out the window. It was cold and the sky was covered with dark white clouds.

What was he doing, he thought. Day after day, the same. He had more money than he knew what to do with, and so now what could life offer? The only thing left was a pursuit of power, but he had no interest in that.

He suddenly felt bad that he had yelled at Taylortoo. She was right, he was selfish, wasn't he? Then, suddenly, out of character for his stubborn self, he knew that a radical change needed to be made.

Within hours, the two of them were in New York City, strolling through Central Park.

It's beautiful, said Taylortoo. So many trees.

They walked past a section of the park where children were using remote controls to steer small boats at the edge of a pond.

Aww, said Taylortoo, look at the cute boats.

It was a chilly, cold afternoon, and it looked like there could be snow.

So, Taylortoo continued, what are we doing here? Don't get me wrong...I'm so glad we're out of the house...it's just I didn't expect it...so spontaneous of you.

I guess I'm still capable of some surprises.

Are we here to visit your sister...Adelaide? Ooooh! Can we go see the play she's in?

No, that isn't it. She's still in L.A. I think. Let me show you why we're here.

They made their way toward Central Park West and 70th, crossed the street, and gazed up at a towering brick building, a beautiful apartment complex with a view of the park.

Well, said August. This is your new home. I bought you your own loft on the tenth floor.

No...August...you're joking. What about us? What about our home in Hartford?

Taylortoo, I know you aren't happy there. You should be free. I'm sorry I never listened to you. I'm sorry I've been so closed-minded.

August, I don't know what to say.

You can be part of those trials now with Genesis. Who knows, maybe they'll be able to give you the kind of life you envision. You were right, I don't know the future. And my vision of it isn't the only one. I was stubborn. And I was scared. I'm sorry.

She ran her cold fingers along his face and kissed him. August, thank you, she said.

Now, they're located downtown in Chelsea, so you'll have to take the subway or a ride-share. If you take the subway, probably the C to—

Okay, okay...I think I can figure it out, August.

I just want to make sure—you know, I'm just worried about you. This kind of thing isn't really done. We're testing new waters.

I know I can make it here, on my own.

I know you can, I believe in you.

They hugged again and then a man showed up to meet them in front of the lobby doors. The three of them went up to the loft and signed some papers, and then the man handed the keys to Taylortoo and the loft belonged to her.

The man left and Taylortoo and August were left standing there in her new home, gazing out at the park.

The loft was empty, but Taylortoo had already envisioned how she would decorate her new space. She'd even picked out and purchased many things online, as the copper ring twirled around her eyes, envisioning her future there.

Thank you, August. I love you.

I love you, he said.

They embraced there in the open expanse of the loft, surrounded by the beautiful walnut floors.

Here, I want you to have this. He took out a figurine from his pocket and handed it to her. It was the blue troll doll. For good luck, he said.

I'm not sure I believe in luck, said Taylortoo.

Well, you'll need it out on your own. I want you to have it.

Taylortoo took the doll. Thank you, she said. Are you sure? I know how much it means to you.

I'm sure. It's yours. Just promise me you'll look out for us when you're running the show. Promise me you'll have compassion.

I'll always remember you, August. I'll always care for you. I owe everything to you. Thank you...this is very nice.

She set the doll on the counter and embraced him one final time.

I'm going to miss you, he said.

I'll miss you too. So, what will you do? she asked.

He thought about it as he looked out the window at the bustling park, and the snowflakes that now fell from the clouds.

I don't know, he said. I might do some traveling, see more of the world. I don't want to spend all my time alone in Hartford anymore. Or maybe I'll return home for a little while, help Amelia fix up that old house. I think something like that would be good for me.

I think so too, August.

They stood there in the open living room, watching all of the bodies move up and down the Avenues, through the park. They watched together as the snow drifted down through the sky and melted on contact upon the concrete surface.

CHAPTER EIGHTEEN

It was the eve of Cupid's day of love, and Amelia and Bobby were on the path toward destruction.

They had protested for days at the Capitol in D.C. with a group of nearly five hundred activists, and had received some national media coverage, but still to no avail.

The Colonial Pipeline Company had found another AI company to partner with and had built a fleet of sentient trenchers and pipelayers to construct the pipeline for them. Construction was to begin at the site in Asheville tomorrow.

But Amelia and Bobby and a small group of REC members had different ideas, as they drove down the highway toward Georgia and the Colonial Pipeline headquarters.

Bobby looked determined and purposeful in the front seat, but Amelia still had reservations about what they were doing.

The darkness settled in slowly, tossing, turning, uneasy, as an exiled lover to the sofa.

Bobby, I think maybe we need to turn around, go home, she said.

We're going home, Amelia. This is our home, everywhere. We belong everywhere and nowhere. What they're destroying, *that is home.*

You know what I mean.

We've been in exile for centuries. We exiled ourselves, walled ourselves away from *home.* You know this. You feel this. We both do. You aren't having reservations are you?

—

This is what we've been talking about—impact, radical action, revolution! This is what we've been working toward. Don't do this to me now. We're almost there, Amelia, we can't turn back.

They crossed the border into Georgia. Amelia thought about it. She wanted to go along with the passion that flowed from him. He had some kind of spell over her. The way he said her name now, *Amelia,* was so commanding; he was so assured in the course of their action. She had not long ago been Professor Wheeler. He'd been steadfast in his adherence to that title and its inherent authority, but she had invited the boundary down and he had shifted the balance of their relationship, and now she was only Amelia, and he was Bobby, and they were stardust children of the Earth, roaming, and had no more use for titles or labels or hierarchies of the exiled world. But, at the heart of it, she could intuit the fear, could feel that at a level that he was too blinded by his righteousness to even acknowledge, he was not so special, not so unique, but was a fearful, common archetype of the rebellious adolescent, acting out—be it at his father or the fast-paced, all-consuming bedlam of the modern world—acting out with the need to be heard. That isn't to say that his objectives were without merit, but in Bobby there certainly was, she felt, the oedipal drive to overthrow. He wanted to overthrow those in power, to rescue an oppressed Mother Earth, to change the story so that he might be the protagonist, one of the driving and deciding factors of her ultimate fate. But for what true means? Was it not so that he might be known as an agent of her salvation? Was the desire not at least minorly influenced, if not deeply rooted, in the great error of critical thinking that tricked him, the delusion that made him believe that her own agency could ever belong outside of her own hands. We had been birthed of her, and we had burned her blood and moved her mountains, but never had her agency dwindled, and whether these were our sins, or gifts that she had granted us for our own journeys, the fueling of our civilizations, only time would tell, but it was always and will forever be the case that if she so desired, if our ungratefulness were too explicit, she could make her agency known and free us from our mortal coils without batting an eye, could erase all trace of our memories and time before breakfast.

I need to pee! said Amelia. Take the next exit.

It was a dilapidated Shell in northern Georgia. They were at the halfway point between Asheville and their target in Alpharetta, the Colonial Pipeline headquarters.

She slammed the car door and walked past the revolving snack-rack filled with Cool Ranch and Funyons and Flaming Hot Cheetos, past the aisle with magazines and lighter fluid and tire-pressure gauges and Evergreen air fresheners and into the yellow corner where the shitters were tucked away.

She pissed into the dusty bowl without touching the seat. What was she doing here? In this gas-station bathroom. Bobby was a righteous child; intellectually she understood this, but watching him drive along the open road, his eyes alert, purposeful, seeing him engineer and organize this effort, how perfectly he had inspired the other members of their faction to have faith in this, had gotten them to fall in line, the three vans following them hauling all of their DIY explosives, their oxidizing and reducing agents, their fragile charged vests, their copper shells and hollowed out suitcases tingling with electric and pressure and homemade Semtex, witnessing him bring this all to fruition, she'd never been more drawn to him. She wanted to give up all of her control. She wanted him to lead her into whatever destruction they were set on course for.

The bathroom sink trickled weak. A babbling brook. A raging stream. How great it had been to see them again, to laugh, to sit around the fire at the edge of the forest, overlooking the river, to feel, if only for that night, as if things might be easy again. But it couldn't be, it never would. Wasn't it easier, this way, following Bobby and his mystical force? Wasn't it better, to be a part of this great change, to let Bobby's insistence on the narrative he envisioned carry her into the future?

She turned the knob. The sink dripped. She walked past the lighter fluid and the magazines. She stole a bag of Flaming Hot

Cheetos on her way out the door. There was Bobby, behind the wheel, an American Spirit loose at the corner of his mouth, the epitome of cool, crafted in the fashion of golden-age Hollywood images.

Bobby, she said, her voice calm and stern and unwavering in its conviction, take us home.

He smiled. He started up the electric engine. Home it is, he said.

CHAPTER NINETEEN

Addy and Ray exited the theater and made their way downtown toward Chelsea. They passed through Times Square. Weaving through tourists taking pictures, couples embracing, Addy looked up at the neon lights of Broadway. She was reminded of everything that had lured her there, the density of bodies, the trust of clustering tight together, the energy, the dreams, the hope that radiated from not only the theater district but the entire city.

She thought of being a mother and what it would mean to raise a child in such a beautiful and crazy city, in such an uncertain world. Then she thought of her own family. She hadn't spoken to August or Amelia since the night of the funeral. She had become so absorbed in Trent's film. She felt bad about it and wondered if she should message Amelia. She wanted to reconnect, she really did, and perhaps it wasn't too late.

If she was going to have a child, she would want to be closer with her own family, only she wasn't sure where to begin. She'd been so used to living life on her own for so long. She took out her phone, but scrolled aimlessly, ultimately deciding not to message Amelia, as they made their way toward an empanada spot on 24th street, where they had reservations for dinner. She would message her after dinner, she decided. But what would she say? What magic words might bring about a real connection after all these years?

To what extent did the motivation behind words and actions mean more than the words and actions themselves? Words contained so much, and so little, she thought. How would her raising of a child be affected by the limits of language, and the motivations beyond the edge of language?

Parents wished to pass on certain values to their children, ways of life that had been passed onto them, value judgments of goodness, of right and wrong, fairness, justice, and compassion, but many had not come to understand what the words truly meant, the history they held, had not done the work to reach the feeling behind the words, and were not living out the values within the shadows of their own hearts, so that in passing said values along to their children, they merely hoped that the children might do better, might be able to one day live out the meaning of the words, might be able to do the difficult work inside to not only pass the words on verbally, but also through example, never quite understanding that it rarely works that way. The light inside has to shine, from each and every one, on the individual level, in order for great change to be felt in the generations of the future, in order for those values to be deeply felt, to develop within the child's spirit. And usually this takes years and years of self-reflection, toiling in isolation, sorting out one's own shortcomings, making sense of one's story, mining the past and imagining futures blooming with love. Children are the greatest lie detectors of all, and words are light as feathers to them, weightless as clouds. It is the motivation beyond the words, the feelings and thoughts carefully tended to beneath the surface, as seeds in a garden; that is what the children can hear, clear and resonant as the chime of a bell, the strum of guitar strings, that is what they can see with their magic eyes, the vulnerability, the belief that lies beyond the physical realm of words, radiating out into the world; that is what they can feel, solid as a stone in the hands, dense and textured and fragile as a shell in the center of their palm.

The secret truth of things is this, she thought: if we are to achieve balance and harmony and to make sense of the chaos that ripples across oceans and permeates each and every culture, then it must first start within. There are entire galaxies in us, planets and continents whose cultures have evolved and been forged in the formative years of childhood; there are warring factions abound in the self. This could all change over the course of a generation—the hunger and the terror and the heartache and the greed. It could change so easily if we are first willing to sort out the battles of the soul. Great change will never be achieved in parliamentary halls or senate chambers or at G7 summits, if not first achieved in individual moments, within the home.

Addy thought about this. She understood that this was what would be required. Yet there was so much doubt in her. Had she blinded herself to it, distracted herself for too long from the scars of the past, with work, with her own ambitions? Had she truly done the work, on an elemental level, to believe and live by the words and values that would be needed to raise a child in this world? She didn't know. That was the scariest part, the not knowing.

They reached the restaurant and were seated at a table, where they sipped their waters and dipped tortilla chips into salsa. She had told Ray about the pregnancy back at the theater, before they left, but hadn't discussed it at length. She knew he was excited, but she didn't know her own feelings, and wasn't sure what direction their broaching of the conversation might take.

There was Ray, in front of her, expecting. He held her hand across the table, after they had finished eating, half-eaten plates of empanadas between them, expecting an answer, yearning for her solidarity, hoping for her to take the leap with him. This was one of those moments, she realized, to give yourself over to something, to plunge into the darkness, the shadows, and trust faith in the face of the unknown, to believe that somewhere along the way light would reveal itself.

Honey, he said. Addy? Are you ready to do this together? I know that we can. I love you.

Every potential path of triumph and catastrophe flashed in front of her eyes, the milestones of crawling, of first steps, of tooth fairies and Santa Claus, of learning to swim, to ride a bike, of graduations, and first loves, heartache and teenage rebellion, of bad decisions, and choices not made, of regrets and resentments, selfishness and cruelty and greed, of perhaps the dissolution of her own marriage, bonds broken, venturing out into the world, the inability to let go, of empty-nesting and loneliness, of some unforeseen tragedy that would leave the child bereft, or—God forbid—losing a child too young, of unimaginable grief and emptiness, of hatred and rage at everything the world might become, of hunger and disease, rock-bottom, feeling lost. She imagined every degree of suffering and stillness that might be ahead on the horizon, and so how could she possibly make a decision with all of these images storming her mind? How could she take the leap with him? How did he seem so calm and assured?

She took a deep breath and saw him across the table, beneath the dim light of the restaurant, the life of the city swarming all around them. She didn't know; but she felt a small, quiet ember within, the blue flicker of a gas stove, and knew that she had to produce words, that he was expecting some kind of answer.

She took a sip of her water and looked him in the eyes, trying to summon some kind of courage. She didn't know what the words would be before she said them, but knew that whatever they were she would have to live with them, would have to do everything to make them true.

She said, finally, I don't know, Ray. I don't know if I'm ready—but I think we should try.

www.ingramcontent.com/pod-product-compliance
Lightning Source LLC
Chambersburg PA
CBHW030132310726
48970CB00005B/1403